The adventure began in

BEYOND LICH GATE

Aitchley Corlaiys—illegitimate descendant of the great
Cavalier Procursus—was chosen to restore the endangered
land of Vedette to greatness. And Aitchley, thrown into
adventures far beyond his control, quickly learned what it took
to be a true hero . . .

Now, the adventure continues . . .

Aitchley Corlaiys must follow the treacherous Harris Blind-
Eye across Vedette to rescue the woman he adores and the
artifacts he needs to complete his quest—for love, for land,
and for the Elixir of Life itself . . .

CATHEDRAL OF THORNS

*The second chapter of a captivating new
adventure in fantasy and magic by the
author of* The Wheel Trilogy
STEVEN FRANKOS

Ace Books by Steven Frankos

The Wheel Trilogy

THE JEWEL OF EQUILIBRANT
THE HEART OF SPARRILL
THE DARKLIGHT GRIMOIRE

BEYOND LICH GATE
CATHEDRAL OF THORNS

CATHEDRAL OF THORNS

STEVEN FRANKOS

ACE BOOKS, NEW YORK

This book is an Ace original edition,
and has never been previously published.

CATHEDRAL OF THORNS

An Ace Book / published by arrangement with
the author

PRINTING HISTORY
Ace edition / June 1995

ISBN: 0-441-00221-8

ACE®
Ace Books are published by The Berkley Publishing Group,
200 Madison Avenue, New York, NY 10016.
ACE and the ''A'' design are trademarks
belonging to Charter Communications, Inc.

PRINTED IN THE UNITED STATES OF AMERICA

10 9 8 7 6 5 4 3 2 1

*To Jacqueline Sledge, who not only laughs at
all my really dumb jokes, but wanted my hours,*

and to the Donkey Girls,

Rachelle (Don't call me "Slick") Hubert,

Kristina Schulze,

*and Julie Cerniglia,
my favorite kartwheeling,
Donkey Dancing partner*

CATHEDRAL OF THORNS

Prologue
The Quest

Aitchley Corlaiys—the only surviving descendant of the great Cavalier Procursus Galen—left his village to search for the magical Elixir of Life, accompanied by the Cavalier's personal smith, a pessimistic dwarf named Calyx. Also joining the young farmer were the elderly Captain d'Ane; the half-human, half-troll, Poinqart; the humanoid fungus, Gjuki; and the dangerous and untrustworthy brigand, Harris Blind-Eye.

Disheartened by the death of his father and the suspected death of the scullery maid, Berlyn, Aitchley undertook the Quest intending to use the magic Elixir on Berlyn rather than on his long-dead ancestor. The Quest started badly—no more than a day out of Solsbury the group was attacked by starving xlves. Using the deadly accuracy of Harris's twin stilettos, Mandy and Renata, the group was able to turn the animals back and continue. The next morning, they overtook a band of would-be rapists and cutthroats, and—much to Aitchley's surprise—rescued Berlyn from their clutches. Now something of a hero to the girl, Aitchley decided to continue the original Quest of resurrecting the Cavalier.

Outside the town of Ilietis, Aitchley found and rescued a fledgling gyrofalc entangled in the bushes. The irascible young bird took off without a word of thanks and flew into the night. Upon entering Ilietis itself, the Quest members were taken

prisoner and forced to serve a slavelike penance. During a
daring night escape, the gyrofalc returned to save Aitchley and
Berlyn from the clutches of a vengeful acolyte and stayed long
enough to get some food before flying off again.

Originally coerced into joining the groups by an explosive
bracelet around his wrist, Harris Blind-Eye attempted to sab-
otage the Quest by forcing Aitchley to venture back into Ilietis
and retrieve the alchemical necklace linked to his bracelet. To
Harris's surprise, Aitchley not only managed to recover the
necklace but also slay the tyrannical Archimandrite ruling the
town.

Defeated by Aitchley's ever-increasing skills, Harris Blind-
Eye then took a more straightforward approach and kidnapped
Berlyn, holding her hostage until Aitchley gave him the necklace. During the ensuing scuffle, Gjuki was stabbed and Aitchley himself was injured. Harris made off with Berlyn, the
necklace, and Aitchley's near-magical shield that once belonged to the Cavalier. Despite a possible concussion, Aitchley
gave chase, taking Poinqart with him, while the others took
the wounded Gjuki into the town of Viveca.

Once Gjuki was safely at a healer, the others found replen-
ishing their dwindling supplies to be difficult when, despite
their credentials, Chief Advisor Paieon refused their request.
Forced to liberate the Baroness Desireah and destroy Paieon's
black market trade with Ilietis, and aided by the healer Sprage,
Patrolman Lael, and a lowly fisherman named Rymel, the remaining Quest members succeeded, but not without cost. The
elderly Captain d'Ane died of heart failure and was replaced
by Sprage.

Now fully stocked, Calyx, Gjuki, and Sprage set off after
Aitchley and Poinqart, hoping to reach the two before they
confronted the villainy of Harris Blind-Eye.

1

Heathaze and Sunlight

*F*our horses thundered across the grassy plains south of Karthenn's Weald. Hooves pounded heavily at the earth, throwing up great clods of dirt, and the tall grasses and springtime array of flowers bowed their respect as the beasts charged past.

The first mount was a *meion*, the rare, diminutive breed of horse bred exclusively by the dwarves of Aa. Seated in its saddle—face drawn up in an unfriendly scowl—rode a dwarf. Silver-black hair covered his head, and a salt-and-pepper beard and mustache tried unsuccessfully to hide the cynical frown on the dwarf's lips. Small, beady eyes peered southward in their displeasure from a face ruddy in complexion, and a huge, bulbous nose—like a rosy gourd of flesh—squatted at the center of his features. A menacing warhammer hung at his belt, and a large sack was tied securely to his *meion*'s flanks as he pushed the beast to even greater speeds.

Behind the dwarf rode the only human of the group. Even from atop his palomino it was obvious he was a tall man, yet his shoulders were stooped and hunched, shortening his apparent height by a few inches. Long black hair liberally streaked with grey flew in the rush of air, and dark brown eyes kept flicking apprehensively from the dwarf to the fast-moving earth beneath his mount's hooves. His lean body was clad all in black, and his clean-shaven features were alight with a kind of gnawing anxiety as his golden horse charged recklessly after the dwarf and his *meion*.

Bringing up the rear were two other galloping horses. One mount carried nothing but supplies, its strong back burdened by food, clothing, and fresh water, while the last horse carried a rider that was neither human nor dwarf.

The third rider was a Rhagana, one of the mysterious humanoid fungus creatures from the dense jungles of the Bentwoods. Nearly as tall as the slouch-shouldered man, the third rider looked more like a tree come to life than his nearest relative, the mushroom. Leathery, barklike skin—a raw umber in hue—covered his lean, humanoid body, and his legs and arms were thin and sticklike. Hair like green lichen sat tangled atop the creature's head, and frondlike strands grew down the sides of the Rhagana's face in moss-green sideburns. Tiny, button-black eyes—like two shiny black pearls—surveyed the wide meadow about them in contemplative silence, and an impassive mien was etched on the barklike countenance of the creature's face.

With a sneer, the dwarf drew his mount to a halt, his gaze trained darkly on the southern horizon. "Don't tell me the kid's gone into the desert," he groaned out loud, slumping despondently in his saddle.

The long-haired human threw the dwarf a sardonic smile. "Well, if the kid didn't go in, his horse sure as Pits did," he remarked.

The Rhagana stretched out a hand to take the reins of the supply horse, his tiny eyes briefly passing over the two men before him. "I believe Master Calyx was speaking rhetorically, Healer Sprage," he announced in a deep, yet quiet voice. "He was not seeking a response."

The dwarf dismounted, throwing a gruff snort back at the Rhagana. "Sprage knows that, Gjuki," he grunted. "He's just trying to be a witling."

Sprage sat back in his saddle, crossing condemnatory arms over his chest. "Why is it that when I make a smart remark, I'm a witling," he wanted to know, "and when you do it, you're just being true to your nature?"

Calyx pushed his way through the knee-high grass that— for him—nearly reached over his head. "Because I'm a dwarf," he answered the physician, "and I've had nearly two hundred years to get it right. You humans wouldn't know proper sarcasm if it crept up and bit you on the butt.''

Sprage offered the dwarf a knowing smirk as Calyx disappeared down among the grasses and weeds, beady eyes carefully searching the earth. When he resurfaced, the look of doom was even darker on the dwarf's features.

''Yeah,'' he said with a heavy sigh of resignation. ''*Meion* chips. That means Poinqart's been this way. Tracks indicate the kid was too.'' He placed a disgruntled hand on his hip. ''Why in the forge would the kid follow him into the desert? I thought he had more sense than that.''

Sprage clambered down off his horse to inspect the prints hidden amongst the foliage. ''Didn't you say he suffered a head injury?'' asked the doctor. ''Maybe he wasn't even aware of where he was going.''

Hands tucked into his belt, Calyx began a defeated walk back to his mount. ''Nah,'' he grumbled in despair. ''That's why I sent the troll along with him. I figured at least the troll would have enough common sense to keep the kid out of trouble.''

From atop his dark horse, Gjuki looked down at the two. ''What we pursue is a young human male in love,'' he announced. ''Having worked at Lord Tampenteire's estate for as long as I have, I have come to learn that this sort of . . . occurrence can be the catalyst for many strange and irrational behaviors. Master Aitchley's pursuit of Harris Blind-Eye into the desert does not seem so odd when one considers the fact that he is very much in love with Miss Berlyn.''

Eyebrows narrowed, Calyx hoisted himself back into his *meion*'s saddle. ''Yeah, but with no food? And with a head injury? When we left to get you to a healer, the kid had about a week's worth . . . maybe less . . . of whatever berries and fruits you guys had found . . . and that's if he was being careful! It's been over three weeks since he went off on his own, so—unless he found some magic well of food somewhere—I'd say it's safe to wager the kid's bordering on starvation right now.'' Small eyes turned southward. ''Why in the forge didn't he just wait for us to show up?''

Turning away from the dried blocks of *meion* dung and fading hoofprints, Sprage returned to his palomino. ''What I don't understand is why this Harris fellow would go into the desert himself.''

Calyx clucked his *meion* forward, continuing southward but at a much slower pace than before. ''What you don't understand is that you've never had the misfortune of meeting Harris Blind-Ass,'' the dwarf answered the healer. ''See . . . this quest is going to take us to a place where—according to this real trustworthy book of myths and legends—there's this Keyless Lock. Now, obviously, without a key, we're gonna need to find a way in, so the lords of Solsbury got together and decided that a skilled locksmith would be handy. Trouble was, so many of you humans were dropping dead of the Black Worm and all those other wonderful diseases that—when it came right down to it—the only person who had the proper skills just happened to be one of the most notorious outlaws in all of Solsbury, So . . . since they couldn't trust Harris to do this voluntarily, they put this bracelet on him to keep him in line. That's why he took Berlyn in the first place. He used her to get the necklace that sets the bracelet off.''

Sprage was nodding as he started his horse after Calyx's. ''Exactly,'' the healer replied, ''and that's why Aitchley followed him. But why go into the desert? The whole point of kidnapping Berlyn was so that he could get rid of the bracelet.''

There was a momentary silence between the three riders as Calyx pondered the physician's words.

''So . . . ?'' the dwarf prompted when no other explanation came.

''So,'' Sprage went on, ''the first thing Harris would want to do is find someone who could remove the bracelet. Someone like an alchemist or somebody. And, the last time I looked, there weren't any alchemists in the Molten Dunes.''

A thoughtful expression replaced the grim look usually on Calyx's face. ''You know,'' he mused, ''you may have something there.'' The dark mien returned to cloud the dwarf's features. ''Still don't see how that helps us, though.''

Sprage's lips twisted in a self-satisfied smirk. ''If Harris kidnapped Berlyn to get the bracelet removed—and *if* he went into the desert to lose anyone following him—the first thing he's going to try to do—desert or not—is head for the nearest town.''

"And that would be the town of Leucos on the eastern rim of the Molten Dunes," Gjuki interjected, nodding his comprehension. "If we were to head directly there instead of following Master Aitchley's trail, there's a very good chance that we might arrive at the same time as Harris or Master Aitchley."

There was a sour pucker still on Calyx's lips as he glanced back at his companions. "That's a lot of ifs to get overly enthused about," he remarked dryly. "And what happens if Harris decides *not* to go to Leucos?"

"Then your quest is over before it really began," Sprage bluntly answered. "Your friend Aitchley dies out in the desert, your locksmith gets away, and you're left standing with your bung-rod blowing in the breeze."

A wry smile crossed beneath Calyx's beard and he clucked his *meion* into a faster gallop. "You've got a subtle way of phrasing things, Sprage," the dwarf quipped. "Come on. Let's see if we can't head 'em off at Leucos."

Four horses thundered off across the grassy plains south of Karthenn's Weald.

It watched them from a far-off ridge, focusing through the imperceptible blur of heathaze and the glare of blinding sunlight. Two figures made their way across the red-brown wasteland, their horses trailing wearily behind them. Harsh winds cut at their faces—throwing up hurtful barrages of dirt and sand—and the desert sun beat down upon them like a cruel and oppressive master.

The first figure was human; a mere youth of seventeen years wearing brown slacks and a brown shirt. The patched and tattered cloak he normally wore was packed neatly away in one of his horse's saddlebags, and he used his cross-shaped throwing ax as a kind of impromptu walking stick as he trudged across the red-brown dirt. A battered and worn hat sat comfortably atop the young man's head of dark brown hair, shielding him from the intense heat from above, and a single feather protruded from the left side of the hat, bent and pale almost as if it had wilted in the extreme temperatures. Yet despite the hat's protection, perspiration streamed in great rivulets down the young farmer's face, and a painful sunburn had formed to join the black, blue, and purple bruises that still slowly healed across his features.

Aitchley Corlaiys looked up at the leagues of barren wasteland before him, all lost in the rippling, shimmering wall of
heathaze. Eyes the color of an ocean's waves squinted against
the harshness of the desert sun, and he was forced to blink
sweat out of his eyes. Soft, powdery dirt—very nearly sand
but not quite—gripped eagerly at his boots, forcing the young
man to exert extra strength to pull his feet free; then he would
step across rocky, hard-baked soil that would trip him up and
send him staggering, drawing an exhausted curse from
chapped and dry lips. Great monoliths of red-brown stone rose
up along the desert floor like the spines of some subterranean
behemoth, and there were spots along the desert landscape
where the ground dropped sharply away in rocky cliffs, offering deadly drops to golden sands and shifting dunes.

The thing watching from many leagues away scuttled once
on spiderlike legs and trained its single glass eye on the figure
following Aitchley.

Despite the distance, it was obvious to the watcher that the
second figure was anything but human. Only some five feet in
height—with bulky shoulders, gangly arms, and hamhock fists
of four warped fingers—the creature walking behind Aitchley
Corlaiys was a hybrid green troll. Born of both human and
troll parents, the half-breed was the dark olive green of most
trolls, yet he stood at least a foot taller than average troll
height. His short, stubby legs moved with difficulty over the
treacherous terrain, and sometimes he was forced to keep his
balance with his long, gorillalike arms. Black, scraggly hair
ringed the bald dome of his skull, and small, wartlike bumps
raised his forehead where eyebrows should have been. Large,
saucerlike eyes squinted against the sun's harsh glare—yellow
pupils in a black iris—and a confused expression of trollish
exhaustion and human despair crossed his inhuman mien.

Poinqart watched with silent gratitude in his mixed expression as Aitchley moved out of the heat and into the inviting
shade of a stony outcropping. The world before them continued to ripple and swim, and Aitchley was no longer sure if
the cause was the curtain of heat before him or the aching
pound that throbbed so insistently at the back of his skull.

Poinqart collapsed into the shade beside the young man, his
tongue lolling from his mouth. "Stay, Mister Aitch," the half-
troll panted. "Murder-kill the snort-horses if we go on."

Aitchley wiped at the dirt and sweat caking his face, wincing as he touched a still-sensitive bruise. "Got to keep going," he barely whispered. "Got to . . . find Berlyn."

Poinqart took a hearty swig from a water flask before answering. "No more food, Mister Aitch," he said in his exhaustion. "We will surely starve-to-die if we stay. Poinqart thinks it stupid-dumb to kill ourselves instead of rescue-saving Missy Berlyn."

Aitchley took the water flask Poinqart offered him and drank greedily of its refreshing contents. "There's still a few berries left," he responded, his voice a little less dry as the water soothed his throat. "And we've got lots of water."

"River-water is not being enough, Mister Aitch," the hybrid tried to explain to his stubborn companion. "Snort-horses have no food, and trolleyes are not enough for you and me to eat. No strength, Mister Aitch, and we fall-down-dead. Vulturebirds will surely pick our bones clean, and then there will be no one left to rescue-save Missy Berlyn."

Aitchley took another long drink of water before stoppering the flask. "So what are we supposed to do?" he snapped at the half-troll. "Give up? Let Harris get away with everything? Let him kill Berlyn?"

Poinqart visibly cringed at his friend's explosive anger, yet found the courage to reply quietly, "Poinqart thinks maybe we can catch him elsewhere-places. Maybe find him when he comes out of the desert. Rescue-save Missy Berlyn then."

"And where is he going to come out of the desert?" Aitchley roared, his sunburned face turning an even darker shade of red, his rage offspring of his weariness and frustration. "I've told you before, Poinqart, I'm not leaving until I've caught that son of a bunghole! If you want to leave—if you want to give up—then you go right ahead and leave!"

"But Mister Aitch . . ." the half-troll pleaded.

"No buts, Poinqart!" fumed the young farmer. "We have water, and that's enough! If you want to go . . . *Go!*"

Many leagues distant, the squat metallic spider-thing could see the look of hybrid sorrow that creased the half-breed's face, and Poinqart sank despairingly against the red-brown stones at his back. "Poinqart will stay, Mister Aitch," the half-troll murmured softly. "He will not leave you."

The argument won, Aitchley turned away from the saddened

hybrid beside him and leaned back into the shadows, his eyes closing. Behind the blackness of his own eyelids, the young man squinted against the pain in his skull and the discomfort his own yelling had caused him. He could feel numerous aches and pains wracking his body, and a numbing exhaustion held him fast in its grip, but he could not allow himself to give up. He had to push himself forward—had to convince himself that there was a chance of finding Harris and rescuing Berlyn—or else he'd just give in to the unrelenting heat and disabling weakness. Or else he'd just lay down and die.

Aitchley cracked open one eye, looking out over the desert before him. Red-brown soil gave way to red-brown soil—all lost in the shimmering veil of heathaze—and, apart from the occasional rock, there was nothing to break up the monotony of the desert's empty horizon.

You really think there's a chance? the young man thought, his pessimism rising up from inside him. You've been pushing your luck for months now, and the Corlaiys luck was never very good to begin with: bad to worse to intolerable. So what in the Pits do you think you're doing? You think you're the bunging Cavalier or something?

The memory of a petite young girl with long, platinum-blonde hair broke through the shroud of weariness and hunger. High cheekbones accented a pert, girlish nose, and a tattered and patched brown shift covered the lean but shapely frame of an eighteen-year-old. Eyes that shifted from light green to ashen grey filled with a kind of emotional beauty that only the eyes could convey, and Aitchley almost felt a wistful smile tug at his chapped and sore lips.

Berlyn, Aitchley's mind mused, and a pang of sorrow touched at his heart. He could remember her standing at the door of the scullery, looking down at him with a concerned smile and a grey-green light in her eyes. Could remember the closeness of her body pressed up against his as they rode together on his horse. Remembered the caress of soapy-white bubbles embracing her pale white flesh, silver-yellow hair damped to dark brown by the rushing stream.

She was the very reason he had agreed to go on this stupid quest to begin with, the young man recalled. He had thought she had died, and he had been ready to journey to the very ends of the living world in order to get her back. And now . . .

Now he was chasing a murdering, thieving, traitorous son of a bunghole with no food and a growing sickness in his head. And for what?

All for the love of Berlyn.

Fear, worry, and hope blazed in grey-green eyes.

Aitchley's fingers tightened instinctively about the water flask in his hands. It isn't fair, the young man concluded, his anger fueling his body with the strength he needed to continue. Berlyn was the best thing to ever happen to me! So what happens . . . ? Typical bloody Corlaiys luck, I lose her! And for what? For a stupid necklace! For a stupid necklace that I didn't even know how to work in the first place! I *knew* I shouldn't have trusted him!

An aquamarine fire ignited in Aitchley's blue-green eyes, and he stared off into the uniform distance of the Molten Dunes. For seventeen years my life was basically nothing more than a cartload of dung, he thought, and I didn't do anything about it. I figured that was my lot in life and I let it happen. But not this time. Life may be unbearable, but that doesn't mean it has to be intolerable. Even I'm entitled to a little happiness, and if that happiness happens to be Berlyn, well, then . . . Gaal damn it! I'm gonna get her back! And I don't care if Harris Blind-Eye has her or all the Daeminase of the Pits! I'm getting her back!

And, many leagues away—stanced atop a mesa of red-brown stone—a glint of silver flashed off the metallic spider-thing, and its single eye stared glassily at the rage and newfound determination that scrawled itself across the sun-burned face of Aitchley Corlaiys.

The smell of his horse was thick in her nostrils, and the rope about her wrists chafed and rubbed against the redness of her sunburn. If the cord about her hands had not been tied securely to the saddle between her legs, there were times when she felt as if she would fall feebly off his stallion.

Berlyn tried to focus through the wavering heat, narrowing eyes that felt as sore and as blistered as her skin. She teetered precariously on Harris's mount, her wrists tied together in front of her and looped about the saddle horn. Perspiration wound down her face and back, and her bare legs stuck wetly and uncomfortably to the leather of the saddle. Harris was nothing more than a dark blur a few steps ahead of her, leading his horse through the wasteland as if taking an early morning stroll. His pace was steady and strong, and he neither stumbled nor tripped, as if unaffected by the hellish temperatures and searing winds.

The stink of the stallion beneath her and of her own sweat mingled with the damp-leather stench of the saddle caused a small frown to form across the blonde's lips. So soon after just getting clean, was all she could think, and, at the time, it seemed a stupid thing to be worrying about. Here I am, she mused more coherently, kidnapped—tied to a horse and forced to ride through the Molten Dunes—and all I can think about is how I smell! How long ago was it that Aitchley and I took that bath at the western Uriisa? Nearly a month, at least. And—almost entirely since then—I've been the unwilling guest of the infamous Harris Blind-Eye. Like I should care about how I look!

Berlyn found the strength to lift up her head as Harris directed his mount into a cluster of wind-sculpted boulders and took shelter in their cooling shade. Casually—without the slightest trace of exhaustion or discomfort—the southern-city bandit undid the knot about his horse's saddle and helped Berlyn to the shaded ground, leaving the rope trailing from her bound wrists. Wearily, the young blonde lay there, relishing the coolness of the shadows as Harris stalked off to his horse and began rummaging through the saddlebags.

Now what? Berlyn wondered to herself as she tried to regain her strength. They had been traveling the desert for a week . . . maybe more . . . and there still appeared to be no chance for escape or release. Aitchley's stolen shield hung brazenly off the cutthroat's shoulders, and there were times when the desert sun gleamed alchemically off the red-gold pendant hanging about Harris's throat. So why keep me a prisoner? Berlyn asked herself. He's got everything he wanted.

Berlyn tried to shift her legs so that the ragged hem of her skirt didn't ride so high on her sunburned thighs. There *was* that, the girl thought darkly to herself, but so far Harris hadn't done anything. Oh, sure, he had grabbed her a few times . . . made a few lewd comments about her body . . . and had touched her in places where she would rather not have been touched by someone like him . . . but that had been the extent of his advances. She wasn't altogether sure, but there was something about Harris Blind-Eye that confused her. Most southern-city scum wouldn't think twice about robbing, raping, and ravishing a young woman—Berlyn should know; she was very nearly the victim of such lawless men if not for the timely arrival of Aitchley. But, despite the fact that Harris had said he preferred women with "a little more meat on their bones," there was something that told her there was more to it than that. Attractive young women were a rarity thanks to the Black Worm's Touch, and she just couldn't believe it was Harris's tastes that were saving her from being violated every hour of every day.

Berlyn leaned her head wearily against a rock, closing her eyes in her fatigue. She could hear Harris shuffling about in his saddlebags, and the high-pitched keen of the hot desert wind screamed and shrieked about the sculpted peaks of their protective outcropping.

"Why don't you just let me go?" she asked tiredly, not even bothering to open her eyes and look at the brigand.

Harris turned toward where she sat, extracting a large pouch of food from his saddlebags and shoving a piece of jerky into his mouth. "Can't be doing that, sweets," he replied cordially. "You wouldn't last a day out there without me."

The weariness in her body made her brash. "I'll take my chances," she grumbled. "You've got everything you wanted; let me go."

Berlyn heard Harris's boots scuff the sandy rocks as he approached and sat nearby. "And what would your boyfriend have to say about that?" the outlaw pressed, offering her a leering grin that she did not see. "Might make him awfully mad if I went and did something as stupid as that."

She didn't know what it was . . . maybe there was a slight hint of something in his voice or a tiny inflection she had never noticed before, but—because her eyes were closed—Berlyn suddenly thought she caught a trace of what was confusing her about Harris's character.

Grey-green eyes slowly opened beneath dark lashes as the blonde fixed a curious gaze on the cutthroat. "You said yourself that we lost him once we entered the Dunes," she remarked, keeping her eyes alert for any change in the bandit's expression. "So why keep me around? I thought I was only here to stop Aitchley from catching up and killing you."

Harris barked a harsh laugh from around a mouthful of food. "Hah!" the outlaw scoffed. "I just kept you around so that if the kid caught up with us, *I* wouldn't have to kill *him*!"

Berlyn refused an offered handful of food. "So why not let me go?" she insisted. "You obviously don't need me anymore."

Still chuckling at her naivete, Harris uncorked a flask of water and took a long draught before answering, "Look, sweetcheeks," he replied, "I'd be more than happy to let you go, but, you know what? I let you go now and you're dead." He swept a hand out behind him at the desert's red-brown desolation. "See that? Ain't exactly Lord Tampenteire's library, if ya know what I mean. I let you go into that—alone and without food—and you're vulture droppings by day's end."

Berlyn's gaze flicked briefly to the saddlebags on the brigand's horse. "So give me some food," she suggested. "You seem to have an ample supply."

A malicious smirk twisted beneath Harris's ragged beard and mustache, and his blue-black eyes gleamed with nefarious pride. "That's 'cause I'm a lot smarter than I look, sweets," he jeered her. "See . . . we've got food 'cause I wasn't stupid enough to get caught back in Ilietis. And if you're going to be dumb enough to send a known thief out to retrieve your horses and your supplies, you can bet that cute plum duff of yours that it ain't all coming back!"

A spark of realization lit in Berlyn's grey-green eyes. "So when Calyx thought the priests had taken some of our food, it had actually been you?" she accused.

Harris's broad smile condemned him. "Ah, you caught me," he mocked. "But it isn't going to last us much longer. That's why it's safer for you to stay with me."

Berlyn couldn't stop the derisive laugh that forced its way past her lips. "Safer for me to stay with you?" she repeated incredulously. "I'd be safer in a pit full of mucid-worms."

An acrid glistening flamed in Harris's dark eyes. "That can be arranged," he threatened her in a low growl.

Inwardly, Berlyn winced, cursing herself for being so outspoken. This was not a man you wanted to get mad at you, she thought to herself, but Harris's attitude sometimes infuriated her. He seemed to have very little—if any—ethics, and did whatever he wanted when he wanted. Over the last few weeks traveling with him, Harris had boasted that kidnapping her was something he had planned after Aitchley had returned victoriously with the alchemical necklace from Ilietis. That meant that Harris had stolen the food from the others long *before* even planning such a solitary outing, and that proved he didn't care what the Pits happened to somebody else . . . So why was he so concerned about her survival?

The blonde flinched as Harris shot out another handful of food. "Here, now," the ponytailed outlaw said to her in more pleasant tones. "Eat something."

Berlyn turned her face away, still angered by the thoughts passing through her head. "I'm not hungry," she lied.

Harris dumped the food into the skirted folds of her lap. "Well, you gotta eat something," the brigand declared. "I don't want you dying on me."

The frustration and anger became too much, and Berlyn was unable to keep the words down in her throat. "Why should you care about people dying?" she spat at him. "You kill people for fun! You killed all those priests! You tried to kill Aitchley!" Grey-green eyes flamed. "You killed Gjuki!"

Harris got up from where he sat, throwing the blonde a cursory glance as he moved to replace his pouch of stolen food. "If I killed the plant-man, I'm sorry," the southern-city outlaw proclaimed with an unfelt shrug. "He came up from behind, and sometimes Mandy's got a mind of her own. Shoulda known better than to try and take Harris Blind-Eye from behind. But don't get me wrong. I didn't do it 'cause I enjoyed it. I did it 'cause I had to." He tied shut his saddlebags and fixed a cruel blue-black eye on the diminutive blonde. "Now eat something," he ordered. "Last thing I need is some maniac kid with a vendetta chasing me all across Vedette 'cause you went and died."

All the frustrated anger . . . all the raging feelings of help-lessness . . . unexpectedly dispersed, and Berlyn felt a stunned enlightenment fill her mind. That was it! She suddenly under-stood. He was afraid of him. Harris Blind-Eye was afraid of Aitchley! For all his posturing . . . for all his boasting . . . Har-ris Blind-Eye was afraid of Aitchley Corlaiys!

Berlyn stared at the ragged and lean figure adjusting the

straps on his horse's saddlebags. So that was it, she mused triumphantly to herself. Harris wasn't touching me because he was afraid of what Aitchley might do to him. And he didn't want me hurt or killed because he was afraid Aitchley might seek revenge and chase him from here to the Pits and back again!

Grey-green eyes drew inquisitive. But why? the blonde wondered. Why Aitchley? Harris was always bragging about his ability to "read" people . . . how he could tell from the way someone talked or the way someone acted what they were really like . . . but what about Aitchley? What was it that Harris Blind-Eye had "read" that made him nervous enough to keep me alive and Aitchley off his trail?

Berlyn settled herself back against a rock, trying not to let her smile show across chapped lips. If Harris Blind-Eye believes Aitchley is capable of coming after us, well, then, who am I to argue with him?

She could almost see the red-violet feather of Aitchley's hat approaching across the ocean of golden sand.

As the blinding sun disappeared behind the flat, arid plain of the Molten Dunes, Aitchley sat strangling the haft of his throwing ax, staring blankly out at the landscape about him. In a few hours, he knew, the heat of the desert would fade, only to be replaced by a cold as biting and as chill as any winter back in Solsbury. It was then he and Poinqart could continue on.

Aitchley lay back, squinting his good eye at the red-brown emptiness surrounding him. Who would have ever thought the desert got cold at all? the young farmer mused to himself, and his hands continued to reflexively tighten about his throwing ax. All the stories he had heard told of blistering heat and burning sand, and—while he could attest to the heat—there were things he had learned about the desert that he had never known before.

Leaning back into the protective shade of a rocky overhang, Aitchley let his thoughts drift back to the day he and Poinqart had entered the desert. They had been riding for nearly two weeks—and the pain in his face and in his head had made Aitchley's thoughts jumbled and his halved vision blurry—

but, even injured as he was, he could not ignore the unexpected beauty of the desert's fringes.

Wildflowers and shrubbery—all awash in a rainbow of colors—had swarmed the flat, otherwise featureless terrain. Ugly brambles that at any other time of the year would have been twisted, skeletal remains were lush and green, dotted with small white buds. There were even a few trees—some no bigger than the shrubs—their gnarled and ancient branches painted with the green of new leaves.

Noting Aitchley's surprise, Poinqart had explained that rain did occasionally fall in the desert and, when it did, such magnificent displays were to be expected. They were also fortunate, for the weather would not be as severe as it usually was. Nonetheless, the hybrid had gone on, the explosion of color and greenery—and the more temperate climate—would not last long. Rainfall was a rare and precious thing in the Molten Dunes, and all the plants and animals had adapted to getting the most out of their brief, springtime respite.

Aitchley pulled himself out of his recollections as the desert steadily fell into darkness around him. Less than three days in, the young man thought, the wild display of plant life and vegetation had started thinning out, growing sparser with each southward league. By the end of the fourth day in the Molten Dunes, they had left all signs of life behind them and had grown accustomed to the red-brown rocks and rusty-hued soil that had become their constant companions. Yet Poinqart had said that—further inward—the desert became even more inhospitable: deadly, rolling waves of nothing but sand. No rocks. No dirt. Nothing but searing, blistering oceans of melted gold.

An involuntary shiver tremored through Aitchley's system as he pulled himself wearily to his feet, his throwing ax doubling as a cane. Even worse than it is now? the young farmer thought dubiously to himself. My feet are sore, my face still hurts, and this sunburn seems to sap the strength right out of me. Not to mention this persistent dizziness . . . and I don't know if it's because we're running low on food or if it's from running face first into the Cavalier's shield. All I do know is that I wish it would go away.

Aitchley glanced at his large black stallion stanced behind him in the rocky shadows. I wish we could ride, but the exertion would probably kill the horses, he mused. Or they might trip on an uneven patch of sand and rock and break a leg, and then we'd really be in the Pits.

Groaning at the various aches and pains prickling at his nerves, Aitchley hobbled over to where Poinqart slept and woke him. Then--taking his stallion's reins in his sunburned hands—the young farmer stepped away from the safety of the rocky outcropping and into the chill nightfall of the Molten Dunes.

They walked the entire night, bundled up against the cold of the desert air like two travelers scaling the northern peaks of the Solsbury Hills. Aitchley tried unsuccessfully to ignore the rubbery weakness pervading his legs and the hot flashes of discomfort radiating from his sunburn in painful contradiction to the icy darkness, but failed on both counts. His stomach made loud growling demands for food they no longer had, and the resulting lightheadedness added to the already vertiginous state of his skull. Sometimes he walked without realizing it—lost in a daze of hunger and pain—yet his addled brain kept up the continuous motion of placing one foot in front of the other. He still could not see completely out of his left eye, but the purpled swelling—as well as other bruises across his face—were slowly fading.

Legs moving robotically beneath him, Aitchley continued across the weird and lurid landscape of an alien world. The blackness of the night was interrupted by a million pinpricks of silver from the heavens, and the two had depended on the moon to offer them sufficient illumination, but, as the days stretched into weeks, the moon began to wane, offering less and less light and making night travel increasingly dangerous. Heavy shadows from surrounding rocks drenched the desert floor like puddles of spilled ink, and the rest of the world was painted a bizarre, otherworldly blue. It was almost like being underwater, thought Aitchley.

As the blazing sun rose above the mountains far to the east, Aitchley doffed his tattered cloak and looked for a place to shelter during the day. He had learned the hard way that it only took a few hours after sunrise for the desert to return to its sweltering heat, and he feared getting caught out in such temperatures again.

A weak tap on his shoulder, and a warped, spatulate finger directed the young man's attention toward a jumble of reddish-brown boulders rising only a few feet higher than Aitchley himself. It wouldn't offer them much protection—especially when the sun reached its zenith and the shadows grew short—but it would have to do. Their nightly trek had taken them in a southeasterly direction, and the usual wind-carved sculptures of rock and stone had become rare. More of the fine, powdery soil covered the ground, and near to their right the ground broke away in jagged cliffs, offering them a panoramic, if also disheartening, view of the shifting ridges of sand that gave the desert its name.

Wedging himself into a small shadowed crack in the stones, Aitchley peered out over the cliffs at the moving, windblown dunes beyond. Do I really want to go into that? he anxiously asked himself. Poinqart said all that sand used to be rocks. Rocks, mind you! Rocks that had been reduced to next to nothing by burning desert sun and freezing desert nights. Chipped and flaked away by hot winds. Blown endlessly up against the cliffs and against each other until there was nothing left but a tiny, redly polished, minuscule grain of sand.

Aitchley gave the rocks at his back an apprehensive glance. If that's what a desert can do to stone, imagine what it could do to me!

Trying to clear his mind of such upsetting thoughts, Aitchley sank back into the meager shade and tried to get some sleep. He could feel his body weakening under the tremendous stress he had subjected himself to—and the weariness and fatigue wracking his youthful frame went straight to the bone—yet he could not fall asleep. Too many aches rubbed his nerves raw, and his mind was too full of worrisome thoughts to really relax. He would no sooner start to drift off when his subconscious would assail him with horrible, imaginary visions of Berlyn, dead and raped, rotting somewhere in the burning heat of the desert . . . or of Gjuki, stabbed and bloodied, unable to get to a healer in time and dead somewhere between the Uriisa and Viveca.

Unable to get to sleep, Aitchley spent the rest of the morning as he had most of his days in the desert: staring blankly at the rising heathaze billowing up from the red-brown earth. He envied Poinqart asleep in the shade beside him—huddled up like a dogling—and wished that he could succumb to the unfeeling embrace of slumber.

It's not bad enough I fail at everything else I do, the young man's pessimism cursed. Now I can't even fall asleep on the brink of exhaustion!

As the sun rose higher and the temperature did likewise, Aitchley removed a flask of water from his horse's saddlebags and allowed himself a long, lonely drink. The cool of the boulders' shade was retreating, and Aitchley could already feel the intensity of the noonday sun beating down on him. It certainly wasn't going to make his food-starved, head-injured dizziness any better, and, in an attempt to save himself some discomfort, Aitchley poured a liberal amount of water over his perspiration-matted hair and plopped his hat back down on his head.

A sudden shape moved out across the shimmering veil of heathaze, dark against the red-gold sands of the dunes. At first Aitchley thought the rippling tide of heat was playing a trick on his impaired vision, and he tried to shake the suspected mirage from his beclouded mind.

Something dark and blurry continued to move at great speed across the desert sands.

Aitchley jumped frantically to his feet, throwing ax in one hand, flask of water in the other. A hot wind blew up from the cliffs—throwing sand and tiny fragments of rock at the young man's face—yet Aitchley kept his gaze firmly locked on the mysterious object speeding across the immensity of the dunes.

"Poinqart!" the young man shouted, never taking his eyes from the shape far below the cliff wall. "Poinqart, wake up!"

With a tired moan, Poinqart cracked one yellow-black eye. "What, Mister Aitch?" the half-troll asked sleepily. "It is not nighttime-wakey-wake."

Aitchley's eyes remained glued to the dunes. "There's something out there," he replied, his voice betraying his disbelief.

Poinqart lifted his head groggily, hamhock hands rubbing at his eyes. "Nothing is out there, Mister Aitch," the hybrid responded. "The desert-steam-heat makes you see-imagine things. Go back to restful-sleep."

Aitchley's grip tightened around his throwing ax. "No!" he argued in his frustration. "There *is* something out there! I can see it!'' He took a step to the edge of his boulder's shadow. ''It's probably Harris!''

Poinqart turned on his side in an attempt to reclaim his slumber. ''Cannot be sneakthief Harris,'' the half-troll murmured tiredly. ''It is too burning-hot for the foul-fiend-sneakthief to live-long-last. Even sneakthief Harris is not that stupid-dumb.''

Aitchley took another step forward, the surprise and wonder drawn across a face marred by sunburn and bruises. ''I'm not imagining things, Poinqart,'' he said. ''I can see him! Come on!''

Poinqart forced himself to sit up as he heard Aitchley's boot scrunch against the sandy-gravel of the red-brown soil. Yellow-black eyes went wide despite the harsh glare of the afternoon sun, and Poinqart watched in worried confusion as he saw his young companion venture out into the blazing heat of the desert's fury.

''Mister Aitch, no!'' the hybrid warned. ''Stay in the cool-dark-shade! Burning-hot will kill you quick, it will!''

Aitchley was deaf to the half-troll's cries. His gaze remained locked on the blurred, heat-obscured object that scuttled through the screen of rippling heathaze. Something was out there, the young man concluded, and it could only be Harris Blind-Eye. It was too big to be anything else.

The full force of the afternoon sun struck the young farmer like a great fist from above, and he nearly swooned, his muddled head struggling to retain its tenuous hold on consciousness. The dizziness of his earlier injury became a harsh buzzing in his ears, and he felt his grip weaken on his throwing ax and water flask before he was able to fight off the impending unconsciousness and move quickly—albeit clumsily—toward the edge of the rocky cliffs.

He's heading eastward, Aitchley noted, battling the incessant heat and his own fatigue as he tried to keep pace along the cliff's ridge. Probably heading for Leucos. Damn this eye! I wish I could see better! I can't tell if he's got Berlyn with him or not! Daeminase Pits! I can hardly tell if that's a horse or not, but . . . what else could it be?

Hurrying along the edge of the cliff—keeping the shape in sight while trying to ignore the burning thickness in the air about him—Aitchley threw a look back at the boulders. Poinqart had gotten to his feet now, his face twisted by a hybrid expression of trollish worry and human terror, but he remained safely in the rocks' shadow.

"Poinqart! Come on!" the young farmer called to his companion, continuing his sideways shuffle along the cliff's edge. "We've got the lousy, no good, son of a bunghole!"

"No, Mister Aitch," the half-breed protested from the shade. "Cannot be sneakthief Harris! Please! Come back!" The hybrid's yellow-black eyes suddenly went wide. "Mister Aitch!" he screamed. "Look out!"

Aitchley could hardly hear the half-troll, the intense heat muffling his senses and thickening his brain. The shrill warning cry from the hybrid reached his ears but hardly registered before Aitchley felt his own weight shift dangerously forward, and abrupt terror flashed in blue-green eyes as the young man looked down fearfully at his feet.

Powdery red and brown soil slid forward beneath Aitchley's boots, trying to take the young man with it as it cascaded over the lip of the cliff and was blown away by harsh winds. A white-hot lance of horror speared through Aitchley's skull as he realized he had stepped too close to the edge of the cliff, and the soft, sandlike earth was gliding downward in a diagonal slant under his weight. Frantically, the young farmer scrambled against the flow of the sand and tried to step away from the cliff, his boots kicking up great clouds of red-brown haze into the stale, hot air.

Stone splintered and cracked as the entire ledge shattered beneath him.

Aitchley managed a single scream as the cliff he stood on broke away and dropped to the shifting dunes far below.

2

Another Glint of Silver

Poinqart blinked. It was no trick of the burning-hot-sun: Mister Aitch was gone.

The half-troll took a tentative step to the shadows' edge, yellow-black eyes locked on the place where Aitchley had been just moments before. A brackish cloud of red-brown dust was all that remained before the hot winds from below the cliffs rose up and blew the haze away, leaving only a jigsaw cleft in the side of the cliff.

Poinqart looked back helplessly at their horses before returning his shocked gaze to the shattered ledge. What was he to do? Mister Aitch was there-no-more. He had been so intent-concerned with what he had thought-assumed to be sneakthief Harris that he hadn't even realized-noticed how deadly-close he had come to the cliff. And now what? What could Poinqart do now that Mister Aitch had fatal-fallen?

Bracing himself against the near physical blow of the afternoon sun, Poinqart stepped out from the boulders' shade and neared the lip of the cliff. The heat struck him immediately—bearing down on him like a fiery weight—but the half-troll forced himself to ignore the overwhelming temperature and shuffle closer to where he had last seen Aitchley.

Yellow-black eyes narrowed to see through the churning heathaze and dust. He could barely squint-see down the sides of the jagged-high-cliffs, the half-troll discovered, and he didn't want to get too-nearby-close or else the same dreadful-fate-fall might claim him as well. Harsh-searing-winds blew up into his face, and there were so many wind-carved-jagged-ledges that Poinqart could hardly see the bottom-ground.

"Mister Aitch?" the hybrid cried over the shriek of the wind, large eyes peering down the length of the uneven cliff face. "Mister Aitch?"

There was no answer save the screaming-howl of the wind.

Poinqart shuffle-stepped closer to the edge. "Mister Aitch?" he called again. "Are you all-right-alive? Can you hear-speak Poinqart?"

The silence that answered his cries filled the hybrid with an arctic chill despite the burning temperature of his surroundings. Sand continued to sift and dribble over the newly formed cut in the cliff's ridge, and every time Poinqart tried to peer over the rim, searing knives of airborne rock stabbed viciously at his eyes.

"Mister Aitch!" the half-troll screamed again, a frightened quiver catching the words in his throat.

Poinqart narrow-squinted his eyes, staring down the red-brown nasty-crags of the cliff's face. Far-down-below—many-many the heights of poor Poinqart—the half-troll could just barely glimpse-see what might be the body-remains of his dear friend. Windblown sand continued to obscure-confound his vision, but the dark shape lying crumpled-still at the base of the cliff grew sharper-clear the longer he stared at it.

"Mister Aitch!" the hybrid called once more, so overcome by worry that he pulled himself to the very lip of the cliff.

Aitchley lay in an unmoving heap at the base of the cliff, his body veiled by the wind and rippling heathaze. Already a blanket of red-gold sand covered half his body, and Poinqart did not like the way the young man's right leg was twisted and bent. His throwing ax lay half-buried in the dunes beside him, and from this height Poinqart was unable to see if the young man still breathed or if he was alive-no-more for certain.

Poinqart feeling-sensed other eyes on the young farmer's unmoving form and looked up, worry-scared, from the cliff. The dark shape Mister Aitch had thought-so-sure was sneak-thief Harris now still-stood-still, shimmering and burbling through the distant heathaze. Although it was no more than a blurry-shadow-shape, Poinqart worried that the question-object had somehow seen Mister Aitch fall and, even now, was think-ing-contemplating some nasty-bad-thought to do Mister Aitch harm.

And if it is sneakthief Harris, the half-troll thought anxiously to himself, how can Poinqart rescue-save Mister Aitch before something nasty-worse is done to him?

Assuming-pray that Mister Aitch is even living-still, the hy-brid gravely added.

Throwing a worried glance along the leagues of cliff to both his left and his right, Poinqart gave a last, fleeting glimpse down the jagged face of the precipice. There was no pathway-route for Poinqart to clamber-climb, he realized with growing trepidation. No way for Poinqart to reach-attain his compan-ion-friend before the burning-hot-sun broil-cooked him or something else foul-nasty-bad got to him.

Large yellow-black eyes filled with tears. "Poinqart is com-ing, Mister Aitch!" the half-troll shouted down into the sands and shrieking winds. "Never worry-fear, Mister Aitch! Po-inqart will not let you die!"

But—even as he tugged at the reins of the reluctant horses—the half-troll couldn't help but hear the falsehood in his own words. There was no way down those jagged, wind-shorn cliffs other than to jump himself, and Poinqart feared that by the time he found a way around his friend would be long-time-dead.

More precious liquid spilled from his eyes and splashed the lifeless sands.

He had been walking for two months now . . . two months that felt like a damnable eternity in the Pits themselves. Two months of begging and stealing . . . of living life like some diseased gutter rat. Reeking of the trash heaps and refuse where he was forced to find his food. Feeling the heavily caked layers of grime and filth that covered his body. Unable to get the rotting stench out of what used to be fine silks and expen-sive fabrics. Knowing he looked little better than the common scum that traversed the road at his side, their faces smeared with their own shit and their bodies wasting away from mal-nutrition.

Nicander Tampenteire scratched fitfully at the thick black

beard that had grown over his once youthful features, his stomach twisting at the sensation of tiny creatures scrabbling about the hairs of his cheek. He could still feel the drying scabs that furrowed across his jawline where he had scratched himself bloody in a convulsive fit of raking fingernails and disgust, and it took all his waning willpower not to rip at his own flesh again as something repugnant and many-legged scuttled out of the way of his scratching fingers.

The young nobleman forced weary legs up a small rise in the road and halted. Dim recognition and surprise lit in his light brown eyes, and he swung his gaze out across the town that had suddenly appeared stretched out below him.

Solsbury, the young noble thought in his stupor, and elation rose in his tired body like a heady aroma.

Forcing weak and weary legs onward, Nicander descended into the level valley of neglected farmlands. Tall weeds grew in place of crops, and there was even a plow or some other such farm tool lying rusted and forgotten among the weeds. All the houses—some no bigger than the Tampenteire privies—stood empty and deserted, their fields unworked and their inhabitants gone. Even the Corlaiys plot was nothing more than a weed-choked rectangle of property, its small house steadily falling into disrepair.

Nicander looked up to where the dirt road became paved with cobblestones, and a sigh of relief passed through his lips. Ahead of him—bathed in the pleasing yellow glow of an afternoon sun—towered the immense Tampenteire estate, its orange and blue banners fluttering in the gentle springtime breeze. Ivy grew in unrestrained anarchy about the wrought-iron gate of the mansion, and his father's favorite garden was as weed-infested and as barren as the farmlands that belonged to his family.

Home, Nicander thought deliriously to himself. Finally home! Oh, for a bath and a change of clothing! A chance to shave off this infernal beard and eat a proper meal! Sleep in a real bed! Eat real food! It was good to be home.

And the first thing he was going to do was demand that an entire squadron of Patrolmen go back to Ilietis and have that Daeminase-spawned Archimandrite's head removed from his body!

Nicander abruptly stopped halfway to the front gate of his

father's estate, a look of worried question spreading across the dirt and filth on his bearded face. The smell of his own body was strong and pungent in his nostrils, and the grime and sores that covered his arms and legs made him wonder what hideous state his face might be in.

Nicander dropped to the ground by the side of the road, his light brown eyes brimming with sudden remorse. I can't go home, he unexpectedly concluded. Look at me! I'm no better than a common peasant who's been steeped in his own piss! What would Father say if I were to walk through the doors looking like this? I'd be a disgrace to the entire Tampenteire family! Why did I ever think that they'd take me back? What would Pomeroy say?

A sudden righteous—and not altogether sane—fury blazed in Nicander's chest, and the young nobleman swung a vengeful eye up at the massive stone keep. Pomeroy! he raged to himself. This is all Pomeroy's fault! He told me to go after the farm boy. Told me it would be in my best interest. This is all *his* doing! I should have him flayed alive and impaled on a rusty spike, the fat balding warthead! He probably wanted me to fail! Wanted to disgrace me! I *told* him I wasn't some simpleton errandboy to go traipsing out across Vedette after Corlaiys! If he believed it was so important that I get the Elixir instead of Corlaiys, why didn't he come himself? Why send me with that inept dunderhead Fain? Daeminase Pits! Pomeroy probably had this all planned from the very start!

The wrath and ire festering inside Nicander Tampenteire unexpectedly turned, redirecting its vengeance on another. No, the nobleman thought foully, not Pomeroy: Corlaiys. This is all Aitchley Corlaiys's fault! He's the one who got me captured back in Ilietis. Him and his little blonde-haired slut! Because of him I was made to work like a commoner. Because of him I lost my food, my horse, my supplies. Because of him I was forced to walk back to my home, begging and stealing like some southern-city filth.

This all Corlaiys's fault . . . not Pomeroy's. I'll see that he pays. Oh, how he'll pay.

Nicander threw a final glance up at the castlelike estate that was his home. No, he concluded direly. There was no way that he could go home now. He would bring shame and disgrace upon the Tampenteire home and name, and he would never become lord himself. What he had to do was clear his name and prove his worth to his father and the others. And the only way he could do that was to beat Corlaiys at his own game. Show the sniveling little plowboy what it meant to be a Tampenteire and prove to his father that Nicander Tampenteire had what was necessary to be the next great lord of the keep.

Nicander forced himself up and turned his back on the nearby estate, retracing his steps down the dirt path out of Solsbury. He would do as Pomeroy had told him, the young noble decided. He would steal the Elixir and use it himself to resurrect the Cavalier, proving to all who mattered that he— Nicander Tampenteire—was worthy of name and rank.

And if Aitchley Corlaiys even *thought* about getting in his way, Nicander would crush him like the feeble little peasant-insect that he was . . . !

Pain. Heat. Cold. Gotthelousynogoodsonofabunghole. Poinqart? Got to . . . Got to find Berlyn. Huh? Can't move my legs. Hot. Hot as the Pits. Howdigethere? Whu . . . Where's here? I don't . . . Ouch. Berlyn. Find. Berlyn.

Fearworryandhopeblazedingreygreeneyes.

Aitchley Corlaiys struggled to lift his head out of the burning sands half-burying his face. The taste of dirt and blood was thick in his mouth—his brain sending scrambled images out through his eyes making it difficult to tell whether he was standing up, lying down, or floating in mid-air—and there was an unsettling, numb coldness in his lower extremities that sent a jolt of anxiety arcing through his mind despite the confusion and delirium that reigned there.

Headhurts. Even worse. Than before. Can't . . . Can't see straight. Got to . . . Got to find Berlyn. I . . . Whathappened? Can't. Think. Straight. Mind feels like mulch.

A vivid memory of falling—of sliding, bouncing, and shrieking uncontrollably down the face of a cliff—flashed briefly across his mind, but Aitchley relaxed when he realized it was nothing more than a dream.

Nodream, a rational part of his brain buried deep within the pain argued. Real. I reallyfell. Poinqart? Huh? I . . . Ow. Yuck. Mouth tastes like. Blood. Phlegh. Tastesawful.

The young man lifted his head—or thought he lifted his

head—and tried to look around. Intense agony speared his neck and forehead at his every movement—and instant vertigo gripped his temples—before his head dropped uselessly back to the golden sands.

Can't . . . Can't. See, the young man thought. Gold. Sand. Allaroundme. Can't . . . Don't understand. Why can't I. See? Too hot. No. Cold. Legs. Can't move my legs.

Weak, rubbery arms tried to pull the young farmer forward, and something protested painfully at his rib cage. Wincing, he fell back into the sands, unable to even roll onto his back, something heavy and unmovable resting on his unfeeling legs.

Cold. The young man recognized the sensation. Legs are cold. What . . . ? Desert. Hot. Can't . . . stay in hot. Find. Shade. Maybe find . . . Whattimeisit? Berlyn? Where did you go? Help. Me.

Fearworryandhopeblazedingreygreeneyes.

Beneath the cruel glare of the desert sun, Aitchley managed to prop himself up on one arm, achieving a brief look around before crumpling back to the searing dunes.

Not good enough, he thought, and he wasn't sure if he had said it out loud or not. Not . . . Sandeverywhere. Got to . . . Ouch. Ribs hurt. Head hurts. Evenworsethanbefore. Can't . . . Can't. See. Joub? Is that you? I . . . Help. Sun. Hot. Sand. Dunes. Die. Me.

Frightening images began to play before the young man's eyes, and he was unable to tell if they were real or imaginary. A million fiery suns burned their image into his brain, and his blurred vision had nothing but league after league of sand to focus on. Somewhere deep down he understood what had happened. Somehow he knew he had survived something but wasn't quite sure what. All he remembered was that he had to get into shade of some sort or else he was going to die. Wind up nothing more than a sun-bleached skeleton picked clean by the vultures.

Helpme, Aitchley tried to scream. Poinqart? Some help one me. Can't. Berlyn . . . I . . . Not fair doesn't bung! Gaal! Some hero hot you are die. Can't. Move. My. Legs. Sands got to die find hot Berlyn. Not a very good swimmer. What? Ribs hurt. Quiet. Don't you heat shadows see that? Gotthelousynogood-sonofabunghole.

The overwhelming pain and unrelenting heat sent Aitchley

reeling in and out of consciousness, bombarding his mind with vivid fever dreams. He was unaware that he kept blacking out, and the phantasms of his subconscious began to overspill into the delirium of his consciousness.

"Has anyone ever told you you have a cute smile?"

Squinting, Aitchley looked up into the sun. But it wasn't the sun. It was Berlyn. Berlyn in a flowing white gown, a dirty cloth from the Tampenteire kitchen held in her dainty hands.

Berlyn? Aitchley inquired, yet no sounds issued from his throat. What are you doing here? You weren't . . .

"You weren't paying attention, that's what you weren't doing." And, suddenly, Berlyn was Calyx.

No, no, the young man tried to answer. I *was* paying attention. I saw him. Saw him. Gotthelousynogoodsonofabunghole. Cliff broke. Wasn't my fault.

But Calyx had already become Gjuki, and Gjuki had melted into d'Ane, and d'Ane had become Poinqart. So many faces. So many voices. Why were they all here? Why weren't they helping him? Berlyn. d'Ane. Joub. Sultothal. Harris. Calyx. Haek. Poinqart. Why wouldn't anyone help him?

A shadow passed over the young man . . . real or unreal he could no longer tell. Too many visions assailed his pain-deluded mind. Too much agony flooded his senses. Shadow. Shade. Real. Unreal. Someone standing over him? Aitchley could not tell. Not that it mattered. He needed to find shade. Real shade. Force his reluctant legs to move. Ignore the pain ravaging his body. This shade hovering above him. This shadow could not be real. It had found him . . . not he it.

Bewildered, Aitchley fought to turn his head—forcing himself to ignore the pain tearing at his neck—and looked up into the sun. So many people stared down at him. So many memories. Berlyn. Calyx. Poinqart. d'Ane. They were all there. Floating. Bubbling. Shifting. Changing. As mutable as the very sands he lay on . . . But there was something else. Something Aitchley had never been before . . . only heard about. Something that glinted silver in the harsh light of the desert sun. Something that stared down at him with a single, glassy eye and took a tentative step forward on lean, spidery legs. Something that could not exist except in Aitchley's pain-clouded hallucination.

The young farmer gaped up at the squat, metallic spider-thing, his eyes seeing but his mind refusing. Just a dream, he thought confusedly to himself. No one. Here. Can't. Can't be. Got to . . . Got to find Berlyn . . .

Unconsciousness finally severed his tenuous hold on reality.

Silver gleamed in the brilliant desert sun—flashing blue-white off the spider-thing's arachnid body—and its solitary eye stared without emotion at the still body of the young man from Solsbury.

Calyx threw a few twigs absentmindedly into the campfire, watching in silence as the flames feasted hungrily upon the dry tinder. The night smelled with the hint of approaching rainfall, and Calyx had noticed regiment after regiment of dark clouds roll in overhead just as the sun had vanished behind the far distant Solsbury Hills. Sprage sat across from him, using the light of the fire to sort through his bag of medicinal herbs, and Gjuki busied himself making supper, throwing together a quick meal for the three men.

His large nose throwing shadows across his face, Calyx glanced up at where Sprage rummaged through his bag. "So you've lived in Leucos before," he commented. "Any idea what we can expect?"

Retying a small bunch of dried *kalreif* shoots, Sprage gave the dwarf a curt shrug of slouched shoulders. "You mean any chief advisors hoarding all the supplies?" he responded wryly. "No, I think we're safe there."

"What about religious zealots forcing us to do penance?" the dwarven smith snorted back.

Sprage feigned a look of thought before replying. "No, none of those either." He put away his herbs and tied his pouch shut. "From what I remember, Leucos wasn't a very big town at all. It's built on the western bank of the Alsace River . . . really not much more than a hamlet. Basic trade is in livestock, and what few farms there are grow mostly grain to feed the kine. The people relied on neighboring towns for their food. Only one regent, if I remember correctly. A viscount. Old fellow. Not in the best of health. I visited his keep on a number of occasions."

Calyx continued poking distractedly at the fire. "So why'd you leave?" he wondered. "A town full of livestock sounds perfect for a man of your skills."

There may have been a trace of melancholy in his movements as Sprage nodded his thoughtful agreement. "It was a
nice place," he replied, "but times are tough. Not much food
was coming in from Viveca or Nylais, and it got hard. Real
hard. People started leaving, and, remember, it's a small town.
When people left, you felt it. There wasn't a blacksmith or a
tanner left. Very few people left working the farms. Things
were not going well. So . . . when a virulent outbreak of Black
Worm started spreading through the livestock, I took the hint.
Lot of other folk did likewise." He shook his head at the
memory. "Tell you the truth, I don't know what we can expect
once we reach Leucos."

Calyx frowned into his silver and black beard. "Sounds
positively charming," he quipped. "Far be it for me to admit
to something good, but I guess it was fortunate Baroness Desireah overstocked us with some of the supplies Paieon had
been hoarding. Doesn't sound like we'll get a ragworm's piss
out of Leucos."

Sprage lay back, folding his arms behind his head. "Yeah,
but still," he said, "at least you made arrangements to leave
our horses there. There's no way we'd be able to take them
through the Bentwoods."

"Yeah, but that also means that whatever supplies we bring
will only be those we can strap to our backs," retorted Calyx,
always quick to point out the dark side of things.

Gjuki joined the two men beside the campfire, handing each
of them a share of dinner. "And you will find that that will
make your journey even more difficult," the gardener proclaimed. "Only the Rhagana find the climate of the Bentwoods
comfortable. Most other races suffer great discomfort. The
weather is hot and humid, and the air is thick with moisture."

" 'The Halls of the Living Mist'!" Sprage dramatically in-
toned.

There was a sparkle of question in Gjuki's tiny eyes as he
turned toward the doctor. "You are familiar with Rhagana
lore, Healer Sprage?" he questioned.

"Well . . . not really," Sprage answered with a hint of red
coloring his cheeks. "I've just read what little has been written
about your people and the Bentwoods, and Rhagana aren't
famous for their vast migration across Vedette. In fact, I'd

never even seen a real Rhagana until your friends brought you to me."

A small smile stretched Gjuki's barklike face. "I am something of a rarity," he agreed. "Not many of my people venture outside the Bentwoods, and those that do return soon after. I am the exception."

"So what made you leave in the first place?" Sprage queried.

Gjuki shrugged lank shoulders. "Youthful curiosity?" he mused. "I really do not know." Pearl-black eyes fixed on the healer. "I know you have a great interest in the Bentwoods, Healer Sprage, but it can be a most uninteresting place. The weather is monotonously predictable and—unless you have an affinity toward heat and rain—miserably consistent. It is so engulfed by its own vegetation that there are no spectacular views of which to speak, and—aside from a few waterfalls—there is truthfully not that much to see."

Sprage nearly got to his feet in his astonishment. "Not much to see?" he sputtered. "Not much to see? What about all the wildlife? All the varieties of plant life?" He tried to blink the shock out of his eyes. "Some scients say that there's more wildlife in a single league of the Bentwoods than in twenty outside of it!"

Gjuki shrugged. "That very well may be," he said, "but you will not see them. They may assault you from the canopy with their calls—perhaps even throw leaves and branches at you for encroaching upon their territory—but the network of trees and vines will prevent you from actually seeing them." A thoughtful glimmer entered his tiny black eyes. "Perhaps that is why there are so many of them?"

Only half listening to the conversation, Calyx had directed his attention to the edge of their makeshift camp. "Speaking of wildlife," the dwarf announced in a low voice, "we're being stalked."

Both Gjuki and Sprage turned to where the dwarf stared, but Sprage could only see the dancing and shifting shadows of their campfire against the foliage. Judging from the way Gjuki rose nonchalantly to his feet beside him, Sprage could only assume that the Rhagana had seen nothing, either.

He was wrong.

"I count three, Master Calyx," the gardener remarked,

moving slowly toward the horses. "Do you concur?"

Calyx gave a contemptuous snort, dimpled fingers rapping across the head of his warhammer. "Three over here," he grunted. "There's probably a hundred more surrounding us on all sides."

Glancing nervously from side to side, Sprage clambered worriedly to his knees. "A hundred what?" he wanted to know, apprehension rising in his throat. "What the Pits are you two talking about?"

Gjuki calmly took the reins of his horse in his coarse, bark-like hands, throwing the frightened doctor a look of impassivity. "Trolls, Healer Sprage," he explained casually. "On the north side of camp."

Sprage rose a little higher. "Trolls?" he repeated, and his voice cracked anxiously.

Calyx shot him an unfriendly glance. "Sit down!" he hissed. "If they think we're going to make a run for it, they might attack."

The fear coursing through the physician's tall frame made it impossible for him to obey the dwarf's gruff order. Dark eyes still unable to see the threat lurking in the brush, Sprage stood up, ignoring Calyx's sneer of warning. "So what are we going to do?" he asked. He threw a questioning look back at Gjuki. "Get to the horses?"

"The horses are probably what they want," Calyx muttered under his breath. "Trolls love horsemeat."

His fear momentarily dampened by his knowledge, Sprage stopped his nervous scan of the campsite and fixed an inquisitive gaze on Calyx. "Since when?" he challenged. "I always thought trolls were afraid of horses."

"*Green* trolls are afraid of horses," Calyx snidely corrected him. "*Brown* trolls consider horseflesh a delicacy."

"Brown trolls?" Sprage echoed with a nervous chuckle. "There hasn't been a tribe of brown trolls in central Vedette for centuries! What makes you think . . ."

There was a sudden shriek from the night-cloaked shrubbery as three shapes exploded out of the darkness. Squat and gangly, the trio of monsters charged straight for the center of camp, long arms flailing. Yellow-black eyes blazed with a hunger and ferocity absent in Poinqart's hybrid gaze, and their wide mouths were drawn back in slavering grins of eager yel-

low fangs. Trollish talons—lost in Poinqart's mixed heritage—
crested their spatulate fingers, and their legs were thin and
rubbery. Their skin was a mottled brown even in the orange-
red glow of the fire, and scraggly manes of unkempt black hair
splayed down hunched and crooked spines as the three beasts
lurched into the small campsite.

Calyx cocked back an arm and caught the first of the creatures in the side of the head, shattering bone in a grotesque
spray of pinkish-white blood. Deadly black talons swung viciously for the dwarf's head, but Calyx ducked effortlessly to
one side, bringing his heavy hammer up and around and splintering the wrist of the second troll.

The third troll trundled past the dwarven smith and ran
straight for Gjuki and the tethered horses.

"Sprage!" Calyx shouted over one shoulder. "Keep it away
from the horses!"

Time seemed to slow as the repulsive creature bounded in
Sprage's direction, eerily lit by the flickering glare of the orange-red campfire. Shadows winked and frolicked across the
crags and pocks of the creature's face, and naked flame glinted
off the viscous saliva drooling from around yellowed fangs.
Dark claws flashed a deadly ebony as the troll lurched nearer,
and Sprage could almost smell the hot, fetid breath that heaved
and panted from its slobbering maw.

Screaming, Sprage threw himself to one side and dived into
the safety of the bushes.

Calyx turned just in time to see the doctor go scrambling
into the underbrush, his hammer slamming into the beaklike
nose of the troll confronting him and dropping the creature to
the dirt. Worry wormed its way through the dwarf's innards
as he turned to follow the charge of the remaining troll, his
own stubby legs propelling him after it. He had to hope he
caught the creature before it did any permanent damage to one
of their mounts. Unexpectedly, however, a lean figure blocked
the troll's path, long, fragile-looking fingers catching the hungry monster on either side of its face and twisting.

Even from where he stood, Calyx could hear the snap of
the troll's spinal cord as Gjuki turned his powerful hands, his
fingers locked around the batlike ears of the repulsive brown
creature.

The troll was dead even before Gjuki released his grasp, its right foot making a final violent spasm before going still.

Wiping his weapon free of troll blood, Calyx shoved his hammer back into his belt and surveyed the trio of corpses with a wry grimace. "Well," he remarked in typical dwarven fashion, "that was fun." He turned reproachful eyes toward the dark bushes. "But what in all QuinTyna's Creation were you trying to prove by running away? If those things had gotten to our horses . . ."

Shamefaced, Sprage dragged himself out from underneath the shrubbery, brushing embarrassedly at the muddy stains caking his knees. "I know! I know!" he retorted, trying to explain away the crimson flush in his cheeks as indignant anger. "But I told you before . . . I'm a coward!" he snapped.

Calyx gave the healer a dismissive wave of his hand. "Yeah, yeah," he growled back, "but I didn't think you were *that* serious about it. I'll guess we'll just have to change that." He returned his attention to the trolls. "Come on, give me a hand with these corpses. Last thing I need is some hungry xlf or something come poking around inside our camp 'cause it got all peckish for dead troll."

Emotionlessly, Gjuki stepped back into the light of the campfire, his horse in tow. "Might I suggest we move on?" he said. "Brown trolls hunt in many small parties of two or three, and if they have returned to the area we are likely to run across more of these scouts if we remain."

Reluctant to touch a dead troll, Sprage looked expectantly at Calyx. "What I don't get is what the Pits brown trolls are doing in Vedette in the first place." He said. "We haven't had problems with brown trolls since . . ."

"Since around the time of the Cavalier," Calyx answered gloomily for the doctor. "Don't you think I don't know that? Dwarves and trolls have *never* gotten along well. We were always at one another's throats—greens and browns—but the browns were always the worst. 'Til Procursus chased 'em up north. Browns haven't come this far into populated areas for nearly two hundred years." He shrugged as if it didn't matter. "All I can say is maybe the winter was hard for them too."

Sprage looked down distastefully at the twisted, rubbery corpses. "Ugh!" he declared. "I don't know if I'm going to be up for this if we have to fight brown trolls every step of the way."

A grim look set itself familiarly onto Calyx's features. "Hey, if you can't stand the heat, back away from the forge," he quipped. He ground out their campfire with an irritated sweep of his boot and stalked to where his *meion* stood nervously tethered to a nearby tree.

As he swung into his saddle, the dwarf threw an annoyed glance toward the healer, clucking his mount forward. "Now," he told Sprage, rankled, "about this cowardice thing: Pay attention . . ."

Screaming. Shrieking. Falling. Spinning.

Aitchley Corlaiys jerked his head up, snapping himself free of the nightmarish memories engulfing his mind. Sand flew off the brim of his hat in great red-gold clouds, and the Molten Dunes touched his sunburned face with a coolness that went rapidly from comforting to freezing.

Seized by a sudden dizziness, Aitchley shut his eyes tightly, propping himself up in a seated position. Sand sloughed off him in great heaps—and his lower half was completely buried in the stuff, making it difficult to move his legs—but he managed to prop himself up against the cliff wall at his back and stare blurrily out at the underwater-blueness of the desert night.

Can't . . . the young man tried to think. Got . . . How. Did I. Get here? Don't remember. Moving?

Questioningly, Aitchley scratched at the dark brown hair beneath his hat, wincing as he touched one of the many cuts and abrasions crisscrossing his scalp. Thought I was . . . gonnadie, he mused dazedly. Out in. The desert. For die sure. How . . . ? How'd I get here?

Trying to ignore a stab of pain from his ribs, the young farmer gave the cliff at his back a curious glance. Don't remember crawling to the cliff, he tried to recall. Couldn't even. Move. Thought my legs . . .

At the bleary thought of his legs, Aitchley dug away at the sand covering his lower half, smiling when he felt his toes wiggling inside his boots. Prob'ly just. Sand, he thought in his relief. Prob'ly just buried. Couldn't. Feel 'em. Before. Thought they might be . . . gone.

An agonized scream suddenly tore through the young man's chapped lips as he tried to pull his legs free of the sand. White-hot misery speared through his right knee—spiraling down through the nerves of his right calf—and his hands made an instinctive grab at his injured limb, his abrupt scream cutting off into a strained hiss.

Broken, the young man understood. Great. Brokenleg. Bloody. Typical. Corlaiys luck. Nowwhatamisupposedtodo? Hurts like the Pits! Can't . . . Ouch. Thisineed?

Exhausted, Aitchley slumped back against the cliff wall, shivering as the arctic cold of the desert washed over him. He was a little more coherent than before, but it was still hard to think. Still hard to accept the fact that he had survived such a fall. That he had somehow managed to get to shade without remembering. How his hat had gotten back on his head without his putting it there. Sometimes he wondered if any of this was real at all. Maybe he had never ventured out into the desert, he speculated. Maybe the old dagger wound in his shoulder had become infected and he had succumbed to fever dreams while battling the infection. Maybe he was really lying in a bed somewhere . . . maybe Viveca . . . maybe Karst. Maybe Harris had never stolen the necklace. Maybe Gjuki had never been stabbed. Maybe Berlyn was standing right beside his bed at that very moment waiting for him to regain true consciousness.

Fear, worry, and hope blazed in grey-green eyes.

Aitchley's eyes sprang open, a rush of determination fueling his injured body with much needed strength. No, he thought resolutely, this was no dream. Berlyn was out there and in need of his help. But what good was he going to be to her lying dead in the desert?

Using the determination reignited in his veins, Aitchley tried to clamber to his feet, using the cliff wall at his back to brace himself up. Dissenting pain tried to keep the young man down, but Aitchley tried to shut out the barbs of discomfort radiating from his legs, his rib cage, his back, and from his head. For Berlyn, he told himself. He had to do this for Berlyn!

With an exhausted curse, Aitchley collapsed face first into the cold sands, trying to blink away the vertiginous stars that exploded behind his eyelids.

Nogood, his pain-filled mind conceded. Can't . . . stand le-talone walk. Some hero you are.

He wasn't sure how long he lay there in his defeat . . . just staring blankly into the dark sands before his face. The extreme fatigue coursing through his body offered him an almost pleasant numbness from all the pain, and he resigned himself to just lie there in its voidlike embrace, watching tiny particles of sand skitter before his own breathing or listening to the sand crunch loudly beneath his ear.

A glimmer of blue-grey steel suddenly winked at the young man from beneath a mound of sand beside him, and Aitchley forced himself to lift his head. A quick sweep of the red-gold terrain uncovered the cross-shaped blade of his throwing ax, and Aitchley hurriedly freed the rest of his weapon from the sands.

My ax! he thought in his excitement. Found my ax! Maybe I can use it to helpmestand.

Even as Aitchley started to prop himself up, he noticed the leather flask half-hidden in the dunes where his ax had been, its cork still in place and its seams intact.

Yes! The young man cheered his luck. Waterflask! Must have landed right on top of eachother! Got water . . . That's enough.

Eagerly, scraped and sunburned fingers tore at the cork, allowing cool liquid to pour down the back of Aitchley's throat. No sooner did the water reach his belly than the young farmer heaved forward, watching through tear-filled eyes as he vomited back up the water he had so greedily drunk.

He shook the flask in his hand, disheartened by the sloshing from within. Not much left, he noted grimly. Got to . . . Got to be. Careful. Take it slow. Can't . . . Can't drink toofast.

Forcing himself to take only a few sips of his water—and giving the puddle of watery vomit a regretful glance even as it soaked away into the sand—Aitchley replaced the flask at his belt and tried once again to stand. This time—his back braced against the cliff—Aitchley was able to get his throwing ax under him and use the shaft of wood as a cane, enabling him to keep most of his weight off his broken right leg. It wasn't easy to do in the shifting, untrustworthy sand—and every time he tried to take a step, the dunes threatened to betray him—but he succeed in hobbling forward a few paces.

Fear, worry, and hope blazed in grey-green eyes.

She needs me, the young man thought, urging himself on. Got to . . . find Berlyn. Got to.

Tapping into his final reserves of strength, Aitchley pushed his ravaged and injured body across the chill landscape of the desert night, staggering through the cold sands after Berlyn. The pain grew distant and obscure as he kept his attention focused on that last fleeting mental image of the blonde—his strength and determination resting on the emotions he had seen in her eyes.

Hope, the young farmer mused. She had had hope. Hope that I would save her. Hope that I would be the hero she longed for. Hope.

He lost track of how long he trudged across the dark dunes, hobbling through the sands like some crippled beggar. The cold bit at his face and hands with a pain all its own, but its numbing chill helped take some of the discomfort from his other aches. Keep centered, the young man told himself. Keep focused. Try not to think about the pain and just do it.

Got to . . . find Berlyn.

A faint pink glow began to fill the eastern sky ahead of him, and Aitchley swung a curious gaze toward the cliffs. He would need shelter to survive the day, he knew. Perhaps a few more steps before stopping for the . . .

Treacherous sand unexpectedly gave way beneath the young man's impromptu cane, knocking him off balance and hurling him down the steep incline of the dune. Red-gold clouds of gritty dust accompanied the young farmer in his uncontrolled tumble down the slope, and pain filled his body with renewed venom. Familiar stars and a nausea-inducing dizziness returned to grip his head, and, for a moment, Aitchley had not even realized he had come to a stop at the bottom of the dune.

The young man blinked stupidly, wishing the world would stop spinning about him. Oh. Ouch, his brain registered. That didn't help.

Pink light grew red as the sun awoke behind the eastern mountains, ready to spread its cumulative heat out across the Molten Dunes. Anxiously, Aitchley glanced back up the incline at the cliffs beyond, frowning with chapped lips at the typical twist of Corlaiys luck.

That was good, he congratulated himself. Now what? Climb back up a mountain of sand with a broken leg? Bloody typical Corlaiys luck.

A menacing blue filled the sky above the young man's head as he tried to climb back up the dune. He fought for at least an hour before giving up, lying flat on his back against the slope of the dune, staring up with blue-green eyes at the early morning light that stretched across the heavens.

Can't . . . Can't do it, he realized in his exhaustion. Had my chance . . . Blewit. Shoulda stayed . . . nearer the cliffs. Stupid! Stupid! Stupid! Deserve to die.

The mental image of grey-green eyes began to fade from Aitchley's mind as the heat rose from the desert's sands.

Gonna die, the young man concluded. Shoulda known it. I'mnohero.

Defeatedly resting his head against the slope of the dune, Aitchley stared up into the blinding blue sky of the Molten Dunes. Suppose there are . . . worse ways to die, he resolved. Just . . . didn'twant to get. To Lich Gate. This way.

A single dark shape passed far overhead, gliding in the thermal updrafts of the desert morning. Aitchley noticed it as the first billowing waves of heathaze washed over him.

Vultures are already starting to circle, he thought morosely. I'm sorry . . . Berlyn. He closed his eyes and waited for the inevitable caress of oblivion.

3

"Thisz Way! Thisz Way! Zstupid Human!"

Something pecked hungrily at the young man's forehead.

Aitchley awoke in the cool shade of the cliffs, his body comfortably blanketed by a thick layer of sand. His throwing ax lay alongside his body, and his hat half draped his face, shielding his features from the burning sun high above. Drunkenly, the young farmer tried to reaffirm his grasp on consciousness, yet the dizziness in his head and the exhaustion wracking his body made it hard to stay alert. The dim, unfeeling void of unconsciousness was a far more tranquil place than this muzzy, obfuscated world of intense heat and unrelenting pain.

Something pecked hungrily at the young man's forehead.

Aitchley managed an instinctive—but weak—wave of his hand. "Ow. Hey. Cut it out," he croaked.

Hidden by the protective cover of his hat, Aitchley heard rather than saw a disgruntled squawk of avian annoyance and a fitful fluttering of wings. What must have been a vulture cheated of its meal scuttled back through the surrounding sands, presumably—Aitchley thought morbidly—to wait for the young man to be properly dead before continuing its feast.

He had just started to drift back into the peaceful blackness of narcosis when something sharp and insistent rapped smartly against his hat-protected head.

"Ow!" the young man yelped.

Aitchley swept out another angry arm, not so much to stop the pain—since the bird could do no real damage through the thick fabric of his hat's brim—but moreso to stop the incessant echoing inside his skull caused by the vulture's pecking.

"Go 'way," the young man muttered through his hat.

Amid another flutter of wings and the flurry of his own delirium, Aitchley thought he recognized the high-pitched, raspy voice that answered: "Awwwk! Eeeed! Eeeed!"

Dazedly, Aitchley cracked open his good eye, pulling his hat away from his face to stare at the red-violet shape that faded in and out of focus before him. Milky blue eyes like turquoise diamonds glittered back at the young farmer, and the fluffy-headed gyrofalc did an agitated dance from one foot to the other as it waited for the young man to get up from his bedding of sand.

"Hungry!" the fledgling announced with an inquisitive cock of its triangular head. "Zstupid place hot! Eeeed! Eeeed!"

Aitchley let his hat fall back over his face, the silence and insensibility of unconsciousness a far·better alternative to the harsh, grating demands of the young gyrofalc. "Go 'way," he snarled at the bird. "I don't have any food."

He could hear impatient talons scrape at the sand as the fledgling hopped closer. "Hungry! Hungry! Hungry!" it squawked. "Eeeed! Eeeed! Eeeed!"

The piercing screech of the fledgling stabbed through Aitchley's skull like a fiery brand, bringing an aching throb to the very center of his brain. Angrily, he grabbed a fistful of sand and flung it without looking in the gyrofalc's general direction, allowing himself a weak—albeit lopsided—grin at the ensuing scream of displeasure.

Quiet returned to the heat-rippled sands of the Molten Dunes, broken only by the shrill keening of the hot wind.

Just as he was about to drift back into the tranquil embrace of unconsciousness, something pecked savagely at Aitchley's head.

"Ouch! Cut it out!"

Adrenaline born of vexation offered the young man a wild boost of strength, and Aitchley bolted upright, snatching his hat off his head and flailing it madly toward the gyrofalc. He could almost swear the fledgling was chuckling as it flapped coyly out of reach, its head craned in a taunting tilt of its feathered neck.

"Hungry! Hungry! Hungry!" the bird proclaimed.

Ire flashed in Aitchley's blue-green eyes at the red-violet nuisance hopping from foot to foot, watching him with glistening blue eyes. The young man's anger momentarily caused him to entertain the thought of throwing his ax at the annoying bird, but his rationale made him think twice. It's just hungry, he told himself with what little compassion he could muster. Who can blame it?

As the adrenaline-induced strength began to fade, another shock jolted Aitchley even further from the serenity of unconsciousness.

Hey! the young man suddenly thought. I'm back under the cliffs! Daeminase Pits! How in Yram the Chaste's virginity did I manage that?

Blinking his astonishment, Aitchley surveyed the desert before him. Red-gold sand continued to surround him on every side—blurred in its veil of shimmering heathaze—yet he was safely in the cool shade of the jagged cliffs. The sun hung high in the cloudless sky, and the wind screamed harsh and hot against his face, but there were no clues to explain how he had gotten back.

Perplexed eyes turned on the gyrofalc dancing beside him. "I . . . How . . . Did . . . How did I get here?" he finally got out. "Did you . . . ?"

Aitchley caught himself in mid-sentence. Did you *what*? he asked himself incredulously. Did you carry me back to the cliffs? Look at him! He's just a stupid little bird. The biggest thing he could probably carry would be a rabbit! Gaal! Is my head that bunged up that I'd seriously think a fledgling gyrofalc could pull me to safety when I couldn't do it myself?

Twisting its head in wordless question, the gyrofalc watched as Aitchley turned his befuddled gaze back on the dunes. So how'd I get here? the young man wondered. Did I crawl back? No . . . I've still got my ax. How could I crawl back holding my ax if I couldn't even walk back? That doesn't make sense. I would have needed both hands . . .

Blue-green eyes scanned the windblown desert. Well, he thought, pursing chapped lips, if I *did* crawl back, there aren't any tracks . . . the wind's blown 'em all away. So how did I get here? Maybe Poinqart . . . ?

The young man stopped himself, frowning at his own musings. No, he told himself. If Poinqart found me, why isn't he here? Or the horses, at least? He wouldn't put me here and then wander off without at least leaving the horses . . . would he?

An explanation tried to form through the dizziness and delirium swirling about Aitchley's brain. But, he continued to ponder, what if Poinqart left the horses behind somewhere to try to find me, and then—once he did—he went back for the horses? That makes sense . . . but would Poinqart leave the horses behind at all? That's not like him. Still . . . it *does* make sense . . . Kinda.

Still wrought with puzzlement, Aitchley shifted his bewildered gaze back to the gyrofalc. "Did you see who brought me here?" he asked the bird.

The fledgling cocked its head to one side, the triangular fluff of feathers on top of his head wavering in the desert wind.

"Who brought me here?" Aitchley tried again, sensing the bird's ignorance. "Did you see who that was?"

Milky blue eyes blinked back without answer.

Aitchley leaned wearily against the wind-carved rocks of the cliff face. This is pathetic, his pessimism hissed at him. I'm relying on a stupid bird with a triangle head to help get me out of this place! He gave himself a mental snort of contempt. Some hero you are!

Forcing himself to remain calm, Aitchley leaned forward, looking down at the fledgling with all the concern he could scrawl across his sunburned face. "You have to think," he begged the bird. "Did you see who brought me here? Do you know where he went?"

Trianglehead twisted his head the other way, his beak hanging open in the desert's heat.

An abrupt idea popped into Aitchley's head. "You know who brought me here?" he tried again. "If you can find him, he's got food."

The gyrofalc's head snapped upright. "Eeeed?" it repeated, interest sparking in diamond-blue eyes.

"Yes, food," Aitchley nodded, trying not to let his own

excitement show. "If you can show me where he went, I'm
sure I can get you some."

Triangulehead began to do an eager hop across the sands.
"Eeeed! Eeeed! Eeeed!" he squawked, flapping wings in fam-
ished anticipation.

A lopsided smile pulled painfully across Aitchley's chapped
and split lips. "Do you know who brought me here?" he asked
again now that he had the bird's attention.

The fledgling nodded its triangular head. "Brought you!"
it parroted. "Zsaw! Zsaw!" It continued to dance across the
cliff shadows. "Eeeed! Eeeed! Eeeed!"

Aitchley hoped the gyrofalc didn't take prematurely to the
sky. "Do you know where he went?" he inquired.

A momentary question lit in the fledgling's eyes and it
stopped its avian jig long enough to give Aitchley a look of
milky blue confusion. "Went?" the bird echoed. "Neverzsaw.
Have to iind!"

With an unexpected sweep of red-violet wings, the gyrofalc
rose up from the dunes, instantly rising to half the height of
the cliffs themselves. Worriedly, Aitchley leapt to his feet, the
sudden pain in his right leg and the vertigo in his head nearly
throwing him back down.

"No! Wait!" he yelled up at the bird. "Where are you
going?"

The gyrofalc hovered effortlessly above the young man, riding the thermals of the cliff. "Have to iind!" it cawed back.
"Iind! Iind! Iind! Hungry!"

Aitchley peered up anxiously at the fledgling. "Once you
find him, are you going to be able to find me again?" he
fretted.

Diamond-blue eyes stared down at the young farmer. "Iind
you!" Triangulehead screeched confidently. "Iind you! No
problem!"

In a blur of red-violet, the gyrofalc spun off into the cloudless heavens, the low whirring hum of its gyre cutting through
the shriek of the wind. Aitchley watched with a sudden start,
impulsively running after the bird and forgetting all about his
broken leg.

"Wait!" screamed the young man. "You're going the
wrong way! That's . . ."

Sand slapped the farmer in the face as he pitched forward,

sentient fire blazing up and down the length of his right leg. Cursing, he watched with pain-filled tears blurring his eyes as the gyrofalc cycloned off into the eastern sky, a fast-moving speck of black against virgin blue.

Frustration joining the pain flowing throughout his body, Aitchley pulled himself back into a seated position and slumped despairingly against the cliff wall. Stupid bird! he grumbled to himself. The dumb thing's going east! There's no way Poinqart could have gotten ahead of me!

Pessimistically, Aitchley pulled his hat down over his face, muttering about the consistency of Corlaiys luck. Oh, well, he shrugged with bleak sarcasm, for a moment there I actually thought I was going to get out of this alive. Should have known better than to trust a bird!

Still, a faint trace of optimism remained burning somewhere deep within all the young man's pain and exhaustion. He saved your life once before, it reminded the farmer. Maybe he *will* find Poinqart.

Aitchley couldn't help the disbelieving snort that escaped his lips. Yeah. Right, he darkly concluded. And I'm the bunging Cavalier.

He closed his eyes and tried to recapture the quietude of unconsciousness.

It wasn't long in coming.

Something pecked hungrily at the young man's forehead, drawing him up out of the halcyon repose of senselessness. Groggily, the young farmer squinted open his good eye, trying to blink the dizziness and sleep from his mind as he stared at the red-violet creature stanced over him.

Copper flashed in the light of the afternoon sun, and Aitchley flinched as a beak rapped sharply against his head.

"Ow!" he exclaimed, opening his swollen left eye. "What? Trianglehead . . . ? Would you quit poking me!"

As the cobwebs retreated marginally to the back of his brain, Aitchley refocused his eyes on the scruffy-looking bird hopping about before him. He was still in the desert, he noted, and he was still alone, but the bird had returned. Maybe he was bringing Poinqart with him . . . ?

Despite the wooziness in his head, Aitchley forced himself to sit up, peering down at the fledgling expectantly. Trianglehead only looked back, shifting happily from foot to foot. His beak hung open because of the heat, but he ruffled out his bright chest feathers as if in prideful boasting.

"Iind!" the bird remarked. "Told you. No problem!"

"Find?" Aitchley repeated in his uncertainty. "You found him? You found Poinqart?"

The fledgling jerked its head to one side, blinking its question without words.

"The troll," explained Aitchley, getting used to the bird's inquisitive head-tilting. "You know? The one who first found you? The one who carried me to the cliffs?"

Comprehension returned to milky blue eyes. "Awwwk!" Trianglehead exclaimed enthusiastically. "Iind him! Iind him! Told you. Told you zso." He made a wing-assisted leap into the air. "Thisz way! Thisz way! Hurry!"

Clumsily, Aitchley tried to pull himself to his feet, finding the sudden movement far too much for his head to bear. With a weak moan, the young man crumpled to the sand, bright stars flashing and imploding behind his eyelids. Despite the fact that his thoughts seemed less muddled than before—although the persistent dizziness still buzzed through his brain like a bothersome horsefly—the exhaustion gripping his body had grown worse. No food. Numerous injuries. Searing heat. It was a wonder the young man could sit up, let alone stand!

Quizzically, Trianglehead stared as Aitchley tried to pull himself back up.

Come on, the young man urged himself. Get up. You can do it. You *have* to do it! Trianglehead found him. He found Poinqart! And Poinqart's got the food . . . and the horses . . . and . . . Get up, damn you! You have to! For Berlyn!

Fear, worry, and hope blazed in grey-green eyes.

A lightninglike shaft of anxiety jolted the young man's system. It didn't work! he realized with growing fear. Through this whole ordeal, that's the only thing that's kept me going: the thought of Berlyn. The fact that she believed I'd save her. And now . . . now . . . Nothing. No strength. No sudden rage. No righteous determination. Nothing!

Aitchley tried to clamber to his knees, momentarily forgot about the shattered bone in his right leg, and collapsed, once again, to the dunes.

"Can't . . . Can't do it," he gasped. "No . . . strength . . ."

Questioningly, Trianglehead hopped closer to where the young farmer lay in the sands, cocking his head in avian puzzlement. "Thisz way," squawked the fledgling. "Hurry! Thisz way! Eeeed! Eeeed! Eeeed!"

Despondency challenged the buzz in Aitchley's head for supremacy, and the young man closed his eyes, a familiar sense of failure rising up to torment him. "I . . . I can't," he told the bird. "I . . . don't . . ."

The gyrofalc skipped nearer, flapping wings in what might have been impatience. "Thisz way! Thisz way!" he screeched. "Hungry! Hungry! Hungry!"

"I know you're hungry!" Aitchley's anger gave him the strength to yell. "I'm hungry too! I haven't eaten in . . . Gaal! No wonder I . . . I don't have . . . the strength."

Something sharp suddenly rapped the young farmer on the back of his head, sending a painful jab through his pain-benumbed cranium. The sudden burst of discomfort succeeded in chasing away the growing despair festering in his mind, and he turned an angry eye on the red-violet bird jumping agitatedly beside him.

"Ow!" the young man declared. "That hurt! Cut it out!"

Trianglehead flapped quarrelsome wings. "Hungry! Hungry! Hungry!" he whined. "Get up!"

Aitchley lay where he had fallen, his weary and sunburned body falling steadily into a kind of numb shock. "I can't!" he snapped angrily at the bird. "I don't have the strength to stand up!"

The gyrofalc's beak pecked him smartly through his hat.

The flicker of pain returned a modicum of sensation to Aitchley's depleted body. "Ouch!" he cursed. "Knock it off!"

"Hungry! Hungry! Hungry!" the fledgling gyrofalc chanted, delivering another blow to the back of Aitchley's head.

Aitchley tried to grab at the bird but it flapped easily out of reach. "I said stop it!" he warned, managing to clamber to his elbows. "I just . . . I can't do it."

Trianglehead paused long enough to regard the young farmer with disdain in his avian eyes. "Zstupid human," the gyrofalc spat. "Make me zsearch then not go. Zstupid place hot! Get up!"

As another blow smacked soundly against Aitchley's hat, a blossoming anger began to churn in the young man's skull. Doesn't the stupid bird understand that I *want* to go? he asked himself. I just don't have the strength anymore. I pushed myself too hard and now I can't even stand up! Yeah. Right. This from the guy who was supposed to save Berlyn from Harris Blind-Eye! I couldn't save her from a three-legged dogling with no teeth right now! I'm completely drained.

Another blow struck the back of the young man's hat.

"Cut it out!" he thundered at the bird hopping tauntingly about his spent body.

"Zstupid human!" the gyrofalc responded. "Zstupid! Zstupid! Zstupid! Iind eeed. You no go. Zstupid! Zstupid! Zstupid!"

Aitchley attempted a wild backhand at where he thought the fledgling was going to strike next but only connected with hot desert air. "Go . . . Go back to Poinqart," he suggested. "Tell him . . . I can't walk. Tell him I broke my leg. Have him come back and get me. Maybe bring my horse."

Trianglehead ruffled indignant feathers. "You go," he retorted. "Went already. You go thisz time. Give you eeed. Zstupid place hot."

The anger and frustration grew. "I *can't* go!" Aitchley raged at the bird. "I can't even bunging stand up!"

"Not my problem," the gyrofalc quipped, pecking the young man tersely on the shoulder.

"Ow! Ouch! All right! That did it!"

Allowing the anger inside him to reach a boiling point—and succumbing to the frustrated rage burning within—Aitchley suddenly found himself standing on one shaky leg, glaring down angrily at Trianglehead. As soon as he realized he had been tricked into getting up, the persistent vertigo attacking his head tried to knock him back down, yet the young man fought the dizziness inside his skull. He'd made it this far, he concluded dourly. He was actually on his feet. If he should somehow have the misfortune to fall, he knew the peckings of an entire flock of Triangleheads wouldn't get him back up.

Clumsily snatching up his throwing ax, Aitchley braced it beside his broken leg and took an uncertain step along the shadows of the cliff. The sands sucked hungrily at his boots—and he hardly had the strength to shuffle along the desert floor—but he managed another unsteady step, keeping close to the cliff wall to brace himself should he stagger.

He tossed a cursory glance over his shoulder at the gyrofalc watching him in avian derision. "How far?" he wanted to know.

Trianglehead launched himself into the desert air and perched on a rocky outcropping above Aitchley's head. "Thisz way," the bird declared, tilting his head eastward. "Not aar."

Aitchley could not ignore the rubbery, untrustworthy shudderings in his left leg. "Not far for you maybe, but I can't fly," he remarked dryly. He gave the blazing orb of orangered flames hanging in the cloudless heavens a disgruntled frown. "We've little less than half a day left," he noted. "Maybe we should wait until nightfall?"

Trianglehead released a snort that reminded Aitchley of Calyx. "Night?" the fledgling echoed snidely. "Zstupid human! What I look like? Owl? Go now. Eeeed!"

Aitchley was quick to nod, unsure if his cloudy head could take any more of the fledgling's high-pitched squawking. "All right! All right!" he agreed. "We'll go now. But I won't be able to walk across the dunes until the sun goes down. How far from the cliffs is he?"

Trianglehead shot off into the sky, angling his body into a blurry whirligig of red-violet feathers. "Not aar! Not aar!" he cawed. "Go now! Eeeed!"

Hesitantly, Aitchley started off across the sands after the spiraling raptor, relying heavily on his throwing ax to keep him upright. His left leg shook with each unsteady step, and he hardly had the strength to keep his right arm locked over his impromptu cane.

Yeah, this is going real well, he grumbled pessimistically to himself. Even if I do make it, I'll probably fall down dead the moment I reach Poinqart.

Bloody typical Corlaiys luck!

The sky grew variegated with reds, blues, and purples as the sun made its lazy way down behind the western mountains. Aitchley Corlaiys continued to trek wearily across the golden sands, hardly noticing the colorful display painted above his head. His eyes remained firmly locked on the ground before him, and his tired and starving body limped and staggered at a clumsy pace beside the cliff wall. He had stopped only twice during his journey, leaning up against the cliff face and allowing himself a few sips of precious water. But now his flask was dangerously low, and the bright colors splashing the firmament caused despair rather than wonder.

"How much . . . How much further?" he called to the bright object whirling through the chromatics above him.

Trianglehead made an impressive circle, banked, and soared out over the cooling sands. "Not aar! Not aar!" he responded.

"You said that about two leagues ago!" the young farmer below him complained. "I'm not . . . I'm not going to be able to make it much further."

Diamond-blue eyes stared down at the young man. "Quit komplaining," taunted the gyrofalc. "Zsquawk like a lledgling. Not aar!"

Aitchley returned his gaze to the sand beneath his feet, careful not to trip or fall. There was an unsettling numbness in his legs and arms, and he could feel the shuddering protests of the muscles in his left leg every time he placed his weight upon it. The disorienting buzz had grown stronger in his head, and bleary images began to play tricks upon his eyes. Twice before he thought he had seen Poinqart and the horses ahead of him, but it only turned out to be the heathaze tormenting him. Now the growing shadows stretching across the dunes added to his confusion, mimicking the color of the young man's horse and fooling him with their shifting, rippling motions.

I'm not . . . I'm not going to make it, Aitchley's pessimism concluded. I might as well give up. Once the sun sets, I'm as good as dead anyway. I don't think . . . I'll be able to survive another night without my cloak or some blankets. It gets . . . awfully cold here at night.

A sudden squawk from Trianglehead pulled the young man free of his depressing thoughts and drew his gaze skyward. Questioningly, his eyes narrowed as the fledgling above him did an acrobatic loop, circumgyrating down so that he hovered a few feet over Aitchley's head.

"Told you zso! Told you zso!" the gyrofalc shrieked enthusiastically. "Not aar, I zsaid! Not aar! Did you listen? Did you? Zstupid human!"

Made eager by the fledgling's promise, Aitchley forced his

legs up a gradual rise in the red-gold sands and stopped at its summit. The cliff wall still towered solemnly on his left—draping the young farmer in the false shadows of the coming night—and the setting sun continued to blaze an array of colors across the sky, but Aitchley had to blink a few times to make sure his pain-addled mind was not fooling him again with imaginary visions and dreamlike mirages.

Cutting a silent green swath through the harshness of the Molten Dunes, Aitchley stared down in stunned admiration at a lush oasis of life. Trees—strange and tall with weird, broad leaves—loomed on lengthy, bamboolike trunks, and thick bushes and shrubs grew in chaotic profusion about a burbling river. For at least a quarter of a mile the greenness stretched eastward, and it tapered like some leafy green serpent striped with blue off into the southern distance.

Aitchley nearly tripped down the slope of the sand, so great was his surprise. Blue-green eyes awash with shock and disbelief, the young man wanted to shake his head to make sure his eyes weren't playing tricks on him but feared the insistent vertigo in his skull might knock him down.

"I . . . Uh . . . Ummm . . ." he sputtered his astonishment.

Trianglehead wheeled excitedly through the multicolored air. "Eeeed! Eeeed! Eeeed!" he cawed raucously. "Time to get eeed!"

Wrapped in a shroud of muted surprise, Aitchley began his descent toward the river valley, his staggering, limping pace slowing as he neared. It was almost as if the young man feared the scenery might suddenly vanish if he walked too hurriedly or uttered something too loudly. After all . . . who had ever heard of a river in the middle of a desert? his pessimism grunted its suspicions. By all definition, it would no longer be a desert.

Aitchley's bewildered gaze used what little daylight was left to scan the flat, arid landscape on every side of him. No . . . it was true, his mind finally grasped. The desert was still desert as far as his eye could see. The only difference was that here—laid out in front of him—a miniature jungle carved the dunes in half.

Unable to contain his excitement any longer, Aitchley broke into a hobbling run, limping urgently into the green valley. All the pains and aches of his body seemed to vanish as he pushed his way through thick foliage, enjoying the feel of springtime buds against his skin and even relishing the pinpricks of discomfort from the occasional sharp branch or bramble. Not even his sunburn could dampen the sensations that sparked his nerves, and the thick smell of the river's waters filled the young man's nose like an aromatic wine.

This is incredible! the young farmer thought. Trees! Water! Bushes! I . . .

An odd-looking shape dangling from a nearby shrub caught Aitchley's attention, and he hurriedly limped to the bush. Eager hands snapped the figlike fruit from its branch and shoved it into the young man's mouth, greedy jaws chewing the dark fruit into a gooey, succulent pulp. The anxious thought that perhaps the figlike delicacies might be poisonous didn't even cross Aitchley's mind until he had already eaten three of the moist fruits.

Above him—milky blue eyes tracking a small lizard through the underbrush—Trianglehead perched on top of a palm, his head craned in that inquisitive avian tilt. "Eeeed!" the fledgling chirped. "Hungry! You zsaid eeed!"

His mouth full of figs, Aitchley tossed the demanding gyrofalc a dark fruit. "You said Poinqart was here," he responded. "Here. Eat this instead."

Effortlessly, Trianglehead snatched the thrown fig out of the air and returned it to his perch, tearing at its dark flesh with a hungry copper beak. The half-eaten fruit nearly smacked Aitchley on top of his hat as the bird threw it away, a repulsed squawk coming from his feathered throat.

"Awwwk!" the fledgling announced. "Zshit! Tastes like zshit!"

"It's food," Aitchley answered, popping another into his mouth. "Shut up and eat it."

"Don't want any that rubbish!" Trianglehead retorted. "Meat! Want meat!" He ruffled indignant feathers. "Kould eat that krap anytime!"

Aitchley nearly found himself smirking at the irate fledgling's demands. I could do with some meat myself, the young man thought, shoveling another fig into his full mouth, but at this point I'll take what I can get. There's some type of food here, and water; even if I can't find Poinqart right away, I'll have better luck staying alive here than out there.

The young farmer gave the darkening desert a last glance, the glare of its red-gold sands turning to a harmless-looking blue.

Still feeling the weariness in his legs, Aitchley hobbled to the river's edge and looked in. The waters were gentle and blue, filling his nostrils with the same odors as those at the Uriisa, and—unbidden—a memory sprang to mind.

Frothy white bubbles hugged slim, slender limbs, yellow-white hair blonde-brown with moisture.

Aitchley trembled at the thought. *Berlyn,* his mind mourned. *I miss you so much. I swear I'll find you ... I'm just sorry it's taking so damn long. I'm no hero. I don't care if the Cavalier was supposed to be my ancestor, I'm not cut out for this. But I swear ... I swear I'll get you back. I swear it!*

A fragment of muddy ground unexpectedly slipped beneath the young man's left boot, interrupting his thoughts with the sudden grip of gravity. Gawkishly, Aitchley splashed into the river, landing with a crystalline spray on his rump. An angry grumble split his lips as he tried to pull himself out, and the taunting laughter from the treetops didn't help his predicament any.

"Zstupid human!" Trianglehead mocked from his palm tree. "No time to take a bath! Klumsy! Klumsy! Klumsy!"

Soaked and dripping, Aitchley crawled out of the water, throwing an acrid glare upward. "Shut up, you stupid bird," he snarled back.

The many hues of the desert sky faded imperceptibly to black and dark blue as the chill of night took hold. Anxiously, Aitchley looked down at his water-soaked boots and pants, feeling the coolness in the air already nipping with arctic teeth at his legs and waist.

Oh, that was real good! his pessimism jeered him. *You find an oasis—a means of keeping yourself alive—and what do you do? You fall in a river just as the sun's going down! What are you trying to do? Be the first man to ever freeze to death in the desert?*

Despondently, the young farmer sat on the riverbank, attempting to wring some of the moisture out of his pants. *Only Aitchley Corlaiys could bung something up this badly,* he concluded glumly. *Should have known better. Everything I try turns to useless mulch. Should never have gone on this stupid quest. Should have stayed back in Solsbury and gone about my complete-and-utter-failure ways.

Shrubbery suddenly parted behind the young man, and Aitchley spun around where he sat, his eyes going wide at the figure that approached him. Fear and wonderment filled the young man with a fiery rush of adrenaline, and every instinct in his head told him to run away, but the river blocked his only escape.

The last rays of the setting sun gleaming off its silver framework, a man made completely of metal stepped through the brush, lenses of smoky grey filters rotating and irising into focus. An articulated hand with five steel fingers reached out for Aitchley's head, joints whirring and humming with hidden gears and servos as it splayed its hand out beneath Aitchley's chin.

The metal man cocked its head in almost the same questioning fashion as Trianglehead and looked down at the young farmer with video camera eyes. "Query: Do you require assistance, Aitchley Corlaiys?" the construct said.

Aitchley could only blink in response.

4

Tin William

From upon a bed of silken clouds, Aitchley Corlaiys floated up out of slumber, his body refreshed and rejuvenated. Bleary, nightmarish images scurried rodentlike through the recesses of his mind—terrifying slow-motion sequences of uncontrolled falling, unbearable heat, and helpless exhaustion—before he pushed them back into his subconscious and closed the door. Dreams, he thought drowsily to himself. Nothing more than bad dreams.

Squinting against the light, Aitchley cracked open his left eye, instantly aware that no purpled or swollen flesh obscured his vision. Just like I thought, he confirmed with a lopsided grin. A dream.

As the grogginess of sleep continued to loosen its hold, Aitchley opened his right eye and looked around. A sudden spear of apprehension lanced through his innards, and he bolted upright in his bed, gaping in wordless wonder at the bizarreness of the room surrounding him.

Strange, tubelike rods of some sort hung mysteriously from the chamber's ceiling, filling the room with harsh, unnatural light. Furniture that resembled bookcases lined three out of four walls, every shelf filled with rows of grey, booklike shapes—like solid covers with no interior pages—and some *thing* with a grill like the Cavalier's visor sat stuck in one wall, humming to itself as it blew a cool breeze into the room.

The fourth wall was the most confusing of all. Even though it was made out of some alien grey substance, Aitchley recognized a desk, but he had no idea what all the funny buttons and levers implanted in its surface were for. And—above the desk and completely filling the wall—Aitchley stared at what appeared to be thirty or forty different windows . . . only something wasn't right. Each window—although they were beside, atop, and below one another—showed different scenes . . . different views. Some were completely black as if curtained or looking out into a moonless night, while others had pictures frozen in place as if they were some sort of odd painting. Still others showed movement: People. Places. Some kind of riot raging in the streets of some town. A ragged shadow slipping expertly past priests in velvet-trimmed robes. Six or seven brown trolls ravenously chasing someone on horseback. A young man and a young woman enjoying an afternoon swim in a river.

Aitchley blinked repeatedly. Hey! his sleepy mind exclaimed. *That's me!*

As the fear gradually turned to wonder, Aitchley pulled himself out of bed and neared the wall of magic windows. There were over thirty different portals showing thirty completely different views, and the more Aitchley stared the more he recognized.

There was Lord Tampenteire's estate and . . . was that *him* walking up to those imposing black gates? And there . . . ! A frozen image of him, Calyx, and General Fain outside the Abyss. Another window showed Harris Blind-Eye and Gjuki talking in low whispers in some gloomy, ice-strewn alleyway. And a fourth revealed a picture of Aitchley—looking halfway to Lich Gate himself by his appearance—limping and hobbling through heavy foliage with the help of a man who appeared to be dressed in full armor.

A vague memory tugged at the young man's mind as he stared at the wall of screens. He recalled something about trees and streams in the middle of the desert, but he was no longer certain what was real and what was not. Like this room, he concluded. I've never seen anything like it. What . . . Where am I?

A portion of wall slid away and the intense heat of the

Molten Dunes poured through the portal like molten lava. Cringing, Aitchley instinctively backed away as a tall, humanoid shape stepped through the door, a familiar red-violet object perching on its metallic shoulder. Another figure scuttled in behind the first, large and squat and scurrying on spiderlike legs into the corner of the room.

Alarmed, Aitchley shrank back up against his bed, wild eyes staring at the freakish creatures entering the room.

Tilting its head, the humanoid shape of metal regarded the young man with emotionless camera-lens eyes. "Query: You are feeling better?" it asked.

The shock and fear stuck the words in his throat. "I . . . I . . . I . . ." the young man stuttered.

Trianglehead flew off the man of metal's shoulder and landed on a bookcase near Aitchley. "Awwwk!" teased the bird. "And you zsay I no zspeak well!"

Aitchley could only blink dimly at the gyrofalc.

The creature that looked like a man took another step into the room, allowing the wall to slide shut behind it. "Statement: The healing process may have left you disoriented," it said in a low, electronic voice like the buzzing of a million bees. "Perhaps you should resume a supine position?"

Bewildered and afraid, Aitchley's hand went automatically to where his sword hung at his hip, and a frigid barb of terror struck his heart when it realized the weapon was gone. His fright expanded when—for the first time—he realized he was completely naked, standing unarmed and nude in front of this new menace.

"Where's . . ." he started to demand, but a new shock cut off his voice.

Hey! he abruptly noticed. I'm standing up! By myself! And . . . And my sunburn . . . ! It's gone! But that's . . . I mean . . . That's not . . . How . . . ?

The steel figure neared Aitchley in concern, a metal hand reaching out for the young man's arm. "Observation: The disorientation of the regenerative matrix and nutrient bath have left you addled," it declared. "Solution: Return to the x-axis before more damage is done to your motherboard."

Hardly hearing the robotic request, Aitchley plopped back down on the soft mattress of his bed, staring in amazement at the painless way his right leg bent at the knee.

This can't be happening, the young farmer argued with himself. This has got to be another stupid dream. Bones don't heal overnight! I could barely walk yesterday, and now I'm jumping around like some spiny leafhopper! And my sunburn . . . where did *it* go?

His astonishment continued to grow as Aitchley stared in stunned bewilderment at his naked body. No, he saw, the sunburn *was* gone. And that wasn't all. Unclothed, he could see every scrape, bruise, and abrasion he had suffered had vanished just as completely. Even the old dagger wound at his shoulder had faded to an almost invisible strip of pink-white scar tissue.

This is impossible! the young man concluded. I've got to be dreaming this! I'm probably lying out in the desert somewhere—dying from the heat—and this is some last, frenzied hallucination before my brain boils in its own blood!

Purposefully, the metallic man clomped stiffly across the room, turning video-camera eyes on the wall of magic windows. "Observation: You are confused," it said. "Perhaps this will help you to better understand."

Aitchley watched mutely as the steel figure stalked toward the grey desk below the walls of windows. And what the Pits is this thing? the young farmer asked himself suspiciously, squinting at the metal humanoid. I must really be hurting badly to imagine something like this. It almost looks like a suit of armor, but it's not wide enough for someone to fit inside. So how does an empty suit of armor with glass eyes walk and talk with no one inside it?

Blue-green eyes narrowed at the glimmering form of metal. The creature stood nearly a foot taller than Aitchley, and its silver body gleamed in the harsh white light of the magic rods overhead. Its head was humanlike in shape—lacking the recognizable bevor or visor of a piece of armor—and, in its place, was a silver ridge that attempted to mock a nose and some sort of triangular grill where the mouth should be. There were no signs of chainmail at the metal joints—only some kind of shiny black material that bent and stretched without difficulty—and none of the more familiar pieces of armor adorned the figure. There were no tassets, cowters, or skirt. It was almost as if someone had built a suit of armor that very nearly mimicked the full anatomy of the human body. The only noticeable difference about the creature were the upraised symbols across its silver chest: TW-O: 114-84-1311825

Aitchley wondered fleetingly if dwarves had anything to do with this construct.

The man of metal made a few quick adjustments at the grey desk and all forty windows blinked simultaneously, revealing an identical image of Aitchley and the metal man trudging through the desert oasis.

"Statement: I found you approximately .427 kilometers from my workstation and assisted you back," the human-shaped creature reported. "Although it conflicts with standard programming to interfere, I placed you in both nutrient bath and regeneration matrix and administered the proper dosage of anxiolytics and analgesics to help repair the lesser damage to your system. I then corrected the error in the osseous tissue of your lower limb and the similar errors in your chest cavity. An intravenous feed helped replenish many of the fluids lost while out in the desert, and I performed numerous computed tomographic scans to ascertain you suffered no permanent brain damage from your fall."

Aitchley watched in dumbed stupefaction as all forty screens cut to a wide-angle shot of someone bouncing, flailing, and sliding down the uneven side of a cliff. It wasn't until he saw his own hat fluttering and spiraling weakly in gravity's heartless grip that the young man realized the person falling was himself.

The picture flashed back to Aitchley and the man of steel entering a large, domelike structure half-hidden among the foliage of the oasis, spiderlike creatures of silver following behind them. Each spider-thing stood about four to five feet in height, and—for some reason—Aitchley found their shape oddly familiar.

The silver man turned away from the wall of magic windows, freezing their movements with a single flick of a switch on his desktop. "Declaration: Permit me to introduce myself," it said. "I am unit TW-O: 114-84-1311825." It focused camera lens eyes on the young farmer. "My programmers call me Tin William."

Aitchley could only gape in wordless reply.

*   *   *

A fat man made his way, wheezing and puffing, up the stone and marble staircase leading to the Guild of Alchemy. Warily, he threw a distrustful glance over one shoulder at the elaborate carriage waiting patiently for him by the curb, its Patrolman driver slumping, bored, in his seat. No one else seemed to notice him as he approached the impressive building, and—with the return of his certainty—he drew his robes about his wide bulk and stalked through the massive double doors.

A pock-faced youth with yellowing teeth met him inside the hall with a simple bow. "Scholar Pomeroy," he greeted the fat man. "Master Epistor is awaiting your presence. This way, sir."

With another bow, the scrawny youth started down a long hallway, not even bothering to make certain the obese scholar followed. Arrogantly, Pomeroy began after the boy, disdainfully screwing up his nose at the various chemical smells that pervaded the corridor. Heavy, rhythmic clanging sounded from locked chambers, and thin wisps of noxious clouds escaped out into the hallway as Pomeroy walked past. The sounds of bubbling cauldrons and steam-rattled lids echoed throughout the wide hall, and Pomeroy could only speculate at what sort of experiments were going on behind the many locked doors of the Guild.

The pock-faced adolescent ahead of him turned sharply to the left and led the overweight scholar down a narrower corridor, leaving the sounds and stench of the Guild's workrooms behind them. At the far end stood a single door, and the scrawny servant-boy offered another curt bow as he pulled the portal open for Pomeroy.

"In here, sir," he said. "Master Epistor is expecting you."

Snorting, Pomeroy pushed his way past the ugly teen and entered into a plush chamber of ornamental rugs and oaken bookcases. A massive desk with intricately carved detail—Pomeroy assumed dwarven—was the centerpiece of the room, but its fine, mahogany finish was obscured by a towering clutter of papers, parchments, scrolls, and vials. Wrinkled, skeletal hands appeared groping behind the disarray, and Pomeroy could barely make out the bent and wizened figure of Alchemist Epistor hunched over his work.

Clearing his throat, Pomeroy caught the Guildmaster's attention.

Alchemist Epistor glared up slowly from behind his jumble of grimoires, texts, and scrolls, his face thin and taut and shrivelled like a prune. A single cruel eye peered up at Pomeroy with an icy cold blueness while the other socket was puckered and soured like a rotting peach, its wrinkled, tightened flesh lovingly clasping a faceted ruby in place of its eye.

"I take it you have received word?" the ancient alchemist queried, and his voice was as dry and brittle as his withered body.

Pomeroy stared down at the old man, trying to keep the scornful sneer off his bloated lips. "No, I have not," he responded, matter-of-factly, "but I see no reason why that should worry us. By my calculations, they should be well through the Bentwoods by now."

Pomeroy thought he caught a mocking smile stretch the old man's lips. "By your calculations, hmmmm?" the Guildmaster echoed, and the scholar could not tell if there was a trace of derision in his tone or not. "Forgive me if I am not reassured by your calculations, Scholar Pomeroy, but I have far too much at stake here to be quelled so easily."

A scarlet flush filled the tutor's cheeks as he caught the underlying insult. "I stand to lose as much as you, Epistor," he snarled back, "and if you are unable to trust my very word, perhaps I . . ."

The elderly alchemist raised a placatory hand, silencing the enraged teacher. "Be at peace, Scholar," he advised. "I did not mean to imply that it was your word that was circumspect. I am more concerned over your choice of messenger."

Pomeroy drew himself up, indignant that his decisions should be questioned. "General Fain is loyal to me," he proclaimed. "He would not dare think of betraying us!"

Epistor's ruby-red eye glinted in the flicker of the lanterns. "That's just the point, now, isn't it?" he responded. "I have found that most Patrolmen tend to be pompous, unthinking, arrogant fools who use their positions of power for the belittling of others. I see no reason why I should consider Fain otherwise. It has been over three months since we have received word, and I begin to wonder if your general has not made some other plans . . . ?"

Pomeroy allowed himself an unfelt chuckle. "You are far too suspicious, Epistor," he remarked. "Fain may realize what

I've sent him out after, but to betray us? What would he do? Sell the Elixir to the highest bidder? Our plan will make us rich beyond dreams compared to the few paltry coin he may receive from a single buyer.''

The alchemist waggled a skeletal finger at the tutor. ''There are others, Scholar,'' he said. ''Skilled alchemists in both Karst and Malvia. He may take the Elixir there.''

''But the most skilled are here!'' Pomeroy replied, unconcerned. ''Only someone of your expertise can duplicate the Elixir of Life!''

''*If* it can be duplicated,'' Epistor added.

The obese scholar gave the alchemist a sideways glance. ''An elixir is nothing more than a combination of liquids,'' he grunted. ''All you need do is break it down into its separate elements and you will be the first man to ever mass-produce a medicinal potion that makes death obsolete!''

Epistor gave the books and scrolls scattered across his desk a one-eyed sweep, his lips pulling downward in an unconvinced frown. ''I do not know,'' he answered. ''I have been reading about this Lich Gate. More specifically, about this Cathedral of Thorns and the treasures therein. There is a great deal of ambiguity in the details. Some people believe this Elixir of yours exists . . . others say it is naught but a panacea that can cure ills but not raise the dead. There are still others that believe this Elixir is the fabled philosopher's stone . . . the legendary substance that can change lesser metals into gold. Whatever its true purpose, all these beliefs bear the unsettling stench of magic about them, and even the greatest of alchemists cannot replicate something that has been that long dead!''

''Magic! Fah!'' scoffed Pomeroy. ''Next you'll tell me you believe in damselflies and jackanapes. Whatever magic there was faded almost four hundred years ago, and the Elixir would have faded away with it! No . . . I'm certain there's a positively simple scientific explanation for this Elixir, and I am counting on you, my friend, to find it. Think of it! Life everlasting in a bottle!'' A greedy gleam lit in Pomeroy's porkine eyes. ''Imagine what someone would pay for that!'' He directed his gaze to the Guildmaster. ''I think seventy thousand gold is a fair price for my delivering it into your hands . . . hmmm?''

Alchemist Epistor returned his attention to the books in front of him, dismissing the scholar with a wave of a withered hand. "Yes, yes," he agreed tartly, "*if* your servant-boy Fain doesn't get any ideas in his head. Now go. Leave me. I have much work to do."

As Pomeroy made his departure, a cruel smile came to the Guildmaster's skeletal mien, the blood-red glare of his faceted eye splashing crimson splotches across the walls of his chambers. And if *my* calculations are correct, Scholar, he thought malevolently to himself, and this Elixir *does* bear the properties of the philosophers' stone, you can have all the money you want, you fat, slobbering fool. Everlasting life is meaningless when I have the means to turn lead into gold!

What might have been wheezing laughter followed Pomeroy down the wide hallway of the Guild of Alchemy; he shrugged it aside as he did the sound of boiling cauldrons.

Aitchley Corlaiys stepped gingerly into his clean and mended pants, overwhelmed at how new his clothes looked. For the past year he had been wearing the same brown shirt and slacks, patching and sewing them himself whenever necessary. Now he could barely find his own previous repairs, let alone the ones made by Tin William's spidery servants.

"Statement: I hope the corrections made on your garments are satisfactory," the robot said. "Tailoring is not part of my basic programming."

Aitchley adjusted his hat more comfortably on his head, its brim not quite as limp as before and the gyrofalc feather just a tad bit brighter. "No, no," he stuttered his awed response. "They're . . . They're fine. I just . . . I just don't get it."

The creature called Tin William made an inquisitive tilt of its head, video-camera eyes staring without emotion. "Query: Get it?" the man of metal repeated. "Syntax error. I do not understand your meaning. Have I not just given you back your clothing?"

Aitchley shook his head, forcing himself to continue this unbelievable dialogue. "No, that's not what I meant," he responded. "I mean . . ." He gave a helpless look at the alien room around him. "All this," he went on with an encompassing wave of a hand. "Why you're here. How you found me. What . . . What this place is."

The glistening humanoid framework of metal lifted its steel

chin in a sudden move of comprehension. "Declaration: I have been negligent," it replied. "Explanation: I am unit TW-O: 114-84-1311825. Primary function: TransWorld Observer. Basic programming relates to study of neighboring universes and correlation of data to be transmitted back to my homeworld of Sphere for further study." It cocked its head to one side. "Query: Does this answer your question?"

Aitchley blinked stupidly. "Uhhhh . . ." was all he could manage.

Tin William's video-camera eyes focused intently on the young farmer. "Exposition: My primary function is to observe," it said, simplifying its answer.

Confusion continued to roil about Aitchley's cranium. "Observe?" he asked back, unsure. "You mean . . . you just watch? You just look at things? But . . . But there's nothing out here to look at. It's all desert. I . . . I don't . . ."

"Declaration: Observation for scientific purposes only," the silver-plated man replied. What might have been a thoughtful pause emanated from Tin William's triangular speaker. "At least . . . primary intent was for scientific purposes only," it added somewhat sheepishly.

Sitting back down on the bed, Aitchley tugged on his newly cobbled boots, still fighting the bewildering disbelief that refused to leave his head. "Are you . . . Are you a scient or something?" he wondered. "Are you doing some kind of secret experiment?"

Tin William stared with unblinking eyes. "Response: Scient? You mean a scientist of your world?" Its silver head shook negatively with the whispering hum of hidden motors. "No, but I was created for observation purposes by men you might consider as such. At last count, thirty-eight thousand TWs had been dispatched to neighboring universes. Originally, what we observed was transmitted only to our scientific CPU until some programmers saw the potential for inexpensive entertainment. Upon doing so, they enhanced the Mainframe and retrofitted all TWs with updated firmware."

Aitchley felt his eyes glaze over. Firmware? he asked himself. CPU? Mainframe? What the Pits was this thing talking about?

The robot called Tin William tilted its head. "Observation:" it said, "You are confused again." It clomped back to the grey desk below the wall of magic windows. "Perhaps this will help."

All forty screens blinked with the same picture:

An ocean of grass extended eastward for as far as she could see, beginning as lonely island patches before expanding into a continent of verdure. Orange-red spires of corrugated mud rose like miniature church steeples through the grass, and a small muddy brook—not much more than two feet deep—burbled and splashed through the tangle of weeds and wild-flowers.

Berlyn took in the beauty around her, hardly able to believe that they had finally left the arid emptiness of the Molten Dunes. There there were no flowers. No dragonflies darting and whizzing over small brooks. No cathedrallike insect mounds. It had been a vast expanse of red-brown nothingness with little or no variation. How Harris Blind-Eye had managed to navigate his way out of that place without getting lost was beyond her.

The sun hung high in the sky as the blonde sat herself comfortably on the bank of the small stream, removing her shoes and placing them beside her. She ignored the ragged figure stanced at her back, no longer as afraid of him as she had been. She knew she was safe so long as Harris feared Aitchley, and—knowing Harris could "read" her—she knew the thief was aware of this. Oddly enough, the southern-city outlaw didn't seem to care, and he had let her ride and sleep no longer bound. It was almost as if the two now shared an uneasy truce . . . a vague understanding of sorts. With his ability to read people, Harris knew when and how far he could trust the scullery maid. And—knowing he could read her—Berlyn knew not to betray that trust.

"Don't do anything stupid now," the lockpick behind her advised. "I'll only be gone long enough to get us something to eat."

Berlyn pulled her tattered skirt up above her knees, resting her feet in the cold waters of the brook. "I told you I'm not going anywhere," she answered tersely. "You go ahead and kill as many harmless little animals as you want."

The blonde didn't see the smirk that drew beneath the hairs

of Harris's ragged beard, but she didn't have to. They understood each other.

"I'm gonna leave the horse with you again," the southern-city thief remarked. "Keep an eye on him, or else we're walking the rest of the way to Leucos."

Berlyn sank back into the grass. "He'll *be* here; *I'll* be here," she sighed her impatience. "Anything else?"

Grinning, Harris snapped down his left wrist and brought Renata into his hand. "Yeah," he answered. "You might not want to sit there."

Berlyn stayed right where she was, stretched out on her back with her feet dangling into the waters of the tiny stream. "Why not?" she wanted to know.

Black steel flashed in the afternoon sunlight, stabbing into the dirt near Berlyn's head and vibrating back and forth with a loud "dwaangg!"

Startled, the young blonde straightened back up, giving the ebony stiletto a surprised glance before narrowing her eyes at its owner. "What the Pits did you do that for?" she demanded.

Harris approached her nonchalantly, jerking Renata free of the earth and inspecting the tip of the blade. Berlyn hadn't noticed beforehand, but sharp black steel now drove directly through the thorax of some pale yellow, many-legged insect.

"Fleshbiters," Harris explained, nodding in the direction of the orange-red pillars of mud. "Bury under your skin and eat you from the inside out." He dislodged the two-inch-long corpse into the grass, not bothering to conceal the smirk beneath his beard. "You might not want to sit there."

Shuddering, Berlyn placed herself a safe distance from the steeplelike mounds and sat down on the other side of the stream. She made certain none of the termitelike creatures crawled in her immediate vicinity before replacing her feet in the cool waters of the brook and reclining back.

Grass and weeds rustled as Harris made his way off across the meadow to hunt, his lean and wiry form melding into the foliage like a fitful shadow. Berlyn didn't bother to watch him, knowing full well that the thief would be back with something she'd have to cook for dinner. She didn't like skinning and cleaning—food preparation had not been her job in the Tampenteire kitchens—but Harris had shown her how to clean, skin, and eviscerate so that none of the meat was contaminated.

He had also shown her the proper way to spit-cook something, which had surprised the young blonde because she had always thought travelers or adventurers caught something, stuck it on a stick, and roasted it over an open fire. Mockingly, Harris had explained to her that it wasn't quite so simple. Cooking an animal over an open flame burned off some of the meat's nutrients . . . hot coals were better. Searing the animal's flesh, however, closed off pores and sealed in natural juices. Even the skewer couldn't be the first sharp stick you happened to find lying on the ground. You had to make sure it wasn't from a poisonous plant, and it helped to sear the skewer as well so its own juices didn't adversely affect the taste of the meat.

Berlyn stretched languorously through the grass, forcing the thoughts of food and evisceration out of her head. She had a chance to relax and clean herself up a bit, and she was going to take advantage of that.

Reluctantly, the blonde forced herself to stand—made sure there were no fleshbiters about—and slipped quickly out of her torn and dirty shift. A warm breeze caressed her body—a western reminder of the nearby desert—and she stepped daintily into the brook, dropping slowly to her knees. Cold water streamed up past her thighs and around her waist, invigorating in its chill, and she set about trying to scrub some of the stink and stains out of her dress. She secretly wished that the stream were larger—or that she had Captain d'Ane's bar of soap— but there was enough room to sit comfortably in the gurgling brook and even wash some of the sweat-caked dirt out of her hair.

Splashing cold water up the length of her arms and across her chest, Berlyn gave her body an unhappy frown. Patches of skin along her arms and legs peeled away as the scaly remains of her sunburn faded, and she had to be careful she didn't rub too hard, since her limbs were still sore and tender. Her platinum-blonde hair streamed far past her shoulders—far longer than she had ever let it grow before—and it was stringy with grease, sand, and sweat, making the back of her neck hot and uncomfortable.

Lowering herself further into the cold waters, Berlyn lay back, letting the stream rush through her long hair. Chill rivulets spread out over her stomach and between her breasts, splashing and frothing as the water passed over her petite body and continued rushing downstream.

The lithe blonde reclined in the tiny brook for nearly half an hour, letting the cool rush of the liquid soothe the aches out of her muscles and joints. Watery tendrils rushed through her hair, allowing her to comb out the tangles with her fingers, and the sweat and dirt from weeks in the desert finally swept away, leaving her feeling clean and refreshed.

A strange sensation suddenly passed through the young scullery maid, and she sat up in the cold waters, grey-green eyes scanning the grasslands about her. Water and damp hair cascaded down her back in icy cataracts, but she ignored the cold and kept a questioning gaze fixed on the meadow. For just the briefest of moments, she had felt unseen eyes upon her . . . as if someone watched her from the cover of the tall grass. Her first thought was of Harris, but, somehow, that didn't make sense. Harris was afraid of what Aitchley might do should Berlyn come to harm . . . why torment himself by spying on her impromptu bath? That could only cause them both trouble.

Apprehensively, Berlyn clambered to her knees, her wet dress clutched tightly before her nakedness. The warm breeze rustled tauntingly through the grasses—blowing over her and causing a wintry shiver to race up her spine as it evaporated the water off her flesh—but there was another kind of chill growing in the young girl's belly, and she stepped tentatively out of the stream and up onto the bank.

Could be someone else, the blonde thought nervously. Harris said we're not too far from Leucos. It could be someone from there.

The frightening image of dirty hands restraining her—the mental feel of rough fingers grabbing and touching her in places where they were not welcomed—returned to haunt her mind. She never wanted that to happen again—never!—and she understood well enough that a young girl was a rare and desirable prize in plague-ridden times . . . whether for southern-city slime from Solsbury or pondscum from Leucos.

Hair slick and wet, moisture dripping off her limbs, Berlyn tried to stay low in the tall grass, her dress still held before her. She couldn't see anyone through the tangle of weeds—and the warm feeling of being watched had faded—but the worry and anxiety continued to churn through her bloodstream.

Not this time, the young blonde firmly resolved. I will not be someone's victim again!

Grey-green eyes surveying the landscape, Berlyn wriggled awkwardly into her water-soaked shift, shivering at the moist embrace of its wet fabric against her skin. A few feet from her, Harris's horse grazed contentedly on the various grasses, Aitchley's shield a comforting blue and gold against the stallion's dark flanks. If I can just get to the horse, I'll be all right, the young girl concluded. I don't care if Harris gets mad or not.

Trepidation trickling through her veins like the water off her dress, Berlyn began a cautious walk toward Harris's stallion, trying to be as casual as her fear would allow. Nonchalantly—although her hands trembled—she pulled her wet hair back into a loose ponytail, nearing the horse as if looking for a cord or rope in which to tie up her hair.

Just a little bit more, the blonde coaxed herself. Almost there . . .

An unexpected howl of hunger and rage caught the young girl by surprise, her own scream adding to the sudden noise. Shrubbery exploded as a gangly creature of mottled brown flesh and stringy black hair launched itself out of the high grasses around her, black talons gleaming in the afternoon sunlight. It looked a little like Poinqart—only much more frightening—and a starving fury flashed in its yellow-black eyes.

Screaming her terror, Berlyn made a wild dash for the horse, stumbling in panic. Her feet tripped and staggered over jumbles of rocks and weeds, and the dampness of her dress stuck the folds of her skirt against her legs as if with a sticky paste. The stallion suddenly seemed a million leagues away, and she could almost feel the hot, fetid breath of the brown troll as she ran madly for the horse.

Frantic hands grasping at the saddle, Berlyn tried to pull herself up onto the horse's back, her fear making her movements clumsy and gawkish. Her heart beat fiercely against her breast, and a wild, white-hot blaze of horror engulfed her in its flames as she swung a terrified look over one shoulder at the approaching troll. Her dress continued to get in the way as she tried to mount up, and the rim of Aitchley's shield also made it difficult to hoist herself into the saddle.

With quivering fingers, the petite blonde tried to undo the

straps holding Aitchley's shield to the stallion's flank, also struggling to hold the horse still as it spied the oncoming troll. Shaking, Berlyn glanced over her shoulder to see the troll nearly on top of her, its yellow-fanged mouth dominating her field of vision.

Blue and gold *gnaiss* wheeled her around the moment the leather restraints fell free, slamming the shield into the leaping troll's face. With a garbled shriek of surprise, the gaunt creature flipped backwards, the momentum of its jump deflected back at it and sending it flying. Astonishment lit momentarily in its yellow-black eyes as it crashed ignobly to the ground, rolling helplessly through the weeds and grasses before coming to a halt near the tiny stream. Angrily, it pulled itself to its feet, chasing the dizziness out of its skull with a single vicious shake of its head.

Berlyn stared in horrified shock as the troll rebounded away from her, dropping the near-magical shield to the dirt. What the Pits . . . ? she started to ask herself.

Sudden terror arced through her body as she noticed the troll lurch to its feet, a vengeful ire flickering in its inhuman glare. Anxiously, she clambered into the horse's saddle, yanking angrily at her skirt as it continued to get in the way of her legs. Fabric tore as a long gash ripped up the right seam of her dress nearly to her hip, but she somehow managed to swing her leg across the stallion's back and grope desperately for the reins.

Starvation's light ignited in the brown troll's eyes as it spied the young girl climb astride the horse, eager saliva streaming from its jaws. It could not let the puny human deprive it of such a succulent morsel of horseflesh, the creature vowed. The rippling muscles. The proud, broad forelegs. The rich, warm blood rushing through its veins.

Sudden pain caught the monster unaware, and it flinched as something pierced its leg. Teeth gnashing, the troll spun about, yet there was no one there. No meddlesome human come to save one of its kind. The woman and horse belonged to the troll, and nothing could get in its way of such a tempting feast!

Another burst of misery speared the beast on the foot, slicing effortlessly through flesh and muscle. And another. And then a third.

Berlyn reined in Harris's horse as she turned to watch the

troll, confusion glittering in her grey-green eyes as the inhuman creature dropped to its knees with an anguished yowl. Thousands of pale yellow shapes had come crawling out of their orange-red towers—eager mandibles sinking into brown, mottled flesh—and Berlyn stared, petrified, as the entire colony of fleshbiters left their mound of dried mud and ate the troll alive.

Shuddering with the movement of flesh-burrowing insects, the troll's corpse crumpled to the grassy earth, splashing in a pool of its own pinkish-white blood.

Tin William froze the image of the half-eaten troll in midframe, taking a personal satisfaction in the composition of the shot. "Declaration: There," it said proudly in its buzzing robotic voice, "now do you understand?"

Aitchley could only stare blankly at the wall of screens, his eyes lost on the video image of the beautiful young girl in the torn and wet dress. "You're a magician!" was all he could shout.

What could have been an exasperated sigh escaped Tin William's speaker.

5

Contractual Obligations

S moky grey lenses irised and refocused. "Query: Have you ever seen a theatrical production, Aitchley Corlaiys?" the creature called Tin William inquired.

Aitchley blinked back without response, his gaze torn between the silver man-shaped form of steel and the frozen picture of Berlyn and the dead troll.

The robot tried again. "Query: Are you aware of morality plays or harlequinades perhaps performed in the center of your town?"

Shock and bafflement kept the answer locked in the young man's throat.

"Query: Dramas? Farce? The traffic of the stage? Operas?" What might have been another sigh escaped the construct's triangular mouth. "Query: Have you ever seen a puppet show, Aitchley Corlaiys?"

Recognition finally lit in Aitchley's gaze.

Tin William continued before the young farmer could interrupt: "Statement: Good, then you will understand something of what I am doing here." The robot turned to its grey desk and punched a few buttons, bringing other still-frame images to the forty screens; Aitchley could only gape in wonder as he saw himself and his friends displayed in various scenes before him.

"Declaration: As with any good play or marionette show, all such works must tell a story, and—known or unknown to us all, Aitchley Corlaiys—our own lives tell such a story. Perhaps it is an uninteresting one—perhaps only the people involved find it compelling—yet there are other stories that a greater majority of the people find intriguing." Emotionless lenses fixed on the young man. "Tell me, Aitchley Corlaiys, what were these puppet shows that you saw about?"

Aitchley sent his mind back twelve years to a festival held in Solsbury. There had been dwarves, and jugglers, and minstrels, and a gaily draped puppet theatre that had captured the young farmer's imagination. Even though he had only been about five years old at the time, Aitchley still remembered much of the celebration quite vividly.

"One was a story about the plague and how it was shown as an ugly old crone who rode on the back of a poor peasant farmer from Karst and made him visit all the other towns so that she could spread her disease," Aitchley recalled. "The others were about the Cavalier."

And—despite his newfound admiration for his ancestor—a familiar taste of bile rose in Aitchley's throat.

"Statement: The Cavalier Procursus Galen," Tin William declared, a steel finger punching one of the many buttons across the desk's surface.

A picture of what Aitchley thought was himself and Calyx filled all forty of the magic windows, each window adding a small piece to the overall picture. It took a moment before the young farmer realized that the dark-haired youth standing beside the grumpy-looking dwarf wasn't him, and a wave of bewilderment washed over the young man as he stared at the giant image of his long-dead ancestor.

Frozen in time by Tin William's magic, Procursus Galen looked down regally at Aitchley, blue-green eyes ablaze with a righteous vigor. A red-violet plume of feathers arced from the glittering helm held in the Cavalier's gauntleted hand, and a familiar oval of blue and gold *gnaiss* adorned the Champion's left forearm. His smile was just a little bit lopsided—and his hair more black than brown—but there was something in the face that bore an eerie resemblance to Aitchley.

Shivering at the sorcery displayed before him, Aitchley peeled his eyes away from the long-dead Cavalier and stared at the mechanism nicknamed Tin William.

The robot either did not notice or chose to ignore the young man's blatant look of horror. "Statement: The Cavalier Procursus Galen," the construct said again. "Never in all the history of your world has there been a greater hero. Even today people still write books, tell stories, and sing songs of his exploits. Would you not then consider his life to be of interest to all?"

Even though he was befuddled and afraid, Aitchley's seventeen-year-old resentment for his ancestor managed to surface. "Big deal," snorted the young farmer. "He was the bunging Cavalier. He couldn't do wrong if he tried."

"Statement: Or so the stories would have you believe," Tin William responded. "But he was a man same as any man born on this world. He lived a life as you now live one. He ate, drank, slept, and excreted."

Aitchley had to stifle a snigger as the sudden thought of the mighty Cavalier straining away on the wooden seat of a privy popped unexpectedly to mind.

Tin William gave the giggling young farmer a warning glance of filtered lenses. "Declaration: He made mistakes as you make mistakes, Aitchley Corlaiys," the robot announced. "But it was just his life. Why, then, do you think so many people are intrigued by him?"

Aitchley snorted again. "'Cause he's the bunging Cavalier," he retorted.

"Correction: Because his life told a story," Tin William answered. "Because it wasn't just a misdirected attempt to survive, as with most human lifeforms. It had a purpose and a goal. A true purpose that wasn't self-serving or misguided. The Cavalier was a true hero."

A sneer crossed one side of Aitchley's lips. "Oh, wow. Big deal," he muttered sarcastically. "Tell me something I don't know!"

Steel fingers changed the picture, and this time it was an image of Aitchley that filled all forty screens, Berlyn and Calyx at his side. "Statement: You too, Aitchley Corlaiys, tell a story of great interest," the metal man declared, "and I have been filming that story from the very beginning. I have—as I have been programmed to do—been observing you from the very start."

A muted sense of surprise returned to the young man's brain as he stared at his own image, a vague feeling of understanding rumbling under all his confusion and fear. He wasn't sure why, but this silver creature didn't strike him as a proper sorcerer, and—even though he had just seen a lifelike picture of his own dead ancestor—magic no longer seemed a viable explanation.

"But what . . . What are you?" Aitchley wanted to know.

"Statement: I am TW-O: 114-84-1311825, nicknamed Tin William by my builders. I am an observation unit brought online 2•821•6 from the scientific/entertainment sector of the world Sphere from a universe completely divergent from your own."

Aitchley stared dazedly at his own giant-sized image. "So . . . So you're not a magician?" he stuttered.

"Statement: My motives are purely technological in operation, Aitchley Corlaiys," Tin William replied. "I record on magnetic tape; my dumb terminals run on solar cells; and I myself have a central processing unit composed of more than one processing chip, the most powerful being the Y-Teq 90986SX. There is no magic involved in my construction."

"So . . . you weren't built by dwarves?"

Tin William offered a motorized shake of his head. "Response: I was not even built in your universe," he said. "Query: Are you familiar with the theory of perpendicular universes?"

Aitchley narrowed a questioning blue-green eye at the robot. "Don't you mean parallel universes?" he wondered.

Tin William shook his head again. "Correction: I mean perpendicular universes," he answered resolutely. "While I do not deny nor refute the existence of parallel universes, parallel universes—by their own definition—cannot meet or allow to cross over any or all living matter, or else they would cease being parallel. Only in perpendicular universes—where the separate dimensions overlapped and actually touched—could we cross over and observe."

Aitchley felt the faint, downward tug of disappointment. "So it's not magic?" he queried.

"Response: No, it is not."

A twinge of despair flickered somewhere in the vicinity of

the young man's heart. "So Berlyn's not on the other side of those windows?" he puzzled.

"Query: Windows?" echoed Tin William. "Correction: These are not windows, Aitchley Corlaiys. They are high-resolution CRTs."

The young farmer blinked. "See our teas?" he repeated. "What kind of talk is that?"

"Explanation: cathode ray tubes," Tin William replied. "Also commonly referred to as VDTs: video display terminals."

"I still don't . . ."

Tin William cut him off with an upraised hand of steel fingers. "Declaration: It is unimportant, Aitchley Corlaiys," the robot said. "All that matters is that you understand my function and my purpose. I mean neither you nor your friends any harm, and—in fact—I intend to help you return your quest to the matter at hand."

Eyebrows narrowed in sudden suspicion over Aitchley's eyes. "Which is?" he wanted to know.

"Declaration: To journey beyond the walls of Lich Gate and retrieve the fabled Elixir of Life!" Tin William proclaimed.

An irrational sense of panic suddenly burst in Aitchley's thoughts. "I'm not going anywhere till I get Berlyn back!" he swore vehemently. "I don't care what . . ."

"Interruption: I am well aware of your desire to rescue your leading lady," the silver construct answered bluntly. "In fact, it has made for an interesting subplot that has increased our ratings share exponentially over the last three weeks, yet it is necessary to hurry things along. Your arrival at Lich Gate could be most lucrative if it coincided with sweeps week."

Aitchley blinked stupidly. "Sweeps week?"

Tin William waved an indifferent hand with the muted whir of gears and servos. "Statement: Unimportant," he said. "Suffice to say it is a time of celebration and competition on my world of Sphere where many TWs override basic programming ethics and moral applications to film the inhabitants of their respective worlds engaging in rites and rituals that would otherwise not be documented."

Aitchley's blinking increased. "Uhhhh . . ."

What might have been an abrupt idea lit in Tin William's

video-camera eyes. "Supposition: Unless, of course, you plan to interface with the heroine once you rescue her?" he prompted.

The words were confusing but their meaning was clear.

"*What?*" Aitchley exclaimed in his shock.

Tin William turned away, the robotic excitement draining from his electronic voice. "Apology: No, no, of course not. Forgive me, Aitchley Corlaiys. I have exceeded my parameters. I meant no offense."

Aitchley tried hard to remain indignant even though a warm flush filled his cheeks; he had been staring a little too intently at the way Berlyn's skirt had ripped up to her waist, hadn't he? "Yeah, well . . . um . . . it's okay . . . I guess." An abrupt realization hit the young man and he turned on the spidery remote still watching him from the corner of the room. "Hey!" he exclaimed. "Has this thing been following us everywhere?"

Tin William threw a cursory glance over a gleaming metal shoulder. "Response: A total of nine different cameras have been tracking your movements, Aitchley Corlaiys," the robot responded. "Query: Why?"

The warmth in Aitchley's cheeks intensified as the mental image of the Cavalier squatting became one of the young man doing likewise. "Well . . . umm . . . just how much do they see . . . er . . . film . . . er . . . whatever?" he demanded.

Emotionless camera-lens eyes fixed on the young farmer. "Statement: As I told you, Aitchley Corlaiys, yours is the story I have chosen to follow," the man of metal declared. "My remotes are programmed to record any and all movements made by you or your companions. They videotape everything."

The heat in his face feeling like the return of his sunburn, Aitchley stared in flustered embarrassment at the forty CRTs. "But what . . ." he started. "I mean . . . There are . . . umm . . . You didn't . . ."

Tin William caught the embarrassment in the young man's words. "Statement: Basic biological functions and physiological minutiae may be filmed but are edited for time and continuity once they are sent here to my workstation. Only events relevant to the plotline need ever reach the airwaves."

Although he didn't understand the words, Aitchley felt the

humanoid figure of steel was trying to reassure him, yet a redness still colored his face. "But . . . But I saw that picture of me and Berlyn," he protested. "When we were . . . ummm . . . when we were taking a bath."

The construct nicknamed Tin William nodded smartly. "Response: Ah, yes. The bathing sequence. A highly rated episode. Nearly as popular as the escape from Ilietis installment. Query: Would you care to see the edited footage?"

His embarrassment growing, Aitchley watched as Tin William brought up a now-familiar image across all forty of the CRTs. "But . . . But we're naked!" he cried.

Tin William threw what might have been a confused look back at the young farmer. "Statement: There is no proviso against nudity so long as it is done tastefully and has bearing on the story," the observation unit explained.

The entire wall of VDTs filled with the videotaped image of Aitchley and Berlyn resting peacefully beside the Uriisa River, their nakedness natural and not at all awkward or embarrassing. Sensations and emotions surged like electricity through Aitchley's mind as he stared up at the massive picture, his eyes roving across Berlyn and the way she lay her head contentedly across his naked chest. He hardly noticed his own nudity as the camera pulled in on their faces, focusing in on the love and happiness on their features.

Low, foreboding music suddenly pervaded the scene as the camera panned guardedly to the right, zooming in on a dark figure crouched menacingly in the bushes. A cold prickle of fear fingered the back of Aitchley's neck as he made out Harris Blind-Eye spying on the young couple resting beside the river, and he turned a frantic glance at the glistening framework of man-shaped steel beside him.

"What the Pits is that?" the young farmer questioned.

"Declaration: Camera 12 detected Harris Blind-Eye concealed in the bushes," Tin William explained. "It made for a convenient cliffhanger ending to that episode."

Aitchley blinked back his surprise. "Harris was spying on us?" he exclaimed. "What the Pits for?"

"Speculation: Probably planning the kidnap of Berlyn," remarked Tin William. "He probably observed your open feelings toward the female unit and decided to use them against you."

"And . . . And you saw him?" Aitchley sputtered, his shock and disbelief swamping his earlier embarrassment. "Why didn't you say something? Why didn't you warn me?"

"Statement: As I mentioned before, Aitchley Corlaiys, it goes against all standard programming to interfere with the course of a story," Tin William answered. "I am only an observation unit. I am not supposed to play an active part. You were not even supposed to be aware of me or my remotes."

"But I am!" argued the young man. "You . . . You rescued me! You brought me here and healed me!"

Video camera eyes focused and refocused. "Only after continued interference by Camera 12," the robot replied matter-of-factly. "I was forced to come to the conclusion that the damage had already been done, and—in the strictest of confidence—a brief cameo on my part could only be beneficial to the continuation of your story."

The electronic words left Aitchley addled. "What?"

Another buzzing sigh escaped Tin William's speaker. "Simplification: You would have died without my help, Aitchley Corlaiys, and your story would be over." The robot fiddled with some levers on the desktop. "Twice—acting of its own accord—Camera 12 carried you to the safety of the cliffs and buried you in the sands." Forty images of a spider-thing kicking red-gold sand onto Aitchley's unconscious form flickered across the VDTs. "When you commanded your bird to search out the person responsible for your continued survival, it led you to my workstation where I had recalled Camera 12 to run an extensive debugging system check on its primary programs." An inquisitive metal hand rubbed thoughtfully at a steel chin. "I am still unable to find fault in Camera 12's programming."

Blinking repeatedly, Aitchley threw a perplexed look at the silver spider-thing squatting in the corner of the room, its glass eye staring blankly back at the confused young man. "But I . . . I don't understand," he said. "I mean . . . if you're not supposed to interfere, why did you? Why save me at all? And what was the whole point of your stupid camera burying me in the sand?"

"Explanation: While the topmost surface of sand in the desert regions of Vedette is unbearably hot for most living organisms during daylight hours—highest shade temperature ever recorded: 58° C—just below the surface, the sands are quite cool. Most desert animals living in burrows are well aware of this fact, and standard survival practices dictate the search for adequate shelter. With no protective vegetation or rockwork to utilize, Camera 12 resorted to burying you in the cooler levels of sand, thereby saving your life and continuing the story."

"But why?" Aitchley asked.

Tin William offered the young man a motor-assisted shrug. "Speculation: I can only conclude that Camera 12 felt guilty," he answered.

Aitchley squinted blue-green eyes in befuddlement. "Guilty?" he echoed. "Guilty of what?"

There might have been a moment where Tin William averted embarrassed eyes from the young man before replying. "Response: Let it be known, Aitchley Corlaiys, that what you thought was Harris Blind-Eye moving across the desert was—in all acuality—Camera 12 moving to another vantage point. Your mental state and inferior focusing ability conspired against you and caused you to fall from the cliff. For that, I am most apologetic."

Lurid memories of burning heat and dark silhouettes brushed fleetingly past Aitchley's mind, recalling exhausted elation and stubborn determination. It hadn't been Harris after all, the young man thought glumly to himself. Poinqart had been right. *I fell off a cliff 'cause I saw some stupid metal spider-thing and I thought it was Harris! I'm such a warthead sometimes! I . . .*

Another memory unexpectedly intruded upon the first.

"Hey!" Aitchley exclaimed, jabbing an accusatory finger at the spider-thing watching him with its single, unblinking eye. "That's the thing Captain d'Ane saw!"

With an almost inaudible whir of servos, Tin William turned to regard the insectlike remote filming them from the corner. "Correction: Improper identification," he replied. "This unit is Camera 4. The unit observed and pursued by the late Captain d'Ane was, once again, Camera 12."

Vague understanding began to light in Aitchley's eyes. "So if this Camera 12 was causing you all this trouble, you just decided to . . ." The low buzzing of Tin William's words suddenly registered belatedly in the young man's ears. "Late?" he blurted. "What do you mean the *late* Captain d'Ane?"

Video camera eyes stared back emotionlessly at the farmer. "Explanation: The unit you knew as Captain d'Ane suffered a fatal systems failure and has ceased functioning," Tin William replied. Steel fingers drew up forty images of an enormous hall with a wide staircase; Aitchley barely noticed the frail, old-looking man sitting slumped on the bottom step. "He expired during the riots in Viveca in the attempt to free the Baroness Desireah from under the influence of her chief advisor." A hint of boastful pride resounded in the electronic voice. "We received a forty-eight share for that night."

An uncomfortable numbness began to seep through Aitchley's rejuvenated body as he stared in stunned incredulity at the video image of Captain d'Ane's lifeless form. A growing sadness roiled up deep inside him, and Aitchley could barely swallow the sudden lump in his throat that tried to release a tidal wave of tears from his eyes. Captain d'Ane? Dead? the young man thought in denial. No! It wasn't fair! Just like his father! Just like Berlyn! Just like everything else that had happened to him on this Gaal-damned quest! It just wasn't fair!

Aitchley turned condemning eyes on the observation unit. "Why didn't you save *him*?" he spat venomously, the words catching in his throat. "If you could save me, why couldn't you save him?"

Tin William twisted his head into what could have been a remorseful pose. "Statement: I am most apologetic for your loss, Aitchley Corlaiys, but there was nothing I could do. Captain d'Ane died from angina pectoris culminating in myocardial infarction. Or—in high-level language—his angina resulted in a heart attack. Angina itself is a symptom, not a disorder, as it may have been caused by any number of things: arteries narrowed by a passing spasm, atherosclerosis, and so forth. It is brought on by exertion, extreme change in temperature, or intense emotional fluctuations, yet it can be relieved by simple rest. Unfortunately—in the case of Captain d'Ane—circumstances would not allow him to rest and his heart was starved of oxygen. This depletion caused the myocardial infarction and his subsequent death."

Tears tried to leak free of Aitchley's blue-green gaze, yet the young farmer refused them. "*Why*?" he howled his anguish. "Why save me and not him? It isn't fair!"

Tin William cocked his head in the opposite direction, video-camera eyes irising as they focused on the young man. "Query: Why, Aitchley Corlaiys?" the man of metal responded. "I thought I made the answer easily accessed: I can make you a *star*!"

Poinqart forced his *meion* through the rain-soaked plains, the heavy black clouds overhead creating a false dusk across the heavens. A light sprinkle still fell from the sky—saturating the tall grass and soaking the half-troll—but the hybrid rode on, throwing an anxious look over one shoulder to make sure Aitchley's black stallion still trailed obediently behind him.

Yellow-black eyes narrowed in a mix of human fear and trollish scrutiny. He could not spy-see the others, the hybrid thought worriedly. Mister Aitch's snort-horse followed-ran behind him, but Poinqart could no longer see the nasty-bad-trolls that pursued him.

Drawing in a strained sigh of relief, the half-troll drew in his *meion*, allowing the poor beast a chance to rest. The gentle pitter-patter of the falling rain against the grass sounded unsettlingly like the soft creep of enemy feet, and a nervous fluttering began in Poinqart's belly as he slid down off his mount and stood in the rain-slicked meadow.

Brown trolls, the half-breed mused, unable to control the fearful shiver that coursed through his body at the words. Nasty-bad-mean, they were. Many story-tales Poinqart had heard while a troll-tadling, but he never thought-feared that he would actually meet one. Brown trolls were not like Poinqart. Hungry-vile, they were. Aggressive and hungry, nasty-bad-trolls made human-peoples worry-fear all trolls. Even friendly trolls like Poinqart. Not until the good-Cavalier-man came and chased all nasty-bad-trolls away did human-peoples become Poinqart's friend. And now . . . Now the nasty-bad-trolls were back, and they had scared-away-chased poor Poinqart from the burning-hot-desert. Scared-away-chased him from poor Mister Aitch, slavering-drool over Poinqart's poor snort-horses.

The hybrid turned apprehensive eyes on the dark plains about him. Somewhere behind all the rumble-black-clouds, the half-troll knew the sun was beginning its night-time-descent. The darkness-gloom now that encompassed him would grow ever darker-bad, and it would be dangerous to gallop-ride once true night fell. The seven or eight nasty-bad-trolls that followed him might catch him then, and poor Poinqart would be eaten-dead and certainly no help to Mister Aitch.

Poinqart turned a curious look southward through the drizzle and murk. The burning-hot-desert-sand was only a few leagues that way, the half-breed knew. He had only left the desert to find hungry-food for himself and the snort-horses and had planned to return once he had moved farther east. He had been unable to find any way down the craggy-high-cliffs to help Mister Aitch and had started heading eastward in the hopes of finding a route down. Leaving the burning-sands was the only way Poinqart could think of to continue moving-ride during the day. And now he was being chased-pursued by nasty-bad-trolls who wanted to gobble-eat him and his horses . . . going further and further away from Mister Aitch all the time.

Poinqart is scared, Mister Aitch, the hybrid thought miserably to himself. Poinqart does not like being out all-by-himself-alone. He wishes you were here.

What might have been the plunk of raindrops on wet grass or the muffled step of a gloom-hidden brown troll sounded on Poinqart's right, and the hybrid was instantly alert. The nervous fluttering in his stomach grew into a fearful triphammer of panic, and the half-troll scrambled anxiously back into his *meion*'s saddle. He didn't bother to look behind him—too scared by his own imagination to find out what the noise had really been—and clucked his horse urgently back into a gallop. Aitchley's stallion followed wearily behind, its heavy hooves plodding sluggishly through the marshy grasses.

The grumble of mud-muted hooves filled the stormy skies as the half-troll and horses rode into the misty gloom of the premature night.

Aitchley sat on the bed in Tin William's editing bay, watching the sun slowly set in all forty of the video screens. The sorrow and loss of Captain d'Ane's death continued to ache dully at his breast, but the young man fought back the tears that wanted to flow. He was no stranger to death—growing up in a world beset by plague, drought, and famine, no one was—but the frustration and guilt of such a demise still churned within him.

"What would you have done? Watched him die, most probably." Words spoken by Captain d'Ane himself to Aitchley after the young man's father had died. And what *would* he have done? The creature called Tin William said that Captain d'Ane had died of some disease . . . some sickness that had affected his heart. Aitchley could no sooner have unclogged the captain's arteries than he could cure the entire world of the Black Worm's fatal Touch.

Aitchley looked back up at the wall of CRTs. Captain d'Ane was dead; life continued on, the young farmer acknowledged. There were other matters that now required his full attention.

A wind he could see but could not feel whistled softly through the tall grass and flowering weeds in the video terminals, and the gigue of crickets sounded sprightly from videotaped shrubbery, and from what Tin William called surround-sound speakers.

The horse bearing Berlyn and Harris Blind-Eye trotted slowly into the shot, the camera gradually pulling in on the petite blonde. There was a kind of soured pucker on her lips—and Aitchley could see where her skin had peeled away in itchy fragments from her sunburn—but she appeared to be unharmed. A festering anger returned to the young man's gut as the camera redirected its gaze and zoomed in on the ponytailed brigand riding in front of the blonde, the fading sunlight glimmering mockingly off the red-gold pendant hanging around his neck.

Aitchley tried to keep the fury out of his voice as he turned to where Tin William stood beside his grey desk; Trianglehead sat watching the screens, perched comfortably on the robot's shoulder. "You said they're heading where?" Aitchley asked.

"Response: They are heading for the village of Leucos," answered Tin William. "At their constant rate of travel, they should reach their destination in approximately two days' time."

A pessimistic frown pulled on Aitchley's lips as he watched the video. "So how am I supposed to catch up?" he wondered, old feelings of despair and failure creeping up inside him. "I don't have a horse, and they're at least a week ahead of me."

"Declaration: You will catch them, Aitchley Corlaiys," the observation unit said. "Have no doubt of that."

A skeptical smirk pulled lopsidedly across one side of the

young man's lips. "Yeah? How?" he queried. "I didn't see any stables out back."

"Statement: You will not need a horse, Aitchley Corlaiys," Tin William declared. "I am sending Camera 12 with you."

An initial barb of panic speared the young farmer's rib cage as he flung an anxious look back at the spidery Camera 4 stanced behind him. "What?" he nearly shrieked. "Why?" He pointed a trembling finger at the insectlike remote. "I don't want one of those things following me!"

"Response: Camera 12 will not be following you," Tin William explained calmly. "You will be riding it."

Trepidation swirled like an ocean's waves through the blue-green of Aitchley's eyes. "Huh?" he shouted. "I'm not riding one of those! I had to take a month of riding lessons just so I didn't fall off my Gaal-damned horse!"

Tin William trained cursory eyes on the video image of the blonde in the ripped dress. "Query: You do want to save Berlyn from the clutches of Harris Blind-Eye, do you not?" the construct asked.

Aitchley felt an abrupt spark of shame bruise his conscience as he looked up sheepishly at the wall of monitors. "Well . . . yeah . . ." he murmured.

"Query: And do you not want to prove to her that you are worthy of her affections by rescuing her and showing her that there are still heroes to be believed in?"

Aitchley shifted under the cold glass glare of Tin William's camera-lens eyes. "Yeah," he answered, blushing.

"Conclusion: Then I do not understand your reluctance."

Embarrassed yet still unsure, Aitchley gave the spiderlike Camera 4 a timid glance before answering. "It's just . . . I mean . . ." A sudden excuse popped into his head. "I thought you said Camera 12 was broken."

"Response: Camera 12 suffers from a small glitch in its programming," Tin William replied simply. "I conclude that this glitch is because it has taken a strange liking to you. Its transport functions are unaffected by this error."

Aitchley gave Camera 4 another glance, his anxiety drowning out his shame. "But . . . But it doesn't look very fast," he objected. "How am I supposed to catch Harris riding on one of those things?"

"Declaration: All video remotes are equipped with a small,

gimbaled rocket capable of attaining hypersonic velocities,''
Tin William proclaimed. ''While such speeds will not be necessary for your purpose, Camera 12 should get you comfortably to Leucos at about the same time as Harris Blind-Eye and
Berlyn.''

A glimmer of question flickered in Aitchley's eyes as he
glared suspiciously at the many-legged camera. He didn't
know whether or not he trusted the device—Daeminase Pits!
He didn't know whether he trusted Tin William or not!—but
if it was able to get him to Leucos in time to stop Harris . . .

The young man swung his gaze on the man-shaped construct
standing beside the wall of CRTs. The video image of Berlyn
riding quietly behind Harris Blind-Eye continued to torment
the young man across the forty screens, and another pang of
guilt furrowed through his thoughts like a plow through fertile
soil.

This may be the only chance I've got to catch them, the
young farmer realistically mused. I'm still stuck out in the
middle of the desert with no horse and no food, so I might as
well agree, right? But . . . I don't understand any of this. I
don't understand why this Tin William wants to help me or
why he's even here! I mean . . . I've seen a lot of weird things
since I've started this quest, but this . . . !

Doubt narrowing his eyes, Aitchley fixed his vision on the
creature called Tin William. ''I don't get it,'' the young man
admitted. ''Why even help me at all? I mean . . . what's in it
for you?''

There might have been a brief pause in the silver metal
robot's actions as it stepped away from its editing board and
removed one of the solid grey books from its immense library
of shelves. ''Declaration:'' it said. ''As I mentioned before,
Aitchley Corlaiys, it is your story I have chosen to follow,
and—judging by the latest ratings we have received—I have
chosen wisely. The people of Sphere cheer and eagerly await
the next installment of your adventures as it adds excitement
and intrigue to their otherwise uneventful lives. Only once before in my experience as a TransWorld Observer have I received such high ratings, and that was when I televised the
exploits of your ancestor, the Cavalier Procursus Galen.''

The robot removed a black rectangle from the hollow interior of the grey box and slipped it neatly inside a mechanical

fissure at the front of the grey editing desk; loud music and thunderous sound effects filled the tiny workstation as Aitchley watched the Cavalier and Calyx struggling up the side of a snow-capped mountain, tendrils of steam coiling about them like so many hazy serpents.

"This is the final episode in the life of Cavalier Galen," Tin William went on, a trace of gloom in his electronic voice. "As you'll see, I had little trouble filming the adventure so long as the Cavalier and the dwarf remained on the mountainside."

Aitchley stared, dumbfounded, as his silver-armored ancestor and the black-haired dwarf rounded a rocky bend and came face to face with an enormous cave, larger than Lord Tampenteire's estate and the Tridome put together. Ribbons of steam wafted up from the cavernous maw, and an echoing rumble in Aitchley's own innards mimicked the worry and fear on the faces of the videotaped adventurers.

"I think we've found it," Aitchley heard Calyx's voice sound from the speakers, his usually gruff tone hushed in astonishment. "Hammer and anvil! He's got to be bigger than anyone's ever thought!"

"Small men may live in very large castles, Calyx," Procursus responded, rising from his crouch. "Do not let the cavern's appearance fool you."

"Fool me, no," the dwarf retorted. "Intimidate me, yes. Are you sure this is really necessary?"

"For the good of the land I've sworn to protect, this monster must be destroyed," the paladin declared. "Singlehandedly, I have managed to stamp out all threats to our beloved land save this one. Today Vedette will never have to live in fear again."

Aitchley stared in muted awe as his ancestor strode boldly forth, gauntleted hands gripped tightly around his silver-grey sword. He watched in similar silence as Calyx shifted the heavy sack across his shoulders and began after him, mumbling something vague into his black beard that the camera's microphone did not pick up.

The hint of gloom in his voice had now become full-fledged despair as Tin William caused the videotaped footage to fast-forward. "Statement: This is my greatest shame, Aitchley Corlaiys," the robot said. "This was the day I was almost cancelled."

Entranced by the visual sight of his own ancestor striding forth to slay Myxomycetes, Aitchley turned his bewildered eyes on the depressed robot. "What?" the young man wondered. "What do you mean?"

"Statement: Watch, Aitchley Corlaiys," the man of metal replied darkly. "Watch and you will see."

Not needing any coaxing from the observation unit, Aitchley returned his attention to the screens. This was history reliving itself before his very eyes! the young man understood. Despite how he felt about the Cavalier, Aitchley was seeing something that—up till now—no one else in Vedette except for Calyx had ever been a part of!

Agitation began to ferment in Aitchley's mind as the camera attempted to follow after the dwarf and Cavalier, yet—at the same time—remain out of sight. The blackness of the cavern opening taunted both camera and young farmer with its massive width but impenetrable darkness, and—no matter how often or how varied its attempts—the remote recording the final battle between Cavalier and Dragon was unable to pierce the murk and get a clear shot.

A thunderous roar shook the speakers, and there was a brief flash of fire from deep within the cave, yet still the camera was unable to see what transpired within.

Tin William ejected the tape, unable to watch any more. "Declaration: Now do you understand, Aitchley Corlaiys?" the robot inquired. "I have agreed to help you so that you, in turn, can help me."

Aitchley blinked, the sight of his own ancestor bravely going to his death replaying itself over and over in his mind. "Help you?" the young man repeated, apprehension gnawing at his innards. "How the Pits can I help you?"

Tin William made an unfelt wave of his hand back at the wall of monitors. "Response: As you have just seen, Aitchley Corlaiys, my camera remote was unable to follow your ancestor, the Cavalier Procursus Galen, into the entrance of the Dragon's Lair without being detected and thereby nullifying all standard programming of noninterference. As a result, I was unable to film the climactic ending to your ancestor's life and was very nearly pulled from observation. I do not want that to happen again."

Bewilderment continued to assail the young man as Aitchley

turned to face the steel figure. "I don't see how I can help you with that," he responded. "That was almost two hundred years ago!"

Tin William offered the young man a curt nod of his head. "Response: One hundred and eighty-seven years, to be precise, Aitchley Corlaiys," the robot agreed, "but your adventure continues even as we speak. I have offered you the use of Camera 12 to aid you in your journey not just as a means of transport but as a fellow traveler so that, when you, too, enter into the blackness and gloom of the Dragon's Lair at the end of your quest, *I* will be there to film it!"

Aitchley blanched, staring wordlessly up at empty screens while visions of steam, snow, and caves flooded his brain. *The Dragon's Lair!* his thoughts screamed at him. Don't remind me! It's bad enough I'm going beyond Lich Gate!

Slumping back onto the bed, Aitchley looked up at the blank wall of CRTs. Still, there was something about seeing the Cavalier in action that stirred the young man. Something that made him yearn for heroes with all the enthusiasm of Berlyn or some naive child. Something that ignited a special spark in himself to do better and try more before giving in to the despair and pessimism always so eager to claim him.

It was understandable why the four lords of Solsbury had sent Aitchley out to resurrect the Cavalier . . . sometimes there *was* a real need for heroes.

I just never thought one of those heroes would be me! Aitchley thought sardonically to himself.

Smoky grey lenses rotated as they focused on the young farmer. "Query: Well, Aitchley Corlaiys?" Tin William interrupted the young man's thoughts. "Do you agree?"

Swallowing hard, Aitchley looked back up at the blank monitors. Even though Tin William had turned them off, Aitchley could still see images of his long-dead ancestor, of himself, and of Berlyn playing across the screens. A familiar determination began to stream once more through the young man's bloodstream, and a distant memory returned vividly to mind.

Fear, worry, and hope blazed in grey-green eyes.

Aitchley swung sharply on Tin William, snatching up his sword belt from the bed beside him and buckling it about his waist. "Yes!" he boldly announced his decision.

The abrupt realization of what he'd done suddenly made him feel like throwing up.

6

Nature's Scales

Nervously, Aitchley stood in the frigid chill of the early morning desert, the anxiety and queasiness still gnawing voraciously at his belly. Trianglehead perched on the young man's shoulder, one grumpy eye half-open as he sleepily scanned the oasis greenery for any signs of food. Tin William stood before the pair, busily adjusting a strange harness to the back of Camera 12's insectlike abdomen. Behind them all—half-hidden in the brush—Camera 4 recorded the whole event.

Aitchley watched Tin William work without comment, uneasily shifting the maroon-colored backpack slung over his shoulders. The backpack had been a gift from the robot—something, the construct had said, left over from when the programmers used to make frequent visits to the various TW workstations before they became self-operational. Inside the pack were strange foods Aitchley had never heard of . . . magically thermostabilized, rehydratable, freeze-dried, and irradiated; just add water and he had a meal. There were also magical items such as a small knife handle without a blade that glowed a brilliant white when shaken, and a cocoonlike blanket that unfolded into a small bed with metal teethlike fasteners up the side. There was even a cylindrical water flask called a thermos that—according to Tin William—kept hot liquids hot and cold liquids cold. What Aitchley wanted to know was, how did it know the difference?

Even though Tin William had briefly instructed Aitchley on the use of all the weird and mysterious items in the knapsack, the young man felt uncomfortable wearing the pack so close to his body. Tin William's magic may not have been proper magic as Aitchley had been led to believe, but having enchanted food and sorcerous lightsticks resting so intimately against his shoulders only caused the young man's apprehension to grow.

Starlight and moonbeams glistened off Tin William's metal framework as the robot stepped away from Camera 12. "Declaration: It is complete, Aitchley Corlaiys," the observation unit announced. "You may be on your way."

Aitchley swallowed hard, blue-green eyes narrowing at the silver-grey harness. "You sure that thing's going to hold me?" he worried, the anxiety expanding. "It looks pretty flimsy."

"Statement; The harness is made from the strongest of tungsten steel filaments," the robot replied. "It is capable of towing a small hopper-barge through the Swampworks without breaking; it will hold you."

Uncertainly, Aitchley neared the waiting camera, the doubt and fear increasing with each step. Magic food on my back and now a magic saddle under my butt! the young man thought sardonically. Is any of this all worth it?

Fear, worry, and hope blazed in grey-green eyes.

The sudden surge of courage and determination sparked by the image of hopeful eyes placed Aitchley in the weirdly shaped harness before another doubt could enter his mind. This is for Berlyn, he reminded himself in earnest. Maybe he wouldn't have to eat the strange foods Tin William had given him—or use the otherworldly tools in the backpack—but he *had* to catch up with Harris if he was ever going to save her. This was something he *had* to do!

The terror ebbed as the young farmer seated himself more comfortably in the silver-grey saddle. He didn't like the way his legs were completely surrounded by the steel-wire mesh—and the sling of metal against his back felt odd and disquieting—yet he pushed the uneasiness out of his head and settled back into the hammocklike harness.

Tin William stepped up to the Camera, steel hands checking and securing the harness straps. "Statement: When you arrive at Leucos, you must wrest the necklace away from Harris Blind-Eye,'' the robot counseled. "Only then will you be able to resume your true quest."

Aitchley gave the construct a wilting glare. "I *know* that," he seethed. "But it's not going to do me any good. He knows I don't know how to set it off."

"Solution: Spin the chain—stone held outward—in a three-hundred-and-sixty-degree revolution until the alchemical pendant begins to emit a phosphorescent reaction," Tin William explained. "Then bring the pendant down on any hard surface to shatter the stone. This will ignite the volatile monads and trigger the explosion in the bracelet around Harris Blind-Eye's wrist."

Aitchley just stared blankly at the man made of metal. "Huh?" he finally asked.

"Simplification: Spin the pendant in a circle until it glows," Tin William said. "Then break the stone. That will set off the bracelet."

The blank look remained on Aitchley's face. "How . . . How the Pits did you know that?" he wanted to know.

If steel could stretch, Tin William would have smiled. "Explanation: As I told you before, Aitchley Corlaiys," the construct remarked, "I have been watching your adventure from the very beginning. There is very little I do not see."

Aitchley blinked glassy eyes. "You were even watching the alchemists?" he exclaimed.

Tin William cocked his head proudly to one side. "Confirmation: I have a total of some five hundred thousand remotes distributed strategically throughout this world," he said. "Even as we speak, they are busy recording the lives and deaths of potential follow-ups to your story. After all, Aitchley Corlaiys, one day your story will end—the adventure will be over—and I will need a mid-season replacement or else be bumped from the fall lineup."

Shaking his head in mild bewilderment—wondering if he'd ever get used to the alien language the man of metal spouted— Aitchley turned away and gazed out over the early morning obscurity of the desert. The underwater-blue of the desert night filled the eastern horizon, and—somewhere far distant—Aitchley knew Berlyn and the town of Leucos awaited him.

An abrupt worry brought the churning back to the young

man's stomach. "What should I do if Harris gets to an alchemist before I get there?" he asked.

Video-camera eyes irised and focused. "Declaration: He will not, Aitchley Corlaiys," the robot responded. "You should arrive at approximately the same time as they do."

"But what if I don't?" the young farmer fretted. "What if I'm a little late? It'd bung everything up if Harris gets the bracelet off."

Emotionless glass eyes fixed smoky grey filters on the young man. "Affirmation: Trust me, Aitchley Corlaiys," Tin William proclaimed. "Harris Blind-Eye will *not* find an alchemist in the town of Leucos."

Frowning, Aitchley turned away, returning his gaze to the eastern horizon. Maybe there was something that Tin William knew that the young man didn't, but it didn't make him feel any better. Probably one of his stupid camera-things was already at Leucos, the young farmer concluded snidely to himself. Probably just waiting for Harris and Berlyn to show up. So how was it supposed to know who was an alchemist and who wasn't?

The nausea gaining strength within his bowels, Aitchley turned an argumentative mien on the silver robot. "But . . ." he started.

"Interruption: Trust me," was all Tin William said.

Aitchley had to bite his tongue in order to keep silent. Trusting someone on blind faith was not something the young man did easily, and the suspicion that he was being misled added to the already troubled rumbling of his innards. He had no reason to believe anything that the strange silver figure told him—nor to do anything that was asked of him. After all . . . what had this Tin William creature ever done for him?

Sheepishly, Aitchley bent and straightened his right leg, feeling a creeping warmth fill his cheeks. Oh, yeah, he mused. There was that.

Ruffling indignant feathers, Trianglehead fluffed himself out against the cold of the desert night. "Talk too much, you do!" the bird squawked irritably. "Go now. Zsooner iind eeed!"

With the low whine of gears, Tin William stepped away from the arachnoid Camera 12. "Agreement: Your bird is correct, Aitchley Corlaiys," the construct said. "The sun will rise in exactly three hours, forty-four minutes, and twelve seconds, and you will be forced to skirt the cliff wall to keep you from the heat.''

Aitchley shuddered; he didn't relish the idea of venturing back out into the inhospitable terrain of the Molten Dunes.

"Statement: You have an ample supply of water and food to sustain you for at least thirty days should the unthinkable happen and you become separated from Camera 12,'' Tin William went on, ''but you should arrive on the outskirts of Leucos in approximately sixty-one hours if all goes according to program.'' The construct looked away as if it had something on its mind but was reluctant to speak. When it finally looked back, Aitchley thought he heard the slightest trace of uncertainty tinge the electronic voice. ''Terminate-and-stay-resident, Aitchley Corlaiys,'' the robot said, and Aitchley could only assume it was a kind of farewell.

A high-pitched whine arose from the rear of Camera 12's body, and the sickening turmoil in Aitchley's belly rose with it. Thoughts of near-panic zig-zagged through his mind, and his pessimism and lack of self-esteem made a desperate attempt to think of as many excuses as possible before the small rocket activated.

I'm gonna die! the young man worried. I can't do this! This is magic! What the Pits was I thinking when I agreed to do this?

The shrill keening of the rocket's engine built as Camera 12 took a step forward.

"Exclamation: Aitchley Corlaiys! Wait!'' a sudden voice shouted.

The whining pressurization of the camera's engine died down as Aitchley redirected his attention to Tin William.

Although the machine was unable to express facial emotion, the young farmer could swear there was a look of contemplative thought on the robot's rigid steel features. ''Declaration: Although it is a greater infraction of standard programming to reveal pivotal plotlines moreso than the actual act of interference, there is something I must tell you.'' The metal man threw an anxious glance over one shoulder before fixing camera-lens eyes on the young man. ''I am first and foremost an observation unit, Aitchley Corlaiys,'' the robot declared. ''All TWs are regulated to certain neighboring dimensional worlds due to some oddity or interesting natural order that previously

was viewed with great curiosity and wonder. We were to observe and acquire as much information as possible in relation
to these natural occurrences and transmit the data to our scientific CPU. When we went syndicated, these priorities became secondary but remained in effect.

"The populace of Sphere have long had an infatuation and
interest in the natural phenomenon many worlds behold as
magic," Tin William continued. "Now, while your world has
long depleted its natural resource known as such, there still
remained a form of natural phenomenon that required detailed
study." The construct tilted its head to one side in a questioning, innocuous way. "Did you know, Aitchley Corlaiys, that
this world was never once subjected to firestorms, earthquakes,
pestilence, or floods? For nearly the entire millennium in
which I have served as TransWorld Observer, the land of Vedette suffered no known natural catastrophe. Magic notwith-
standing, there is not other world in all the history of TW
cataloging to boast such a claim. And yet—in less than two
centuries—this ecosystem has broken down. Blight, famine,
arefaction, and plagues have been the output."

Aitchley stared vacantly at the robot.

Tin William gave another nervous glance over his shoulder.
"Statement: Life and death are part of the natural order, Aitchley Corlaiys," the construct said. "When a species interferes,
disaster is the only result."

Aitchley licked lips that had suddenly gone dry. "So what
are you trying to say?" he wanted to know, his own fears and
worries suddenly seeming small and insignificant against the
ominous words of the observation unit.

Empty video-camera eyes fixed on the young farmer.
"Statement: There is a precarious balance at work in all
worlds, Aitchley Corlaiys," Tin William proclaimed, and an
echo of desperation tainted the buzzing, inhuman voice. "A
regenerative cycle. Birth and death. Growth and decay. Destruction and creation. But these are forces only Nature can
control in its myriad ways. No single species must ever cause
this balance to lose its integrity."

A dread of dark design wormed its way through Aitchley's
innards at the robot's warning, even though he didn't fully
understand.

A steel hand of concern unexpectedly clutched Aitchley by

the wrist. "Declaration: There are some things that were not meant to be tampered with, Aitchley Corlaiys," Tin William implored. "Be wary of Nature's scales."

Aitchley hardly heard the small rocket scream into life behind him or felt the sudden acceleration that pressed him back into the comforting embrace of the mesh harness. His mind was filled with the mysterious words left to him by the enigmatic creature called Tin William.

What was all that about? the young man wondered. Life and death? Birth and growth? Some things not meant to be tampered with? It almost sounds like he doesn't want me to finish the quest! But . . . but that's stupid! Why give me all this stuff? Why help me at all if he didn't want me to finish? Why not come out and just tell me not to go?

A mental scoff chased the growing doubts and anxieties from the young man's mind with a forced air of indifference. Who knows? he shrugged to himself with false apathy. Who cares? I've got more important things to worry about.

Fear, worry, and hope blazed in grey-green eyes.

Flying at subsonic speeds over the gently rolling waves of the desert's sandy ocean, Aitchley leaned into the shriek of the wind and rocketed eastward toward Leucos.

The stars were just beginning to glitter through the velvet-blue veil of early evening as Calyx dragged his heavy sack closer to the burgeoning campfire, his ruddy face drawn up in an expression of constipated annoyance. Seated beside the fire, Sprage watched with grim suspicion in his dark brown eyes as the dwarf plopped down next to him, rummaging and grumbling through his bag. Something vaguely positive slipped free of the dwarf's lips as he pulled himself free of his sack, and a cold slap of clammy unease sparked sympathetically against the back of Sprage's neck.

"Ah, ha!" the smith proclaimed. "I thought I still had this thing."

Relaxing a little, Sprage narrowed his eyes at the slender shaft of black steel, carved with an array of dwarven glyphs and designs, that had appeared in Calyx's grip. It didn't appear sharpened or dangerous in any way, and the healer leaned a little closer in his interest.

Calyx turned the innocent-looking object over in his hands.

"It's called a *navaja*," he told the curious physician.

Sprage flinched unexpectedly when one of the dwarf's stubby fingers triggered a hidden catch and released a wicked-looking blade onto the haft of the weapon.

"It's a pretty common weapon in Aa," Calyx went on casually, as if hardly aware of the eight-inch blade that had snapped threateningly into place. "Nothing fancy. Just a double-edged folding blade." He offered the weapon to Sprage. "Here. You take it."

Sprage visibly shied away from the knife as if it might bite him. "I'm not taking that!" he cried. "I'd probably cut my own fingers off!"

A look of sardonic contempt crossed Calyx's features. ":So?" he countered. "You're a healer . . . sew 'em back on again."

Sprage continued to scoot away from where the dwarf held out the *navaja*. "That's just it," he answered, an anxious churning roiling through his intestines. "I'm a healer, not a swordsman. It would be against my ethics to carry a weapon."

"Ethics, schmethics!" grunted Calyx. "You're a coward! If you plan on coming with us the rest of the way, you've gotta be able to take care of yourself!"

"I *can* take care of myself," Sprage retorted. "I've done it for over thirty years and I didn't have to go around stabbing people to prove it!"

"Who said anything about stabbing people?" Calyx shot back, his patience beginning to wear thin. "You need a way to defend yourself in case you get into trouble again. A *navaja* is a harmless little weapon that . . ."

"Harmless?" Sprage interrupted with an apprehensive bark of laughter. "How can a weapon be harmless?"

With a well-practiced flick of his wrist, Calyx tossed the blade point-first into the soft soil near Sprage's feet. "As I was saying," the dwarf impatiently ground out, "a *navaja* is a harmless little weapon that dwarven children carry for protection." He leaned in close to Sprage, his beady eyes catching the orange-red gleam of the fire. "There are things out there, Sprage," he said in low, menacing tones. "Things that you probably wouldn't want me talking about. Things that'll chomp your head off and worry about proper dining etiquette afterward. I don't care whether you're a dwarf or a human, you need a way to defend yourself. After all . . . the next time we get attacked by brown trolls, you might not have a bush to crawl under.''

The memory of the hideous trolls remained fresh in Sprage's mind, and he gave the weapon a tentative look. His lips pulled down as he reached out for the knife, but the vivid recollections of fear and panic actually seemed to fade as his fingers curled uneasily around the ebon hilt.

The expression on Calyx's face wasn't so much triumph as it was relief. "Now it's just for protection," the dwarf reminded him. "Having a *navaja* doesn't make you the Cavalier. I can teach you how to throw it if you want, but it's primarily in case something gets past me or Gjuki.''

Sprage nervously nodded his understanding, dark brown eyes locked on the knife in his grasp.

Gingerly, Calyx indicated a small lever at the base of the hilt. "That's the catch," he told the doctor. "You have to release the spring in order to open the blade, but be careful not to put your hand over the front. The blade *is* double-edged.''

Fear began to slither back into the physician's gaze. "Why?" he queried. "What does that mean?''

Calyx offered the doctor an awkward grin. "Nothing. Nothing, '' he responded curtly. "Just . . . be careful.''

"Why?" insisted Sprage. "What would happen if I held my hand over it?''

Calyx tried to hide his embarrassment by coughing into a curled fist. "You might kuff your finkuffs cough," he wheezed in phoney respiratory distress.

Sprage eyed the smith suspiciously. "What?" he demanded.

A frustrated mien of defeat overtook the dwarf's features. "You might cut your fingers off," he repeated more understandably.

The *navaja* practically jumped out of Sprage's hand and landed uselessly in the grass. "No! No way!" the doctor concluded. "There's no way I'm going to carry that thing!''

Calyx gave the discarded weapon a distasteful scowl before returning his dwarven glare to the physician. "Come on, Sprage," he snorted. "I bet half the instruments in your satchel are dangerous if not used properly. What's the difference?''

"The difference is that that's a weapon!" the healer retorted. "And I refuse to . . .''

At the edge of their campsite, face turned westward, Gjuki rose from where he was preparing dinner. The deep blues and purples of the darkening sky stretched languidly across the firmament, but there remained enough residual light to make out the shadowy outline of nearby trees and grass-laden meadows around them.

"Master Calyx. Healer Sprage," announced the Rhagana. "Forgive my interruption, but someone is coming."

Their debate momentarily postponed, both Calyx and Sprage clambered hastily to their feet. The sky continued to fall steadily into darkness—shrouding the neighboring hillocks in gloomy shades of blue—yet a fast-moving shadow darted in and around the various copses of trees in their direction. The growing thunder of nearing hooves began to rise in volume—no longer drowned out by the smith and healer's raised voices—and Calyx's hand dropped cautiously to the heavy warhammer slung at his belt.

Gauzed in the blue-black murk of early night, two horses suddenly appeared near the impromptu camp, briefly illuminated by the small fire at its center. Squinting, Calyx noted the thick sheen of foam surrounding the horse's bits—and only one horse actually held a rider—but the quick flash of orange-red light that brushed away the shadows was enough to confirm the dwarf's speculations.

"Poinqart!" the smith yelled with sudden urgency. "It's us! Stop!"

Startled—hardly even aware of the small camp and fire to his right—Poinqart drew his *meion* to an uneasy halt, Aitchley's stallion obediently stopping behind it. Wild, yellow-black eyes filled with hybrid surprise at the sight of the dwarf, healer, and Rhagana, yet half-breed trepidation continued to swirl in his gaze as Poinqart threw a fearful look over one shoulder at the darkening meadow behind him.

"Mister Calyx-dwarf!" the hybrid cried in his abrupt recognition, nearly falling in his haste to dismount; he threw another glance westward. "No time to chat-talk! Many nasty-bad-trolls are chasing poor Poinqart! Hurry! Hurry-quick! We must run away!"

Taken aback by the hybrid's rabid terror, Calyx barely reacted quickly enough to catch the half-troll before he collapsed in utter exhaustion. "Whoa, whoa!" the dwarf said. "Slow down a bit. You're not going to be going anywhere anytime soon.''

Led away from his *meion* and forced to sit down, Poinqart tried to resist but couldn't find the strength. "No. No time,'' he protested wearily. "Nasty-bad-trolls will be here soon! Poor Poinquart fell asleep! Creep-skulk-up on him, they almost did!''

Without word, Calyx demanded a flask of water with an impatient wave of his hand from Sprage. The healer, however, remained gaping at the exhausted hybrid, his unease growing as Poinqart's half-breed features reminded him of other, more dangerous creatures.

Gjuki stepped in and gave a flask of water to the dwarf.

Calyx waited as the half-troll took a long, thirsty draught from the flask. "Now think a moment, Poinqart,'' the dwarf suggested. "Where's Aitchley?''

A heavy sigh escaped the half-troll's lips as he wiped his mouth with the back of a four-fingered hand. "Mister Aitch is gone,'' the hybrid declared sadly. "Tumble-lost in the desert, he is. Poinqart tried to rescue-save him—-Poinqart tried!—-but the nasty-bad-trolls got in Poinqart's way!''

A familiar frown passed beneath Calyx's beard. "What do you mean he's lost?'' he asked. "Lost how? You mean dead-lost?''

Poinqart shook his oversized head. "Poinqart does not know,'' he answered apologetically. "Mister Aitch tumble-fell off a cliff, and Poinqart does not know.''

Inhaling deeply, Calyx straightened to his full height, throwing a perturbed look westward. "So we'll have to go back to the desert, then,'' the smith muttered gravely to himself. "I *told* the kid it was a stupid idea to go off on his own.''

"Actually, Master Calyx, it was Captain d'Ane who suggested . . .'' Gjuki began to correct.

The dwarf shot the Rhagana a fierce glance, and even Gjuki knew better than to continue that line of discussion. Grumbling unhappily, the smith started kicking loose dirt onto their campfire, spreading darkness across the plains with each shuffle of soil.

The growing blackness spurred the terror inside Poinqart. "No!'' the half-troll screamed, jumping to his feet. "We cannot go back to the burning-hot-sands! The nasty-bad-trolls will hungry-catch us!''

Calyx moved away from the dying fire and headed for his *meion*. ''If there's any chance that Aitchley's still alive, we've got to . . .''

A horde of dark shapes suddenly exploded out of the surrounding blackness, the hunger in their yellow-black eyes glistening in the red-orange glow of the fading embers. More shapes rose up along their right, and the sound of eager, approaching footsteps broke the night, no longer muffled or concealed by ravenous stealth.

Calyx gave the score of monsters a disgruntled look. ''Well,'' he shrugged haphazardly, ''so much for that idea.''

Ice crystallizing along his spine, Sprage bent down and snatched up his fallen *navaja*.

Birds sung merrily in the afternoon warmth of their leafy canopies—and there was even the arrhythmic rapping-tap of a woodpecker nearby—as Berlyn rode behind Harris toward the western outskirts of Leucos.

The blonde brushed a strand of hair out of her face, grey-green eyes scanning the column of trees enclosing them. They had found a small dirt path only a little after dawn and had followed its winding, serpentine route through the ever-increasing forest for nearly half the day but, so far, the young girl had not yet seen another single person traversing the road. She had glimpsed the off-white of sheep placidly grazing on the gentle slopes and grassy knolls off in the distance, but had seen neither shepherd nor dogs to keep the herds from straying.

A gentle wind rustled through the trees, passing invisible fingers through Berlyn's long hair as she continued to ride in silence. She was grateful for the breeze—it kept the unwashed stench of Harris Blind-Eye away from her nose—but an unsubstantiated unease began to swell in her belly. Although she was unsure how far they were from the town, she suspected they should have seen something other than just sheep by now. In fact, for the better part of the morning the only sounds she had heard had been the constant springtime courting of the birds in the trees and wind-rustled leaves.

For some reason, that didn't sit well with her.

A sharp elbow from Harris unexpectedly poked her in the

ribs, and a wordless finger directed her attention to a church steeple rising above the forest. The sun/moon emblem atop the tower marked it as a temple to the Twin Sisters, but there was a tattered black banner flying just above the symbol, snapping sporadically in the spring breeze.

Harris sucked thoughtfully at his teeth. "That's a bad sign," the outlaw murmured to himself.

The apprehension in Berlyn started to spread. "What?" she wanted to know. "What's a bad sign?"

The thief's finger indicated the threadbare banner. "That," he said matter-of-factly. "Some towns fly a black flag to warn travelers and merchants of plague. Means to stay the Pits away."

Berlyn noted with growing anxiety that Harris made no attempt to rein in his horse. "So why aren't we stopping?" she inquired nervously.

Harris gave her a curt shrug. "Guess you can just say I'm an optimistic blackguard, sweetcheeks," he jeered her. "Besides . . . I'm not planning on staying all that long. I'm in. I'm out. You're the one that's gotta wait around for loverboy to show."

The worry began to haunt Berlyn with repressed memories, and she hoped Harris didn't feel her involuntary shudder. She'd seen firsthand what the Black Worm could do once someone had been Touched. She'd seen the black pustules and buboes swell like dark eggs in the armpits, neck, and groin of Rael and Mrs. Faustine back in the Tampenteire kitchens. Observed the dark rash that spread all across their bodies like ebony worms burying under their flesh. And she had been so terrified by the sight—by the very closeness of the dread disease—that she had done something she would have never thought herself brave enough to do: She had left the Tampenteire estate to try to find a safer life elsewhere.

The young scullery maid shivered again in her fear. The Black Worm's Touch didn't care who it took. Rich and poor. Young and old. It took them all. And now she was riding right into a plague-stricken town with absolutely no say in the matter.

Harris's dark horse broke through the cover of trees and trotted lightly into the narrow streets of Leucos. Empty shops and deserted houses faced them on every side, and the warm breeze had a ghostly way of rattling half-open doors and dark, curtained windows. A few sheep lying lazily in the middle of the road gave the newcomers an uninterested stare of ovine intelligence before settling back down to sleep, yet there remained no other signs of life.

The black flag snapped and cracked above their heads from atop the church steeple.

"What . . . What happened here?" Berlyn asked timorously.

Even without seeing his face, the blonde could tell a frustrated grimace clouded Harris's mien. "Gaal-damned bunging whoresons," was all the brigand cursed under his breath, directing his horse down another unpaved road.

More of the same awaited them down every street: empty buildings—long uninhabited—and desolate dirt roads swept clean by the passage of the wind. Once they passed what appeared to be the bodies of cattle lying lifeless along the side of the street, their bones picked clean by scavengers and time, but still saw no hints of humanity. The town of Leucos was completely empty.

Drawing his mount to a stop near the center of the small village, Harris Blind-Eye slid gracefully out of the saddle and stood glaring at the empty houses around him. There was a large hostel before him—windows dark and door firmly shut—but natural instincts prodded the outlaw toward it. Hostels and taverns were always the best places to glean information, the cutthroat knew, and they always boasted the greatest amount of people in which to remain securely anonymous. But—even here—the hostel, as was the rest of the town, appeared to be completely deserted.

Warily, Harris unstrapped the blue-and gold shield from his horse's flanks and slung it over his left shoulder. Berlyn dropped to the ground beside the thief, watching with wide, awestruck eyes as the thief moved quietly across the earthen street.

"Where is everybody?" the blonde asked in a timid squeak.

Harris stepped cautiously toward the abandoned hostel, Mandy gripped readily in one hand. "Gone, I guess," he answered her without drawing his gaze away from the building. "Heard about this sort of thing once before. Used to be a town south of Ilietis . . . along the coast. Black Worm wiped out nearly the entire population. Those that didn't die, fled. Nowadays, there ain't much left but a few footpaths and some rotting timber. Not even drawn on a map anymore." Blue-black eyes scanned the empty windows. "Looks like pretty much the same thing happened here."

The horror encompassing Berlyn's brain was nearly too much, and the girl felt herself almost swoon. A whole town! Her mind reeled. A whole town had fallen to the Black Worm's Touch!

The scullery maid hugged herself, trembling fearfully. I want to leave, and I want to leave *now*!

Harris kicked angrily at a small rock. "Daeminase Pits!" the lockpick swore in his frustration. "This bungs things up real convenient-like, doesn't it?" He threw a fiery gaze up at the deserted inn. "I suppose we can always head north . . . toward Nylais."

A sudden hand fell upon Berlyn's shoulder, startling her out of her thoughts. A split-second of turgid panic raced through her system, but then she felt how gentle the hand was . . . how protectively it moved her back beside Harris' horse and out of the way of impending danger.

Mind-numbing shock shattered the young girl's composure as grey-green eyes rested on the young man who had suddenly appeared beside her. A lopsided grin answered her awestruck gaze, and blue-green eyes—the color of an ocean's waves—peered into her own, instantly quelling any fears or worries clawing at her insides.

Tugging at the drooping brim of his hat, Aitchley turned his attention away from Berlyn and confronted Harris Blind-Eye, a steely hardness coming into his youthful stare. "You're not going anywhere, *scout*," the young man snarled, making the brigand's favorite nickname a venomous insult.

Harris Blind-Eye spun about, blue-black eyes going wide in unexpected surprise.

Aitchley tightened his grip on his sword and throwing ax, a lopsided smirk thrown defiantly at the lockpick. "Got a problem with that?"

7

Showdown in Leucos

Harris took an arrogant step across the street, trying to intimidate the young farmer with a malignant, blue-black glare. "I'm impressed, scout," the outlaw admitted. "You managed to sneak up on me without me knowing. Should've kept coming, though. Now that I know you're here, you're dead meat."

Aitchley offered the lockpick a confident, albeit lopsided, smirk. "I don't think so," he responded. "I saw what happened to Gjuki when he tried to take you from behind. I'm not that stupid."

A ragged eyebrow raised on Harris's forehead. "Hmph," the brigand snorted. "You've got some smarts, then, puck. Hate to have to kill you."

Aitchley tightened his grip on his sword. "You can try," he growled.

Harris took another wary step forward, his arrogance diminishing. This ain't working, the outlaw noticed dourly. Something about the kid's changed . . . drastically. This ain't the same unscarred mudshoveler who was afraid to take a shot at a starving xlf. This is someone who means business and plans on getting it . . . and that means I'm bunged!

Blue-black eyes flicked anxiously to the cold grey steel in the young man's hand. Now what? the southern-city thief asked himself, his own fear mounting. Fightin' fair ain't my style. I'm more used to the quick stab for the eyes or for the privates than I am fightin' hand to hand. Makes the getaway that much easier. Won't work here, though. Could try for the girl again . . . or maybe my horse . . . That might stop him. But the kid's standing in the way of both of 'em. So what do I do?

Harris hefted the weight of the stiletto in his right hand. He had seen Aitchley effortlessly take down five men because of the threat they had posed to the girl; Harris Blind-Eye was not one to gamble against such odds . . .

Encouraged by the brigand's thoughtful silence, Aitchley took a challenging step forward. "This doesn't have to be difficult," the young man declared. "Just give me the necklace and we'll . . ."

Black steel unexpectedly screamed toward Aitchley's face.

Aitchley froze, his muscles locking into place at the sight of the ebon blade shrieking toward him. Time seemed to slow as blue-green eyes followed Mandy's deadly trajectory through air suddenly as thick as treacle, and the young man's thoughts became a whirlwind flurry of panic and frenzied regret.

Daeminase Pits! I knew this wasn't going to work! I'm dead! Maybe I can duck? Use the shield! Use the shield? I don't have the damn shield! Dung! I'm sorry, Berlyn. I told you I wasn't much of a hero!

There was a low-pitched whir from somewhere nearby, and a flash of red-violet color came swooping in from out of the trees, snatching the weapon in mid-flight and carrying it up to the roof of the nearby hostel.

Harris squinted in malevolent surprise at the small gyrofalc that flapped to a clumsy landing atop the hostel rooftop, Mandy clutched harmlessly in its talons.

Overcome by a great wave of relief, Aitchley glanced up at the triangular-headed fledgling. *That* had been a gamble, the young man concluded, exhaling pensively.

Milky blue eyes fixed accusingly on the young farmer, Tri-anglehead ruffled his feathers in avian pride. "Told you! Told you I kould!" the bird cawed boastfully. "No problem!"

A caustic sneer twisting his lip, Harris pulled his gaze back to earth. "Pretty neat trick, scout," he complimented Aitchley derisively. "You train him to do that?"

Aitchley tried to shake himself free of his lingering fear.

"Didn't need to," he answered. "Instincts. Gyrofalcs catch a lot of their prey in mid-flight."

Harris gave the young farmer an acknowledging nod, his self-assuredness returning with each frightened quiver tainting the young man's voice. "Expect maybe he can do it again?" the cutthroat wondered, snapping his left wrist down and bringing Renata into his grasp.

Blue-green eyes widened even though Aitchley continued to wrestle with his fear. Don't let him know you're afraid! he screamed at himself. He can sense it, remember? He's not going to throw it at you . . . he's bluffing. If he throws it, and Trianglehead catches it, he's weaponless. He knows it, and you know it. So stop shaking!

Wishing his legs didn't feel so much like wet rope, Aitchley tried to look the brigand in the eye. "You're a betting man," he said, using the lockpick's previous words against him. "Odds aren't in your favor."

Harris weighed Renata in his palm, mocking deep thought. "Maybe," he mused. "Maybe not."

So quick that Aitchley was barely able to follow it, black steel once again launched from Harris's hand. Frigid, arctic terror lanced like an icy blade through the young man's gut, and a horrified scream tore involuntarily from his throat as he leapt insanely at Harris, sword flailing above his head.

"*NO!*" the young man screamed. Like black lightning, Renata streaked through the afternoon sky, catching Trianglehead in a sudden explosion of red-violet feathers. With a hapless squawk, the fledgling pitched backwards, Mandy falling from his grasp and skittering back down the sloping rooftop toward the street.

Wolflike, Harris leapt wildly for the falling stiletto, catching the sudden movement of activity behind him out of the corner of his eye. Blue-gold *gnaiss* flowed onto his left arm like magic, catching Aitchley's sword in mid-descent and jolting the young man backwards. Quick, callused fingers caught Mandy as the knife spiraled off the roof to the ground, and Harris spun back around, just in time to block another downward sweep from Aitchley's sword.

Tears streaming from his eyes, Aitchley brought his sword down on the Cavalier's shield in the same way Archimandrite Sultothal had, grimacing each time as the near-magical deflec-

tion tried to rip the weapon from his hands or his arms from
their sockets. Uncontrollable anger swamped the young man
with a berserkerlike rage, and he bit into his own lower lip as
he struck vengefully at the outlaw hiding behind the dwarven
shield.

"You lousy, no good, son of a bunghole!" Aitchley yowled,
sword striking shield in an arrhythmic clang of steel against
gnaiss.

Bloodied feathers wafted earthward.

Harris tried to regain his footing and bring Mandy into play,
yet the incessant attack against the shield stymied him. He
barely kept his balance under the insane onslaught, and a cold
flake of fear began to settle in the cutthroat's mind.

Uh, oh, Harris mused angrily to himself. Tried to take out
one threat and get Mandy back, and I wound up pissing the
kid off . . . Exactly what I didn't want to do. Daeminase Pits!
Kid's got strength! Gonna have to end this quick.

Black steel lashed out from behind the safety of blue-and-
gold *gnaiss*, grazing Aitchley across his right arm. The young
man hardly heard the fabric of his shirt tear or felt the brief
caress of metal against his flesh, his mind too caught up in his
hatred for the southern-city scum before him. This son of a
bunghole killed Trianglehead! was all Aitchley could think. If
it hadn't have been for the gyrofalc, I'd be lying dead somewhere out in the Gaal-damned desert!

Fear growing, Harris staggered back two paces, clumsily
blocking another blow. Dip me in piss and roll me dung! the
lockpick swore to himself. I missed!

Slim hands wringing in nervous anticipation, Berlyn
watched from a safe distance near Harris's horse as Aitchley
pressed his attack, forcing Harris closer and closer to the abandoned hostel. Steel flashed in wicked arcs above the young
man's head, crashing down on the Cavalier's shield with cam-
panologic thunder, and Berlyn stared in enraptured awe at the
young farmer who had come to save her life. A few feathers
continued to drift down around the two as they fought, and
the blonde couldn't help the lump that formed in her throat.
That poor little bird, she thought sadly; her gaze hardened on
Harris. I hope Aitchley kicks his butt good!

Swearing, Harris Blind-Eye stumbled in his backward retreat, his left arm beginning to feel the jarring blows of Aitch-

ley's barrage. Sweat began to form across his dirtied brow as heavy as the apprehension forming in his gut, and Harris gave a startled glance at the hostel wall that suddenly pressed up against his back.

Magical bloody shield, my left dangleberry! the cutthroat grumbled to himself. This ain't going right at all!

Waiting until Aitchley drew back his sword for another powerful, overhanded swing, Harris braced his feet up against the wall and leapt, propelling himself forward, shield held out at arms' length. He caught the young man unprepared, blue-and-gold *gnaiss* catching the edge of Aitchley's weapon and throwing him backwards into the street. Stars imploded behind his eyelids as the young farmer crashed to the ground, his hat spilling off his head in a sudden tornado of dust and gravel. The Cavalier's shield clattered uselessly beside him.

Shaking the dizziness from his head, Aitchley looked up just in time to see Harris turn on his heel and disappear into the desolate gloom of the empty hostel. Good move, that, the young man thought to himself, still just the slightest bit disoriented by the blow. Too bad I didn't think of that when Sultothal was beating the mulch out of me!

As the young man slid the Cavalier's shield onto his left forearm, soft hands suddenly rested on his shoulders, gently restraining him from getting up. Questioningly, the young farmer cast a quick glance behind him, unable to stop the lopsided smile of reassurance that came to his lips when he stared into Berlyn's concerned features.

"Let him go, Aitchley," the blonde pleaded. "He wants you to follow him."

Despite the tender hands trying to prevent him, Aitchley pulled himself to his feet. "I know that," he replied, plopping his hat back down on top of his head, "but we need him. We can't finish the quest without him."

Solicitude flashed in grey-green eyes. "Forget about the quest," Berlyn implored. "Let him go."

Hesitation and doubt nearly shattered the young man's resolve, but he looked closely at the petite scullery maid before him, narrowing blue-green eyes at her anxious mien. Her worry and concern were genuine—and he probably could have given up and let Harris go free without her thinking any less of him—but he knew, somewhere inside her, she'd be disappointed. Maybe he'd walk away unharmed if he let Harris escape, but what kind of hero would that make him to her? To Lord Tampenteire and the others? To Tin William and all the people he said were watching?

Besides . . . there was the matter of avenging Gjuki and Trianglehead.

Aitchley forced himself to tear his eyes away from the care and affection burning in Berlyn's gaze. "I . . . I can't," he told her, almost apologetically. "There's too many people counting on me."

A look of intense sadness creased the young blonde's face, yet she squeezed the young farmer's hand in wordless understanding. "I was right, then," she said with a strained smile. "I *do* have my own Cavalier." She leaned forward and her lips touched his. "Be careful."

Aitchley cursed the lopsided smile he was sure made him look like a complete muggwort. "I'll be all right," he replied, and was slightly surprised by the confident surety in his own tone. Then he spun on his heel and ducked hurriedly into the gloom of the abandoned hostel after Harris.

The murk and mustiness closed about the young man almost immediately, embracing him in the false twilight of empty desolation. A fine layer of dust and dirt coated the wooden floor like a fragile brown-grey rug, and afternoon sunlight tried desperately to push its way past drapery yellow and stiff with age and neglect, succeeding only in casting the interior in dull, jaundiced illumination. A few pieces of furniture remained in the front hall—also varnished with a fine layer of dust—and Aitchley could see some damage where vandals or would-be thieves had overturned tables and bookcases in their search for something of possible value.

Reminding himself of his purpose, Aitchley straitened bluegreen eyes through the bilious lighting of the front hall, reaffirming his grip on his sword. Faint scuff marks through the carpet of dust offered an easy trail to follow, winding their way through the diseased sunlight and gloom to a staircase steeped in shadows.

Floorboards moaned their protest as Aitchley stepped cautiously down the hall, wary eyes trying to pierce the darkness. *He wants you to follow him*, the young man heard Berlyn's warning resonate through his mind. Harris could have just as easily run for his horse instead of the hostel, Aitchley knew. The hostel just offered him a better way to get rid of the young man in typical southern-city scum fashion.

Aitchley swallowed hard, his unease stopping him in the middle of the room. There were a number of doors along the hallway, all closed and ominous, and the staircase itself was cloaked in blackness. Harris could be hiding anywhere, the young man worried. And he still had at least *one* of his knives. One wrong move and Aitchley's quest was as good as over!

Regardless of his apprehensions, a self-righteous anger that was beginning to grow very familiar to the young farmer rose up inside him. Images of bloodied feathers wafted through his mind, accompanied by a memory of white Rhagana blood and a look of terror in grey-green eyes. Harris has caused everyone so much pain recently—including my own nearly botched trip back into Ilietis—that he deserves to get his hand blown off! the young man snarled steadfastly to himself. If he wasn't so damn important to the quest, I'd use the necklace the instant I got it back!

Spurred on by his rage, Aitchley resumed walking forward, trying to step as lightly as possible on the creaking wooden floorboards beneath his feet. Harris's footprints led him closer to the dark stairs, and the young man followed, his desire for vengeance growing with each determined step.

Struck with a sudden suspicion, Aitchley halted at the bottom of the stairs, blue-green eyes scanning the blackness around him. There were a few patches of disturbed dust on the bottommost stairs, yet they didn't appear to go any further than the fourth step. Questioningly, Aitchley turned to look further down the hall, his gaze fixed on the dust-littered floor. A single door rested beyond the staircase, but no matter how hard he strained and squinted through the gloom Aitchley couldn't see any prints going that way. An inquisitive line of thought, however, began to whisper through his brain.

If I was Harris Blind-Eye, where would I hide? the young man asked himself. Would I go upstairs where I might possibly get trapped? Or would I try to make it *look* like I went upstairs so that the person following me followed a false trail while I was still hiding downstairs? That way I could get out to my horse and get away while the person following me wasted his time upstairs.

Smiling lopsidedly at his logical reasoning, Aitchley stomped loudly up the first four steps, throwing up great clouds of grey-white dust. He stopped on the fourth stair—neatly concealed in gloom and shadows—but continued to walk in place, treading lighter and lighter so that it sounded as if his footsteps were trailing away.

His smile growing more self-confident, Aitchley dropped into a crouch on the stairs, eyes locked on the shadowy corridor of the first floor. Come on, Harris, he mentally coaxed the closed door. All-out's-in-free.

The sudden creak of protesting wood above him was his only warning as the young man turned just in time to see a dark shape launch itself from the second-floor landing, black steel stabbing for his eyes. A half-choked scream of surprise escaped the young farmer's lips as he tried to stand, and he could see the triumphant glimmer of victory in Harris's eyes as the southern-city outlaw leapt directly at him.

Blue-and-gold *gnaiss* unexpectedly interceded between the two, rescuing Aitchley from the stiletto striking for his face. Harris's leap, however, sent the wiry brigand straight into Aitchley, slamming the shield up against the young man's chest and forcing him backwards. Stanced as he was on the stairs, Aitchley was barely able to release another half-garbled scream before both men went tumbling down the steps.

Shadows and shapes flashed chaotically past Aitchley's eyes as he fell over backwards in an uncontrolled somersault, his head smacking the wall in the narrow confines of the staircase. Vertigo seized him roughly by the throat, and he heard steel clatter uselessly to the ground, unsure whether he had dropped his sword or whether Harris had dropped Mandy.

All the air rushed out of his lungs as the young man crashed back to the first floor, Harris spilling on top of him. Terrifying images of his own death went shrieking through his mind as he expected the final blow that would end his life, but—when he felt Harris scramble hurriedly off him—the young man cracked open a bewildered eye to see the rogue dive desperately for his fallen stiletto.

Get him! Get him now! the young man's brain screamed at him.

Even before Aitchley could manage to sit up, Harris had rolled back to his feet, Mandy glinting a deadly black in his right hand. "You're starting to become a real nuisance, scout," the southern-city thief remarked, taking a threatening step closer.

Suddenly realizing the bandit stood between his sprawled feet, Aitchley scissored his legs shut. "Get bunged," he retorted, catching the lockpick at the back of the knees.

Struck from behind, Harris pitched over backwards, his own head rebounding off the hostel wall. A startled grunt slipped past the brigand's lips as he slid dazedly to the floor, and Aitchley took that opportunity to scrabble frantically to his feet, fingers curling nervously about his sword.

An unexpected boot suddenly caught the young man in the groin, throwing him brutally back to the ground.

Harris Blind-Eye sprang to his feet, blue-black eyes resting cruelly on the downed young man. "Learn to take a hint, puck," the outlaw advised. "Stay down."

Another boot slammed into the side of Aitchley's head.

Blinding pain wracked the young man's body, threatening to send him teetering to the brink of unconsciousness. A hellish fire raged between his legs—turning all the muscles of his body into limp, rubbery, useless things—and a persistent ringing in his skull overwhelmed him with agonizing peals of discomfort and misery. Somewhere—on the fringes of rationality—he knew he was as good as dead. Harris had won. Dropped him to the ground with a typical southern-city blow to the bung-rod, but still the young man fought on. Still he fought against the unbelievable agony radiating outward from his crotch and bringing with it the foul, tangy taste of bile to the back of his throat.

Wondering why the final blow never came, Aitchley struggled to lift his head, catching a last glimpse of Harris as the lockpick ran back out the front door. Intense pain continued to ravage his body—and someone had replaced all the blood in his veins with molten lead—but Aitchley managed to stagger sickly to his knees, his hands still instinctively clutched between his legs.

Some hero you are, his pessimism commented with bleak ridicule. What the Pits did you think you were doing, anyway? Taking on Harris Blind-Eye! Are you that much of a blind muggwort? He's *the* most notorious outlaw in all Solsbury! Did you seriously think you could beat him in a fight?

Finding the strength to prove his dark thoughts wrong, Aitchley lurched awkwardly his feet. *Who says I have to beat him?* he asked himself rebelliously. *All I have to do is get the necklace back. Once I do that, he falls back into line.*

You think it's as easy as that? his pessimism nearly laughed at him. *What's to stop him from stealing it from you when you're not paying attention? Or slitting your throat while you're asleep and running off with it? Or maybe he'll just kidnap Berlyn again and . . .*

A sudden lightning bolt of terror struck the young man. *Berlyn!* he realized in abrupt horror. *She's still outside!*

His concern for the blonde scullery maid helping him block out some of the pain, Aitchley staggered drunkenly for the door, using his sword to help keep him upright. His thoughts were a sudden turmoil of worry and near panic, and his own imagination assaulted him with images of Berlyn once again trapped in Harris's arms, a razor-sharp blade pressed obscenely against her throat.

Half-pushing, half-falling, Aitchley burst out the hostel door, his fear and anxiety at a boiling point. "*Blind-Eye!*" he roared, and the unforgiving hatred in his own voice startled him.

Harris halted halfway across the street, throwing a single look of tedious disapproval back at the enraged young man. Anticipatively, he readied Mandy in his grasp, but a discerning glance back at his horse told the brigand he could probably make it to the stallion before the kid caught up to him.

All Aitchley saw was the outlaw resume heading toward Berlyn.

With a vocalized yowl of infuriated worry—and knowing he wouldn't reach him in time—Aitchley jerked the blue-and-gold shield off his left arm and flung it out across the street, its rounded surface skimming smoothly over the uneven dirt road. Like a runaway wagon wheel, the dwarven shield caught Harris at the back of the heels, its near-magical deflection snapping the lockpick backwards and hurling him to the ground. A stunned curse broke the rogue's lips, and he swung a furious eye up at the young man charging toward him.

"That was real stupid, scout," the downed thief said. Black steel glimmered in his hand. "Now you don't have nothin' to hide behind."

Mandy jumped like something alive from Harris's fingers, deadly black steel flaming ebony as it streaked for Aitchley. Horrified, Aitchley skidded to a frantic halt, eyes wide at the on coming missile. This time, he knew, there could be no escape. He had foolishly thrown away his shield in an over-ambitious attempt to save Berlyn, and there was no irascible little gyrofalc to save his worthless life now. Not even throwing himself to the ground would save him from the pitch black death hurling toward him.

A sudden roar and whoosh of blue flame exploded out of the shrubbery, drawing the young farmer's attention away from the oncoming stiletto. Glinting steel unexpectedly threw itself in Mandy's path, deflecting the blade with its own body and causing the weapon to ricochet off in an abrupt clangor of metal against metal, dropping harmlessly in the dirt.

As his fear subsided and his anger grew, Aitchley returned his attention to Harris and stepped out from around Camera 12. "Give me the necklace," the young man ground out.

Trying to blink the shock and bewilderment out of his eyes, Harris hurried to his feet, unable to tear his gaze away from the insect-shaped device that had come to Aitchley's rescue. "What . . . What the Pits is that thing?" he wanted to know.

Aitchley took another menacing step forward. "Give me the necklace," he repeated, his fury growing as his benumbed brain finally registered the fact that this southern-city slime had just tried to kill him . . . twice!

Harris took an unsteady step back. "I . . . I . . ." he sputtered.

Aitchley closed the gap, hand tightening around his sword hilt. "Give me the necklace."

Actually frightened, Harris Blind-Eye took another step backwards. "Hey, look, now, puck. No hard feelings?" He attempted an exaggerated smile of rotting teeth. "I was just kidding, you know?"

Stepping nearer, Aitchley retrieved his shield from the middle of the street and slung it back over his arm. "*Now*, Blind-Eye," he snarled through clenched teeth. "Give me the necklace."

There was a sudden blur of motion as Harris Blind-Eye spun about, darting with serpentine speed back toward his horse. The sudden shriek of surprised fear from Berlyn stopped

Aitchley dead in his tracks, and the young man's anger threatened to consume him wholly as he glared at where Harris held the blonde in his dirty grasp, a scarred and calloused hand clutched about her pale throat.

"Okay, scout," the lockpick remarked, some of the confidence returning to his voice. "I don't know who you've been dealing with lately, but call off your armor-plated whatchamacallsit. From now on, I'm calling the shots."

Despite himself, Aitchley took a single defiant step forward, eyes ablaze with an inferno of blue-green fire.

Harris's fingers tightened around Berlyn's neck, forcing a half-choked gag from the girl's lips. "*I'll kill her, puck!*" the outlaw screeched, and Aitchley could hear the high-pitched panic tinging his words. "*Don't think I won't! I'll snap her neck like a bunging twig! Now . . . back off!*"

Aitchley halted, his knuckles white about the grip of his sword.

Nervous eyes flicking to where the strange, alien form of Camera 12 squatted motionless behind the kid, Harris forced himself to relax. "Now, here's the deal," he said, exhaling heavily. "I get on my horse, the girl lives. You try to follow me, she dies. Got that?"

"Get this," Berlyn suddenly snarled, slamming her elbow up and back into Harris's face.

With a crunch of breaking cartilage and a spray of red, Harris Blind-Eye crashed backwards into the bushes, both his hands going to his injured nose. He tried clumsily to regain his footing—to find his bearings as quickly as possible—but the unexpected blow to his face caused a vertiginous wrench of pain that continued to muddle his senses. A string of profanities bubbled through lips smeared with his own blood, and he cracked open one wrathful eye, catching sight of the slender blonde as she jogged gingerly away from where he lay.

Girl or not, the southern-city outlaw thought foully to himself. The little bunghole is *dead*!

The toe of a boot suddenly caught the brigand alongside the face, driving his face back down into the shrubbery. Another blow struck him near the kidney, and when he tried to rise a third smashed into his jaw, clacking his teeth together with such force that he nearly bit his tongue off.

Dazed and bloodied, Harris felt strong hands grab him by

the front of his shirt, hoisting him effortlessly off the ground. Sheer hatred burned in the blue-green eyes above him, and the expression on the young man's face was one of barely restrained murder.

Shaking the thief in his grasp like a rag doll, Aitchley glared down at the defeated rogue. "Now here's the deal," he growled menacingly. Rough hands tore the necklace from around Harris's throat. "There's *no* deal!"

Despite the looming threat of impending unconsciousness, a jeering smile still managed to pull across Harris's split and bloodied lips. "Big deal," the lockpick spat, one side of his face already starting to puff and swell. "You still don't know how to use the damn thing."

Aitchley pulled the bandit up close, nose to broken nose with the cutthroat. The cold fire burning in the farmer's eyes was so intense that it seared straight through the outlaw's pain-clouded and fuzzy brain to the most basic of survival instincts beneath. "You wanna try me?" the young man challenged.

Harris's smile stretched above a beard striped with blood, comprehending without words. "Well, well, puck," he mocked, barely conscious. "Looks like you've got some backbone after all."

Aitchley's eyebrows narrowed in rabid disgust. "And you're just lucky we need you alive," he cursed.

The trunk of a tree suddenly slammed into his face, and the world went black for Harris Blind-Eye.

When consciousness returned, Harris was almost reluctant to receive it. Fiery patches of discomfort burned about his face and head, and crusty, brittle streams of dried blood were caked along the sides of his face and in his ragged beard. A tooth wriggled loosely on the right side of his mouth, and the flesh about his right eye was so swollen he was unable to pry open that eye. It had been a while since he had been beaten this badly—probably the day the Patrol finally succeeded in catching him—and he had to convince himself it wasn't all just a bad dream as he squinted open his left eye and looked about him.

A grumpy-looking dwarf stared back at him, dark mirth gleaming in his beady eyes. "Naw. Too bad," the dwarf quipped, straightening up and walking away from the now-conscious brigand. "He's still alive."

Still fighting off the painless oblivion of unconsciousness, Harris gently shook his head and blinked a questioning eye. He sat against a tree—judging from the chunks of missing bark, it was probably the same one the kid had rammed his face into—with his hands tied securely behind his back. He knew just by feel that both concealed sheaths at his wrists were empty, and his neck ached from where the pendant's chain had been forcibly ripped from around his throat.

A cluster of horses had been tethered outside the abandoned hostel during Harris's bout of senselessness, and the rogue immediately recognized the fungoid Rhagana and squat half-troll standing nearby. A tall man with stooped shoulders and long, grey-black hair stood beside the strange, metal spider thing that had come to the kid's defense, and the kid himself was sitting, side by romantic side, with his girl, an unhappy-looking fluff of bandaged feathers perched on the young man's shoulder.

"I thought I killed that stupid bird," Harris muttered, forcing words through painfully swollen lips.

Taking a seat on the ground beside the kid, the dwarf offered the lockpick a malicious smirk. "You almost did," he answered. "Trouble is, though, Sprage here's a healer. He specializes in animals."

The tall man in the black smock gave the bandit an unfriendly glance. "If it's any consolation to you," he mocked grimly, "he won't be flying for a while."

"Azszshole!" the gyrofalc swore at Harris from across the street. "Peck your eyesz out, I kould!"

Harris noted the kid remained unsettlingly quiet, blue-green eyes fixed on the rogue with an unfriendly glare.

"So what's the story?" the southern-city outlaw queried, trying to ignore the kid's hate-filled stare. "We're all one big happy again?"

"Actually, it was just blind luck that we found you," replied the dwarf, a grin of satisfaction on his lips from the brigand's unfavorable condition. "See, we got chased by a whole bunch of brown trolls, and we couldn't get around them to look for Aitchley, so we figured we'd head here. Maybe find someone to help us get them off our tails. Imagine our surprise when we found you lying in the bushes with your ass kicked in!"

Harris felt fresh blood flow as he forced a supercilious smile in reply. "Yeah. Must have been hilarious."

"Not half as hilarious as the predicament we're in now," Calyx continued with typical dwarven pessimism. "We were supposed to pick up more supplies and leave our horses here before heading into the Bentwoods, but—since there's no one else in town—that's gonna be a little hard to do, isn't it? It'll also look like Berlyn'll have to come with us."

Harris mocked sadness. "Awww," he jeered. "I'm crushed."

"Yeah, figured you might be," retorted Calyx. He gave the young man sitting silently beside him a cursory glance. "Now here's where the real problem comes in," he went on. "I say just leave the horses and start off on foot—we've got plenty of extra supplies thanks to Baroness Desireah—but Sprage, being the animal lover that he is, won't hear of it. See . . . maybe I didn't mention this before, but, sometime around mid-morning tomorrow, the trolls should be catching up with us. Now, normally, in a town, you'd be safe from such an attack, but, since there's no one else here, it won't take long before the trolls figure that out and start swarming in after us. So, here's where you make your decision: Do you come with us and behave yourself, or do we leave you for the trolls?"

Blue-black eyes tried to scry through the dwarf's ultimatum. "You won't leave me here," Harris proclaimed with arrogant surety. "You need me for your stupid quest."

Calyx gave Aitchley another glance before shrugging. "Not really," he said. "See that weird silver thing over there?" A stubby finger indicated the arachnid camera. "It specializes in picking locks."

Suspiciously, Harris glanced at the spidery construct, eyebrows knitting together over swollen eyes. Whether it was his own pain-benumbed state or the veil of possible truth in the dwarf's statement, the thief was unable to read the dwarf properly. Instinctively, he knew this alien creature was no lockpick, but something nagged him from the back of his mind that this metal . . . thing could certainly replace him.

Trying to ascertain whether he had become expendable or not, Harris Blind-Eye turned his gaze to Aitchley; a mien so cold as to be set in marble remained on the young man's face, offering no easy answer to Harris's dilemma.

Wishing he had some better sense of what his captors were up to, Harris gave the dwarf a rope-bound shrug. "Sure," he agreed with feigned amicability. "I'll come with you . . . but I'll want my girls back."

Calyx shook his head in refusal. "Nuh-uh," he replied. "You might get 'em back if you can behave yourself, but, until then, you're gonna have to rely on us to save your worthless butt. Oh, and if you're thinking of stealing them back, one of us is going to be carrying one of your weapons at all times, but you won't know who and you won't know when. And even if you happen to see somebody with 'em, we'll be switching them around every few days or so just so you don't get any ideas. Same with the necklace . . . and Aitchley's told us all how to set it off."

Scowling, Harris clenched impotent fists behind his back, his ability to read people despising the truth in the dwarven smith's words. These people were getting to know him too well, the rogue decided with a frown. Like that bungholer Fain, they had cut him off at every turn, making the threat of losing his hand greater than the potential success of any escape plan. Even if he tried to get Mandy or Renata back, he might lose before he had a chance to figure out who had the necklace.

Gradually, however, a bizarre sense of admiration began to seep through the cutthroat's displeasure, and he flashed the dwarf a complimentary smile through a beard caked with dried blood. "Pretty ingenious plan, scout," he said. "You think of that all by your lonesome?"

Calyx smiled back. "Naw," he said with another shrug. "Actually, it was the kid."

Harris Blind-Eye blinked his surprise as Aitchley's stone-cold mien finally gave way to a readable expression.

Victory, Harris read in the young man's smile. He had faced down Harris Blind-Eye and had won.

8

Into the Bentwoods

Across a thin carpet of dead leaves, Aitchley Corlaiys trudged through the Bentwoods, leading his horse behind him. He could still hear the distant drip and spatter of that afternoon's rainfall as it continued to wind its labyrinthian way through the intricate green maze of leafy drip tips on its attempt to reach the forest floor. In its place, a thin mist curled and roiled through the trees, shirking and balking around the shafts of sunlight that speared lancelike through the nearly impenetrable canopy of trees overhead.

A veritable cacophony of noises assaulted him from high above, an incredible choral arrangement of hidden animals and birds. Insects clicked and sizzled from their hiding places among the ferns and aerial roots, and giant trees surrounded the seven quest-members on all sides, their massive trunks buttressed to support their enormous weight like the flanges on the head of some titanic mace. Spectacularly colored butterflies fluttered and danced through the columns of white sunlight, and great ropelike vines and corded lianas draped and dangled curtainlike across the jungle, sometimes forming great woody lassos where the tree that had supported them had long since fallen.

Aitchley wiped at the sweat collecting beneath the brow of his hat, directing his attention to the people around him. Gjuki led the group, finding safe footpaths for them and their horses around writhing, shallow roots, dead leaves, scattered ferns, and hopeful seedlings. Sprage walked beside the Rhagana, his head craned upward at the network of greenery and lattice of leaves looming high above. Aitchley and Berlyn followed, the latter safely mounted on the metallic back of the spidery Camera 12. Her hair was tied back in an impromptu ponytail, and her torn dress clung wetly to her diminutive frame from the heavy moisture in the air, but she was unharmed. Their first day into the Bentwoods, however, the humidity had almost proven too much for the young girl; Aitchley was just thankful they had the silver-grey construct scuttling along with them . . . not that he was faring much better. He didn't know what was worse: the searing heat of the Molten Dunes that sucked the very perspiration off your forehead, or the drowning humidity of the Bentwoods that stuck your clothes to your body and made you feel like you were walking through atmospheric quicksand.

Behind the two teenagers shambled Poinqart, his hybrid face contorted in a mixed mien of trollish discomfort and human exhaustion. His stubby, oddly proportioned body made walking over the uneven forest floor difficult, yet he had the use of his long, gorillalike arms to help him should he stumble. Calyx, walking behind Harris and bringing up the rear, had no such conveniences. Since entering the Bentwoods, Aitchley heard the dwarf's curses and oaths grow progressively more imaginative as he tripped over rotting vegetation, staggered over leaf-hidden roots, and clambered over fallen trees nearly as high as he was. The ruddy complexion to the smith's face had deepened to an almost burgundy hue, and the rivulets of sweat cascading down his features had shortened his anger and heightened his frustrations.

"This is pointless," the dwarf grumbled out loud, slapping irritably at an overhanging heliconia leaf. "We're lost and we- 're gonna die."

"We are not lost, Master Calyx," Gjuki impassively responded from the front of the group. "And we shall surely not perish." Tiny, pearllike eyes sought out the dwarf. "Would you care to stop for a while?"

Perspiration dripping from his large nose, Calyx gave the Rhagana a nasty scowl. "Naw, what's the point?" he retorted.

"You walk, you sweat; you sit still, you sweat. Besides . . . we're not sure if the trolls aren't still following us."

An apprehensive knot formed in Aitchley's stomach as he turned a questioning blue-green gaze on the dwarf, eliciting a disgruntled squawk from the fledgling resting on his shoulder. "Do you think they'd follow us into the Bentwoods?" the young man wondered.

Calyx shrugged and nearly tripped over a whiplike extension of green-black pepper vine. "Who knows?" he replied. "They've followed us this far. I guess it's been a real long time since they've seen horses."

Gjuki trained tiny black eyes on the forest ahead of them. "In any case, we shall soon find sanctuary, Master Aitchley," he reported. "In perhaps another day's time, we shall be crossing the Mistillteinn River, and only the Rhagana know of the bridge built across its deadly current."

Calyx frowned abysmally beneath his beard. "Great," he responded tartly, "and I'll probably fall in and sink!" He wiped futilely at the bands of sweat forming across his brow. "You know, I've spent centuries in front of a forge and I've never felt heat like this." He turned perplexed eyes on Gjuki. "You people actually live here?"

A faint, wistful smile stretched the Rhagana's lips. "My people are not the only things living here," he said. "In as small a distance as one league, you may find as many as fifteen hundred species of flowering plant, seven hundred and fifty species of tree, four hundred species of bird, one hundred and fifty species of butterfly, one hundred species of reptile, and sixty species of amphibian. The numbers of insects are so great that they can only be guessed at."

Slapping ineffectually at something buzzing hungrily around his face, Calyx muttered, "Tell me something I don't know."

For what might have been the first time in their eight days since entering the Bentwoods, Sprage pulled his attention away from the treetops above him. "That's an awful lot of animals for so small an area," he remarked. "How come I haven't seen anything yet?"

"As I told you before, Healer Sprage," answered Gjuki, "you may hear them, but you will not see them." He glanced up into the cathedrallike vault of leaves and branches overhead. "All the activity takes place up there," he continued, pointing skyward. "There are animals living in the highest branches of the canopy that in their entire lives will never touch the forest floor. They eat, mate, and die within the tree-tops, and the most you can hope for is a quick glimpse or, perhaps, a silhouette leaping from tree to tree."

"Is there any way we can get up there?" Sprage asked.

Picking his way carefully through a patch of begonias, Gjuki replied, "There is a way, but it takes time and great strength. Were we not trailed by trolls, I would demonstrate, but we have no time."

A look of despair crossed the healer's face as he trained longing eyes on the green far above him. "So humor me, then," he said. "If we had the time, what would I see?"

A thoughtful look came over the Rhagana's usually placid mien as he responded: "If you were to climb to the very tops of the trees, it would be like stepping out of a long, stifling tower staircase onto the castle parapet itself. The humidity and constant shade of the forest would be replaced by fresh air and bright sun-shine, and an ocean of treetops would spread out before you in waves of brilliant green. Here and there, towering above the can-opy rooftop itself, are giant trees—emergents, that live in a dif-ferent climate from their brothers and sisters below. In those trees you might catch a glimpse of a blue-crested hawk—a huge pred-ator large enough to catch monkeys but with wings short enough for easy maneuverability through the branches.

"As you descend lower—back into the canopy itself—you would be surrounded by a maze of green pathways, hollows, and niches, all of which provide a wide array of habitats for the myriad creatures which live there. You would find mosses and algae growing abundantly across the tree trunks and branches, and plants that grew atop the mosses. You would see bromeliads and other epiphytes, their roots dangling down the sides of the trees never to touch soil, and other, carnivorous plants that form great pitchers—larger than Master Calyx him-self—that catch and eat the variety of insects that might fall into its liquid center.

"Perhaps you might catch sight of a few monkeys—slow-climbers or howlers. Perhaps a diminutive leafdweller. Hun-dreds of birds would surround you, their calls loud and piercing across the impenetrable green. Or perhaps you might see some of the brilliantly colored frogs that—like birds—hop among the branches and leaves, taking refuge and spawning young in water-filled bromeliads.''

"Frogs in trees?" Berlyn voiced her wonder. "I thought frogs lived on the ground.''

A small fungoid smile met the young girl's disbelief. ''In the Bentwoods, all life adapts to the trees," Gjuki explained. ''As you can see, the forest floor is a dangerous place. A few ferns, a littering of fallen leaves and flowers, some seedlings that hope for enough sunlight to, one day, grow tall enough to reach the canopy. Not much protection for a solitary frog here. His chances of survival increase, however, if—like the other animals—he can seek shelter in the heavily protected canopy."

There was a hint of skepticism in his dark brown eyes as Sprage turned to regard the Rhagana. "Well, what I don't understand is if it's so hard to see through the trees, how does anything up there ever find a mate?''

Gjuki gave the healer an acknowledging nod. "The Bentwoods is Nature at its most confusing," he said. "True, tree trunks and foliage obscure vision, and continuous rains wash away scents, but the forest animals have adapted to even that. Now, while some do resort to scent markings, they are laborious to apply and maintain, and visual displays cannot be widely seen through the dense leaves. This makes sound signals the easiest to send, and canopy animals produce some of the loudest of all animal noises. Male and female slowclimbers sing long duets, their different calls fitting together so perfectly that it is easy to assume there is only one creature singing. Great howlers—in the morning and early evening—rumble and growl like approaching thunder, and stilt birds produce eerie wails that in early days my people thought were the spirits of the dead bemoaning their loss of life. There is even a bird no bigger than a thrush that sits all day at the tops of the trees reproducing the sound of a cracked anvil being clouted with a hammer so piercingly and insistently that it is sometimes hard to be heard over.''

Yellow-black eyes wide at the diversity overhead, Poinqart turned on their fungoid guide. "Mister Gjuki-plant," the hybrid commented, "Poinqart used to hear when he was a tadling-troll of other creature-things in the Bentwood-trees. Poinqart's mother-care used to say there were evil-bad flowers and fly-high snakes.''

A gruff bark of laughter sounded from Harris's swollen lips.

"Oh, yeah, right," sneered the brigand. "Flyin' snakes. There's one for ya, plant-man! Bet your jungle ain't got that!"

"Actually, it does," Gjuki replied, taking a small bit of satisfaction in proving the outlaw wrong. "There is a species of snake in the Bentwoods that has learned how to fly."

Aitchley blinked in astonishment. "It has wings?" he exclaimed.

"No has wings," Trianglehead chided from the young man's shoulder. "Zstupid human, zsnakes no have wings."

A faint smile touch Gjuki's lips as he glanced back at the young farmer. "Your gyrofalc speaks true," the gardener replied with just a trace of humor in his voice. "The snake looks no different from any of its reptilian brethren. It is a small, slender animal with greenish-blue scales, yet it, too, has adapted to life in the trees. Not only can it climb the trunks of trees with consummate skill, it is also capable of launching itself off a branch and flattening its body so that—like a woman's hair ribbon or leaf—it is caught by the air and held aloft. Then, by twisting its body or extending its scales, it is somewhat able to direct its flight toward another tree and land, unharmed, upon its trunk."

Ducking under a strand of vivid green lichen, Calyx muttered, "Well, I don't see how it could miss with all these damn trees about!"

Ignoring the unhappy dwarf, Sprage tilted his head back up toward the forest canopy. "I've also heard about flying squirrels and lizards that use folds of skin to glide from tree to tree," he remarked.

"Yes, and there is also a species of frog that uses oversized flaps of skin between its toes to float from one tree to another," Gjuki added.

Berlyn exchanged bewildered looks with Aitchley. "Tree frogs *and* flying frogs?" she blurted. "Don't any of the frogs here live in the water?"

Gjuki offered the attractive blonde a widening smile. "As a matter of face, Miss Berlyn, yes," the Rhagana answered. "In fact, the giant toads of Mistillteinn Falls grow to about the size of a small dog."

"Better hope that they don't think you're a passin' insect," Harris jeered at the girl from the back of the group.

Protectively, Aitchley moved in closer to where Berlyn sat

upon Camera 12, his hand resting instinctively near his sword. "I'd say you'd have more to worry about being mistaken for an insect than she would," the young man snapped.

Harris raised a scraggly eyebrow over his purple and black eye. "Ooooo!" he shuddered in mock fright. "Looks like someone's still a bit testy, aren't we, scout?" He gave the young man an insincere grin. "I said I was sorry."

"Yeah, sorry that you couldn't kill me," Aitchley spat.

A nefarious gleam lit in Harris's blue-black eyes. "Hey, a man can try, can't he?"

Flashing the southern-city outlaw a reprehensible look, Sprage returned his eyes to the rain forest overhead. "So what's this flower Poinqart's talking about?" he questioned. "I've heard of snakes and xlves that might be considered evil-bad, but never a plant."

Stepping around a burgeoning tree fern, Gjuki swept tiny black eyes across the sea of greenery about him. "Nothing in Nature is truly evil," the Rhagana answered stoically. "While one creature must kill another, it is only its own survival that drives it thus. Even the giant strangling fig tree that lodges its seed high in the trunk of another tree, lowering thick roots that—in essence—will become its trunk as it wraps these wooden tendrils about its host tree until smothering it and depriving if of all life-giving sunlight, only does so to survive. However, there is another plant in the Bentwoods that—like the strangling fig—is parasitic in nature but with a more . . . aggressive tendency.

"Called the Rafflesia, they are the world's biggest flower, yet—like the Rhagana—they have become sentient. Because the soil of the Bentwoods is so nutrient-poor, the Rafflesia begin their lives by leeching sustenance from a neighboring tree until reaching maturity. Then—to supplement their great size—they become carnivorous like the giant pitcher plants I mentioned beforehand. Tethered to their host tree, the Rafflesia hunt the denser part of the Bentwoods, roaming as far as their roots will allow. Yet, despite the role they play in Nature, they seem to take a great deal of pleasure in tearing their prey apart with their thorny, vinelike appendages. No other creature that I know of seems to derive as much satisfaction in the death of its prey as does the Rafflesia . . . except, of course, your race, Healer Sprage, and I mean no offense."

"None taken," Sprage said with a wry smile. "It's no great secret that men, dwarves, trolls, and even Entamoebae are prone to war,"

Calyx glanced up with a caustic frown drawn beneath his beard. "Hey, speak for yourself," he muttered. "Dwarves don't bash one another over the head just because somebody might look at us sideways!"

The healer's smile grew fiendish. "No?" he queried tauntingly. "Then what was all that about the dwarf-trollish war I kept hearing about?"

The sweat-streaked face of the dwarven smith darkened as he flustered momentarily. "That was well over two centuries ago!" he protested. "And what kind of people *don't* get into a little skirmish when they come into contact with another race for the first time?"

Gjuki drew himself up proudly. "In well over a millennium, the Rhagana have never . . ."

Calyx shot the gardener a fierce glare. "Oh, shut up!" he ordered.

A malicious snicker escaped Sprage's lips at the dwarf's predicament. "So what's the matter, Calyx?" the doctor teased. "At least I can admit that my people are stupid."

"Dwarves aren't stupid!" the smith retorted, self-consciously adjusting his belt and warhammer. "We're just . . . I mean . . . Maybe it's because there was none of this plague and stuff to occupy our time!"

Sprage's snicker became a harsh laugh. "Oh? You mean you were bored?"

"No, we weren't bored!" the dwarf barked. "There was the Dragon, but . . . well . . . I guess he wasn't as bad as everybody made him out to be. I mean . . . so he burned a few villages and he ate a couple of people, what's the big deal, right? It's not as bad as all this plague, famine, and drought!"

"Nothing in Nature is truly evil," Gjuki said again.

Sprage's smile remained pinned on Calyx. "Still doesn't explain why the dwarves and trolls couldn't get along," he jeered.

Calyx's mouth worked, but no true sounds issued forth. "I . . . We . . . They're . . ." he tried.

Defeated, the dwarf grew silent, leading his *meion* through a red-yellow patch of flowering ginger. "This is pointless," he grumbled under his breath.

Night in the Bentwoods wasn't much different from during the day. Noises still bombarded them from high above, raucous and guttural, and the air remained thick and heavy with moisture. No soothing wind could penetrate the solid wall of foliage surrounding them, and the darkness of the night was full and deep, all light blocked out by the dense canopy of leaves overhead.

Doffing his hat and wiping at the sweat accumulating on his brow, Aitchley removed the maroon-colored backpack from his shoulders and set it gently on the forest floor, unzipping the strange, teethlike fasteners up the side. Although he had been loath to experiment with the number of odd and alien items given to him by Tin William, Berlyn's youthful enthusiasm had gotten the better of him, and the two had emptied the knapsack and rummaged through its contents like two small children on the Feast Day of Karnahkarnaz-Leh-Cuns-Ulterlec. Among the array of unfamiliar objects, they had found a small square of greenish-brown canvas labeled "Envirochamber: © Y-Teq 4•82•3." With just a few clicks and bends of strange, hollow metal tubing, the two discovered that the small square of canvas would expand into a domelike shelter with enough room for Aitchley, Berlyn, and even Calyx to sleep inside. Although the dwarf declined the invitation—and Aitchley, in his naivete, didn't understand why—he and Berlyn had slept in the tent every night so far while in the Bentwoods. There was even a small box sewn into the side of the canvas reminiscent of the strange, grilled device that had blown cool air into Tin William's desert home that kept the interior of the tent at a constant, comfortable temperature.

As Aitchley set about building the dark green tent, he threw a curious blue-green gaze at the relatively bare forest floor. "What I don't understand," he said out loud to those around him, "is why there aren't more leaves on the ground. Don't these trees shed their leaves?"

Preparing supper nearby, Gjuki glanced up at the young farmer. "Of course they do, Master Aitchley," he replied. "There is no such thing as an evergreen leaf. However, unlike most regions of the world, there is not a change of seasons

here as we know it. It has often been said by my people that
there are only two seasons in the Bentwoods: wet and slightly
wetter. This means there is no climatic cue for the trees to
shed their leaves, but this is not to say that they don't. Each
species has its own timing. Some drop leaves every six
months. Others after every twelve months and twenty-one
days. Still others do so piecemeal, one branch at a time at
intervals throughout the year.''

Reclining on the cool, metallic back of Camera 12, Berlyn
queried, ''So why aren't there more leaves on the ground?''

''Nothing is wasted in the Bentwoods, Miss Berlyn,'' Gjuki
answered her, sifting his barklike hands through the thin layer
of fallen debris. ''The heat and moisture in the air amply suits
the conditions for decay, and the forest floor is simply teeming
with life. Bacteria, molds, and even certain kinds of insects
work diligently to break down and use all of the leaf's precious
nutrients. Even my own kind—the fungi—proliferate, their filaments enmeshing the entire forest floor beneath the leaves in
a network of hairlike hyphae. While in the cold climate of
Solsbury, a leaf may decay in about a year's time—or a pine
needle may take seven years to rot—a leaf from the Bentwoods will completely decay within a mere six weeks of landing on the ground. Such decay fuels the forest, yielding
nutrients for reuse—as much tissue dies as is produced—so
the Bentwoods is forever in a sort of dynamic balance. Disturb
this balance, and one may see what a fragile place the Bentwoods truly is.''

An uneasy feeling of déjà vu roiled through Aitchley as he
heard the similar words of the mysterious Tin William echo
resoundingly through his brain. ''Balance?'' the young man
repeated unsteadily. ''What do you mean?''

''The Bentwoods is an ancient and mysterious place, Master
Aitchley,'' the fungoid gardener explained. ''Not even my
people know all its secrets. What we do know is that there is
a give-and-take between all living creatures of the forest more
intimate than in any other region. Disturb this symbiosis and
havoc will prevail.

''For example,'' the Rhagana went on, ''Here there are trees
that rely on the protection of ants for their defense, and, in
reply, form empty compartments along their branches in which
the ants can live. Remove the ants, the tree has no protection

of its own; without the tree, the ants have no place to live. Here there is also a species of orchid that depends on a single species of bee to pollinate its flower, and, in response, it rewards the bee with an aromatic perfume which the bee then uses to attract a mate. Without the bee, the orchid is not pollinated and cannot reproduce; without the orchid, the bee is unable to attract a mate, and so it, too, cannot reproduce. And, lastly, there are lowly fungi that may grow at the base of great trees—trees higher than the Tridome itself—leeching away some of the trees's nutrients, and yet, at the same time, the tree also takes from the fungus some of the nutrients it gleans from the debris of fallen leaves.''

Shiny, pearl-black eyes looked up at the night-cloaked canopy overhead. ''There is a fragile equilibrium to the entire world, Master Aitchley,'' he concluded, ''but nowhere is it more prominently displayed than here in the Bentwoods.''

With an enigmatic anxiety churning about his stomach, Aitchley tried to return his full attention to the canvas structure before him. He didn't understand why he suddenly felt so uneasy—or what it was about Gjuki's words that made him remember Tin William's final warning—but he didn't feel much like eating when supper was finally ready. Instead, he sat quietly off to one side, lost in his thoughts, poking disinterestedly at his food.

What had Tin William meant? the young farmer mused. Why help with the quest if it was going to make something bad happen? Perhaps Aitchley should have told his friends exactly what the strange silver creature had said to him. So far he had only told them that the robot had saved his life in the desert and had given him the arachnid Camera 12 as a mount. He had told them nothing about the magic windows and their intimate pictures or about the construct's departing words. Somehow, neither seemed notably interesting at the time and—more importantly—Aitchley had feared his companions might laugh at him or think him mad.

So now what? the young man asked himself, vexed. Am I supposed to figure this out for myself? I don't know anything about balances or the Bentwoods! All I know is how to grow crops, and I don't even do that very well! How am I supposed to figure out what the Pits Tin William meant when I'm stupid? What was he trying to say? That using the Elixir would be bad? That it might throw something out of balance? What? If I used the Elixir here in the Bentwoods, what's the worst thing that would happen? Maybe a few trees would lose out on some nutrients. What's the big deal?

With a gnawing trepidation, Aitchley swung his eyes up to fix on the gaunt form of Gjuki. "Well . . . what would happen if something did happen?" the young man asked, and it felt as if all the butterflies of the Bentwoods had suddenly invaded his stomach. "What if . . . like . . . the ants didn't protect the tree?"

Smiling at what he assumed to be the young man's youthful curiosity, Gjuki replied, "There are some trees that, in fact, are unable to attract a colony of ants. Of these trees, many suffer great damage from leaf-eating insects and some even perish."

"What if crawly-ants didn't even exist at all, or what if something killed-destroyed them all out?" Poinqart queried.

"Then the tree would adapt to another method of defense," Gjuki answered. "It would take time—and the entire species would be in threat until then—but Nature has ways of realigning the balance."

Nature's scales. Aitchley heard the buzzing drone of Tin William's voice reverberate throughout his memory. *Be wary of Nature's scales.*

"What if something worse happened?" the young man asked, and his voice caught nervously at the back of his throat. "What if something . . . bigger happened?"

Gjuki's eyes glittered through the darkness. "Something bigger?" the Rhagana echoed, and a grave thoughtfulness entered his tone. "If something bigger were to happen, Master Aitchley, the Bentwoods would be destroyed. Only the insulating factor of the trees creates the Halls of the Living Mist. Without those trees—and without that mist—this land would be as barren and as empty as the Molten Dunes themselves."

"Are you serious?" sputtered Sprage. "The soil here is that poor?"

"The soil of the Bentwoods is exceptionally poor," Gjuki responded. "That is why the balance of life is so vitally important here. All things—living and dead—make the Bentwoods what it is. The trees are the very foundation of life, but they, in turn, are nurtured by the constant rains and heavy humidity. However, it is the trees themselves that keep the moisture in, constantly recycling each storm and each downpour, stealing back vital nutrients that—even as the rain falls— the water tries to wash away and steal for itself. Remove one or the other and—unlike the ants and their tree that, given time, could adapt—the Bentwoods would be no more.'

The unsettling rumbling in his gut growing to an acidic tumult, Aitchley gave the dark trees above him a worried glance. You just had to ask, didn't you? his pessimism jeered at him from deep inside his mind.

Plagued by dreams of destroyed worlds in which no one but himself was to blame, Aitchley awoke to the sounds of screaming coming from outside the tent. A frigid barb of terror tore the veil of sleep away from the young man's eyes, and he hastily scuttled outside, grabbing up his sword and shield as he left.

Body alive with adrenaline, Aitchley clambered frantically to his feet, the Cavalier's shield flowing almost magically onto his left forearm. The heat and humidity still hung in the jungle air like an oppressive curtain even though very little of the early morning sunlight managed to pierce the trees, and Aitchley had to squint to make out the chaos of what had once been their camp.

Dimly lit by faint pinkish light, a horde of gangly brown monsters had swarmed into camp, iron-taloned hands tearing greedily at the flesh of dead horses. Someone—Aitchley couldn't tell who—hurried past the young man, leading two wild-eyed mounts eastward and back into the jungle, and Aitchley could hear a string of profanities that could only be Calyx sprouting through the gloom. Another horse, untethered and panic-stricken, galloped past the young farmer in terror, heavy hooves thundering off into the jungle undergrowth.

Grey-green eyes wide, Berlyn poked her head out of the tent. "Aitchley!" she cried. "What is it? What's wrong?"

Aitchley gave the blonde a concerned glance. "Stay there!" he warned. "I'll . . ."

An inhuman silhouette suddenly launched itself out from among the trees, yellow fangs slavering for Aitchley's face. With a cry of fear and surprise, Aitchley stumbled back, shifting his body so as to bring his shield around. Unexpectedly,

strong metal legs caught the brown troll upside the head,
crushing its skull and slamming its lifeless body into one of
the buttressed trunks standing pillarlike around them.

Aitchley threw a grateful smile into the blank, glassy-eyed
stare of Camera 12 before returning his attention to Berlyn.
"Get on," he ordered the girl, motioning toward the camera.
"Grab whatever supplies you can and go!"

Hesitation sparked on the scullery maid's attractive features.
"But what about . . ." she started.

"Go!" Aitchley roared, spinning about and rushing off toward the imperiled horses.

Worry and fear ignited in the young girl's breast as she
watched the young farmer rush off into the jungle murk, none
of her usual romantic notions running through her head. This
wasn't some dream where the handsome Cavalier rescues the
lady fair, she admonished herself, hurriedly disassembling the
tent and shoving it into Aitchley's backpack. There was nothing glamorous about swordfights and danger . . . she understood that now. Captain d'Ane was dead, and she had seen
Aitchley put himself in far too many dangerous situations . . .
usually trying to save her.

No, there was nothing romantic about heroes anymore . . .
There was only an anxious fear that Fate would take away the
young man Berlyn had fallen love with.

Hardly aware of Berlyn's apprehensive gaze on his back
Aitchley tried to fight down the boiling horror that burned
through his veins, the jungle humidity adding to the perspiration swelling about his sword hilt. Vauge shadows and silhouettes battled against a backdrop of green, and, twice,
Aitchley slipped in the blood of dead horses.

"Calyx!" the young man yelled. "Where are you?"

Bone shattered somewhere on Aitchley's right, and the
young man turned northward to see a heavy warhammer flatten
a trollish skull. "Kid! Over here! Get . . ."

Panic gouged the young farmer's thoughts as he started for
the dwarf, his pessimism conjuring up all sorts of fatal reasons
for why the smith's words had been cut off.

A sudden figure abruptly blocked Aitchley's way, and he
very nearly launched the Cavalier's shield into Harris's already
injured face. "My girls!" the bandit shouted over the din,

callused hands grabbing Aitchley by the front of his shirt. "Give me my girls back, puck!"

Alarm suddenly overrode Aitchley's mind, and he momentarily forgot all about the horde of attacking brown trolls, faced with the angry visage of Harris Blind-Eye. It was the gruff voice that abruptly sounded beside the young man's knee that helped pull him free of his stifling fear.

"I told you to grab a horse, Blind-Butt!" Calyx snarled from beside the young farmer. "Me and the kid can handle the trolls!"

His confidence reestablished, Aitchley jerked himself out of Harris's grasp. "You heard him," the young man snapped. "Grab a horse and get the Pits out of here!"

The brief pause in Harris's movements spoke volumes, and, for a moment, it was frighteningly easy for Aitchley to "read" the lockpick's thoughts. Now was hardly the time to try to make another run for it, Aitchley could see the brigand thinking. No weapons, no supplies, no idea where he was. No . . . he'd have to wait for a more opportune time to try to make another escape.

Aitchley jabbed a threatening finger under the outlaw's bearded chin. "Don't even *think* about it!" he warned, shoving the rogue aside.

Sword a gleaming arc of silver light, Aitchley chopped sideways at an approaching troll, taking no satisfaction in the way the monster's arm separated at the elbow and flew, sticklike, across the forest. Howling, the wounded creature dropped to his knees, spittle foaming about its fang-rimmed maw.

His hammer splintering the troll's forehead, Calyx gave the young farmer beside him a grim smile. "Some fun, eh, kid?" he jested.

Aitchley was in no mood for the dwarf's sarcasm as the blue-and-gold disc on his left arm whipped him about and sent a troll rebounding back into the foliage. "When you told me brown trolls were chasing you, you didn't tell me that *all* the brown trolls in the world were chasing you!" he exclaimed.

Calyx's warhammer backhanded another troll into a small tree. "Sure, I did," he quipped. "Right after I said they'd catch up with us and eat us for lunch." Beady eyes squinted through the pink-grey light of early morning. "You didn't happen to see Sprage, did you? There's an awful lot of bushes around . . . I was just wondering which ones we should start looking under.''

Aitchley felt an ache fill his right arm as his sword cut deep into mucid brown flesh, striking bone and sending a painful jolt up along the young man's limb. ''I think I might have seen him leading two horses away . . . I'm not sure.''

Calyx shook his head dismally. ''Not good. Not good,'' the dwarf grumbled. ''We've lost two horses for certain. One *meion*. Did you happen to notice if one of the horses Sprage had was the supply horse?''

''I didn't really have the time to stop and ask!'' Aitchley retorted.

The dwarven smith frowned beneath his salt-and-pepper beard, warhammer fracturing a groping, claw-tipped hand. ''Probably wasn't,'' he muttered bleakly, answering his own question. ''Probably the first horse that got killed. Means we'll be without food.'' He shook his head in projected defeat. ''I told you we were all going to die.''

Barely ducking a ravenous mouth of yellow fangs, Aitchley drove his sword through the soft, yielding flesh of a troll's guts. ''We're not dead yet,'' he told the pessimistic dwarf beside him.

More brown forms rose up through the ferruginous morning light.

''*Yet*,'' Calyx gravely echoed.

The Bentwoods was a chaotic blur of green as Berlyn clung to the back of the insectlike Camera 12, Aitchley's knapsack slung across her back and Trianglehead clutching frantically to her shoulder. The hollow cold of fear lodged in her breast, and her own heartbeat sounded loud and furious in her ears as she threw an apprehensive glance behind her, her sweat-slick hair whipping cruelly into her face.

''I can't believe we just left him,'' she worried out loud. ''He'll be killed!''

''Better him than usz,'' Trianglehead cawed, flapping useless wings in an attempt to stay balanced.

The young blonde turned angry eyes on the rumpled bird. ''How can you say that?'' she scolded. ''He's saved both our lives!''

Trianglehead offered her an avian shrug, nearly losing his

grip on her slim shoulder. "Zstupid to zstay and iight," he said. "Typikal human thing to do. No zstay . . . no die."

Biting down on her lower lip, Berlyn suddenly jerked on the reinlike mesh hooked about Camera 12's thorax, bringing the spidery machine to a halt.

Trianglehead regarded the blonde with milky blue eyes. "What you do?" the gyrofalc wanted to know.

Berlyn pressed her bare leg up against the camera's cold, steel flank, trying to steer the construct as if it were a horse. "I'm going back to save Aitchley!" she declared bravely, tugging resolutely at the reins.

Red-violet feathers ruffled, Trianglehead gave the rain forest a disconcerting look as Camera 12 headed back the way they had come. "Humansz," the fledgling muttered, shaking his crest of triangular feathers in unspoken disgust.

Aitchley vaulted over a coil of vines and saplings, one hand on his head to keep his hat from flying off. Beside him, Calyx shoved his way through the greenery with breakneck indifference, muttering his displeasure as beads of moisture flew off disturbed leaves and splashed into his face.

Aitchley tried to throw a quick glance over one shoulder. "Do you think they're following?" he questioned.

Calyx pushed a dangling liana out of his way as he continued running. "I doubt it," the dwarf remarked. "They're probably too busy right now munching on our horses to give *gnaiss* shavings about us. But don't worry. As soon as they finish their meal, they'll be right on our asses again!"

Recklessly, Aitchley jumped a tangle of shrubbery and almost plowed into a small row of bamboo. "What about that river Gjuki mentioned?" the young farmer queried. "You don't think that'll stop them?"

"Come on, kid," Calyx said with a smile, "you're asking a dwarf here!" He shoved his way through a latticework of vines and brambles. "Brown trolls don't have enough sense to know when something's out of their reach. The bastards have been following us since Viveca! You think a stupid little river's gonna stop them from trying to get the rest of our horses?"

Lost for an answer, Aitchley did not reply as the pair continued running through the dim morning light of the Bentwoods.

"Besides," Calyx went on, "Sprage may have been teasing before, but there's a reason dwarves and trolls didn't get along for so long . . . and this is it! Only a brown troll would be so . . . Ow!"

Fearing the worst, Aitchley skidded to a frantic stop, fixing his eyes on the dwarf behind him. "Calyx?" he inquired. "Are you all right?"

Frowning, the dwarf looked away from a nearby leaf, an embarrassed grin drawn on his lips. "Yeah, I'm okay," he said. "Something stuck me, that's all." The smith fought his way clear of the shrubbery. "Come on, kid, we can worry about it later. Right now we . . ."

A sudden look of confusion scrawled across the dwarf's face as he nearly lost his balance, his ruddy complexion fading to an unhealthy pink.

Aitchley took a step back toward the dwarf, abrupt worry creasing his features. "Calyx?" the young man asked again.

The color draining rapidly from his face, Calyx looked up weakly at the young farmer. "You know, kid . . . all of a sudden, I don't feel so good . . ."

Aitchley took another worried step forward as the dwarf unexpectedly crumpled to the forest floor.

"*Calyx!*" he screamed.

9

The WorldDweller Returns

With heavy misgivings, Sprage fought his way through the underbrush, tugging at the reins of the two horses behind him. Perspiration caused by terror mingled with perspiration born of humidity, and the healer's breathing came in long, difficult gasps as he tried to take in heavy gulps of air with lungs that felt waterlogged. Behind him—eyes still wide with fear—the physician's palomino and the supply horse reluctantly followed the doctor, their nostrils quivering as they searched the humid air for any trace of pursuing trolls.

Exhaustion finally burning away the last reserves of his strength, Sprage slumped up against a tree trunk, grasping both reins in one hand. "Oh, this is real good," he muttered out loud to himself, throwing a despairing look over one shoulder at the maze of trees behind him. "Like I'm supposed to be able to find my way back?" He ran his free hand through grey-black hair thick with sweat. "*Not* a good way to start the morning!"

A sudden rustle of foliage sparked the terror back to life within the physician's breast, and he pushed himself clumsily away from the tree, an anxious hand diving to the dwarven *navaja* at his belt. Black steel flashed once in the morning sunlight as the slim knife slipped free of both belt and sweaty

fingers, spiraling end over end to disappear into a clustering
of ferns and sedges.

Sprage glanced up as the figure of a troll broke through the
greenery. "Oh, bung!" he swore venomously.

A nasty scowl on his healing lips, Harris Blind-Eye shoved
his way through the Bentwoods, battling through overhanging
heliconia leaves and narrow, leafy saplings. He gripped the
reins of Calyx's *meion*, callously jerking the small horse over
the entangling vines and leafy-green obstacles in their path.
He entertained the thought of leaving the stupid beast behind—
after all, it was only slowing him down—but the purple-blue
bracelet about his right wrist stopped him. The bracelet had
become a threat again, the southern-city lockpick understood.
Unless he could figure out which of them had the necklace,
he was stuck being the obedient little rotgrub that Fain had
forced upon him.

Fain! Now there was a man who deserved twin daggers
through his eyes! It was all his fault that Harris was on this
stupid quest! He could have been sitting warm and comfortable
back in the Abyss, content to outwit the jailers and pick any
lock he wanted to so long as he didn't try to go outside—he'd
tried that once . . . still had the scars from the dogs to prove it.
But this . . . Daeminase Pits! Even the dank, smelly claustrophobic Abyss was better than this!

Harris swung an angry fist at the leaves around him. Shouldn't've gone soft! the brigand cursed himself. Should've
killed the kid when I had him down back in Leucos! But, no!
What do I do? Kick him in the head like some namby-pamby
schoolboy! And where's it gotten me? Stuck back on some
damn fool's errand for some make-believe Elixir without my
girls and with a tribe of starving trolls on my butt! Bloody
bungin' marvelous!

A dark smile pulled its way across the rogue's swollen lips
as he continued through the forest. Next time I'll know better,
he grimly mused. Next time the kid dies first . . .

Throwing a fearful look over one shoulder, Aitchley could
hear the mass of brown trolls scrabbling through the undergrowth after him, their roars and howls of hunger drowning
out the usual jungle cacophony. More sunlight pushed its way

through the tangled mesh of trees overhead, bringing with it more heat, and the young man wiped irritably at the streams of sweat that poured down his face and into his eyes as he tried to lift the still form at his feet.

"Calyx!" the young farmer grunted. "Can you walk? I can't . . ."

Calyx half opened one beady eye, his vision bleary and fogged. "Procursus?" he mumbled deliriously. "I can't . . . feel my legs."

Struggling, Aitchley tried to position himself beneath the dwarf's arm but was unable to stoop that low because of the smith's smaller stature. "No, it's not Procursus. It's me, Aitchley. Come on, Calyx. You've got to get up. You're too heavy to carry."

The dwarf managed to fix his one-eyed gaze on the young man. "Somethin' t' do with our mass," he explained, his speech slurred. "Why we sink. Too much weight . . . tiny little body."

A dark brown form raced through the jungle nearby, separated only by a sparse column of trees.

Aitchley tried to keep down the panic that gnawed at the edges of his calm. "Come on," he pleaded with the dwarf, "you've gotta get up. It's only a matter of time before they find us."

A glimmer of understanding broke through the dwarf's daze. "Leave me," he rasped. "Maybe they . . . won't notice."

"Yeah, right," Aitchley retorted, wrestling with the dwarf's weight, "and maybe Harris Blind-Eye's trustworthy. Come on, Calyx. Up we go!"

Straining, Aitchley managed to pull the dwarf half off the ground, still trying to wedge his shoulder beneath the dwarf's. Unexpectedly, a villainous yowl tore through the Bentwoods, and Aitchley looked up just in time to see a snarling brown troll crash free of the foliage, yellow-black eyes aflame with an inhuman hunger.

Steel was instantly in the young man's right hand; blue-and-gold *gnaiss* in his left.

No longer supported, Calyx crashed back to the dirt.

"Oh, Calyx!" Aitchley apologized, momentarily shifting his attention back to the dwarf. "I'm sorry!"

The smith winced. " 'S okay," he mumbled. "Can't feel my skull either."

Drooling, horseflesh caught between its fangs, the brown troll took a slow step forward, its ravenous gaze locked on the young man and dwarf. Warily, it moved forward, staying well out of reach of Aitchley's weapon as it circled the pair on gangly legs. Abruptly, it halted, throwing back its domed head to release a warbling cry that pierced the wall of greenery that was the Bentwoods.

Perplexed, Aitchley took a threatening step toward the howling troll, throwing a curious look back at Calyx. "What's it doing?" he wanted to know.

"Callin' his friends," Calyx answered. "Go on, kid. Get the forge out of here. I'll be all right."

Aitchley reaffirmed his grip on his sword. "You'll be troll turds by evening," he snapped back. "I'm not going anywhere without you."

Grumbling, Calyx forced himself to try to sit up. "Stupid and stubborn," the smith muttered to himself. "Yeah . . . you're Procursus's descendant, all right."

An answering wail suddenly echoed the first as the forest came alive with movement. Raw fear shot through Aitchley's veins as more howls split the moisture-filled air, their starving, unnatural cries growing in volume as the trolls neared their quarry. Even if only a few found them, Aitchley knew he'd be outnumbered. Without Calyx's warhammer at his back— and without a couple of dead horses to occupy the others— the young man knew he'd be overrun by the murderous horde.

Spurred on by the adrenaline pulsing through his system, Aitchley suddenly launched himself forward, hurling himself at the single troll ahead of him. What might have been a startled shriek escaped the monstrosity's mouth as it caught sight of the young man leaping toward it, and it made a desperate attempt to turn and run before silver-grey steel slammed into the back of its neck and severed its spinal cord.

Pink-white fluid sprayed as Aitchley spun, spotting another troll bursting out of the foliage. An agonizing screech rent the Bentwoods as the young farmer's sword tore across the troll's face, puncturing one eye and slicing off half its nose. Pale blood frothed and spumed as the creature staggered back into the greenery, its cry of hunger now one of misery.

"Kid," Calyx warned weakly. "Watch your back."

Obediently, Aitchley turned, instinctively ducking the pair of trolls that came leaping out of the forest's cover. Even as they sprang, Aitchley's shield caught one in mid-leap, redirecting the creature's own momentum and throwing it bodily through a few small trees where it lay, lifeless, at a base of a giant emergent. The other impaled itself on the young man's upraised sword, a feeble scream fleeing its lips as the blade tore through organs and flesh to peek coyly out of the monster's back.

Sweat streaming down his face, Aitchley wheeled back in the direction of their abandoned camp, readying himself to face the dark tide of figures that shuffled and scrambled about the tangle of brush. He could feel the adrenaline-induced strength in his limbs starting to fail, and his own dark thoughts rose up as he spied the inhuman silhouettes pushing their way ever closer through the green.

Not a chance, the young farmer's pessimism concluded dourly. We're dead.

Unexpectedly, something large and silver exploded out of the plant life on Aitchley's right, its single glass eye fixed rigidly upon the young man. A beautiful young blonde clung desperately to the thing's back, her hair and dress billowing out around her, and a look of relief momentarily crossed her features as she saw the young man stanced defiantly below her.

Camera 12 kicked viciously at the oncoming trolls, catching two and throwing them brutally back into six others.

"Aitchley!" shouted Berlyn. "Are you all right?"

Aitchley hurriedly sheathed his sword and returned to Calyx's side. "I'm fine," he replied brusquely, "but Calyx has been hurt!"

Berlyn clambered down from the wire-mesh harness, dainty hands trying to help Aitchley lift the motionless smith. "Hurry up! Hurry up!" the red-violet fledgling perched atop her shoulder cawed. "Trollsz are koming! Trollsz are koming!" The gyrofalc shook his head dismally. "Zstupid humansz! Make usz dead, you have!"

Berlyn gave the apprehensive bird a warning glance before helping Aitchley pull Calyx off the leaf-strewn ground. "What happened to him?'' she asked, grey-green eyes filling with worry at the weakened dwarf.

''I don't know,'' Aitchley said with a shrug. ''We were running and he got stung or something. I don't know.''

Barely retaining his hold on consciousness, Calyx offered the young scullery maid a cynical grin. ''Jus' my luck,'' he slurred. ''Live to be three hundred and twenty-eight years old an' I get killed by a caterpillar.''

Berlyn's eyes widened. ''A caterpillar?'' she repeated.

Calyx tried to nod but didn't have the strength. ''Real ugly-lookin' one,'' he said, his smile deepening. ''All green an' spiny. Damn thing musta been poisonous.''

With great effort, Aitchley and Berlyn managed to sling the dwarf across the smooth back of Camera 12. ''You're not dead yet,'' the young man said as a consolation, pulling himself into the saddle behind Berlyn.

Calyx's smile vanished. ''*Yet*,'' he ominously repeated.

Trying not to hyperventilate, Sprage dropped to one knee to search for his weapon, giving the troll in front of him an unfriendly sneer. ''Daeminase Pits, Poinqart!'' the healer declared. ''You scared all four humors out of me!''

Poinqart bent over to help search for the lost *navaja*. ''Poinqart is sorry, Mister Healer-Sprage,'' the hybrid apologized. ''Poinqart did not mean to frighten-scare you.''

Hoping that the flush of red in his face didn't show too prominently, Sprage recovered his dwarven blade and waggled it threateningly in Poinqart's direction. ''Yeah, well, you're just lucky I don't know how to use this thing,'' he responded. ''Somebody else might have mistaken you for one of those blasted brown trolls!''

''Poinqart is no nasty-bad-brown-troll,'' the hybrid retorted, offended. ''Poinqart is a friendly-green-good-troll. Poinqart hates the nasty-bad-trolls, he does!''

Sprage swung a cursory look at the forest. ''That makes two of us,'' he quipped. ''Come on. Let's get the Pits out of here.''

Compliantly, Poinqart fell into step behind the healer, staying well out of the way of the two horses in Sprage's grip. It was funny, the physician mused to himself, noticing the hybrid's reluctance. Brown trolls loved nothing more than the taste of horseflesh, yet green trolls were deathly afraid of horses. Strange how two races that were so similar could also be so different.

A low rumble reached the physician's ears as he pressed further into the Bentwoods, and he cocked his head questioningly to one side, trying to filter the sound out from the ruckus of calling birds and whirring insects overhead. Whatever was out there murmured like constant thunder but, from what he could see through the canopy, there wasn't a cloud in the sky. Apprehensively, the healer started to change course, deciding that whatever was out there was something he didn't want to run into.

Poinqart suddenly bounded ahead of the doctor, gangly arms flailing above his head. "No, no! This way! This way!" the hybrid declared, hurrying toward the sound. "Poinqart knows!"

Some of the color drained from Sprage's face. "Poinqart knows what?" the healer argued, dark eyes nervously flicking to the curtain of plant life around them. "I thought you'd never been here before."

"Poinqart hasn't," the half-troll admitted, taking a few more enthusiastic steps toward the source of the noise. "But Mister Gjuki-plant said we must find the go-across-bridge to go over the Mistillteinn River-stream."

Skepticism drew itself on Sprage's features. "Yeah? So?" he queried.

"So Mister Gjuki-plant also said there was a water-tumble-fall in the Bentwood-trees," the half-troll went on excitedly. "Told Poinqart that you could listen-hear it through almost the entire Bentwood-forest. Grumble-rumble must be the water-fall!"

The doubt remained on Sprage's face. "I don't remember Gjuki saying anything other than there were giant frogs at the Mistillteinn Falls," the healer protested.

Poinqart gave the physician a crossed expression of trollish exasperation and human perplexity. "Before you joined," explained the half-troll. "At the Uriisa River, we were." He turned back in the direction of the distant sound. "Quickly-come, Mister Healer-Sprage," he said, sprinting through the meshwork of vegetation. "Poinqart knows the way! Poinqart knows!"

Dreading the worst, Sprage began a slow shuffle after the

hybrid, mulling over his fate. Not that things would be any better even if the half-troll is right, the healer thought. Gjuki said only the Rhagana knew where the bridge over the Mistillteinn River was located. Be just our luck to reach the river and get cornered by brown trolls.

Nervously, his grip around his *navaja* tightening, Sprage hurried after the eager hybrid.

Berlyn flinched involuntarily as an overhanging branch of a nearby sapling brushed fleetingly past her, arousing an angry squawk from the red-violet bird perched on her shoulder. Rankled, the fledgling ruffled his feathers and reaffirmed his hold, his triangular crest rising and falling in unspoken agitation. His talons clutched painfully to Berlyn's shoulder—and she tried not to let her discomfort from the bird's weight show—as she looked over her shoulder at the young man riding behind her.

"Are you sure it knows where it's going?" she asked, glancing down at the cold metal between her legs.

Aitchley offered the blonde a small, lopsided grin. "Trust me," he assured her. "Camera 12 has great eyesight. If I said take us to Gjuki, it'll take us to Gjuki."

Berlyn ducked an octopoid strand of dangling moss, provoking another vexed yawp from Trianglehead. "I just don't see how anything can know where it's going through all these trees," she frowned. "It makes my head hurt."

"Keep your eyes down," Aitchley advised, recalling something Gjuki had told him their first day in the Bentwoods. "Look at the ground; not at the trees."

Berlyn's frown deepened. "Like that would make finding your way any easier?" she grumped.

"No," Aitchley agreed, "but it'll stop your head from hurting. Besides, Camera 12 knows where it's going."

Without comment, Berlyn lowered her gaze to the fast-moving forest floor. She didn't understand why Aitchley put so much faith into the strange mechanical beast below them—after all, the thing only had one eye!—and if she couldn't tell east from west in this jumble of trees, how was this brainless hunk of metal supposed to find Gjuki in all this mess?

Feeling disheartened that they were lost—and knowing unwary travelers had died in far less dangerous terrain—Berlyn continued to cling wordlessly to the tungsten harness strapped to Camera 12. Unexpectedly, the wall of vegetation suddenly dropped away from around them, hurling the two teenagers and the dwarf out into a lush clearing of vivid green grasses. A wide river dissected the glade—its current a thundering rush of white water and churning foam—and, somewhere off in the distance, Berlyn heard what sounded like continuous thunder rumbling through unseen clouds.

Aitchley's grip around the young girl's waist tightened affectionately. "See?" he boasted. "I told you so."

Peeling her surprised gaze away from the mighty river, Berlyn suddenly noticed the tall, gaunt figure that stood by the riverbank, mossy green hair billowing in a gentle breeze. Quizzically, the Rhagana turned, fixing tiny black eyes on the approaching camera. Frondlike strands of green fluttered down the length of the creature's jawline and also down its bare, sticklike legs, and it cocked back a thin arm, leathery fingers curling around the shaft of its spear.

"Aitchley!" Berlyn exclaimed, fear seeping into her voice. "That's *not* Gjuki!"

The spear flew toward them.

Harris Blind-Eye paused, ducking as low as he could among the sparse shrubs and foliage of the rain forest floor. A good place of concealment—one of the giant buttressed tree trunks of an emergent—stood uselessly a few feet away, far too great a distance to cover before whatever was coming through the brush reached the southern-city outlaw. Grimacing, Harris resigned himself to stay low, throwing a nasty glare at the *meion* behind him that all but gave away his hiding place.

Oh, well, the brigand decided with a heartless shrug. If it's a bunch of trolls, the stupid animal'll make a good decoy.

An unexpected hand landed upon the rogue's shoulder from behind, and Harris nearly let out a shout as he whipped about, instinctively snapping down wrists to release knives that were no longer there.

A small smirk drew across Gjuki's tree-bark features as he placed a long, silencing finger to his lips and motioned for the lockpick to follow him. "This way, Harris Blind-Eye," the Rhagana said. "We wish to go east. Not west."

"Yram's bunghole!" the thief swore under his breath.

"You nearly scared me out of a year's growth, plant-man! Haven't you learned by now it's not safe to sneak up on me from behind?"

Gjuki's smirk became a rare smile. "Be fortunate I hold no grudge against you, Harris Blind-Eye," the fungoid gardener replied, "or else I would leave you to the trolls you were so blithely walking into."

A brief glitter of unease flickered through Harris's blue-black gaze. "Yeah, well . . . ranger, I ain't," he announced.

Leading his horse and Aitchley's almost soundlessly through the shrubbery, Gjuki started in the opposite direction. "No," he agreed, "you are not. It would serve you well to remember that should you ever decide to strike out on your own again."

A half-restrained sneer crossed beneath Harris's raggedy beard as the southern-city bandit followed. Bracelet or not, the plant-man's got a point, he mused sourly to himself. I'm stuck. I wouldn't last two days in this place alone, and the plant-man knows it. Even if I could get back my girls and the necklace, what good would they do me? I'd still be lost. And I don't suppose the plant-man would give in to coercion, either, what with me stabbing him before and all.

Harris shoved his way through the dense foliage, unhappy with his newfound revelation. Awww, bung! he swore to himself. Looks like I'm along for the entire rest of the ride!

Sprage stopped at the edge of the forest, unable to shake the unsettling paranoia that inhuman eyes watched him from behind. Joyfully, Poinqart raced ahead of the healer, short, stunted legs carrying the half-troll through the grass-covered clearing. Thunder sounded in both their ears as a huge waterfall spilled to their right, at least a league away but still sprinkling the air with its mist. Great clouds of silver-white foam bubbled and churned off the sides of immense cliffs, roaring and booming as it fell to the Mistillteinn River far below, and—if it hadn't been for the insistent fear surging through his system—Sprage might very well have been impressed.

Doing a happy little dance through the grass, Poinqart swung his attention back to the doctor. "This way, Mister Healer-Sprage!" the half-troll declared merrily. "Didn't Poinqart say he knew the way?"

Sprage stepped uncertainly into the clearing, unable to get the feeling out of his mind that they were being watched. "We're not out of the woods yet, Poinqart . . . or so to speak," he remarked. "We still have no idea where the bridge is. Or the others."

"Who needs the cross-over-bridge?" the hybrid responded, his mouth opened wide to taste the faraway spray of the titanic falls. "This is where Mister Gjuki-plant and the others will come. All we need do is patient-wait for them."

Patient-wait for them, Sprage muttered gloomily to himself. Not an easy thing to do with a tribe of hungry trolls chasing you. What do we do if they catch up? Jump in the river? There's no way anybody could swim that. Not only is it at least a league wide, the current looks relentless!

A tree unexpectedly detached itself from the Bentwoods, striding gracefully out into the clearing. At first Sprage thought Gjuki had found them, but then he noticed the creature wore no clothing and that its mossy green hair was tied back in a long, lichen ponytail. Its expressionless mien only served to heighten the physician's fear as another Rhagana came at him from behind, a cold, impassive mask on its barklike face.

Sprage's eyes nearly popped from his skull. "Poinqart!" he screamed, running like a frightened child toward the river.

Frustration and agony tinged the scream that ripped through the brown troll's throat as the barbed spear drilled its breast, splintering bone and piercing soft, vital organs. Pink-white blood splashed to the grass as the monster crumpled to the ground, taloned fingers clutching for the three figures seated upon the back of Camera 12.

Berlyn made a face as a lake of pale blood burbled up around the monstrous corpse. "Oh, yuck," she said.

Expressionlessly, the unclothed Rhagana stalked past the two teenagers and retrieved its spear, wiping its blade clean on the grass. "I trust no harm has come to you?" it asked in a low, gravelly voice.

Aitchley tried to blink some of the shock out of his eyes. "Uhhhhh . . ." was all he got out.

Spear in one hand, the Rhagana approached. It wasn't as tall as Gjuki, Aitchley noticed, and its arms and legs appeared to be thinner, but its skin was the same color and texture.

Because it wore no clothing, he could see there was absolutely no trace of genitalia on its body, and Aitchley felt a momentary flush of embarrassment fill his cheeks as he realized he was staring intently—and rather stupidly—at the smooth, featureless skin between the creature's legs.

No wonder Gjuki didn't understand the dangleberry joke! The young man finally understood.

Obviously not concerned with the sex or lack thereof of the Rhagana, Berlyn slid delicately off the cold, metallic back of Camera 12 and approached the creature. "Can you help us?" she asked. "We're lost, and our friend's been hurt."

The Rhagana's tiny eyes flicked to where Berlyn indicated the motionless dwarf. "A dwarf and two Pink Ones," the fungus said with a vague smile. "I should say you are lost. It has been at least a quinquennium since either of your two species has graced the Halls of the Living Mist. What brings you this way?"

"Well, we're not actually lost," Aitchley answered, stepping down behind Berlyn. "We're more like separated. See, we have a guide, but, when the trolls attacked us, we just kind of . . . ran. Calyx told everybody else to try to take a horse, and we don't know where Gjuki went, so . . ."

An abrupt flash of emotion illuminated the Rhagana's gaze. "The WorldDweller has returned?" the creature demanded, twiglike fingers clutching eagerly at Aitchley's arm. "Is what you say true?"

Not waiting for an answer, the humanoid fungus turned quickly on its heel, beginning a quick, noiseless sprint along the banks of the great river. "Quickly, Pink Ones!" it called back to them. "Bring your ailing friend and your strange beast! I must alert the others! The WorldDweller has returned!"

Watching the Rhagana run animatedly through the grass, Aitchley traded bewildered glances with Berlyn. "Was it something I said?" the young man wondered out loud.

10

Valley of the Diamond Rains

Surrounded by azure stone and charcoal rock on one side, and an impenetrable wall of water on the other, Berlyn and Aitchley followed the slender, unclothed Rhagana over the Mistillteinn River, Calyx's unconscious body slung over the back of Camera 12's abdomen. Berlyn's eyes were wide with wonder as she stepped lightly over blue-grey stones slick with moisture and phosphorescent green-blue algae, the roar of the Mistillteinn Falls filling her ears.

A wall of white water curtained the rest of the world from the young scullery maid—spilling from cliffs nearly a mile high—forming a liquid barrier between her and the Bentwoods. Instead, she tiptoed carefully through an otherworldly cavern of cerulean rock and eerily-glowing sphagnum, winding her way through toadstools and boleti that reached as high as her waist.

Behind the Mistillteinn Falls, the young girl thought to herself in awe. Known only to the Rhagana—and, perhaps, to a few giant toads—there was a gigantic cavern behind the falls themselves. Although made slightly treacherous by the constant spray of moisture—and incredibly noisy as the thunder of the falls rebounded and echoed off the blue-grey walls of the cave—the bridge was built right out of the cliffs, safely hidden from outside view. It was almost entirely natural as well. Except for a few vines to serve as handrails and a few steps chiseled here and there in the stone, the cavern was a natural formation of rock eaten away by the steady and insistent shrapnellike spray of liquid.

Stepping around a puffball that stood as tall as her chest, Berlyn trailed the Rhagana ahead of them. They hadn't said anything since entering the hidden cave—the rush of the nearby falls made speech a near impossibility—so they still knew very little about their fungoid guide. So far all they had learned was its name: Eyfura. Even still, the young girl was not afraid. She had known Gjuki all her life—she had grown up in Lord Tampenteire's castle with the gardener as a constant companion. In fact, she could remember spring days when she and other children would be left to sit outside in the castle gardens, kept safe by the watchful eye of the Rhagana, so she knew she had nothing to fear from the strange creature before her. Only a day before Gjuki had said Rhagana had never reacted violently to a new race . . . or, at least, that's probably what he was going to say before Calyx had interrupted him.

Calyx, the young girl mused, throwing a concerned look at the tiny body draped over Aitchley's metallic mount. I hope he's all right. Eyfura recognized the sting—said it was caused by a changingworm and, while painful, was not usually fatal—but Calyx's small size made it easier for the poison to have that much more of an effect on him. Not to worry, the Rhagana had told them. There was a simple cure of a paste made from mashed truffles.

All but screaming to be heard over the rush of water, Aitchley tapped the Rhagana ahead of him on the shoulder. "How much further?" he queried.

"Not far," the Rhagana leading them responded. "The river only stretches about two leagues wide at this point. A simple stone's throw."

"A simple stone's throw?" repeated Berlyn, astonishment coloring her voice. "Two leagues wide is only a simple stone's throw?"

The fungoid creature offered her a faint smile. "The Mistillteinn River is nearly fifteen hundred leagues long. Fifty leagues wide at its estuary. Throughout most of the Bentwoods, the river varies from half a league in width to two and a half except when the floods occur."

Berlyn caught the inflection in the Rhagana's voice. "Why?" she asked. "How wide does it get when it floods?"

Eyfura's smile widened. "It can reach widths of ten leagues across during the rainy season," the humanoid fungus declared. "Fortunately, floods of that magnitude do not occur in these parts."

Finding it difficult to carry on a conversation without constant shouting, the three dropped back into silence, Berlyn wrestling with the disbelief that had taken root inside her brain. Ten leagues? she thought to herself incredulously. That was thirty miles! Well over a full day's worth of walking! Imagine! Crossing a river for an entire day!

Still swaddled in shock, Berlyn hardly noticed when she and Aitchley walked free of the hidden cavern and back out into the hot, humid morning of the Bentwoods. The Mistillteinn Falls thundered at her back, and thick, lush grasses grew as high as her hips, yet the soil beneath her feet was muddy and saturated by the unceasing spray of water. A flight of stone steps was chiseled out of the steel-blue rocks beside the river, winding down into a fertile valley cloaked in the shadows of the falls' great cliffs, and Berlyn felt her breath catch in her throat as she stared down into the mist-enshrouded center of the valley below.

Garbed in the grey scarf of shadow of the high mountain wall sat a tiny village, the granite staircase twisting down into its hazy middle. Crude roads wound in and around the buildings—and Berlyn could even see what looked like someone riding a cart drawn by two strange, piglike animals with long, elephantine snouts—but what gripped her full attention were the buildings themselves.

Protected by a wall of immense rock on one side and a barrier of gigantic trees on the other, enormous mushrooms flourished in the perpetual mist and constant shade of the Mistillteinn Falls, their umbrellalike pilei glistening with a fine sheen of moisture. Rhagana moved and bustled about the streets of their city, entering the giant mushroom houses through arched doorways carved in their fleshy stalks, and strange fungi lampposts dotted the roads, crested with strange lichens and mosses that illuminated the pathways with unearthly pulses of blue and green bioluminescence.

Each mushroom house stood at least twelve feet high—the

smallest still towering over Berlyn by about a foot—and their
hollow stalks were wide and roomy. A neverending display of
fragmented rainbows flickered and blinked overhead through
the continuous spray wherever the sun crept past shadow and
gently touched the mist, and each drop of water seemed to
hang forever in the air, shining like free-floating pearls in the
midmorning sky.

Berlyn and Aitchley stopped at the top of the stairs, mouths
dropping open in astonishment. Unimpressed, Trianglehead
rustled wet feathers.

Eyfura extended a slender arm outward, gesturing down the
granite staircase with rare Rhagana pride. "Welcome to the
Valley of the Diamond Rains," the creature said. "Quickly,
now. Let us prepare for the WorldDweller's return."

Tugging at the hem of her skirt so that the wet fabric
wouldn't impede her legs, Berlyn started down the stone steps
after the fungus. She heard Aitchley let out a muttered curse
behind her as his boots found a slick patch of glaucous algae—
and the ensuing avian oaths from Trianglehead who had, once
again, taken up residence upon the young farmer's shoulder—
and she tried to hold back her giggle. They had gone from the
horrifying events of that morning to the comforting safety of
an inhabited town, and even if the trolls could find their way
across the river they'd never be desperate enough to attack a
populated village. Not even hunger made them that bold.

Feeling the tension and fear drain free of her system, and
relishing the wonderment that had moved in to replace it, Berlyn continued down the rocky stairs. The valley below her was
filled with an assortment of sights and smells, and the young
girl drew them all in eagerly: the sweetly sour odor coming
from the giant mushrooms; the moist dampness in the air; the
sparkling, colorful bands that danced and frolicked amid the
sunbeams; the thick smell of rotting vegetation. Even the constant spray from the falls was a welcome relief. Whereas the
humidity of the valley was nearly as bad as within the giant
trees of the Bentwoods, the continuous drizzle from the titanic
waterfalls touched her skin with cool, teasing fingers, giving
her the feeling of a refreshing rainfall despite the tropical temperatures.

As Berlyn's feet reached the marshy soil of the valley, she
noticed a crowd had gathered to welcome them. Many Rha-

gana—all without clothes and all looking pretty much the same—stood at the base of the stairs, tiny black eyes aglow with anticipation. Leathery brown faces watched without emotion, but there was an unmistakable electricity of excitement in the misty air as the two teenagers entered the Valley of the Diamond Rains. Odd, Berlyn couldn't help but think to herself. There didn't appear to be any Rhagana children. All the fungi that clustered in restrained eagerness around them were about the same height and build as Gjuki.

A human figure suddenly pushed his way through the press of Rhagana, ebullient hands waving above his head. "Hey! Hey!" Sprage shouted at the youngsters, grabbing each enthusiastically by an arm. "I'm glad you're okay!" He swung an excited look at the village behind him. "Can you believe this place?" he asked the two. "I've never seen anything like it! It's incredible! And it's completely natural! Baugi was telling me it grew right up out of the ground!"

Before they were able to respond, another form forced its way through the mist and crowd, engulfing the two teenagers in a powerful bear hug of gorillalike arms. "Mister Aitch! Missy Berlyn! Poinqart is so happy-glad to see you! Worry-feared you were slobber-eaten, he was!"

Ribs groaning in protest, Aitchley pried himself free of Poinqart's embrace. "We weren't slobber-eaten, Poinqart," he assured the hybrid. "We're fine."

A tall Rhagana with a moss-green ponytail trailing down its lean back stepped forward, sticklike fingers upraised in an open-palmed greeting. "Welcome, Aitchley QuestLeader," the creature said, its voice almost identical to Gjuki's. "I am Gjalk DarkTraveller, and it is my honor to receive you into our village. I am pleased Eyfura SpearWielder was able to bring you here unharmed. She is our greatest sentinel."

Berlyn blinked her own surprise as Aitchley blurted, "*She?*"

Grey-green eyes narrowed at the slender Rhagana holding the spear. Aside from being a bit thinner, how could you tell? the scullery maid wondered.

"We are all excited that your journey has brought you to our village," the Rhagana called Gjalk DarkTraveller went on, "and we eagerly await the return of the WorldDweller."

Berlyn caught the look of pessimistic worry that scrawled

briefly across Aitchley's face. "Well . . . uhh . . . I'm not sure
we can stay," the young man said in his uncertainty. "Calyx
is still hurt . . . and Gjuki's still out there . . ."

Gjalk placed a comforting hand upon the young farmer's
shoulder. "Worry not, Aitchley QuestLeader," the Rhagana
said. "We shall take your companion to Tufa HerbMother
straight away . . . It would hardly do to have one of the
WorldDweller's companions become one with All That Is on
such an auspicious occasion. And waste no fear on the
WorldDweller himself. He will be along as surely as Pahoe
GoldenOrb chases the Night'sEye from the sky."

Even as the ponytailed Rhagana led them away from the
stone staircase and into the shelter of the mushroom village,
Aitchley faced the fungus with an apprehensive look on his
features. "How can you be so sure?" he asked.

A tight smile stretched Gjalk's lips. "If there was anything
I was ever sure of, Aitchley QuestLeader, it is my own brother.
Come along now. We must prepare for the WorldDweller's
return."

In an awed silence, Berlyn followed Aitchley and the others
into the dry warmth of one of the giant mushrooms.

There was a great celebration when Gjuki and Harris arrived
at the Rhagana village later that afternoon, unlike any Berlyn
had ever seen before. Large gourdfuls of a powerfully sweet
drink the Rhagana called nectarwine were passed around—
instantly making the young scullery maid feel woozy and light-
headed—and a huge feast of uncooked, rotting meats and vegetation was placed out in honor of the WorldDweller's return.
Fortunately, Gjalk DarkTraveller had enough foresight to prepare some food for the non-Rhaganas visiting his village, but
the idea of eating roasted grubs and spitted spindleworms
didn't sit well with Berlyn's stomach . . . nectarwine or not.

After the feast—as the setting sun drew the valley into even
deeper shadow—the Rhagana gathered in a ceremonial circle,
sitting all seven members of the quest in places of honor. A
quartet of Rhagana musicians entertained them with lively music played on hollowed reeds and strange stringed instruments,
one of which used the emptied shell of an armadillo as its
sounding box, and Berlyn was even able to coax Aitchley—
with the help of the potent nectarwine—to join her and the

many fungoid figures dancing in wide, handheld circles about them.

Laughing and giggling—made giddy by the Rhagana drink—the two teenagers lost themselves in the celebration. All thoughts of brown trolls, quests, and magic elixirs left their minds, chased away by the intoxicating nectarwine, leaving them with nothing but their own youthful exuberance. Not since the Uriisa River had Berlyn enjoyed herself this much, and she even noticed Gjuki dancing nearby, his hand intertwined with Eyfura SpearWielder's, a small grin on his usually stoic features.

Illuminated by the eerie posts of blue and green mosses, Berlyn hardly remembered the rest of the night, her memory befuddled by her happiness and the taste of fermented honey and water. She didn't even remember staggering with Aitchley to a giant mushroom with blue and grey markings across its umbrellalike cap—snickering and snorting as they tried to help one another through the mud and darkness and usually wound up tripping over each other. Nor did she recall actually arriving at the toadstool, crawling into its warmth and dryness and snuggling up against the young man beside her. All she remembered was the single kiss they shared and falling asleep in his strong, caring arms.

Berlyn awoke by herself the next morning, a dull ache at the back of her head and an unpleasant fuzziness coating her tongue. Groggily, she lifted her head off the soft, fleshy floor of the giant mushroom and looked about her, taking a moment to realign her senses. Trianglehead was the only one else in the room—perched judgmentally on a small mantle of mushroom stalk, milky-blue eyes fixed unblinkingly on the young girl.

Berlyn ran a hand through her tangled and tousled hair, trying to blink the aftereffects of the nectarwine from her head.

"Diszguszting," Trianglehead remarked from his perch, shaking his head with a derogatory furl of his red-violet crest.

Berlyn winced at the fledgling's grating voice. "Where's Aitchley?" she wondered.

The gyrofalc gave her an uncaring shrug of bandaged feathers. "What kare I?" he retorted. "Piszszing or puking. Take your pick."

Scratching her tongue up against her front teeth in an attempt to remove the uncomfortable taste lingering in her mouth, the scullery maid propped herself up into a seated position. "I must look a mess," she muttered to herself, trying to smooth out some of the wrinkles from her torn and rumpled skirt.

"Like bird zshit with paraszitesz," Trianglehead declared.

Berlyn narrowed a grey-green eye at the bird. "Thanks," she answered tartly, forcing herself to stand.

Feeling a little better once she was on her feet, but having to chase the tingling beginnings of pins-and-needles out of her left foot, Berlyn stepped out of the giant mushroom and back into the heat and humidity of the Rhagana village. The deafening roar of the giant waterfall nearby played havoc with her tender head, and she practically walked with her eyes shut against the bright morning sunlight, as she maneuvered through the misty valley toward a circle of people seated ahead of her.

Reclining back comfortably in a chair carved from the cap of a giant toadstool, a recovered Calyx offered the young blonde a friendly wave. "Another survivor staggers through the carnage," he teased. "Heard you had a party without invitin' me."

Unconcerned with decorum or proper etiquette, and not wanting to sit in the marshy soil, Berlyn dumped herself into the chair where Aitchley sat, curling up on the young man's lap. "You can't tell?" she answered the dwarf.

"Don't feel too bad," Aitchley said, shifting awkwardly beneath her. "Sprage and Harris are still out cold."

Berlyn only grunted in reply, burying her head in the young man's shoulder to try to block out some of the jungle's persistent noises.

"I hope the celebration for my return did not cause you any undue stress, Miss Berlyn," Gjuki remarked, leaning forward in concern.

"Speaking of which," interrupted Calyx, "why didn't you ever tell us you were the Rhagana equivalent of the Cavalier?"

What might have been a momentary flicker of embarrassment glittered in Gjuki's eyes. "Life in the Bentwoods is hard but not particularly eventful, Master Calyx," he replied. "Most Rhagana believe that the World Outside—your world—is a much more confusing and disorienting place to survive. My living there has earned me this much misplaced admiration.''

Seated beside his brother—or SporeKin, as the Rhagana called it—Berlyn noticed Gjalk DarkTraveller nudge Gjuki good-naturedly in the side. ''The WorldDweller humbles himself,'' the ponytailed Rhagana said. ''Throughout all time as we know it, no Rhagana has been able to last a blink of the Night'sEye in the World Outside. Only Gjuki WorldDweller has survived for so long in such a harsh, unfriendly place.''

''It is only a matter of tolerance,'' Gjuki responded. ''The World Outside is not as frightening as we were all led to believe.''

''Say what you will, WorldDweller,'' Eyfura SpearWielder remarked, ''but it is a place where I will not go.'' She shook her head in muted disbelief. ''All that wasted activity and corrupted lands . . . I would never begin to understand the Pink Ones' desire to do so much and accomplish so very little.''

''All life is driven to survive as best it can,'' Gjuki answered, and Berlyn thought she caught the gardener look shyly away from the female. ''Humans are unable to live at peace with All That Is and constantly struggle against it. They do not understand the subtleties and intricacies of Nature that we take for granted. They try to adapt the world around them rather than adapt *to* the world around them.''

Almost so low as not to be heard, Aitchley grumbled, ''Be wary of Nature's scales; there are some things that are not meant to be tampered with.''

A Rhagana named Baugi PathFinder gave the young farmer an acknowledging nod. ''Sound words from a Pink One,'' the creature complimented him.

Sitting as she was on his lap, only Berlyn heard the young man mutter: ''Yeah. Too bad I don't know what the Pits they mean.''

Unaware of Aitchley's pessimistic grumblings, Calyx returned his attention to the five Rhagana seated around him. ''Enough philosophizing,'' he said. ''We've got work to do.'' Rummaging through his large sack with enough clinking and clattering to drown out the Mistillteinn Falls—or so it sounded to Berlyn—the young blonde watched as the dwarf extracted a crudely drawn map from his bag. ''We're looking for a place called the Shadow Crags," the smith continued, beady eyes on the fungi before him. "You say you've actually been there?"

The object of Calyx's question, Gjalk DarkTraveller nodded once. "It lies less than a full blink of the Night'sEye to the southeast," the ponytailed Rhagana replied. "Unfortunately, the way leads through the EverDark."

Calyx shifted his questioning gaze to Gjuki. "EverDark?" he queried.

A grim visage momentarily darkened Gjuki's mien. "The EverDark is an even denser portion of the Bentwoods," he explained, "where very little light, if any, passes through the canopy. There the vegetation grows so thick that sharp blades of flint or steel are required to cut through the undergrowth."

"Which is why, I guess, we have Thiazi BladeWalker here?" Calyx commented.

A slender, shorter Rhagana nodded in wordless affirmation at the dwarf, a wicked-looking arc of metal resting across its bare knees.

Female, Berlyn noted to herself with some surprise. She was getting better at being able to tell the difference between the Rhagana sexes.

Although his brother was grim-faced, no such worries clouded Gjalk DarkTraveller's expression. "Although a place of mystery and danger before the WorldDweller's departure," he said, "the EverDark has been extensively mapped and explored. Myself and Baugi PathFinder know the way well."

"Let me guess," Calyx said sarcastically. "DarkTraveller, right?"

Berlyn suddenly felt Aitchley shift worriedly beneath her. "Hey, isn't that where those giant flowers are?" he fretted.

Baugi PathFinder gave the young man another nod. "You are well versed in the world of the Rhagana, Aitchley QuestLeader," the creature said. "Indeed, the EverDark is home to the Rafflesia, but fear not. The DarkTraveller and myself know the way well enough to skirt the Rafflesia's domain and stay well out of harm's way."

Calyx gave his sketchy map an unhappy frown. "What about these Shadow Crags?" he queried. "What can you tell us about them?"

"Very little, I'm afraid," Gjalk DarkTraveller answered. "Called the Mountains of Solid Blackness by the Rhagana, they exist outside the influence of the Halls of the Living Mist, so none have ever explored them. From what I have seen of them, they are not as high as most mountains—and no white fur coats their peaks as with some hills—but they are jagged and sharp, jutting up from the ground like the giant stone teeth one finds in caverns."

"A mountain range of stalagmites," Calyx murmured darkly to himself. "Sounds positively charming."

The image of dark hills rising up like brown troll fangs churned through her mind as Berlyn gave Calyx an anxious look. "So how are we supposed to climb them?" she wondered.

Calyx gave the girl a cynical glare. "What do you mean *we*?" he asked back gruffly. "*You're* not going anywhere!"

11

Talk for the Eyes

Berlyn jerked her arm free of Aitchley's concerned grasp, forcing the young man to jog in order to keep up with her rankled pace.

"Come on, Berlyn," the young farmer pleaded. "You're being unreasonable."

Ire gleaming in her eyes, the blonde spun, transfixing the young man with a smoldering glare. "*I'm* being unreasonable?" she repeated harshly. "I'm unreasonable? All I said was that I wanted to come along. What's so unreasonable about that?"

Aitchley threw a helpless glance behind him as if somebody might come to his assistance, but he was all alone. "It's just that . . . I mean . . ." He gave another anxious look over his shoulder. "You know it's not safe," he finally said. "We've been trying to find a safe place for you to stay since Ilietis."

"And I've managed on my own," the scullery maid snapped back. "If we're over halfway there, I don't see the harm in continuing."

"The harm?" Aitchley blurted. "The harm is that we're going beyond Lich Gate! Don't you get it? We're going someplace where nobody's ever been before! Who knows what kind of dangers there might be?"

"Yeah, who knows?" Berlyn answered back bitterly. "Maybe there won't be any at all . . . or maybe there'll be so many that you'll never make it out of there alive. Did you ever stop to think about that, Aitchley Corlaiys? Did you?"

Even though he had—many times—Aitchley tried not to let the uncertainty show on his face. "Look," he replied, exhaling heavily, "this quest is no place for a girl. Gaal knows I don't even want to be here myself!"

"Eyfura and Thiazi are going," Berlyn shot back, eyeing the young man captiously. "They're both girls."

"They don't count," Aitchley sputtered, still looking helplessly about him. "They're Rhagana."

"Rhagana *females*," Berlyn countered.

Aitchley sputtered a few more times before he was able to get the proper words out of his mouth. "Yeah, but they won't be going beyond Lich Gate," he argued. "They'll probably stop once we reach the Shadow Crags. You want to come the whole length of the trip."

"And why not?" the blonde argued, placing adamant hands on shapely hips. "You're going, aren't you?"

"Not 'cause I want to!" answered Aitchley. He threw useless arms up into the humid air. "Daeminase Pits, Berlyn! What do you want from me? It's stupid to do something you know is dangerous!"

Berlyn narrowed querulous eyes at the young man. "So what does that make you, then?" she sneered.

She knew it was a low blow—knew firsthand what Aitchley thought of himself and how fragile his self-esteem was—but, LoilLan take her, she was angry!

Aitchley tried unsuccessfully to conceal his hurt expression. "I'm going because I have to go," he replied softly, eyes downcast.

"What about Gjuki or Calyx?" Berlyn insisted. "Or Poinqart? They don't *have* to go."

"They're going because they're trained," Aitchley answered. "They can hold their own in a fight."

Grey-green fire ignited in Berlyn's gaze. "Oh, yeah?" she spat. "And if it wasn't for me, you and Calyx would be troll food right now!"

A brief glimmer of hesitation flickered in Aitchley's ocean-blue stare as he faced the young girl. He didn't understand why she was so suddenly angry—or why she wanted to come on what was undoubtedly the most foolishly dangerous quest ever since the Pilgrimage of Folly—but he had come to the conclusion a long time ago that she was safer being away from him rather than with him, and he wasn't going to change his mind now . . . despite her objections or his own feelings.

"Look," he finally concluded, running a weary hand through the hair underneath his hat, "stay here and take care of the horses. If everything goes well, we should be back in a month or two."

Pink lips set into what could only be considered a deadly pout. "Take care of the horses?" Berlyn echoed, eyebrows knitting together. "What am I now? Some kind of bunging stablehand?"

The oath caught Aitchley off guard, silencing him in wide-eyed shock.

Berlyn pressed her advantage, jabbing a furious finger at the young man's chest. "You are, without a doubt, the most infuriating, uncaring, selfish, inconsiderate muggwort that I've ever met in my entire life, Aitchley Corlaiys!" she screamed at him. "You think you're the only one who can go off and put himself in danger? You think I'm going to sit here and do nothing while you're out there risking your life for some stupid quest that I could give a whore's moneypouch about? Well, two can play at that game! You'll see! You'll be sorry!"

With an angry swirl of her torn skirt, the young blonde turned sharply on her heel and stalked away, dainty fists clenched tight at her sides. Dumbed, Aitchley could only watch her storm off, a look of muted astonishment on his face. Then, slowly—his ears still burning from the harsh words that had escaped her lips—the young man returned to where Calyx and the others still sat gathered in a circle, a look of surprise even on the usually expressionless faces of the Rhagana.

Slumping into his mushroom chair, Aitchley pulled his hat down over his eyes and sank back further into his seat. "Well," he quipped morosely to those about him, "that went well."

With an agitated squawk, Trianglehead barely hopped out of the way of the maroon-colored backpack that flew across the single chamber of the mushroom house, flinching as the bag struck the wall behind him and rebounded off.

"Awwwwk!" shrieked the bird. "Kut it out!"

Vindictively, Berlyn picked the backpack back up and flung

it, once more, across the length of the toadstool, taking very little satisfaction in the way it bounced, undamaged, off the fleshy walls of the giant fungus. "Treat me like a little girl!" the scullery maid muttered wrathfully to herself. "I'll show him."

Flapping useless wings, Trianglehead scuttled frantically out of the angry blonde's way. "Knock it off!" the fledgling demanded. "Zstop it! Zstop it! Zstop it!"

Heedlessly, Berlyn stomped over to where the backpack had landed, snatching it up by its straps and hurling it into the opposite wall. " 'Why don't you stay here and take care of the horses?' " she grumbled to herself, deepening her voice in a bad impression of Aitchley's. " 'We'll be back in a month or two.' " She grabbed up the backpack again. "Yeah, right. A month or two. If you live that long!"

Releasing a premature squawk, Trianglehead ducked, but another throw never came. Questioningly, the bird straightened up, staring in avian confusion at the young girl, who had sunk slowly to the ground, angry tears starting to stream from her eyes.

"Stupid muggwort," the blonde sulked. "Stupid, selfish . . . warthead!"

In what could have been either concern or curiosity, the bandaged gyrofalc hopped clumsily over to where the scullery maid sat, her legs drawn up to her chest and her arms wrapped around her knees. Tears continued to trickle down her face, rimming her eyes with red, and she hardly noticed the little bird as it came nearer, its triangular head cocked quizzically to one side.

"Why you kry?" the fledgling wanted to know.

Sniffing, Berlyn rested her chin against her knees. "Aitchley Corlaiys is an insensitive, idiotic ragworm," she proclaimed.

The gyrofalc cocked his head the other way. "Know that," he responded. "Why you kry?"

Although she tried to suppress it, Berlyn couldn't help the tiny smile that found its way to her lips. "He won't let me come the rest of the way," she told the fledgling. "He's acting like I'm incompetent or something."

Questions remained bright in the bird's milky blue gaze. "Why you want to kome?" he wondered. "Don't underzstand. Dangerousz to kome, yesz?"

Berlyn's faint smile turned down. "You sound just like Aitchley," she frowned.

"No zsound like Aitchley," Trianglehead replied, shifting from foot to foot. "Juszt curiousz. Why you want to kome?"

Berlyn wiped at her nose with the back of her hand before answering. "Because he's going to get himself killed on this stupid quest," she said tartly. "He's going to go off to Lich Gate, and die, and I'll never see him again!"

Trianglehead risked hopping a little closer. "Think zso?" he asked.

Berlyn fixed challenging eyes on the fledgling. "He'd be dead already if we hadn't gone back for him," she pointed out.

The gyrofalc twisted his head inquisitively. "Zso you think he die if you no kome?" he probed.

The ridiculous truth of the statement momentarily tripped up Berlyn's indignant anger. "Well, I . . ." she started.

"You think you have to take kare of him like zsome nezstling or zsomething?" the bird pressed.

Berlyn felt her cheeks flush. "I . . ." she tried again.

Diamond-blue eyes met her gaze. "What you are? Mother hen?" the gyrofalc snorted sardonically. He shrugged flightless wings. "Let him go. Zstay here where be zsafe."

"That's not the point!" the blonde snapped, feeling her rage build back up behind her breast. "He didn't even give me the choice! He just told me what to do like I was his little sister or something!"

Trianglehead turned his head sideways and Berlyn could almost swear she saw a grin spread on his copper beak. "Oh. That point," the fledgling declared, feigning sudden comprehension. "He act like mother hen, *you* get piszszed."

"I'm not acting like a mother hen!" Berlyn retorted, her frustration increasing as the gyrofalc taunted her. "I just want to come. What's so wrong with that?"

Trianglehead shrugged with the same mocking undertone to his movements. "No thing wrong with that," he answered noncommittally. "He want you zstay. What zso wrong with that?"

"I don't want to stay!" Berlyn shouted.

"He no want you kome," Trianglehead responded with another shrug. "What you do now?"

A glimmer of malicious thought sparked in Berlyn's eyes at the gyrofalc's question. "I'll go out on my own," she grumbled under her breath. "Show him how *he* likes it. Let him sit here and worry about whether I'm dead or not!"

Trianglehead blinked at the young girl before him. "That zstupid," the bird said. "Why riszk own life? Pretty zstupid trick you really die."

"Well, what else am I supposed to do?" the scullery maid wanted to know, the tears starting to well back up in her eyes. "I want to come but he won't let me!"

As if uninterested, Trianglehead stretched out a wing and started grooming his feathers. "Don't let him go," he answered simply.

Berlyn sank back against the wall with a harsh, sob-choked laugh. "Sure," she sneered. "If it was that easy, I wouldn't be sitting here right now!"

The gyrofalc gave the young blonde a look of withering scorn. "All humansz thisz zstupid?" the bird asked in avian contempt. He ruffled his crest in wordless rancor. "Liszten, you want to go, he no let you. He want to go, *you* no let *him*."

"Well, how am I supposed to do that?" Berlyn queried. "I already tried talking to him and he . . ."

"Tch, tch, tch, tch, tch," Trianglehead interrupted her, shaking his head disdainfully. "Talk no good if one hasz no earsz. Talk muszt be for the eyesz."

Confusion permeated the grey-green of Berlyn's stare. "Talk for the eyes?" she repeated. "I don't understand what you mean."

Sighing, Trianglehead made an awkward flapping leap back up to his perch of protruding mushroom stalk. "Zshow him you want to go," the bird explained. "Zshow him you go, or he no go."

"But how am I supposed to do that?" Berlyn wanted to know.

Eyes closed—his head nestled under his bandaged wing—Trianglehead only responded: "Eeeed?"

A small smirk drew across Berlyn's lips to chase away her befuddlement.

The shrill cacophony of the Bentwoods filled the pinkish-grey morning sky, vying with the growling thunder of the Mis-

tillteinn Falls as they competed for dominance of the dawn.
Yawning, Aitchley stepped out of his mushroom house, slinging his maroon-colored backpack over one shoulder as Camera
12 scuttled out of the mushroom hut behind him.

It had been odd sleeping alone, the young man thought as
he meandered down the Rhagana pathways toward Gjalk's
house. He hadn't realized how used he had gotten to Berlyn
sleeping beside him, her body snuggled against his, sharing
their warmth even when such warmth wasn't needed. He could
only hope she understood his need to keep her safe. He didn't
want her coming not because he didn't enjoy her company—
quite the opposite!—but because he didn't want anything bad
to happen to her. That was something he just couldn't live
with. In all his seventeen years, very few things had meant
much to him—in such bleak times it was just downright stupid
to get emotionally attached to something that LoilLan could
so easily take away—and now that he had found something,
now that someone meant a great deal to him, he'd be damned
if he was going to put her in any unnecessary risks. After all,
this was his stupid quest. If something happened to her, it
would be his fault, wouldn't it? He could only hope Berlyn
understood this, regardless of her anger.

Despite the early morning hour, Rhagana already bustled
about the young man, walking leisurely down their streets on
communal errands and chores. That was something the Rhagana did that his own people didn't, the young farmer noted.
Unlike humans, the Rhagana all worked together. The entire
village shared all the chores like one big family, and—also
different from humanity—there were no ruling classes. Each
Rhagana, male or female, was completely equal in the eyes of
All That Is and among each other. No one gave orders. No
one served another. They just all did the required work and
lived in complete peace and harmony with nature.

As if unlocking a small door to his subconscious, Aitchley
heard the buzzing drone of Tin William hiss through his cranium: *There are some things that were not meant to be tampered with*, it said. *Be wary of Nature's scales.*

A frown creased Aitchley's lips at the words. Something
was different, the young man mused, pondering the enigmatic
message. Something in the way Tin William had worded it
and the way he had said it the other day . . .

A sudden wave from a nearby toadstool doorway pulled Aitchley out of his thoughts and back into the humid morning of the Rhagana village. Waving back, the young man approached the giant mushroom, immediately noticing the unhappy scowl painted beneath Calyx's salt-and-pepper beard.

"'Bout time you got up," the dwarf admonished the young farmer. "We'll never get out of here by noon with all you people sleeping in so late." He jerked a thumb over one shoulder. "Why don't you go make yourself useful and help Gjuki sort through the provisions? Remember, take only what we need. We're gonna be carrying all this stuff ourselves without the horses along."

Aitchley gave the dwarf an understanding nod but turned a curious glimpse at the silver-grey construct stanced behind him. "What about Camera 12?" he suggested. "We could always strap a few supplies on him."

Calyx gave the arachnidlike construct a skeptical glance. "And have it break down on us halfway there?" He shook his head curtly. "Naw. Maybe load it up with a few of the extra supplies Desireah gave us, but the real vital stuff we'll have to carry ourselves. We'll probably break our backs doing it, but it's the price we'll have to pay."

Nodding again, Aitchley turned and left the dwarf's company, trying hard to hide his smirk. Calyx could be so worrisome at times it was almost funny, the young man thought to himself. *He's the only person I know that, if I ever saw him happy, I'd get worried!*

Camera 12 following him like a puppy, Aitchley headed for the open stretch of valley the Rhagana had set aside for the quest-members' horses and their own piglike uiptyrs. Gjuki, Aitchley saw, was already there, removing weaponry and setting aside saddles, and another Rhagana—a lean, skeletal male called Hugi UiptyrFriend—tossed handfuls of food to the snorting, grunting animals.

Wading through the swinelike press of uiptyrs, Aitchley neared Gjuki and the horses, giving his own black-and-white stallion an affectionate pat on the nose.

"Welcome, Master Aitchley," Gjuki greeted the young man. "I surmise Master Calyx has sent you to assist me sort through the provisions?"

Aitchley answered with a nod, unslinging his backpack as

he lowered himself to one knee. "That's what he wants," he replied, pushing an uiptyr away that sniffed curiously at the young man's backpack.

Gjuki returned the nod. "Yes," he agreed. "Master Calyx is quite concerned over the state of our supplies. He is afraid we will either bring too much and load ourselves down, or not bring enough and starve before reaching our goal."

Aitchley reached out for the first of the saddlebags full of food. "He's a dwarf," he responded with a good-natured shrug. "He's got to worry about something."

"Indeed."

Sudden question exploded in the young farmer's brain as he picked up the first of the leather saddlebags given to them by Baroness Desireah, and he quickly tossed it aside to pick up another. Both Gjuki and Hugi noticed the young man's abrupt anxiety as he snatched up yet a third pouch and threw it aside to grab a fourth.

"There is a problem, Aitchley QuestLeader?" asked Hugi UiptyrFriend.

Bewilderment contorted Aitchley's mien as he grabbed up a fifth saddlebag. "I . . ." he began, but his own perplexity cut him off.

Quizzically, Gjuki reached out to pick up a saddlebag. "Is something wrong with the provisions, Master Aitchley?" the fungoid gardener wondered.

Aitchley threw the fifth saddlebag, unopened, onto an ever-increasing pile. "They're all . . . They're all empty!" he sputtered. He trained a curious eye on Gjuki. "You didn't empty them or something, did you?"

Fleeting surprise glistened briefly over Gjuki's pearl-black eyes as he inspected the empty pouches for himself. "No, I have not," he said, confusion tainting his voice. "Equally as strange, your throwing ax was not with the rest of your provisions, and yet I notice you are not in possession of it. You didn't happen to leave it in your quarters, did you?"

His own astonishment almost made him miss the obvious. "No, I . . ."

"A theft in the Valley of the Diamond Rains," Hugi UiptyrFriend said with a disparaging shake of his head. "Never in my life have I heard of such a thing happening. We must bring this to the attention of the entire village."

A slow anger began to burn through Aitchley's surprise. "Yeah, sure. You go ahead and do that," he snarled. "I'll be right with you . . . right after I go and kick somebody's ass in!"

Gjuki watched with little emotion as the young farmer pushed himself angrily to his feet. "You know who the culprit of this most grievous deed is, Master Aitchley?" the Rhagana questioned.

Aitchley's hand coiled expectantly around the hilt of his sword. "You're damn right I do," he fumed, "and I bet he thinks he's pretty damn clever if he can steal one of my own weapons to use against me!"

A hint of confusion lingered in Gjuki's eyes as he watched the young man run off down the marshy streets of the village before rising to follow.

Instincts alerted, he was on his feet seconds before the young farmer stormed across the threshold of his mushroom lodgings, wrists snapping down instinctively despite the vacant sheaths beneath his sleeves.

Aitchley's face was red with rage as he burst through the arched doorway of the giant toadstool, one hand still resting on his sword hilt. "All right, Blind-Eye!" he shouted vengefully at the outlaw. "What'd you do with them?"

All trace of sleep purged from his system, Harris scrabbled to his feet. "What'd I do with what?" he shouted back in his defense.

Steel scraped against leather as Aitchley extracted his weapon. "Don't play games with me, Blind-Eye!" the young man roared. "The supplies! My throwing ax! What have you done with them?"

Blue-black eyes wide with ignorance, Harris took an uneasy step backwards, arms stretched wide and fingers splayed. "I haven't the foggiest what you're talking about, scout," he responded. "I ain't touched nothing and I ain't touched no one since we got here!"

Consumed by his fury, Aitchley took an intimidating step forward, accenting his words with vicious jabs of his sword. "I bet you think you're cute, don't you?" he raged. "I bet you think it's *real* funny!" He took another threatening step forward. "Didn't you learn anything at Leucos?"

The look of fear was unmistakable in Harris's eyes as he backed up against the mushroom's wall. "Hey, hey, hey! Calm down, puck!" he advised. "Truth to tell, I don't know what the Pits you're talking about!"

Hatred flashed in Aitchley's blue-green glare. "You expect me to believe you?" he snarled. "What do you think I am? Stupid?"

A sudden voice sounded over Aitchley's shoulder. "Believe him," it said.

Still charged with an anger-induced adrenaline, Aitchley turned on the newcomer, eyes ablaze with aquamarine fire. Unexpected befuddlement successfully doused much of his rage, but there was still a hint of ire tinging his voice as he glared at the petite figure leaning confidently in the doorway. "Berlyn?" he questioned. "What . . . ?"

Assuredly, Berlyn crooked one leg across the width of the mushroom's doorway, unconcerned with how much flesh showed as her torn skirt fell away from her thigh. "Believe him," she said again, an unnatural smugness in her tone. "Harris didn't take the supplies."

Aitchley could only blink at her.

Berlyn shouldered the young man's throwing ax. "I did."

Acrimoniously, Aitchley paced back and forth across the floor of the giant mushroom, unable to quell the unsettling queasiness that roiled through his bowels. Calyx watched him from the comfort of a toadstool chair, beady eyes glimmering in the bioluminescence of phosphorescent lichen. From outside, the night sounds echoed and reverberated through the darkened canopy of the Bentwoods—and the growling rumble of the Mistillteinn Falls was a constant thunder that filled the valley—yet Aitchley heard neither. His thoughts were too caught up in the beautiful young girl standing before him and the frustrating rage that ate away at his innards.

Uncharacteristically calm, Calyx regarded the two youngsters with thoughtful eyes. "You tried getting her to tell you where she hid 'em?" he asked Aitchley.

Impotent fists curled and uncurled at the young man's sides. "Yeah," he grumbled.

"And you tried talking her out of coming?" the dwarf asked.

Teeth ground together. "Yes."

"And you explained you don't get proficient with a weapon from one day's worth of practicing?"

"Two days," Berlyn corrected with a sneer, "and you can stop talking like I'm not in the room."

Calyx shrugged indifferently at the blonde's retort. "Then it's settled," he said. "Berlyn comes with us."

Aitchley wheeled on the dwarf in his abrupt panic. "No!" he all but screamed. "She can't come! It's too dangerous!"

Calyx offered the young farmer a genial, albeit strained, smile. "She's got us by the pubes, kid," he quipped. "There's not much we can do that we haven't already tried."

"Just give me a few more days," Aitchley pleaded, throwing a worried look at the diminutive scullery maid. "I'll figure out where she hid them."

Calyx released a heavy sigh as he pulled himself from his chair. "Look, kid," he replied. "We're wasting too much time as it is, and I want to be well on our way back before the start of summer. If Berlyn wants to come, we'll just have to let her come."

The apprehension he felt created even more turmoil in his already turbulent stomach as Aitchley begged, "But . . ."

"Besides, she's better with your throwing ax than Sprage is with his *navaja*, and we're letting *him* come!" Calyx continued. He headed for the door. "Now, if you'll excuse me, I believe the two of you have something to discuss."

Aitchley could only watch as the dwarven smith strolled out the door and vanished into the night. Awkwardly, the young man remained staring out into the blackness, his back to Berlyn. He didn't know what Calyx thought he had to say to the girl—the only thing he was sure of was that he was worried sick about the blonde and absolutely furious that she didn't seem to care.

"What would you do if Lord Tampenteire sent me to Aa in the middle of the winter?" the scullery maid behind him suddenly asked.

Perplexed, Aitchley turned to face her. "Huh?" he asked.

"What would you do if Lord Tempenteire sent me to Aa in the middle of the winter?" she asked again.

A small smirk drew across half of Aitchley's lips as he suspected where the blonde was going with this line of questioning. "Lord Tampenteire wouldn't send anybody across the

Solsbury Hills in the middle of winter,'' he responded, trying to undermine her argument.

A similar smirk stretched pink lips. ''Just like he wouldn't send anybody beyond Lich Gate,'' she countered. Her eyes met his. ''Now, for argument's sake, what would you do if Lord Tampenteire sent me to Aa in the middle of the winter?''

Aitchley gave a noncommittal shrug. ''Nothing,'' he replied. ''Even if Lord Tampenteire *did* send you, he wouldn't send you alone.''

''No more than he'd send a farmboy beyond Lich Gate who hadn't even picked up a sword before then,'' she said, her smirk growing. ''So let's say he does send me alone. What would you do?''

Still seeing where her argument led, Aitchley answered with another shrug. ''I wouldn't let you go,'' he declared.

''But I'd have to go,'' Berlyn replied. ''He's our lord; we're his servants. If he tells me to do something, I do it. Just like you're doing.''

''That's different.''

''Is it?''

The frustration churning through his thoughts made it difficult for Aitchley to make his point. ''Yeah. Sure it is!'' he said. ''Lord Tampenteire didn't send me by myself!''

''You looked pretty alone when I saved you from those trolls a few days ago,'' Berlyn responded smugly. ''So what would you do if Lord Tampenteire sent me to Aa?''

Aitchley scowled at her confidence. ''I'd make sure he sent some men with you,'' he stated.

''What if he didn't have any men to sparc?'' the blonde wondered.

''Then I'd go with you,'' Aitchley answered, his ire beginning to get the better of him.

''And what if I didn't want you to go with me?'' Berlyn baited him.

''Then I'd go anywa . . .'' Aitchley tried to cut himself off but was unsuccessful.

Berlyn took an eager step backwards, stabbing an accusatory finger at the young man. ''Hah!'' she chided him. ''You'd go anyway! That's what you were going to say! That's exactly what I'm doing!''

''No, it's not!''

"Yes, it is!"

"This is different!"

A trace of indignant anger sparked back to life in Berlyn's eyes. "Ooooooh, you're just impossible, Aitchley Corlaiys!" she accused. "This is only different because I'm the one who wants to come and you're the one who's not letting me!"

Aitchley tried to think of a response but his brain failed him. She was—he noted grimly to himself—right.

"If things were really different, and Lord Tampenteire was sending me to Aa in the middle of winter, I'd like to think that you'd do everything you could think of so that you could come with me, wouldn't you?" the young girl argued.

Despite himself, Aitchley felt his head bob in gentle agreement.

"All I'm doing is the same thing!" the attractive blonde explained. "I just want to come with you so that *I* know nothing happens to you." She gave a quick glance at the throwing ax in her hands. "I'm not pretending I know how to use this thing—that I could protect you from something that you couldn't save yourself from—but you heard what Calyx said: I'm better with it than Sprage is with his weapon! Why won't you let me come with you?"

Because I love you? Aitchley considered shouting at her. Because I'm afraid the only good thing to ever come into my life will be taken away from me if I let you come? Because I've already spent a month chasing after you and Harris . . . not knowing if you were alive or dead . . . worrying every step of the way? What do you want from me, Berlyn? I've never even had the chance to be happy! You want to take that away from me as well?

It took a second before the young man realized he had said the words out loud.

Tenderly, Berlyn reached out and grasped the young farmer's arm, compassion and understanding misting her eyes. "I don't want to lose you either," she said softly.

Trying to hide his embarrassment in a facade of indifference, Aitchley turned sharply away. "Oh, all right!" he finally conceded, throwing his hands up into the air. "You can come! But you've got to promise to stay out of the way! And if I ever tell you to get to safety again, you get to safety! No coming back and looking for me, understand?"

The blonde forced her gaze earthward, trying to keep the victorious smile off her lips. "All right," she agreed.

"And you stay on Camera 12," the young man went on imperiously. "And stay either between me and Calyx or somebody else. Never wind up without somebody on either side of you!"

Berlyn nodded again, the warm thrill of giddiness filling her slender frame.

A faint flush of red colored Aitchley's face when he finally turned to face her. "And tell me where the Pits you hid the damn supplies so we can sort through them!" he demanded sheepishly.

Still beaming with triumph, Berlyn bent over and tossed the young man his maroon-colored backpack, no longer able to keep the happy grin off her features. "Sometimes the best hiding places are the most obvious," she told him matter-of-factly.

Stunned into silence, Aitchley knelt down and unzipped the knapsack, staring in wordless stupor at the hoard of supplies crammed into its canvas interior. "I thought it felt heavier," he remarked. "But where's the rest of them? And where's the stuff that's supposed to go in here?"

Skipping playfully to the door, Berlyn threw the young farmer a ravishing smile. "In the cave behind the Falls," she said.

Momentary surprise flashed in Aitchley's eyes. "In the cave . . . ?" he said, flustered. "But I had them check the cave . . ."

"Really, Aitchley," Berlyn teased, "sending Eyfura to check the cave . . . Don't you know we girls have to stick together?"

His mind still benumbed by shock, Aitchley hardly heard the young girl as she stopped in the doorway and gave him another loving smile. "Oh, and Aitchley . . . ?" she called.

Aitchley threw a puzzled look over one shoulder.

"I love you, too."

From atop his perch, Trianglehead shoved his beak grumpily under one wing and shook his head sadly. "Zstupid humansz," he groused to himself.

12

Toward the Shadow Crags

*E*mbraced once again by the claustrophobic humidity of the Bentwoods, Aitchley was grateful when Gjalk DarkTraveller called for a halt. For the past one and a half weeks, Aitchley had tripped and staggered his way through the chaotic jumble of vines, shrubs, and networking of roots that was the EverDark—an even denser, more overgrown section of the Bentwoods—his feet sore and tired and drenched in his own sweat. Without the luxury of the horses, and burdened by the extra weight of supplies across his shoulders, the young man had hated every moment since leaving the Valley of the Diamond Rains, and was surprised to hear himself wish they'd hurry up and get to Lich Gate already. Aitchley also made his clumsiness more apparent, unable to stop throwing worried glances behind him at the petite blonde straddling the cool metallic back of Camera 12. Despite the heat and oppressive foliage, however, Berlyn continued to wear a smile of victory across her lips, her bearing unaffected by the stifling heat, overwhelming humidity, and minatory shroud of trees. She proudly kept Aitchley's throwing ax propped against her shoulder, and—as if to accent her new role as adventurer—she had torn off the sleeves of her dress, revealing pale, slender arms that now, Aitchley fretted, faced an even greater risk of being cut or scratched by the groping green tendrils of vegetation about them.

Or worse, the young man thought, stung like Calyx had been.

Swinging in a wide arc, Thiazi BladeWalker made a small clearing for the eleven. "Gjalk says we shall stop here for the night," she announced, sheathing her machete.

Questioningly, Calyx narrowed beady eyes through the thick cover of trees, squinting at the deep, greenish gloom of the EverDark. "Looks like there's a few hours of sunlight left," he noticed. "Why are we stopping so soon?"

Gjalk DarkTraveller gave the smith a single nod, his mossy ponytail bouncing across his shoulders. "You are correct, Calyx MetalShaper," the Rhagana declared, "yet we approach the sporing grounds of the Rafflesia, and—seeing as they are nocturnal—it would not do us well to enter into their territory once night falls."

Eagerly shrugging off the packs of supplies strapped to his back, Sprage sank to the vine-entangled ground, propping himself wearily up against a tree. "What's to stop them from venturing out a little further than their normal territory if they spot food?" the healer worried.

Gjalk turned black eyes on the physician. "The Rafflesia are not as ambulatory as you or I," he explained. "They are restrained by their root system that only allows them free rein up to a certain distance. By stopping here, we should be well out of their thorny grasp."

Wiping dirty streams of perspiration from his face, Harris asked, "If you know where they all live—and they can't get away 'cause of their roots—why don't you just wipe 'em all out?"

"Exterminate an entire species just for our own convenience?" the Rhagana called Baugi PathFinder exclaimed. "That is not the Rhagana way, Harris BlindEye."

Harris gave the fungus an indifferent shrug. "Didn't say it had to be your way," he snorted. "Just said it'd make your jungle a whole Pits of a lot safer."

Emotionlessly, Gjuki turned to regard the braceleted outlaw. "The Rhagana live as one with All That Is, Harris Blind-Eye," the gardener replied. "Do you not remember our earlier discussion concerning drastic changes and their effects upon the Bentwoods' environment? Even a creature as menacing and as dangerous as the Rafflesia plays its part. To remove them would be to upset the balance of the EverDark. If they were exterminated, who would hunt the smaller animals who in turn hunt the insects who in turn feast upon the leaves, both living and dead? Populations would grow unchecked without the Rafflesia's influence, and the entire Bentwoods would fall seriously out of balance. You would have us do that just for the sake of convenience?"

Diffidently, Harris turned away from the Rhagana. "Whatever," he grunted with a shrug. "Forget I even mentioned it."

Removing his backpack now laden with extra supplies, Aitchley observed the others around him with a sudden anxiety, a nervous rumbling stirring his innards. Was this what Tin William was talking about? he wondered to himself. Would somehow using the Elixir cause something like this to happen? No, that's ridiculous. We're talking about a whole race of creatures here; the Cavalier is just one man. Surely bringing him back from the dead isn't going to make something fall seriously out of balance . . . Is it . . . ?

Gentle hands touched Aitchley's shoulders, bringing him up out of his thoughtful worries, and he turned to see Berlyn at his back, his throwing ax looking heavy and awkward in her dainty grasp. Smiling, she gave the leaf-hidden heavens above them a quick glance before returning her grey-green gaze to the young man before her. "Since we've got a little time before the sun goes down," she said, "I was wondering if you wouldn't mind giving me a few tips on how to use this thing."

Aitchley gave the weapon in her hands a cursory glance, unable to stop the lopsided smile that pulled across his face. "Sure," he said with a shrug, "but it's not going to be easy."

Berlyn puckered pink lips at the young farmer's concern. "I can take care of myself, Aitchley Corlaiys," she replied, and although she was teasing there was also a trace of seriousness in her voice.

Aitchley shrugged again. "Whatever you say," he remarked, and the pair stepped aside to find a small clearing in which to practice.

As the sky hidden overhead slowly melded to dark blues and deep purples, Berlyn rubbed painfully at her right shoulder, trying to chase away the aches and pains that had invaded her joints. Aitchley sat on the ground nearby, his back up against a tree, commenting on her technique. Sprage had also come with the two teenagers to practice throwing his weapon, and Calyx had accompanied the healer to give him a few pointers on using the *navaja*.

As the throwing ax flipped end over end through the jungle—taking a small chunk out of the tree they were using as a target before falling to the ground—Aitchley shook his head dismally. "Overhanded," he told the young blonde before him. "You have to throw it overhanded."

Berlyn massaged her shoulder more vigorously, stalking over to where the ax lay on the rain forest floor. "I'm trying!" she snapped back, her fatigue starting to play upon her patience.

"Trying's not good enough," answered Aitchley. "You've got to just do it."

A sardonic laugh sounded from where Calyx was showing Sprage how to throw the *navaja*. "Now there's the fire calling the forge hot," the dwarf mocked. "Wasn't too long ago that I remember a certain someone who was afraid to even try."

Aitchley felt a warm flush of color fill his cheeks as Berlyn's eyes fell questioningly upon him. "That was different," he replied in his defense. "We were being chased by xlves then."

Calyx's grin widened. "Oh, I wasn't talking about the xlves," he jeered. "I was talking about your own practice sessions. Sheesh, kid, if I had pushed you as hard as you're pushing Berlyn, you would have stormed off and refused to come out for a fortnight! Give the girl a break!"

Aitchley fixed the dwarf with an accusatory glare. "We weren't in the middle of the Bentwoods when you were teaching me," he answered argumentatively.

"No," agreed Calyx, "we spent most of our time in the Tridome . . . which meant you had three full meals a day brought to you by servants and slept in a warm bed surrounded by four sturdy walls. Not quite the same thing as marching through a jungle eating cured meats and sleeping on dirt, is it? If you felt tired at the Tridome, imagine how Berlyn must feel."

Running a weary hand through sweaty hair plastered to the back of her neck, Berlyn shouldered the throwing ax. "It's okay," she told the dwarf defiantly. "I can take care of myself."

"I'm not saying you can't," Calyx replied. "I'm just trying to figure out what suddenly makes the kid think he can."

An indignant anger brought about by embarrassment filled Aitchley with righteous pride; Calyx was making him look stupid in front of Berlyn . . . just like Pomeroy and Nicander! "I made it through the desert by myself, didn't I?" the young man challenged. "And I got the necklace back from Sultothal. I even beat Harris. What more do you want?"

So unexpected that he didn't even see it, Sprage's *navaja* flashed from Calyx's fingers, embedding itself in the tree behind Aitchley's head. The abrupt *bwaaang* of the ebony blade as it slammed into the bark resonated throughout the young man's skull, and he hadn't even had enough warning to pull the near-magical shield off his shoulder and onto his arm.

Startled, Aitchley tumbled over into the undergrowth, trying to turn his frightened duck into a defensive roll. "What the Pits are you . . . ?" he swore.

Calyx sent the young man a knowing smile, retrieving the knife and handing it back to Sprage. "Never get cocky, kid," the dwarf advised. "No one's ever that good."

Awkwardly, trying to regain some of his composure, Aitchley straightened his hat. "I'm not getting cocky," he retorted. "I'm just . . ."

"Acting like a jerk?" Calyx finished for him. "Now get off your butt and join in the practice. You're not the Cavalier."

Grumbling, Aitchley pulled himself to his feet. "I never said I was," he muttered, an old anger returning to his breast.

A smug smile crossed beneath Calyx's beard. "Good," the dwarf replied. "Now this time *pay attention*!"

On their twenty-fourth day in the EverDark, the confusing tangle of overhanging vines and corded lianas began to draw back, the tight foliage thinning out around them. Trees began to grow with more space between them, and more and more shafts of brilliant white sunlight pierced the retreating canopy and struck the forest floor. Even the heavy moisture in the air began to lift, escaping through the gaps in the once claustral treetops.

As he walked free of the eastern edge of the Bentwoods, Aitchley could feel the ground beneath his feet rise gently upward in a subtle incline.

Gjalk DarkTraveller stepped through the thinning trees, tiny button-black eyes fixed on the eastern horizon. "As we promised, Aitchley QuestLeader," the ponytailed Rhagana announced. "The Mountains of Solid Blackness."

Squinting into the reddish-pink light of the morning sky, Aitchley stared across a wide, dew-swept plain of grass. Evil-looking mountains of black rock cracked the eastern skyline, impaling the rubious morning light with ebony spears, and—while no snow covered their peaks—a roiling, churning mantle of greyish-white fog hovered ominously over the Shadow Crags like cerecloth above a corpse.

Thiazi BladeWalker slipped her machete into the small belt she wore about her otherwise naked waist. "It appears your journey to the mountains will be an altogether effortless one," she said, eyeing the open plain ahead of them.

Calyx was dwarvenly pessimistic. "That's what I'm afraid of," he remarked. "Lots of open space for something to attack us."

"Your fears are unfounded, Calyx MetalShaper," Baugi PathFinder replied. "There exist no predators you need concern yourselves with upon the OceanGrass. The largest animal here is the gefjun, a large, flightless bird that eats insects."

"Flightless bird?" Sprage wondered, his curiosity aroused. "You mean like a chicken?"

"The gefjun is far bigger than a chicken, Healer Sprage," Gjuki informed the physician. "An adult male gefjun stands as tall as you or I."

Sprage let out a low whistle of admiration. "That's one big chicken," he commented.

"Big chickens or not," Calyx said, continuing to frown at the grasslands, "I got a bad feeling about this."

"You've got a bad feeling about everything," Sprage observed sardonically.

"It's kept me alive," Calyx answered back.

"It's kept you paranoid," the healer responded wryly.

Gjalk stepped between Sprage and the bickering Calyx, turning his pearl-black eyes on Aitchley. "Although it may do little to assuage the MetalShaper's misgivings, Eyfura and I would like to ask your permission to accompany you on the rest of your quest. The regions of the Mountains of Solid Blackness and beyond have never been explored by Rhagana,

dwarf, or Pink One, and we would be most honored to say we
were among the first to do so."

Aitchley blinked stupidly a few times at Rhagana. "I . . .
uhh . . . ummm . . . What are you asking me for?"

Gjalk blinked back. "You are the QuestLeader, are you
not?"

"Well . . . yeah . . . I guess . . ." the young man floundered.
"But . . ."

"You'll have to forgive Aitchley," Berlyn teased from atop
Camera 12. "He's not very good at accepting new members
into the quest, but I'm sure he'd be glad to have you along."

"As would I," Gjuki put in, clasping his hands about his
brother's arm. "It has been far too long since you and I have
ventured out together across unexplored territories like adven-
turesome young nubs."

Grunting, Calyx shifted the packs across his back and started
out across the leagues of wild grasses. "Fine. Wonderful," he
muttered dourly. "Two more people to suck up our provisions." He practically vanished into the high grass. "Now can
we kindly get out of here before we're attacked by a flock of
giant chickens?"

Unable to stop himself, Aitchley glanced warily about before starting out after the dwarf, stepping carefully through the
knee-high ocean of grass and leaving the humid confines of
the Bentwoods behind him.

Wiping away the perspiration that collected beneath the
brim of his hat, Aitchley looked up at the jagged black hills
that grew steadily more imposing with each step. Although
carpeted with grass, the plains on which they walked rose
steadily upward, bringing them ever nearer to the ominous-
looking Shadow Crags. There were no trees at all on what the
Rhagana called the OceanGrass—Gjalk said this was due to
heavy flooding of a river to the north—and, although not as
bad as the Bentwoods, the empty stretch of grasses was uncomfortably hot.

Beside him—seemingly unaffected by the heat—Berlyn and
Poinqart engaged in an impromptu game of tag, both running
circles about the young man and causing Trianglehead to ruffle
agitated feathers when they dashed too near. How the two of
them found the energy, Aitchley would never know, nor would

he understand how they kept their balance. One of the more infuriating aspects of the OceanGrass, Aitchley learned from embarrassed experience, was that the grass-hidden earth was practically littered with holes and burrows of tiny, gopherlike animals the Rhagana called biarki. How the tiny mammals survived the floods Gjalk described eluded Aitchley's understanding, but it didn't stop the young man from making his natural grace apparent and stumbling and lurching as his feet tried to navigate the unseen labyrinth of mounds and ditches.

Grumbling as his boot snagged yet another hole, he was slightly surprised when a questioning voice sounded close to his ear. "Why are hillsz zsmoking?" Trianglehead asked from the young man's shoulder.

Murmuring a curse, Aitchley turned away from the treacherous soil and glanced up at the nearing mountains. "That's not smoke," he told the fledgling. "It's just mist."

Milky blue eyes blinked their disagreement. "Z'not miszt," the bird argued. "Know miszt. That not miszt."

Aitchley squinted at the greyish-white haze that floated over the barren mountaintops. "Well, it's not smoke," he replied. "There's nothing up there to catch fire."

Walking beside the young farmer, Eyfura SpearWielder trained tiny black eyes on the Shadow Crags. "I believe your gyrofalc is correct, QuestLeader," the Rhagana said. "A mist would have burned away as the morning grew late; the mountains do appear to be smoking."

Blue-green eyes narrowed at the black hills. "How can a range of mountains be smoking when there's nothing on them to catch fire?" he inquired.

Despite their game, Poinqart had been listening to the young man and now stopped beside him, yellow-black eyes turning toward the east. "Mountain-fire-rock," the half-troll said in a low voice. "Poinqart has heard many fable-tales about such nasty-bad-places."

"Mountain-fire-rock?" Aitchley echoed his uncertainty. "What do you mean?"

There was a dark grunt from the head of the group. "Volcanic," Calyx snorted pessimistically. "Great. Just what we need."

"Perhaps there is no need for any undue alarm, Master Calyx," Gjuki suggested. "In all Rhagana history, there has never been any mention of volcanic activity this close to the Bentwoods. Perhaps it has gone dormant.''

"Then why's it still smoking?'' Calyx wanted to know.

"Dying volcanos have been known to produce vents of steam and hot springs,'' Gjalk explained. "Perhaps that is where the smoke originates.''

Calyx didn't sound very convinced. "Perhaps,'' he muttered ruefully, "but when I get my butt hairs singed off by a massive eruption, I know who I'm gonna come and complain to!''

With his own trepidation growing at every step, Aitchley trailed the others closer to the basalt rock formations of the Shadow Crags. He had heard of volcanos before—heard stories of mountains as fierce and as destructive as the Dragon itself—but he had never seen one. Volcanos didn't exist in Vedette. Maybe east of the Bentwoods or even further south than the Molten Dunes, but certainly not in Vedette. And now . . . Now he was voluntarily walking toward something as dangerous and unpredictable as the Dragon itself? He needed to be alive when he passed through Lich Gate!

Wrapped up in his new fears, Aitchley's foot caught on the lip of a biarki burrow and sent the young man stumbling, throwing a red flush across his cheeks to compete with the anxieties churning through his body. Angrily, he threw a perturbed glance back at the grass-hidden hole before returning his gaze to the ominous black mountains ahead of him.

Bloody typical Corlaiys luck, he mused grimly to himself.

A light tap against his leg pulled Aitchley up out of sleep, shattering the peaceful cordon of slumber from around him. Groggily, the young farmer lifted his head, looking toward the half-opened flap of the Envirochamber with eyes encrusted with sleep. Berlyn slept soundly beside him—barely visible in the darkness of the tent—and, if it weren't for the glittering starlight that washed the OceanGrass with silver splendor, Aitchley might never have seen the dark, gaunt specter that sat crouched at the tent flap, one menacing hand clutching the young man's leg.

"Rise and shine, scout,'' a gruff voice hissed through the blackness. "We've got troubles.''

Instinctively, Aitchley bolted upright, immediate worry coursing through his body at the sound of Harris's voice. Still addled with sleep, frantic thoughts of slender black stilettos and venomous blue-black eyes filled the young man's head, and it took a moment before Aitchley remembered that the braceleted thief had, hopefully, learned his lesson.

Despite his mental reassurances, Aitchley still directed his sword at the southern-city brigand. "What is it?" he demanded.

Harris leaned away from the naked blade, cautiously redirecting its point with one callused finger. "Not me, you damn fool," the lockpick swore quietly. "Outside."

Aitchley was unable to keep the suspicion from his mind as he eyed the rogue. "What?" he wanted to know.

Harris started to back silently out of the tent. "Don't know," he said, shrugging. "Just know that we're bein' watched."

"Watched?" Aitchley repeated, crawling toward the tent flap after the thief. "Watched by who?"

Harris gave him another muted shrug. "Don't know," he answered in a whisper. "All I know is we're being watched, and I don't like it."

As he pushed his way out of the Envirochamber, Aitchley was momentarily startled by the large silver object blocking his way, its single glass eye glazed and unblinking.

Harris gave the silvery construct a perturbed glance. "Oh," he said to the young farmer, "and would you tell your metallic watchdog to leggo my leg?"

Perplexed, Aitchley followed Harris's disgruntled gaze to where one of Camera 12's spidery limbs clutched the lockpick's left foot, restraining the outlaw from fully entering the young man's tent and doing any harm.

Aitchley couldn't help the lopsided smirk that pulled across one half of his lips. "Let him go, Twelve," he told the machine. "It's all right."

Obediently, the camera retracted its leg, allowing Harris to scuttle off to one side, his lean and wiry body staying low to the ground. Aitchley tried to follow with the same stealth and fluidity and wound up making enough noise to wake the Daeminase. "Where are they?" the young man inquired as he reached Harris's side.

A brief glimmer of confusion contorted Harris's bearded face. "They were over there," he said, stabbing a rigid finger eastward through the darkness. "Can't tell . . ."

"You're sure you saw someone?" Aitchley wondered, his suspicion growing.

"Never said I saw someone," Harris snapped back in a low whisper. "I just said we were bein' watched."

"If you never saw anyone, how do you know we were being watched?" Aitchley insisted.

A feral look gleamed in Harris's dark eyes. "It's a feeling I get, puck," he explained. "Kinda like a burning sensation at the back of my neck. What? You've never had the feeling that someone was starin' at you?"

"Not when there wasn't anybody around to stare at me," Aitchley answered tartly, cautious eyes on the brigand.

"Look, scout," retorted Harris, "I know what I felt, and my feelings are never wrong." He threw a quick scan across the high grass. "Why don't you go wake up your little dwarf friend? I'll see if I can't find any tracks."

Warily, Aitchley scurried over to where Calyx slept on top of a woolen blanket, keeping one eye on Harris. He didn't trust the southern-city scum—Daeminase Pits! The man had tried to kill him twice!—but, without his knives and with the bracelet around his wrist, Harris needed to rely on the young man for his own protection. It probably killed the outlaw to do so, but if he wanted to get to Lich Gate in one piece he had to place his own life in somebody else's hand. It didn't make sense for him to try something detrimental to his well-being now.

Forcing his gaze away from the dark figure of the lockpick, Aitchley roughly shook Calyx awake, clamping one hand over the dwarf's mouth when his beady eyes snapped open in sleepy ire. Through the silver light of the stars—and the faint greenish-yellow glare of the setting moon—Calyx spied the young man and gave him a wordless nod, removing the farmer's hand from his lips.

"Problems?" the dwarven smith inquired.

Aitchley gave a halfhearted shrug, glancing over at where Harris had seeped imperceptibly into the darkness. "Harris seems to think so," he replied.

Calyx snatched up his warhammer. "Good enough for me," the dwarf responded. "Blind-Butt's instincts have helped him get this far up the evolutionary ladder. What's he thinking?"

"That we're being watched," Aitchley said, his mouth twisting into a skeptical sneer at how quickly Calyx believed Harris.

The dwarf looked around at the high grass walls enclosing them. "Could be. Could be," he mumbled softly to himself. "Was he sure it just wasn't giant chickens?"

"Just told me we were being watched and then went sneaking off over there someplace," Aitchley said with a disinterested wave.

Calyx got to his feet but stayed in a low crouch. "All right," he said, tiny eyes fixed on the grasses Aitchley had indicated. "Stay here. I'll see if I can't find him."

Aitchley nodded his understanding and took a few clumsy, duckwalk steps back to allow the dwarf to pass. Unexpectedly, his heel caught the edge of a biarki burrow and knocked him backwards, pressing him up against something hidden in the grass. A startled exclamation ripped his lips as he felt the object move, and he threw himself forward with a sudden burst of adrenaline. Dirt spumed into the air as he spun around to face whatever it was behind him, and Calyx came immediately to the young man's side, warhammer gripped in ready hands.

Illuminated by the silver glow of the thousands of stars overhead, a young woman rose up out of the dark grass, midnight-blue eyes trained belligerently on the young man and dwarf. Her skin was an odd, blue-grey hue in the metallic whitewash of the heavens, and long, straight hair the color of pitch streamed over naked shoulders to the middle of her bare back. Her breasts were bare, round, and firm and crested with grey nipples, and she wore only a small loincloth made from some coarse-looking, transparently ribbed material. It took a moment before Aitchley realized she wore only the shed dark skin of some large reptile between her blue-grey thighs as she took another step forward, gesturing with a sharpened black rock in her right hand at the darkened field around her.

A dozen more silhouettes rose up from the grass like shapely ghosts, their grey skin glistening in the starlight, their naked breasts capturing Aitchley's seventeen-year-old attention. All of them held knifelike fragments of black stone in their grasp.

A pessimistic scowl draped beneath Calyx's beard. "Uh-oh," he grumbled. "Looks like penance time again!"

13

Communication Problems

With just the tiniest whisper of disturbed grass, the blue-grey woman stepped forward, shapely legs sluicing through the foliage as soundlessly as Harris moved through the night. Even though he could have been in danger—even though the black rock knife in the young girl's hand was chiseled to a razor-sharp point—Aitchley couldn't pull his gaze away from the supple framework of blue-grey flesh in front of him. Not the way the starlight played across the smooth muscles of her stomach, nor the way the triangular wisp of discarded snakeskin moved gently between her legs, giving the young man tantalizing glimpses of firm thighs and the shadowed places beyond.

"Put your tongue back in your mouth and pay attention." Calyx's voice was a harsh whisper in the young farmer's ear. "We could be in some serious trouble here."

Aitchley tried to blink his eyes free of the young woman, succeeding only in pulling his wide-eyed stare from her crotch to her naked bosom. "What?" he asked in his innocence. "They're only girls."

Calyx answered with a derisive snort. "Only girls?" he parroted. "Remind me to tell you about certain kinds of spiders we have up in Aa if we get out of this one alive."

Slender legs sifting silently through the high grass, the girl in the snakeskin loincloth took another step forward, eyebrows narrowing over midnight blue eyes. *"Hwaet r'ko dhir,"* she demanded.

A look of befuddlement filled both their faces as Aitchley and Calyx traded almost comical looks of confusion; the expression passed quickly over Calyx's features. "Oh, great!" the dwarf declared. "They don't even speak the language!"

Despite the full, round breasts and curvaceous hips wreaking havoc with his seventeen-year-old imagination, Aitchley felt the beginnings of cold dread settle icily in his stomach. "So what do we do now?" he worried.

Calyx's mien was nihilistic. "Die?" he offered as a suggestion.

Unexpectedly—like black smoke issuing up from the ground—Harris Blind-Eye rose up out of the grass behind the young woman, one hand snaking around her bare midriff while the other snatched away her rock weapon.

"Now, then, sweetcheeks," the lockpick rasped in the girl's ear, "let's try this my way." He pressed the sharpened stone up against the base of her jaw. "Call off your friends and maybe we can talk."

Although surprise registered briefly across her features, the girl's posture grew defiant. Despite Harris's entrapping arm about her waist, her back straightened proudly and her head tilted slightly back as she stared down at the knife held against her throat. The only emotion that flickered across her face was a fleeting pout that Aitchley recognized as one of silent condemnation.

Contemptuous disdain scrawled itself across Calyx's face as he glared at the girl and outlaw. "She doesn't speak the language, Blind-Ass," the smith snapped irritably. "How's she supposed to do what you want if she doesn't understand you?"

A sneer twisted beneath Harris's facial hair. "She can understand this, can't she?" he retorted, pulling the young woman up against his body and pricking the grey skin of her neck with the tip of her knife.

Calyx turned away with a sharp shrug. "Wonderful," he grunted jeeringly. "Our first contact with a new race of people, and the only thing we can understand is fear and mutual loathing."

Although the anxiety continued to churn like melted snow through his gut, Aitchley pulled himself slowly to his feet, his eyes fixed on the young girl in Harris's grasp. She stood no taller than Berlyn—making her look small and helpless in the brigand's grip—and, judging from the lean, muscular build of her body and the pert, firm roundness of her breasts, she couldn't have been much older than Aitchley himself. Maybe even younger. And the attractive pout that had crossed her features . . . Even though these lips were grey and this skin was an odd metallic blue, Aitchley had seen that pout on Berlyn's lips just a few weeks ago when they had been practicing back in the Bentwoods.

Startled by the calm that sounded in his own voice, Aitchley stood up and said, "Let her go, Harris."

Ragged eyebrows knitted together across the rogue's forehead. "Now don't be lettin' a pair of naked tits addle your brainpan, puck," the southern-city outlaw responded sagely. "She was the one spying on us, remember?"

The resolve continued to sound strongly in Aitchley's voice. "I remember," he replied. "Now let her go."

Questioningly, the braceleted thief threw a curious look at Calyx before returning his wary gaze to the young man. "I don't get it," he admitted, unable to read the conflicting emotions racing across Aitchley's mien. "A moment ago she was ready to cut your face off." Blue-black eyes narrowed suspiciously. "What do you know that I don't know?"

Aitchley shook his head curtly. "Nothing," he answered tartly. "It's just a feeling I've got, okay?" He trained sarcastic eyes on the bandit. "What? Haven't you ever had a feeling before?"

Hearing some of his own words come back at him, Harris gave the young man a malicious grin. "Your funeral, scout," he remarked, and he released the young girl in his grasp.

As soon as the lockpick's arm drew away from her middle, the young woman in the snakeskin loincloth made a quick leap forward, putting some distance between herself and Harris before spinning around to fix the ponytailed outlaw with an accusing glare. Then, curiously, she turned back toward Aitchley, her eyebrows still narrowed but the look of anger subsiding.

Calyx watched with like expectation. "Okay, kid," he said, arms folded judgementally across his chest. "Now what?"

A sudden cartload of apprehension overturned in Aitchley's

stomach as he confronted the young girl before him. Good question, he asked himself sardonically. Now what? A second ago he had felt nothing but compassion for the exotically attractive young woman in Harris's grasp . . . but that had been while she was held captive. Now—now that she was free— all his previous worries and anxieties returned to haunt him.

What if I've made a mistake? his pessimism raved. What if she *is* dangerous? What if she orders the others to attack now that she's free? What if the other women—despite how young and beautiful they may look—charge into camp and kill us all? What if Harris was right? What if seeing naked boobs has addled my senses? Maybe I should have let Harris handle things his way, and yet . . .

Aitchley's gaze flicked to Calyx before returning to the blue-grey girl stanced in front of him. And yet, he continued to muse, there's something about what Calyx said that bothers me. "Fear and mutual loathing." Is that the only thing we can understand? Ever since leaving Solsbury, that's about all I've seen, and—after listening to Gjuki and Sprage back in the Bentwoods—I'm almost ashamed to be human, but if the Rhagana can interact with new races peacefully, why can't we?

Strengthened by the resolve of his own thoughts, Aitchley returned his full attention to the slender figure before him. The girl still regarded him with caution in her dark blue eyes, and there was a hint of tension in her supple limbs, but she remained where she was, facing the young man expectantly. Tentatively, Aitchley chanced a single step forward, flashing what he hoped was his most amicable—albeit lopsided— smile.

"Uh . . . hi," he said, and felt instantly stupid. "I'm . . . uh . . . Aitchley."

"And I'm little Mary Dimple-Ass," Harris jeered in a strained falsetto from behind the young girl. "Please take me home and plow my fields, farmboy."

"Knock it off, Harris," Calyx ordered brusquely. "At least the kid's trying."

The southern-city outlaw answered the dwarf with a cynical snort. "Trying what?" he retorted. "You said yourself she doesn't speak the language. What's the point of trying to be nice to her if she doesn't understand?"

"That *is* the point," answered Aitchley. "If you're mean to her, she just knows you're mean. She doesn't know why. But if you're nice, maybe it's because you're just nice, and she won't have anything to worry about.''

Harris sucked disinterestedly at his teeth. ''Wouldn't know about it,'' he sneered. ''Never tried bein' nice.''

''Now there's a shock,'' grunted Calyx.

Determined, Aitchley forced himself to ignore the pony-tailed lockpick and return his attention to the young girl. He knew his tone of voice was important—knew a dogling didn't understand words but could be praised or punished by tone of voice alone—and he had run across a deaf merchant once in the marketplace of northern Solsbury, having to explain himself through a variety of hand gestures and head shakes. But, while that had been relatively easy—after all, he only had to point to the item he wanted and show how much money he was willing to pay—this was a bit more complex. He wasn't asking this girl for a new coulter, he was trying to establish a much more abstract communication. So how do you ask someone who doesn't understand you where they came from or what they're doing there? Worse yet . . . how do you tell someone who doesn't understand you where *you* came from or what *you're* doing there?

The beginnings of exasperation came riding up out of the young man's thoughts as he stared blankly at the girl before him. This is impossible, he heard his pessimistic side conclude. Fear and mutual loathing *are* easier to understand.

Frowning as the defeatism beat back his earlier resolve, Aitchley returned a critical gaze to the blue-grey woman. She continued to stand proudly before him, a glimmer of curiosity in her eyes, but there was a growing agitation in her stance as she continued to glance every now and then at the other blue-grey warriors standing nearby. There was no indication that the girl they had disarmed was the leader—Corlaiys luck dictated she most probably wasn't—but the others were not attacking regardless, probably waiting to see if their comrade was in danger before making the charge into camp and killing everybody in it.

A band of sweat began to form beneath Aitchley's hat as his pessimism conjured up even darker images. He had to do something soon, he decided. Twelve women with sharp rocks weren't going to stand in the middle of a field in the middle of the night forever. Sooner or later—regardless of their friend's predicament—they were going to make a move.

Licking at lips gone suddenly dry, Aitchley directed his gaze to the girl before him. "Uh . . ." he tried again. "We're . . . um . . . not going to hurt you." He tried another smile. "Where are you from?"

The girl did not respond, but there was another supercilious scoff from behind her. "This is ridiculous," Harris declared, pushing past the young woman and heading back toward the center of camp. "You'll be here all night trying to get this dizzard to understand you." He stalked back to his blanket. "I'm going to sleep."

Aitchley wasn't going to say anything—he'd probably do better talking to the girl without Harris's snide and mean-spirited commentary—but a sudden movement alerted the young man's instincts. It wasn't much . . . just a glint of blue and purple as the southern-city outlaw shoved his right hand into a pocket, but it was enough to kindle a spark of caution in Aitchley's mind and turn his attention away from the scantily clad female in front of him.

"Hey, wait a minute," the young man ordered the thief. He stretched out an open hand. "Give me back her knife, Harris."

A look of feigned befuddlement pulled itself across Harris's lean features. "Give you back her what?" he asked in his fraudulent confusion. "I don't know what you're talking about, scout."

Aitchley kept his hand outstretched before him. "Her rock, Harris," he insisted in a firm voice. "Give me back her rock."

As if suddenly remembering something, the southern-city rogue delved his right hand back into his pocket, making an exaggerated "O" with his mouth as he pulled free the girl's weapon. Then, peering at the stone with forced innocence, he looked up to meet Aitchley's gaze. "Hey," he said with a sheepish shrug, "it's just a rock, scout. What's the fuss?"

Aitchley waggled his open hand. "Give it to me, Harris," he demanded. "You're not supposed to have any weapons till this quest is over."

Even though the OceanGrass was lit only by the stars overhead, Aitchley caught the false mask of geniality melt away and the flash of raw hatred that flared in its place. "It's just a sharp rock, puck," Harris snarled viciously, slapping the rock flat side down in the young farmer's palm. "Don't see the harm in me having it. For all you know, I could've been picking 'em up for the last ten leagues. Maybe my pockets are just full of 'em!" Angrily, the braceleted lockpick stared hard at the young man. "So what are you going to do with it anyway?" he sneered. "Give it back to the bunghole so she can finish cuttin' your face off with it?"

Although it was meant to be an insult, Aitchley looked down at the basalt in his hand, Harris's remark reverberating through his head. What would he do with the rock? the young man mused. There was really no need for him to keep it—just so long as Harris didn't have it—but throwing it aside could be considered an insult to the young girl watching him. After all, it was her rock. So what if he did give it back? Couldn't that be regarded as a sign of trust? Wasn't it a way for the young farmer to show the blue-grey girl that he and his friends meant no harm if he returned her weapon to her?

Then again, his pessimism hissed in a hoarse whisper, it was also a good way to get his face cut off!

Hesitantly, Aitchley stared down at the crude weapon in his grasp, blue-green eyes drinking in the details. Great care had been taken to sharpen the rock to a dangerous point, and the stone seemed to gleam with a glossy ebon finish where each little flake had been chipped away. It could very easily cut flesh, Aitchley noted, and probably even leather, and if he returned it to the young girl his life could once again be in serious jeopardy. But how else could he convey that they meant no harm? Harris was right . . . He was wasting his time trying to talk to her with words she didn't understand.

Apprehensively, the young man turned back to face the blue-grey woman. His eyes kept jumping from her face to the knife in his hands, and he tried to ignore the incessant fluttering of nervous butterflies throughout his stomach as he took an uncertain step forward. The young girl continued to watch with question in her eyes, and it didn't help Aitchley's composure any when she spotted the knife in his hand and tensed her body in wary reply.

Swallowing hard, Aitchley slowly extended his left arm, gently taking her hand in his and holding her palm splayed outward. Then, nervously, he placed the knife in her open hand and stepped back, praying to whatever gods that might be listening that the girl's first response wasn't to slice open his throat.

Pitch-black hair—as glossy as the basalt rock knife in her hand—fell down around the girl's face and shoulders as she stared down at the weapon back in her grasp, her expression hidden from Aitchley by her luxurious tresses. Then, slowly, she drew her head back up, midnight-blue eyes trained on the young man before her.

Her smile was one of the most beautiful Aitchley had ever seen.

In a wet snap of dislocated vertebrae, the body convulsed fitfully one final time before going limp, dangling in his grasp like a broken marionette in black velvet trim. Scowling with disgust, General Ongenhroth Fain let the priestly corpse fall free of his fingers and slump to the hay-strewn floor with a muffled thud. Then, silently, he picked up the acolyte's fallen trident and stepped over the body, making his cautious way through the early morning light and into the dimly lit stables.

Cursed priests, the Patrolman thought foully to himself. They had delayed him long enough. The Corlaiys bastard was surely halfway to Lich Gate by now, and it was imperative the general find the whoreson before he managed to reach his goal at the Dragon's Lair. It would not behoove a general of the Patrol to be beaten by a north-side mudshoveler . . . not when there was so much at stake.

A grim frown settled itself across Fain's lips as he selected a healthy-looking mare from the stables and set about saddling the animal, cursing under his breath at the palsied, shaking weakness of his own hands. Sixteen-hour shifts of washing the plague-dead, the general mused gravely. Months of near starvation. Quarters strewn with filth and filled with disease. Lesser men would surely have died. As it was, he had no idea what had happened to the Tampenteire brat—certainly the snot-nosed little dogling was dead—but he knew the Corlaiys boy and all his friends had escaped. It had been almost a stroke of good luck that Fain had been sentenced to the penance of bodywashing. There he could keep an eye on the ancient old war hero that accompanied the boy, and when Fain awoke one morning to find the decrepit old captain gone, he knew Corlaiys and his little band of bung-ups had escaped to continue their journey. Only it hadn't been so easy for Fain to get free. A new Archimandrite had come to power—something the general couldn't help wondering if Corlaiys wasn't somehow responsible for—and security measures around the town had been increased. It had taken the Patrolman this long just to gather up a few meager supplies and ascertain the location of the nearest stables.

Allowing his self-righteous anger to give him strength, General Fain pulled himself into his saddle and jerked brutally at the reins. They would learn, he swore darkly to himself. They would all learn to never underestimate someone as clever and as resourceful as General Ongenhroth Fain. Even that fat, bloated tutor back in Solsbury would learn. No longer burdened with the squawking little lordling, General Fain was free to pursue his own venture in this little game, and it wasn't something as trivial and narrow-minded as stealing away the magic Elixir from Corlaiys in order to mass-market it. Those were thoughts for lesser men . . . Those were thoughts for men who had no dreams of real power . . . Who didn't know what to do when liquid life was placed in their hands.

But Fain knew. Oh, yes. He knew. The Elixir of Life went back to an age when magic was real, and wasting its sorcerous properties on a false legend from two hundred years in the past seemed almost criminal to the Patrolman. No . . . he had much more far-reaching goals than that. This was magic they were talking about here. This was a source of energy that had the power to bring the dead back to life. Any dead . . . no matter how decomposed or ancient the bones were. Imagine what it would do to someone who still lived . . .

General Fain directed his mount through the dark streets of Ilietis, hardly acknowledging the blood-garbled scream of an initiate who fell beneath his stolen trident. Ongenhroth Fain, lord and master immortal, the Patrolman thought vainly to himself. Yes . . . he liked the sound of that. But there was another, more pressing reason to have the Elixir. A reason that might dash his hopes like a fragile crystal goblet on hard marble floors.

Hooves thundering beneath him, Fain rode his horse out of Ilietis and into the surrounding forest, scratching absentmindedly at the dark rash that had already started to spread over the back of his right hand.

Another reason altogether . . .

* * *

The sun rose bright and yellow over the ensiform peaks of the Shadow Crags, showering the black foothills with warm morning light. Purposefully, Aitchley tried to keep his eyes on the smooth ebony rocks below him rather than on the shapely, nearly naked buttocks clenching and flexing ahead of him, but he found his attention sorely divided. The ground beneath his feet climbed upward in a gradual slope—rounded and glossy like black glass—yet its surface was a twisted, corded mat that resembled solidified porridge more than rock. Another kind of rock—sharp and jagged and hued a dark red—blanketed the hill to Aitchley's left, but their slender young guides kept them well away from that side of the slope. Aitchley had already learned the hard way that—quite different from the black stone they walked across now—this other rock cut like broken glass across bare hands or even through the tough leather soles of his boots. The flat plains of the OceanGrass stretched far below them.

Pointed shadows moved across the landscape as the sun rose higher, some of its brightness muted by the swirling, churning layer of mist above the mountains. Pools of scalding hot water tiered the foothills, some trickling down the ropelike rocks to form tiny cataracts of steaming liquid, their surfaces decorated by dancing, twisting spirals of vapor. The sweetly sour stink of algae drew up from the bottom of these pools despite their temperatures, and there was a stench of hydrogen sulphide that coated some of the larger rocks with lurid yellow encrustations of sulphur.

Aitchley shifted his attention back to the young girl clambering expertly over the foothills in front of him. It was hard for him not to notice the way the morning sunlight glinted off the almost metallic blue color of her flesh and the tantalizing swing of her tiny wisp of snakeskin that fluttered back and forth, offering quick glimpses of her well-sculpted rear end. There was even a subtle glimmer of what could have been amicability in her eyes when she threw a curious look over one bare shoulder at the young man trailing behind her.

A sudden jab caught Aitchley sharply in the ribs. "Blot your chin," Berlyn scolded the young farmer, the green in her eyes flaring a little brighter.

In response, a crimson warmth spread through Aitchley's

cheeks. "What?" he inquired in what he hoped was innocence. "I . . . I wasn't doing anything."

"You were only staring hard enough to make your eyes bug
out of your head," Berlyn retorted.

Almost slipping on the inclining rock, Aitchley briefly returned his attention to the slope in front of him and accidentally caught a glimpse of naked breast. The heat and color of
his face felt as scalding as the pools of steaming water around
them. "I . . . I . . . I . . ." he flustered.

"That's what I've always liked about you, kid," Calyx remarked from behind him, his ruddy complexion darkening as
he huffed and puffed his way up the hill. "You always say
exactly what's on your mind."

The dwarf's sarcasm did nothing to help ease the young
man's embarrassment. "No, I was just . . ." he tried again. "I
was just thinking . . . I mean, I was just wondering where we
were going. I . . . I still don't see a village or anything."

"Perhaps these females live on the eastern face of the
Mountains of Solid Blackness and have only come this way
to hunt," Gjalk speculated. "Perhaps that is where they take
us now."

Wheezing at the exertion of their climb, Sprage shook his
head. "Doesn't make sense," the healer disagreed. "Why
climb all the way over an entire mountain range just to hunt?
And with no visible provisions?" He shook his head again,
throwing one of their slender guides an appreciative glance.
"No, I'd wager they probably live somewhere up in the mountains themselves. Maybe in a cave or something."

Nervously—using his long, gorillalike arms to help him
climb—Poinqart followed the long-haired healer, throwing apprehensive glances up at the shifting, boiling cloud of mist that
hung over their heads. "Poinqart is worry-scared," the hybrid
proclaimed, crossbred emotions contorting his face. "Mountain-fire-rock is a nasty-bad place to be. Poinqart fears we may
all burn-up-die."

Tiny black eyes glistening, Eyfura SpearWielder gazed up
at the pyramidal mountains looming before them. "I believe
the WorldDweller was correct in assuming the volcano has
grown extinct," she said. "Hot springs appear to be all that
is left of its thermal activity."

"Hope so," Calyx muttered gravely. "Hate to think I was

gullible enough to follow a group of half-naked females into
an active volcano.''

His mind echoing similar dark thoughts, Aitchley continued
to clamber up the slopes of corded black rock, trying not to
think about where they might be going and also trying—unsuccessfully—to keep his eyes away from the shapely forms
of their young guides. The backs of his legs began to ache as
the sun rose higher in the sky above them, and they climbed
for a half an hour more before coming to a small rise that
leveled out into a black plateau. Sheer walls of stone surrounded them on three sides—so steep they practically seemed
to shoot straight up into the sky—and a look of weary resignation crossed Aitchley's features as he stared up at the impossible climb before them.

"Now what?" the young man muttered dismally, wondering how a group of thirteen young women could scale such
cliffs without rope . . . or wings.

As if sensing the despair that tinged the young farmer's
voice, the girl leading them—the same one Aitchley had given
her knife back to—took a step back and touched the young
man gently on his arm. "*Tee yon,*" she said in what Aitchley
assumed was reassurance, and she led him across the black
rock to where a small opening was carved in the floor of the
mountain.

A sudden bout of claustrophobia grabbed the young man
around the throat as he stared at the chiseled opening. It was
hardly wider than a biarki burrow! His mind panicked. And
he couldn't even see into its black-rock depths. For all he
knew, it could be a trap. Some deep pit that the girls wanted
to throw him in!

A flare-up of shame burned away at the young man's abrupt
fright, and he felt his face redden as he heard Calyx's words
about fear and mutual loathing echo through his head. Well,
he thought morosely to himself. This was my idea. I was the
one who wanted to prove that we could get along with a new
race. I guess this is where I have to prove it.

Still hearing the whispering rasp of his pessimism hiss horrible possibilities at the back of his brain, Aitchley sat down
beside the opening, his legs dangling into the chiseled pit. The
hole, he noticed, was much bigger than he initially thought—
and there was probably even enough room for Camera 12's

rounded bulk to squeeze through—but it was still impossible to see much detail through the gloom of the cavern. It all looked completely black, and the position of the rising sun continued to throw early morning shadows of conical mountain peaks across the plateau where they stood, only adding to the murk.

"Oh, well," Aitchley mumbled, pushing himself off the lip of the hole and jumping down into the darkness.

He hit bottom almost immediately, the sudden shock of hitting solid ground throwing his legs out from under him and plopping him unceremoniously on his backside. Good-natured laughter sounded from about him, and he spotted their youthful guide's face at the hole in the cavern's ceiling, an alluring smile drawn over grey lips as she turned around and backed carefully into the hole, bare feet finding the ladder rungs carved painstakingly into the wall near the opening.

Aitchley snatched up his hat, which had fallen from his head, and dumped it back over tousled hair, scowling at the sore spot on his rump and the sympathetic one that jabbed at his pride. Stupid hole, the young man grumbled. No wonder I couldn't see how deep it was. It's as black as the rock around it.

His curiosity aroused—and making the attempt not to stare at the shapely round backside of the blue-grey girl backing down into the cavern—Aitchley directed his attention to the cave he had entered. Lumpy black rock, as ropelike and as gnarled as those up above, made the cavern floor an uneven maze of twisting stone and knotted basalt, and millions of tiny stalactites hung from the rolling, wavy ceiling like falling water frozen in place. A faint glimmer of eerie greenish-blue light twinkled down the length of the oblong chamber, splashing otherworldy shadows across the nodular walls, and Aitchley could see a black shape etched into the cave as if a tide of water had rushed up against the rock and imprinted its image in the black stone.

The young man turned as his friends gathered around him, similar expressions of awe on their features. "Where . . . Where is this place?" the young farmer wondered.

"I believe it is called a lava tube, Master Aitchley," explained Gjuki, his deep voice resonating off the furrowed walls. "And it would appear that these women have made it their home."

"But . . . But what is it?" Berlyn queried, her eyes alight with amazement. "I mean . . . I've never seen a cave like this before."

"Perhaps because it is not a true cave as we know them, Miss Berlyn," the Rhagana gardener replied. "This chamber was formed by a river of molten lava that cooled and hardened as it went, first its banks solidifying, then its surface skinning over to form an insulating ceiling while liquid rock continued to rush through its interior. If you look closely, you may even see spots along the wall where the lava splashed up against the cavern's sides like tidal marks, and these tiny stalactites overhead are not caused by mineral-rich waters but are, rather, small droplets of lava hardened into stone."

With a certain amount of trepidation coloring his eyes, Aitchley resumed following their guides down the oblong tube. "Uh . . . There isn't any chance of this lava coming back, is there?" he worried.

A brief smile passed over Gjuki's face. "No, Master Aitchley," the gardener answered. "All the lava has long since drained from this place. We are quite safe."

Although he had never had any reason to doubt the Rhagana's words before, Aitchley couldn't help the unsettling quaver of anxiety that twisted through his bowels as he trailed the slender young girls through the wide chamber. Despite the faint greenish-blue glow ahead of them and the tiny circle of light above them from the cavern's opening, the lava tube was a scary place of black rock, imposing gloom, and surreal shapes. Aitchley had only heard of volcanos before, and the thought that he was walking through a tunnel formed by melted rock was just too unsettling to fully comprehend. After all, he had seen rocks—everybody had seen rocks!—but *melted* rocks? He just couldn't imagine temperatures hot enough to melt rock and form a cavern this wide. He half expected the tunnel to suddenly fill back up with a boiling torrent of red-hot liquid stones . . . or orange-yellow . . . or white . . . or greenish-blue. Daeminase Pits! He didn't even know what color melted stones were!

Still struggling with the uneasy grumblings of his belly, Aitchley fixed his eyes on the blue-grey girl walking ahead of him. Her bare feet stepped confidently over the uneven black rock of the cavern floor, heading purposefully for the dim glow at the end of the tunnel, and Aitchley tried to convince himself that there was nothing to worry about. *She lives here, right?* he thought, trying to console himself. *She certainly wouldn't be walking into any kind of danger, would she? I mean . . . whatever this place is . . . however it may have been formed . . . she's not going to walk to her own death, right?*

Right?

The anxiety refused to retreat as Aitchley followed their guide down the long, eerie tunnel, his footsteps echoing like the steady drip-drip of falling water around him. Gradually, the greenish-blue glow grew brighter, and the nine quest members came to a wall of black stone. A small hole—much like the one that had led into the lava tube—was chiseled out of the rock, and, lifting her leg through the circular opening, their slender young guide pulled herself through the archway and motioned for Aitchley to do the same.

Ducking through the portal, Aitchley was struck dumb by what he saw on the other side. Smooth rock—unlike the lumpy braids of dried lava of the tube and mountains—lined the floors and walls, all cast in the bright bioluminescence of green-blue lichen. Many passages led off in a variety of directions, some sloping downward while others climbed upward at sharp inclines, and some connected to other chambers by chiseled round doorways cut into the rock. There were even a few basalt pillars lining the rocky corridors, detailed carvings decorating their bases with ebony pictures and strange, craggy runes.

Other blue-grey women stopped to stare as the nine quest members clambered into their subterranean community, wonderment filling their midnight-blue eyes. Not all were dressed like the thirteen who had accompanied them, although a loincloth of shed snakeskin did appear to be the apparel of choice. Others, however, wore large gefjun feathers in their hair or tied to their arms, and some had necklaces of bone and basalt dangling between bare blue breasts. One older woman—Aitchley guessed her age to be about thirty—wore a cloak or shawl of some sort made from the same grey-black skin that made their loincloths, and a pang of anxiety shot through the young farmer's system when he realized the long trailing cape had

no seams or separations and that its entire length was made
up from a single shed snakeskin.

Aitchley was still too stunned to move as their guide stepped
forward and began to talk to the matron in the snakeskin cloak.

"What do you think they're talking about?" Berlyn whispered in the young man's ear.

Aitchley watched apprehensively as the young girl and older
woman communicated with one another in their strange, alien
language, their gazes occasionally flicking back to regard the
nine quest members. "Who knows?" he answered the blonde
with a shrug. "Hopefully it's not how to serve us for dinner."

Trying not to let Aitchley's paranoia affect her, Berlyn returned her attention to the two women, her fingers curling
nervously around the shaft of her throwing ax. She had tried
to remain calm throughout much of the morning—she didn't
want Aitchley to know how scared she had actually been—
but she didn't like the way that so many of the blue-grey
women stared at her. Maybe it was her hair, she decided.
While every one of the Grey Ladies—as she had come to call
them—seemed to have long black hair and dark blue eyes, she
had yellow-white hair and grey-green eyes. But she couldn't
help thinking that maybe it was more than just that. Maybe it
was the paleness of her skin, or the clothes she wore . . . and
why hadn't anyone else thought it odd that—even here in their
strange underground village—there didn't seem to be any Grey
Men?

None of Berlyn's worries abated as the nine continued their
trek, led now by their guide and the woman in the snakeskin
cape. Without words, the group followed the two down a series
of long tunnels and wide chambers, passing the cavern homes
of many blue-grey women and even walking through a large
area where meals were being prepared before coming to a
cavern guarded by two women. Both guards wore large silver
rings pierced through their right nipples—the very sight making Berlyn cringe and place an instinctive hand over her own
breast—and, unlike the stone-wielding women who had accompanied them from the OceanGrass, these women held
crude spears much like Eyfura's in construction.

Although a glimmer of surprise and instant suspicion ignited
in their eyes at sight of the nine, both guards stepped aside for

the older woman in the snakeskin cloak and allowed them all to enter.

A whistle of admiration escaped Sprage's lips as he stared in amazement at their new surroundings. "Will you get a load of this place?" he murmured out loud, craning his head about in an attempt to drink in all the details.

A similar jolt of awe passed through Berlyn's frame as she stepped through the rocky opening, staring in astonishment at the great circle of stone that encompassed them. Great crusty scales of phosphorescent lichen clung to the high walls, lighting the massive chamber with greenish-blue light, but the ceiling rose up so high that the young scullery maid couldn't see it through the ensuing gloom. A number of blue-grey women sat at the center of the stone amphitheater, seated around a great throne of black rock. Many were heavily decorated with silver-grey jewelry or gefjun feathers, and all carried themselves with an air of royalty. The woman in the throne, however, was dressed in far greater splendor than any of her court.

The queen of the Grey Ladies sat in a high-backed chair of glossy basalt, a huge crown of gefjun feathers encircling her head. Silver earrings pierced both earlobes and, unlike her subjects, she wore a loincloth made from soft biarki fur rather than coarse snakeskin. Shining armlets of bronze clung to her blue-grey flesh, and necklaces of bone, silver, and basalt draped the valley between full, round breasts.

"Daeminase Pits," Berlyn heard herself whisper. "She's beautiful."

The open-mouthed stares from most of the men of the group confirmed the blonde's remark.

Calyx's attention, however, was on the number of dark openings riddling the edges of the amphitheater like so many giant wormholes. "Who cares what she looks like?" the dwarf snorted. "If one of those tunnels leads to the outside, we might not have to climb over these mountains after all."

The smith's statement was enough to pull some of Aitchley's focus away from the gorgeous young woman on the throne. "What do you mean?" the young man questioned.

Calyx gave the otherwise preoccupied young farmer a disapproving look. "What I mean is, one of these tunnels might cut through the entire mountain range," the smith replied. "All we'd have to do is find out which one."

"And how are we supposed to do that?" Harris Blind-Eye replied snidely. "Maybe you didn't notice, but there are an awful lot of caves and tunnels in this place."

A look of gloom returned to settle its familiar way across the dwarf's ruddy features. "Yeah, yeah, I noticed," the smith quipped. "But you can't fault me for hoping once in my life-time!"

Harris wasn't about to let the dwarf get away with his accidental burst of optimism. "And even if there was a tunnel that went all the way through to the eastern face of the mountains, who's gonna tell us?" the outlaw challenged. A contemptuous wave of disgust took in the amphitheater of blue-grey women. "They don't speak the language, remember?"

"There are other ways to communicate," Sprage responded pragmatically. "Gestures. Head movements. Even using your eyebrows." He waggled his own as if to demonstrate. "They *are* the most mobile features on our faces."

"Or," a sudden voice in front of them said, and all nine were surprised to see the splendidly dressed queen step down off her throne, "you could just ask."

14

Battu *for* Ta

I t was one instance where Aitchley found his voice before Calyx. "You can understand us?" he blurted.

The gorgeous blue-grey young woman before him gave the farmer a brief nod of acknowledgement, stepping daintily down off her throne. "I know your language," she replied simply, offering a curt shrug that—seeing as she was topless—was one of the nicest shrugs Aitchley had ever seen. "You are not the first such creatures to pass this way."

An eager light of anticipation sparked in the young man's eyes at the thought that their communication problems were over. "Then you know what we were saying," he realized. "You'd know if there was a cave that led through the mountains, right?"

A small smile traced its way across the girl's lips. "I would know," she answered with a gentle nod.

Despite the enthusiasm building in the others, there was a look of dark cynicism passing over Calyx's face like bleak thunderclouds. "Whoa, whoa, whoa," the dwarf advised. "Since when have creatures such as ourselves passed this way?" He pinned beady eyes on the young queen. "Nobody I know of has ever been to the Shadow Crags before . . . dwarf, human, or otherwise."

The faint smile did not fade from the young girl's lips. "Not

in recent years, no,'' she agreed. "But they have come nonetheless. That is how some of us speak your language.''

Calyx continued to shake his head in disagreement. "Still
doesn't make sense," he argued. "Whether it was a long time
ago or not, we'd have heard about it. Maps. Stories. Maybe
even the fact that a race of blue women live here.''

The smith's sarcasm was lost on the young queen. "Those
who came were few,'' she explained. "And most chose to
stay.''

Obvious surprise colored the dwarf's mien. "Stay?" he echoed. "What kind of explorer just stays? Who were these people, anyway?''

A look of deep thought filtered through the young woman's
eyes. "They came many, many years ago, long before the
Mother Snake disappeared from the skies," she said. "Back
in a time when we lived further inside the mountains. They
told us of their journey and of your great god, Gaal, and how
they wished to join him beyond the Canyon Between, but
many were sickly and tired and chose to stay with the *Kwau*
and become one with the tribe instead of completing their
quest.''

"Quest?" Aitchley repeated uneasily. "There was another
quest that came by here?''

The young man was startled when Sprage unexpectedly
snapped his fingers together in sudden comprehension. "The
Pilgrimage of Folly!'' the healer abruptly understood.

Dark blue eyes fell upon the physician. "Yes,'' the young
queen responded. "That is the word they used.''

"Which word?" sniped Harris. "Pilgrimage or folly?''

A mixed expression of trollish confusion and human agony
scrawled over Poinqart's face as the half-troll faced the *Kwau*
ruler. "But Poinqart does not understand," the hybrid admitted
meekly. "Poinqart remember-thought that Mister Turetart said
everyone on the Folly-Pilgrimage dead-died.''

"Apparently not everyone," Sprage speculated. "Some obviously made it this far.''

"Some, yes," the blue-grey queen said, "but not many. Of
the twelve who arrived, only nine lived, and three of them
continued their journey to the Canyon Between.''

Skepticism kept Calyx's gaze dark. "But that was over five
hundred years ago!'' he protested. "You can't seriously expect

me to believe that you people remember all that."

A small smirk twisted the girl's lip at the dwarf's disbelief. "And, yes," she said in subtle mockery, "they even told us of the funny little men with the disagreeable dispositions." She stepped away from her throne and headed toward one of the many openings in the amphitheater wall. "Come," she instructed. "We may speak further of this matter within my chambers."

Without hesitation, Aitchley followed after the shapely young woman, Calyx stomping along beside the young farmer.

"Who's a funny little man?" the dwarf grumbled under his breath.

Berlyn sat cross-legged on a carpet of moss and gefjun down, trying not to stare at her surroundings or her host. The others sat around her on the ground—the only furniture she had seen had been the queen's basalt throne—but the thick layer of feathers and moss kept them buoyed comfortably off the chamber's hard stone floor. The young woman who was the *Kwau*'s ruler sat at the front of the group, her legs tucked under her, and Berlyn tried to keep the envious glint of jealousy out of her eyes as she drank in the nearly perfect sculptured details of the blue-grey girl's body.

Not a bit of fat on her, the young blonde noted sullenly to herself. Not a line or a wrinkle. No wonder Aitchley's gawking at her like a kid staring at a platter full of sugar apples. And how can they all walk around without any tops on? It's . . . It's . . . It's depressing, that's what it is!

Trying not to think about her own moderate chest size, the scullery maid turned her attention to the chamber they sat in. It appeared to be natural in formation—as did all the tunnels, caves, and capillarylike corridors that ran through the mountain—and was brightly lit by the scalelike encrustations of green-blue lichen growing upon the walls. The air was warm but fresh, hidden vents probably keeping the air from getting stale, and there was a small wash basin carved into one rock wall and filled with sparkling water. A band of detailed carvings ran across the width of all four walls, and—unlike the jagged runes she had seen on the basalt pillars when they had first arrived—Berlyn noticed that many of the engravings were of tiny pictures that might, if you followed the line in a particular direction, tell some story.

Also in the room stood another young *Kwau*, a single hoop earring of silver piercing her right earlobe—probably signifying some rank or position of some sort, Berlyn assumed—but wearing the skimpy snakeskin loincloth that the hunting party had worn. A single gefjun feather was tied in her pitch-black tresses, and Berlyn guessed that her age was somewhere around fourteen or fifteen . . . perhaps younger. Her blue-grey breasts were round but small, and her youthful hips had yet to flare out in a sure sign of womanhood, but she carried herself with an air of maturity despite the glimmer of fascination that shone in her deep blue eyes.

The queen of the blue-grey women, who said her name was Winema, settled herself more comfortably on the cushions of moss and feathers and threw a curious gaze out across the nine members of the quest. "Would I be correct in assuming that you are on a pilgrimage yourselves?" she asked candidly.

Still muttering about past indignities, Berlyn saw the look of panic spread across Aitchley's face when the young man realized Calyx wasn't going to answer for them. "Ummm . . . more or less," the young farmer replied. "We're heading in the same direction, anyway."

"So a passage through the mountains would be beneficial to your cause," the young ruler observed.

Aitchley shrugged. "It wouldn't hurt," he remarked bashfully.

Tiny eyes glittered in the green-blue glow of the bioluminescent lichen as Gjuki turned to face the young women. "Does such a corridor exist?" the Rhagana wondered.

Although a look of amazement was etched on her youthful features, the young girl behind the queen nodded curtly. "There is such a passage," she answered, "but it is *ta*. Forbidden."

Berlyn felt a sudden chill of apprehension scurry its way up her spine. "Forbidden?" she echoed. "Why?"

Despite her abrupt anxiety, the young scullery maid still noted the odd look the queen gave her before replying. "Many years ago the *Kwau* lived deep in the heart of these mountains—some say at the very center of the world itself—but it has been many centuries since we have ventured that far into the earth. These mountains are riddled with catacombs and caverns, and even the most skilled of *Kwau* could get lost within its black rock depths.''

"But you said three of the pilgrimage had gone on," Berlyn was quick to point out. "How'd they do that if they didn't climb over the mountains?''

"The passage that leads to the Canyon Between had not yet been sealed off in those times," the younger girl commented. "As the years have gone by, the *Kwau* have moved up through the mountains, choosing to live closer to the surface than down below it. And as we have moved, certain branches and corridors have been sealed off so that no one would become confused and lost in the ancient, unused passageways of our ancestors.''

"But this tunnel is still there?" Aitchley questioned.

Queen Winema nodded once. "The tunnel still exists," she said. "It is only a matter of lifting the *ta* and allowing you free passage.''

Aitchley didn't like the sound of that. "So how do we do that?" he wanted to know.

The young queen shrugged, and Aitchley tried not to be too visibly distracted. "We must bring the matter before the *kel*," she explained, "and a vote will be taken. If the *ta* is lifted, Taci has already agreed to guide you through the passage.''

"So why the vote?" inquired Sprage, glancing briefly at the younger girl who had volunteered to be their guide. "If Taci wants to take us, why don't we just go?''

A look of anxiety creased the youthful Taci's face. "You do not understand *ta*," she said firmly. "To break *ta* would be *dheu*. Death. Only a full agreement of the *kel* can break the *ta* and give us safe passage.''

"So how do we go about doing that?" the healer wondered, recognizing a bureaucracy despite the blue-grey skin.

"I shall call a meeting of the *kel* to be held immediately in which we shall discuss your request," Winema said. "I will need the leader of your group, though, to argue your case.''

Berlyn could almost see the apprehension devour Aitchley alive, causing the color to drain out of his face as the others all looked at him. Nervously, the young man tossed a glance at Calyx, but the dwarf was too busy still grumbling about being called a funny little man to notice. Berlyn could almost hear the worriedly frenzied thoughts of complete failure undoubtedly whizzing through the young. man's brain, and she wished there was something she could do or say to help ease the young man's fears and assure him that he would not fail them.

Throwing a nervous glance at the others about him, Aitchley forced himself to meet Winema's gaze. "I . . . I guess that's me, then," he declared.

There was a momentary peal of silence as both young women exchanged glances before laughing out loud, and Berlyn noticed the way Aitchley's pale features hurriedly took on a warm red hue.

"What?" the young farmer demanded, embarrassed but not knowing why. "What's so funny?"

Apologetically, Winema tried to stifle her laughter by placing a dainty blue-grey hand across her lips, yet the unconstrained mirth in her eyes continued to tease the young man. "I'm sorry," she said in between giggles, "but I said the *leader* of your group. Your *gwenn*. The *Kwau* do not recognize males as *gwenn*. The very meaning of the word connotes 'female ruler.' "

"Well, then . . . I . . ." Aitchley flustered, trying to hide his embarrassment. "If you didn't mean me, who did you mean?"

Winema stabbed a rigid finger forward. "Her," she replied. "Your *gwenn*."

Berlyn blinked hard at the finger pointing right at her face.

All the previous thoughts she had assumed had been roiling about in Aitchley's skull now tornadoed through Berlyn's mind in a whirlwind of confusion and worry. Anxiously, she sat with her back against Winema's throne, Taci beside her, occasionally whispering brief translations in her ear of the *kel*'s discussion.

The *kel*, Berlyn learned, was a group of thirteen women, all of whom held some position of authority in the *Kwau* tribe. She didn't pretend to fully understand the way the blue-grey women ran their village—Daeminase Pits! She could hardly keep straight which had more power: a viscount or a duke!— but she did understand a few things. Men, Taci had told her, were not allowed in the women's village—they were *ta*—and were kept separate. Only during the rite of *jwher* were the males necessary . . . and Berlyn didn't need to ask for a translation to understand that! Also, there was a kind of unspoken understanding between the females. While their primitive dress and crude weaponry made Berlyn think these people may have been prone to violence, she was surprised to learn that the *Kwau* never fought amongst themselves. That, too, was *ta*.

Worriedly, Berlyn drew her attention away from the beautiful blue-grey women arguing in their strange language all around her and cast her gaze to the far wall of the amphitheater. Despite the rules that males were not allowed where the females lived, Winema had allowed the other members of the quest to stand at the entrance of her private chambers and observe. It was a special occasion, the queen had explained, much like the one five hundred years ago, and the other *Kwau* needed to see Berlyn's *bru* or family tribe. The fact that the scullery maid was *gwenn* of such a large number of males gave her an added level of influence—not even the queen had such a number of males in her own *bru*—and the fact that many of the quest-members were not even human only added to the mystique. Even Berlyn's yellow-white hair was enough to put some of the *Kwau* in a state of near-disbelief, and many of them were beginning to refer to her as *Gwenn* Luyan, which—as Taci had told her—translated roughly into calling her some sort of moon goddess.

Berlyn tried not to pay too much attention to the foreign debate that was going on around her. Most of the *Kwau*, it seemed—although reluctant to lift the *ta* on the ancient passageway—had agreed for some reason or another to do so and let the group go on, but there was one woman who, even now, continued to argue vehemently against it. Taci told her her name was Cilka, and Berlyn didn't know what her problem was, but the woman defiantly did not like her.

Cilka, like the other *Kwau*, was a beautiful woman probably younger than twenty years of age. She was as exotically attractive as the other girls—although taller than most—and, judging from the silver ring pierced through her right nipple, Berlyn assumed she was the leader of the guards or some sort of military captain. Right then she was arguing with Alaqua, the young girl Aitchley had befriended back in the Ocean-Grass, and the term *"reu'dheu"* kept coming up. Taci had whispered that *reu'dheu* meant "Red Death," but it still

didn't help the young scullery maid make any sense of what
was being said.

Berlyn caught the eye of Aitchley standing behind Camera
12, a look of concern carved on his features. He tried to flash
her a lopsided smile of reassurance, but the young blonde
could tell it wasn't heartfelt. Poor Aitchley, she thought almost
humorously to herself. He worries about everything. If he
wasn't worrying about having to do this himself, he's worrying
about me having to do it!

There was a rustle of agitated feathers above the young
girl's head. "Thisz isz zstupid," Trianglehead proclaimed
from the arm of Winema's throne. He cocked his head at the
gefjun feathers the *Kwau* had given Berlyn to wear in her hair.
"You look like a krow'sz butt," the fledgling remarked.

Berlyn pursed her lips at the gyrofalc. "Thanks a lot," she
retorted, craning her neck to look up at the bird. "Now be
quiet. This is important."

Trianglehead shuffled across the arm of the chair impatiently. "Not important," he decided. "Zstupid."

Knowing better than to argue with the bird, Berlyn bit her
lip and stayed silent. She wished that the *Kwau* hadn't been
in such awe of the fledgling and that she could have left the
bird behind with Aitchley, but no *gwenn* had ever had a tamed
gyrofalc as a part of her *bru* before. By wearing the fledgling
like an ornament on her shoulder, both Gjuki and Sprage had
hoped that Berlyn could strengthen her influence on the *kel*
. . . or, at least, strengthen the rumors of Luyan and her godly
abilities.

Something was suddenly said by the statuesque Cilka that
drew a collective gasp from the other members of the *kel*.
Urgently, Taci leaned over and whispered in Berlyn's ear:
"The *kel* is *ctyewe*. Deadlocked. Cilka refuses to acknowledge
you as a member of this tribe. She says the threat of the Red
Death is too great to risk helping an *udse*—an outsider—such
as yourself. She will not agree to lift the *ta*."

A sudden dam of worry broke free in an overpowering rush
that swamped Berlyn with a horrible feeling of failure. I'm
going to ruin this for everybody, the young girl thought dismally to herself. We'll never be able to use this passage, and
it'll be all my fault.

Heavy desperation lit in the scullery maid's eyes. "Isn't

there something I can do?'' she queried.

Taci looked helpless. "The other members of the *kel* have accepted you as a member of our tribe," she said. "Only Cilka disputes your right. If you so wish it, you can challenge her word by declaring *battu*."

"*Battu*?" Berlyn repeated, her desperation growing with each passing moment. "What's that?"

"Ritual combat," explained Taci. "Very rare."

The scullery maid blanched, an electrical jolt of fear momentarily dampening her predicted failure. Ritual combat? she asked herself in horror. I'm no fighter! She tossed a cursory look at her throwing ax. I've got a superior weapon, but I don't know how to use it properly. And, besides, this Cilka's some sort of captain of the guards! It's not like she'd be a slouch if it came to fighting!

Apprehensively—the thought of impending failure heavy in her mind—Berlyn flicked her gaze toward Cilka before returning her attention to the young girl by her side. "What does this *battu* entail?" she asked in her uncertainty. "I mean ... how is it decided?" A frightening thought struck her. "It's not to the death, is it?"

"Not by intention," Taci replied. She flung an unpleasant glare at Cilka. "*Battu* is decided when one combatant concedes. Sometimes, and with great remorse, this does not happen, and death is the end result."

An arctic terror welled up in Berlyn's throat. Oh, great, the young blonde moaned to herself. Either I bung up here or I get killed fighting with their stupid captain of the guards! Nomion's Halberd! Now I can understand why Aitchley's so frantic all the time!

Desperately, Berlyn returned her critical gaze to the arguing *Kwau*. "Is there ... Is there anything else I can do?" she quailed. "Something else that can get Cilka to change her mind? I mean ... I don't really want to fight her, but if that's my only alternative ..."

Taci muffled her sudden laughter. "Oh, no, *Gwenn* Berlyn," the young girl explained merrily, "*Kwau* do not fight *Kwau*. That is *ta*. Do you not remember that I told you so?"

A veil of confusion abruptly masked the young blonde's thoughts. "Yeah, but you just said ..."

"*Battu* is ritual combat, but it is not between *Kwau*," Taci went on. "Cilka's champion would face your champion to determine the outcome."

Like a heavy weight lifting off her shoulders, Berlyn felt a wave of relief wash over her. "You mean *we* wouldn't actually be fighting?" she questioned. "We'd each pick a champion— like, what? One of the men from our *bru*?—and they'd do the actual fighting?"

Taci nodded. "Yes, of course." She smiled brightly at the young scullery maid. "What else are men good for?"

The beginnings of an idea began to evolve in Berlyn's brain. "Then tell this Cilka that I challenge her to *battu*," the blonde instructed. "Tell her that if I win, she'll agree to lift the *ta*."

Taci's smile grew into one of admiration. "She would have no other choice, *Gwenn* Berlyn," the young girl responded. "If you triumph in *battu*, you have proven your word to be *deru*. Undisputed truth. Cilka would have no choice but to obey you."

An unexpected fire of determination fanned to life in Berlyn's chest. "Good," she said, her idea coalescing more and more. "Then go ahead and tell her."

As Taci turned away to translate Berlyn's challenge to the other *Kwau*, Trianglehead ruffled his feathers and stuck his head disinterestedly under one wing. "Like I zsaid," the fledgling grumbled, "zstupid."

A great commotion filled the amphitheater as the young girl speaking for Berlyn made a sudden statement and all the women in the great chamber started speaking at once. One of the women, a tall girl with a silver ring piercing her right nipple, took the news with a sudden arching of her back, but a nefarious grin stretched across her grey lips as she turned to regard the area where Berlyn sat. Solemnly, she offered the blonde a menacing nod of acceptance and turned quickly on her heel, stalking past the place where Aitchley watched the unfolding drama with the rest of the quest.

"Gaal damn it," the young man swore unhappily under his breath. "I wish I knew what the Pits they were saying!"

"It would appear they have come to some agreement," Eyfura observed, "but I am unable to tell if that is a good thing or a bad thing."

"Probably bad, if you ask me," Calyx put in. "That one

gilt didn't look like she was gonna give in for all the salt in Malvia. And then she just turns and walks away ... ?'' He shook his head in pessimistic prognostication. "We're doomed, I tell you. Doomed."

Sprage turned a sardonic eye on the smith, a wry smile twisting his clean-shaven features. "You're just little dwarven sunshine today, aren't you?'' he taunted. "I just think you're still mad about being called a funny little man."

"Let's not poke at open sores, Sprage," Calyx shot back. "There's a little matter of hiding under bushes that I could keep bringing up if I felt so inclined."

"Go right ahead," the healer teased. "At least I can learn to stop hiding under bushes; you'd still be a funny little man."

Aitchley waved a silencing hand at the two. "Quiet," the young man snapped. "That girl's coming back."

He didn't know why, but a cold chill clamped around the base of his spine as Aitchley watched Cilka return to the amphitheater. A confident smirk was drawn on the blue-grey guard's face, and her expression was haughty and self-assured as she returned to her position in front of Winema's throne. Behind her—Aitchley noticed with an increase of anxiety—trailed a blue-grey man of rippling muscle.

"What ..." the young man started to ask the others but was quickly shushed into silence.

Trying to fight the rising panic in his throat, Aitchley turned back around to stare at the blue-grey man. Like the women, he wasn't particularly tall—perhaps a little shorter than Aitchley--but it only served to compact his muscular framework of metallic blue flesh. His hair was short and black, and he clutched a crude ax with a basalt blade in one blue-grey hand. He wore no clothing at all—not even a skimpy loincloth of snakeskin—and Aitchley couldn't help but notice the way the green-blue glow of the lichen seemed to outline all the flexing, rippling arcs and curves of crafted sinew and mighty thews. Daeminase Pits! It even looked like the man's dangleberries had muscles!

His anxiety growing, Aitchley turned back to his friends. "What ..." he tried again.

The other quest-members motioned for the young man to be quiet as Winema pulled herself to her feet, raising bare arms for their attention. Her deep blue eyes sought out the eight

people at the edge of the amphitheater, and she gave them a
formal bow of her head as she said, "*Gwenn* Berlyn has challenged Cilka to the ritual combat of *battu*. The battle is decided
when one opponent gives in or is no longer able to continue
the fight." She turned imperiously on Berlyn. "*Gwenn* Berlyn," she instructed, "please select your champion."

Aitchley swallowed hard as Berlyn stood up and approached. Somebody's got to fight this guy? the young man
thought, panicking, staring in amazement at the mass of blue-
grey muscle swinging his ax in eager anticipation. What was
Berlyn thinking when she agreed to this? Surely she doesn't
think *I'm* gonna fight him! I mean . . . look at him! The guy's
huge! Maybe Poinqart, but certainly not me! Maybe not even
Poinqart! This guy looks like he might even be too much for
a half-troll!

The growing nervousness set the young man's stomach on
edge as Berlyn drew nearer, looking beautiful in her torn and
sleeveless dress and decorated by gefjun feathers. He didn't
like the way her grey-green eyes seemed to focus intently on
his general direction, and he prayed fervently that she wasn't
pinning this whole bantu or baktu or whatever it was on him.
She knew that he wasn't a real fighter—knew he wasn't even
a very good farmer—but . . . Oh, no! He had made such a display of acting like he knew what he was doing back when they
were practicing in the Bentwoods! And Berlyn had always
been caught up in that damn romantic notion that Aitchley was
her own personal Cavalier . . . She hadn't taken all that seriously, had she? She didn't truly think the young farmer was
as accomplished and as undefeatable as Procursus Galen, did
she?

Gefjun feathers bobbing in her hair, Berlyn stopped before
Aitchley; sheepishly, the young man tried to make his body
small behind Camera 12's arachnid frame.

"There," Berlyn announced, pointing proudly. "This is my
champion."

Aitchley blinked hard at the finger pointing in his direction.

15

Apology Accepted

Head bowed and eyes downcast, Aitchley Corlaiys trudged through the dark, musty corridor of rock with a discernible shuffle to his step. He didn't feel much like joining in on the excitable chatter of his comrades, and, every time he looked up at the blonde walking ahead of him, he felt a sharp jab of shame lance through his pride. He was more content to hang back, silently brooding, and let the darkness and solemnity of the ancient passageways hold him safely in their gloomy embrace.

"Absolutely ingenious," Calyx continued to heap praise upon Berlyn. "That big oaf never even had a chance."

"Poinqart thinks it laughing-funny," the half-troll said with a look of hybrid humor on his face. "Poinqart only wishes he was as clever-smart as Missy Berlyn."

Aitchley noticed the hint of red color Berlyn's cheeks. "It wasn't all that special," she demurred coyly. "I just did what I had to do to get us here."

Calyx made a rude noise at the girl's modesty. "Yeah," he exclaimed in rare enthusiasm, "but to pick Camera 12 as your champion . . . ! That guy never even knew what hit him!"

A pang of resentment bubbled through Aitchley like curdled milk. Oh, yeah, he mused nastily to himself. Berlyn's just *so* smart. Stupid Aitchley would have never have thought of anything as clever as having Camera 12 fight that big muggwort!

Noooo! Not Aitchley! He was too busy *hiding* behind Camera 12 because he thought Berlyn was gonna pick him!

The young man shook his head in self-disgust. I'm an idiot! he condemned himself. What kind of a bunged-up, muddle-headed, ragworm would even *think* of picking me to fight that guy? And now I'm acting all pissed off 'cause Berlyn *didn't* pick me and went and did something as smart as picking Camera 12! So what's my problem? Am I mad at her for making me look like a fool 'cause I thought she was gonna pick me, or is it because she did something that I would have never have thought to do? I don't know! All I do know is that I'm an idiot . . . and I've probably blown whatever chance I may have had with Berlyn because of it!

Sullenly, the young man trailed the others through the abandoned tunnels of the *Kwau* ancestors, uninterested in the dark, fusty corridors. He didn't care that there were pictographs and glyphs dating back nearly four hundred years on the walls, nor was he listening very intently to Taci's warnings about fissured or weakened floors and ceilings. He was in a Mood, and he had gotten very good at it over the last seventeen years of his life.

As the animated discussion continued on around her, Berlyn threw a concerned glance over one shoulder at the young man plodding along despondently behind her. He was in another one of his deep funks, she understood, but it never ceased to amaze her how inappropriate those moods could be. The last time she had seen him so visibly depressed, he had just successfully recovered Harris's amulet from Archimandrite Sultothal and had escaped unscathed. At least that time Berlyn had had a river to help her cheer the young man up . . . this time it looked like she'd have to do it on her own.

Trying not to be too obvious, Berlyn slowed her pace, dropping back from the front of the group to join Aitchley at the rear. Even though he knew she was there, the young farmer did not acknowledge her presence and kept his blue-green eyes glued to the dark, featureless floor of the caverns.

A tinge of worry glinted in the scullery maid's eyes as she turned a forced smile on the young man. "Is something wrong?" she wondered.

Aitchley kicked at a loose stone. "No," he replied, a rude curtness to his voice.

Berlyn watched the stone skitter off into the darkness and gloom. "Oh," she answered back, a barb of Calyx-influenced sarcasm invading her tone, "I just thought there was something wrong. I mean . . . you haven't spoken a word to me since I beat Cilka in *battu*."

Although he had managed to depress himself, the young man was unable to turn his resentment on the petite blonde. "Well, what am I supposed to say?" he wanted to know. "Nice job? Good going?" He threw the ground an unpleasant frown. "Absolutely brilliant idea choosing Camera 12 to be your champion?"

"Is that what this is about?" the blonde suddenly asked back. "You're mad at me because I won?"

The sheer stupidity of the words almost snapped Aitchley free of his melancholy. "No!" he responded sharply. "I'm just . . . I mean . . . It's just that . . ." He dismissed her with an unfriendly wave of his hand. "Awww . . . forget it."

A defiant anger blossomed behind the young girl's breast. "No, I will not forget it, Aitchley Corlaiys," she scolded him. "I do something good, and, instead of being happy for me, you get into another one of your moods." Eyebrows knitted above grey-green eyes. "What would you have preferred I do?" she interrogated. "Lost?"

As more and more of the young blonde's logic made its way past the young man's dark side, the peaceful escape into despairing solitude slipped away from him. "No," he replied, his voice losing some of its edge. "It's just . . . What I mean is . . ."

"The least you could do is say that you're glad you let me come along!" interrupted the blonde. "If it wasn't for me, you wouldn't even have had a female here to talk to the *kel*!"

"That's not true," Aitchley's melancholy argued. "We would have had Eyfura."

The look of abrupt shock and subsequent rage that crossed Berlyn's face made Aitchley wish he had kept his mouth shut. "Eyfura?" the young blonde nearly shrieked. "The *Kwau* don't even recognize Rhagana as male or female—they just think they're some kind of weird tree people! Daeminase Pits, Aitchley! They're not even built the same way we are! What were you going to do to convince the *Kwau* that she was female? Have her show them where her bunghole's *supposed* to be?''

The young man's depression all but dissipated before the scullery maid's sudden onslaught of angry logic and gynecological references, leaving him floundering in a sea of fragmented protests and apologies. ''I . . . uh . . . I mean . . . ummm . . .''

Grey-green fire rose higher in Berlyn's stare. ''That's what this is about, isn't it?'' She unexpectedly understood. ''You're mad at yourself because you almost didn't let me come along.'' Her eyes transfixed him with her accusation. ''That's it, isn't it?''

Aitchley stared guiltily at the cracks and fissures crisscrossing the stone floor beneath his feet. ''Ummm . . .'' he said in his defense.

An expression of smug certainty drew across Berlyn's attractive features. ''That's it,'' she said again, confirming her own beliefs. ''You're upset because you almost left me behind, and, if you had done that, you would have never been able to use this tunnel.'' She shook her head in muted astonishment. ''I don't believe you,'' she admitted in her awe. ''You're mad at yourself for something you *didn't* to?''

Aitchley felt his stupidity grow at Berlyn's chastisement. ''Well,'' he answered sheepishly, ''I guess . . .''

He was interrupted by a sudden report—like a split-second crash of thunder—and the young man felt the ground unexpectedly drop beneath his weight. Startled, he stared down at where the floor had started to splinter and break below him.

''Oh, bung,'' he managed to swear before crashing through the ancient rock into the blackness beyond.

Berlyn's scream followed the young man down into the darkness, rebounding and resonating throughout the ancient cavern. Warm air rushed up around him—bringing with it an unpleasant memory of falling and spiraling uncontrollably down the face of a jagged cliff—and Aitchley tried to shift his body to scc where he was falling. He had left the yellow-orange glare of Taci's torch far above him, but tiny flecks of lichen grew even here, illuminating the young man's plunge through a cylindrical larynx of black stone with an eerie green-blue haze of luminescence.

Another scream from Berlyn drew the young man out of his

own shock and fear, and he spun in mid-air to see the young blonde falling beside him, the torn and tattered folds of her skirt billowing up around her like the remains of a ragged parachute. Desperately, the young man tried to reach out and take her hand, but she remained just out of reach. He knew deep down inside it wouldn't make a difference one way or the other—plummeting straight down at such speeds, they were sure to splatter once they hit bottom—-but he had to make the try. He hated to think they were going to die without first being able to ask Berlyn to forgive him for being such a warthead.

Something unexpectedly halted their fall, catching them in netlike fibers that bounced and sagged with their sudden weight. A bewildered woof of escaping air expelled itself through Aitchley's mouth, momentarily bringing bright lights to the darkness behind his eyelids, and the young farmer just lay there, winded, the net they had landed in still swaying and bouncing beneath them.

Berlyn lay beside the young man, grey-green eyes staring up at the vast expanse of blackness through which they had fallen. "Where . . . What happened?" she gasped in a tiny little voice.

"Guess we should have been paying more attention to what Taci was saying," Aitchley attempted to joke, still trying to get his breath back.

Feeling a gust of warm air strike her bare thigh—and realizing that her skirt had fallen away and was showing far too much skin--Berlyn tried to sit up and rearrange her dress, yet something yanked brutally at her hair when she tried to do so.

"Ouch!" the young scullery maid exclaimed. She tried to pull her arm free. "Hey!" she abruptly realized. "I can't move!"

Questioningly, Aitchley tried to turn his head to look at her and found his hat stuck tight to the springy, meshlike netting. "Wha . . . Hey! Neither can I!"

With a soft, wet, squishing sound, Aitchley managed to tear one arm loose from the strands of silver netting and roll on his side to look at Berlyn. The blonde lay perpendicular to the young man, the torn seam of her dress parting down the entire length of her naked right hip, and her hair was splayed out behind her and also stuck to the strange trawl that had caught them. Sticky strands of some gummy substance clung to Aitchley's free arm and shoulder, and the young man stared hard at the gooey strings that held him and Berlyn helpless to the very thing that had saved their lives.

Aitchley tentatively touched a line of netting and felt his hand stick to its viscid surface. "What in the Pits . . . ?" he mumbled out loud, tearing his hand loose.

A sudden weight caused the net to sag, and Aitchley looked questioningly at Berlyn. The young blonde, however, was pinned and unable to move, barely able to turn her head to look in the direction of the sudden weight. Curiously, Aitchley slipped out of his glued hat—wincing as he tugged out a few hairs—and turned as well, squinting through the dim green-blue glow at whatever had clambered onto the silver net with them.

Six gemlike eyes glimmered in the faint green-blue nimbus of the lichen, large, yellow-white legs probing delicately at the edges of its web. Chelicerae as thick as Aitchley's arm quavered expectantly, and a hungry flame blossomed in the giant spider's many eyes as it stepped out further onto its web and toward its prey.

Aitchley felt Berlyn's shudder of revulsion reverberate through the silver webbing. "Bugs," the young girl observed with obvious distaste. "I hate bugs!"

Pedipalps waving, the spider advanced.

Frantically, Calyx skirted the edges of the cave-in, beady eyes peering through the impenetrable blackness of the shaft. Even with the crackling light of Taci's torch poised strategically above his head, the dwarf was only able to skim the surface of the pit's darkness, his grim mien growing ever darker with each passing second.

Harris pulled himself out of a crouch at the lip of the pit. "They're gone, scout," the southern-city outlaw declared. "Shaft's at least a quarter of a league deep."

"They're not gone," Calyx retorted, his misplaced optimism becoming apparent. "They're fine. Trust me." Beady eyes fixed on the red-violet shape napping contentedly on Camera 12's back. "You," demanded the dwarf. "Bird. Fly down there. See if you can find them."

Perturbedly, Trianglehead drew his head out from under his

wing and trained contemptuous diamond-blue eyes on the dwarven smith. "Get paraszitesz," the fledgling remarked. He fluttered bandaged wings as if to remind Calyx. "Kan't, remember? Zstupid human klipped my wingsz."

Hardly disheartened, Calyx quickly turned his attention to Sprage. "You, then," he demanded once again. "Do you still have that rope you used back in Desireah's castle?"

Sprage had to blink a few times, the dwarf's urgent brevity momentarily clouding his brain. "Uhhh . . ." he answered unsteadily. "I . . . I think so. It should be in one of the packs."

Even as the smith started a quick inspection of their supplies, the long-haired healer added, "But it's not going to be long enough." A somber expression creased the physician's features. "Face it, Calyx," he said sadly. "They're gone."

With Calyx too busy searching through their belongings, it was another voice that answered for the dwarf, the sorrow and despair in its tone echoing off the ancient rock walls. "No!" Poinqart protested with hybrid conviction. "Mister Aitch and Missy Berlyn are not alive-no-more-dead! Poinqart knows such things! Poinqart believe-agrees with Mister Calyx-dwarf! Both of Poinqart's friends are well! Poinqart has seen Mister Aitch tumble-fall before, and Mister Aitch turned out fine!"

Solemnly, Gjuki placed a comforting hand upon the half-troll's bulky shoulder. "I am afraid that circumstances speak differently this day, Master Poinqart," the Rhagana gardener said softly. "It would appear that a grave misfortune has befallen us all."

The half-troll jerked himself away from Gjuki's touch, yellow-black eyes flaring with determination. "No!" he roared his defiance. "Poinqart will show you! Poinqart will show you all!"

And, so saying, the hybrid leapt into the pit after his friends.

The vibrations along the length of the web increased as the enormous spider drew nearer, stopping every now and again to test the strands of its web with inquisitive, plucking motions. Horrified, Aitchley could only watch as the giant arachnid advanced, struggling futilely with the sticky strands that kept him pinned on his back. Berlyn struggled alongside him, tugging frantically at the cemented folds of her skirt and at the gooey tendrils of adhesive that entangled her hair and her legs.

Bloody typical Corlaiys luck, the young farmer mused gravely to himself. Only Aitchley Corlaiys could survive a fall like that and still wind up being eaten by a giant spider! Bloody, bunging typical!

A sudden idea unexpectedly pushed its way through the young man's pessimism, and he forced himself to sit up as far as the webbing at his back would allow. The spider was nearly on top of him—he could clearly see all the fine, yellow-white hairs that covered its grotesquely oversized body—and he hurriedly threw his shoulders back, slipping his arms free of the maroon-colored backpack he wore. A wild burst of adrenaline surged through the young farmer's body as he felt Tin William's knapsack slide off his shoulders—the pack still locked in a gooey embrace with the silver web but the young man now free—and he desperately jerked out his sword, spinning in the web to meet the oncoming monstrosity.

A garbled hiss escaped the giant spider's mouth parts as Aitchley's sword slashed a bloody groove across its face, causing it to draw back in sudden alarm. Green venom drooled in viscous globs down the length of the creature's ebon fangs, and it scuttled sideways in its web in an attempt to circumvent the young man's weapon and attack.

Legs still glued to the silvery webbing, Aitchley threw his upper body forward, lunging with his sword at the giant spider's legs. A piercing, high-pitched squeal reverberated throughout the dark shaft as the spider stumbled forward, one of its many legs severed. Pale blood spattered the webbing, and the monster staggered drunkenly off its guidelines, accidentally sticking two of its own legs to its web.

Earnestly, Aitchley swung again, but the spider hurriedly retreated, green-black fire flashing in its numerous eyes. Berlyn released a frightened squeak as one of the spider's legs dropped down close to her head, but the creature continued to back away, what might have been arachnid annoyance glinting in its eyes.

Thrashing wildly, Berlyn managed to tear most of her hair free of the web's sticky grip. "Now what do we do?" she asked breathlessly, eyeing the spider that had warily retreated into the shadows.

Aitchley cut repeatedly at the webbing stuck to his legs, yet the silver strands were undamaged by his ceaseless blows. "I'd like to get us the Pits out of here,'' the young man grunted, continuing to hack and slash. "Can you see how far off the ground we still are?"

Causing the web to bounce and sway, Berlyn managed to roll halfway over on her side, grey-green eyes peering through the gloom of the dimly lit shaft. "Not very; I think I can see my throwing ax." Aitchley caught the tinge of self-reproach that soured her voice. "I'm not sure."

Sudden motion caused the web to lurch and shift even more, and Berlyn looked up to see the giant spider reemerge from its murky den, drawn back out by instincts and the young girl's movements in its web. A frightened scream tore instinctively from the back of the blonde's throat as the yellow-white monstrosity came lumbering down the web at her, and she began to struggle more violently against the sticky strands and threads that continued to hold her hostage.

Managing to rip one leg free of the goo, Aitchley readied his sword. "This is all my fault," he told the blonde remorsefully. "None of this would have happened if I wasn't acting like such a jerk."

Berlyn was too frightened to accept his apology.

The arguing stopped as a high-pitched keening arose from the blackness of the cave-in, and even Poinqart stopped struggling in Gjuki's powerful grasp that held him suspended over the lip of the pit as the inhuman scream faded into echoes around them. A very human scream followed, and all seven of the remaining quest-members threw inquisitive glances at one another before directing their gaze on the shattered stone floor at their feet.

"It is not possible," Gjalk DarkTraveller said with rare Rhagana awe. "How could they survive a fall such as this?"

Sprage risked a quick peek into the darkness. "Maybe it's not as deep as it looks," he suggested, making quite sure he didn't step too close to the edge even though he was standing safely behind both Harris and Eyfura.

Still dangling over the edge of the pit—held aloft only by Gjuki's right hand clamped protectively upon his shoulder—a hybrid look of trollish anger and human determination crossed Poinqart's olive-green features. "Who cares if it is deep-fardrop or not?" the half-troll insisted, resuming his struggle in

Gjuki's grip. "Mister Aitch and Missy Berlyn are all-right-
alive, and Poinqart must hurry-run to their aid!" Yellow-black
eyes swung accusingly on Gjuki. "Release Poinqart, Mister
Gjuki-plant!" the hybrid demanded. "Let-him-free now!"

Even as a contemplative look of uncertainty drew over the
Rhagana's usually impassive mien, a smug smile stretched beneath the silver and black hairs of Calyx's beard. "You heard
the troll," the dwarf quipped. "Let him go."

Gjuki's fingers relaxed their grip.

Molten panic burned through Aitchley's mind, leaving behind a seared and charred lava flow of pessimism and failure.
His right leg remained entangled in the silvery strands of the
giant spider's web, and, no matter how hard he tried or how
far he stretched, he could not reach Berlyn to save her. If the
spider came toward the young girl's legs, Aitchley might have
a chance to catch it with a wild swing, but if it went for her
upper half—as Aitchley feared it would—he knew only too
well that he'd never be able to reach her . . . not unless he
somehow managed to finish pulling himself free or grow an
extra three feet in length!

Its wounded leg drawn beneath it, the spider was more cautious in its approach, plucking tentatively at the many silver
strands of its enormous web. Aitchley didn't know exactly
what it was doing—probably sensing where he and Berlyn
were caught by its many-legged touch—-but it seemed to the
young man that the giant arachnid was almost taunting him.
Tug a few times at a strand of web. Make sure the weight is
still there. Take a cautious step forward. Tug a few more times.
Still out of reach? Good. It was almost as if the horrid creature
knew Aitchley wouldn't be able to reach it and was savoring
its coming victory.

An abrupt idea forked through the young man's growing
despair like a shaft of blue-white lightning, and he turned
quickly to the backpack he had left imprisoned in the sticky
netting. Quick fingers jerked at the black, teethlike fasteners
Tin William had called a zipper, and the young man only
prayed that he remembered correctly. He had very nearly lost
track of whose turn it was—although that sometimes helped
because it made him that much harder to "read"—but he felt
a tiny rush of relief pass through his system as he spotted the

evil wink of black steel concealed among his many supplies. Hastily, he pulled Renata free of his backpack and carefully weighed the blade in his hand. He had tried throwing it before and he hadn't been all that successful—he could remember quite vividly how the knife had gone sailing harmlessly past Initiate Haek's right shoulder—but he had managed to hit an acolyte in the head with the stiletto's hilt. And this was hardly some scrawny, power-mad priest coming at him! This was a giant spider. Even if he only managed to hit the eight-legged monstrosity with Renata's hilt, it might be enough to scare it away from where Berlyn lay trapped. After all, he'd never seen a spider attack when startled.

Then again, his pessimism was obligated to add, I've never seen a spider as big as a horse before!

Trying to ignore the yowling catcalls and sniggering ridicule of his own thoughts, Aitchley tested the weight of the black blade in his hand one last time before launching the weapon forward. With a faint whistle, the stiletto tore through the musty air, spinning end over end as it streaked for the spider's already wounded face.

Of course, the young man's pessimism took this time to add, you could have always checked to see if Harris's knife had any better luck cutting at the webbing than your own did.

An iceberg of despair and hopelessness replaced Aitchley's stomach. What a muggwort! he cursed himself. I didn't even try . . .

Renata suddenly slammed blade first into one of the spider's many eyes, sinking through its gemlike surface in a splatter of blood and vitreous humor. Instantaneously, Aitchley's fear turned to victory, and he allowed himself a small cheer of good fortune as the giant arachnid went stumbling backwards.

"Yes!" the young man exclaimed happily, throwing a triumphant fist up into the air as he watched the spider lurch sideways.

Turning on the young farmer's vibrations, the monstrous spider changed direction and headed purposefully for the young man, streams of pale liquid gurgling down its hideous face.

Aitchley's feeling of triumph turned quickly back to fear. "No!" he contradicted himself, fumbling to return his sword to his right hand.

Steel winked flirtatiously as the young man's weapon bobbled precariously in his sweat-slicked grasp before dropping out of his hands altogether and disappearing through a gap in the web.

Oh, that was *real* good, the young farmer berated himself, watching the sword clatter to the gloom-enshrouded earth below.

The movement of the monstrous spider as it drew nearer pulled at the many strands of the web, drawing Aitchley down into the slope caused by the creature's weight. Unexpectedly, something dark and heavy dropped down from above, landing on the spider's hairy back and causing the entire web to heave and buck violently. Aitchley could barely hang onto the sticky threads and cables, and he realized with some chagrin that he had somehow managed to adhere himself back to much of the web.

With a sound like escaping steam, the massive arachnid hissed its annoyance and drew up on its back legs, rearing like some repulsive stallion. Its front legs wavered in the air above its head, trying futilely to dislodge the sudden weight that had crashed down on top of it, but the dark shape riding the spider's cephalothorax ducked beneath the flailing limbs and sent a hamhock fist slamming into the back of the monster's head.

Effortlessly, Poinqart's four-fingered fist punched through the spider's chitinous skull, sending a fountain of blood skyward. Convulsions shook the webbing as the enormous spider crumpled forward, its arachnid brain squashed beneath the half-troll's inhuman strength. Legs continued to twitch in fitful spasms long after the creature was dead, sending sympathetic vibrations out across the silvery strands still clinging to Aitchley and Berlyn.

Poinqart slid happily off the gigantic corpse, his face contorted in a hybrid expression of trollish joy and human misery. "Greetings-salutations, Mister Aitch," the half-troll declared. "Poinqart is happy-glad to see that you and Missy Berlyn are all-right-alive. Nasty spider-bug try to hurt Poinqart's friends?"

Still in a kind of awed shock at how easily the half-troll had killed the spider, Aitchley allowed himself to sink back into the hammocklike embrace of the giant web. "It tried," he answered as exhaustion slowly crept into his joints. "Now can you help us just get the Pits out of here?''

Relaxing back against Tin William's knapsack, Aitchley could sense the subtle shifting and swinging of the silver web. Or—more important—the lack thereof.

Squinting through half-closed eyelids, Aitchley looked up at where Poinqart still stood beside the spider's giant cadaver, trying to read the mixed emotions that twisted the hybrid's face. It wasn't until Aitchley recognized a look of sheepishness or embarrassment that he realized they weren't out of trouble yet.

Timidly, Poinqart looked up from where his stumpy feet stood upon the web. "Uhhh . . . Poinqart is sorry, Mister Aitch," the hybrid apologized, "but Poinqart is stick-stuck."

Berlyn lay back against the webbing, a good-natured sigh passing through her lips. "Apology accepted," she said.

Aitchley smiled crookedly when he realized the young blonde was looking at him and not at Poinqart.

16

A Sense of Adventure

Courteously, Aitchley helped Berlyn climb down out of the giant spider's web, standing below her as the blonde crawled awkwardly to the edge and slowly backed her way to solid ground. Helpfully, Aitchley kept one hand poised behind her as she clambered down, yet a flush of color warmed his cheeks when the scullery maid floundered and he instinctively reached out to steady her, his web-sticky palm clinging a little longer than he had intended to her shapely backside.

Clumsily, Poinqart followed behind the two, the web sagging and dipping beneath his ponderous weight. Although Aitchley had discovered that not all of the web was sticky—not even a giant spider was immune to its own glue—Poinqart continued to have difficulty traversing the silver strands, his stunted legs and large feet faltering as he tried to tightrope his way across the nonadhesive guidelines.

As the half-troll finally lumbered free, there was an unexpected yodel of daredevil bravado from above, and the web suddenly launched into an uncontrollable fit of bouncing and swaying as Calyx dropped down out of the darkness into its gooey embrace. A look of disgust crossed the dwarf's ruddy features as tendrils of gummy webbing adhered to his arms and legs, but he flashed the two teenagers and the hybrid a heartfelt smile of greeting as he started a slow crawl to join them on the rocky ground.

"Seemed the easiest solution," the smith answered their unspoken question once he was back down on the ground. "There was no way we could've pulled you back up."

Retrieving his fallen sword before Calyx could make a rude observation about it—and hiding Renata back in Tin William's knapsack—Aitchley turned a curious eye on the dwarf. "So what do we do now?" he wanted to know.

Calyx gave the young man a noncommittal shrug. "I don't know," he responded with unusual good humor. "Wander these caves forever until we die?" He swung tiny eyes on the velvety blackness surrounding them. "We'll figure something out."

The web suffered another violent tremor of vibrating lines and quivering strands as Taci landed nimbly in its grasp, her torch held safely above her head, its naked flame crackling and popping in the rush of warm, musty air. Eyfura and Gjalk were the next to drop into the web's embrace—faint expressions of astonishment and exhilaration on their respective faces—and they were followed swiftly by Harris, who hid his emotions behind an impassive mien of dirt and old scars.

Trying to be polite, Aitchley helped hoist Taci down from the web by placing his hands beneath her arms, flustering once more as his sticky hands adhered themselves quite intimately to her naked upper half. "I . . . uh . . . So," he stammered as if to steer their conversation away from the fact that his hands were momentarily glued beside her bare breasts, "you can still . . . ummm . . . get us out of here, right?"

Taci slid herself free of the web as if instinctively knowing which strands were smeared with glue and which were not. "Most paths that lead eastward all reach the same *sta*," she said. "The same destination." She turned dark blue eyes on a narrow funnel of stone to her right. "Although I am not familiar with this route, I am certain it will still take us where we want to go."

A sparkle of whimsy lit in Calyx's beady eyes. "How can you be certain of something you're not familiar with?" he teased in typical dwarven fashion.

An abrupt voice cut through the high cavern, a hundred million echoes bouncing and somersaulting off the indigo rocks. "Master Calyx," Gjuki's deep, near-emotionless voice announced from the blackness above them, "it would appear we have a slight complication on our end." There was a short pause as the Rhagana's words slowly faded into the darkness. "It seems Healer Sprage refuses to make the jump."

Aitchley recognized the look of irritated impatience that began to twist its way across Calyx's face. Grumbling, the smith stomped to the shadowy center beneath the giant silver web, glaring up into the impenetrable blackness of the stony shaft. "Sprage!" the dwarf yelled irately. "Get your sorry butt down here!"

"Not a chance!" came the response of a hundred echoes. "I'm not jumping down into some pit! What do you think I am? Crazy?"

Both Aitchley and Berlyn started giggling as Calyx threw them a look of consummate exasperation, his mouth bobbing up and down like a marionette's as he mimicked Sprage's protests. When the echoes had died once again, the dwarf returned his beady-eyed stare up the rocky shaft, folding adamant arms across his chest. "Listen," he shouted up into the pitch, "this is the only way we can stay together! There was no way we could've pulled the kid back up! You said so yourself!"

"Doesn't mean I'm gonna jump!" Sprage's voice sounded from the darkness. "What if the web breaks?"

"The web's not going to break!" Calyx retorted, his complexion darkening even in the faint light of Taci's torch. "It didn't break for any of us! What makes you think you're so special?"

"That's just the point, isn't it?" the echoes argued. "What if there's been too much stress put on the web? All you people jumping down there . . . You're crazy if you think I'm gonna jump!"

"Oh, for QuinTyna's sake, Sprage!" Calyx barked his annoyance. "Get down here or I'll climb back up there myself and drag you down by the ears!"

"No way," came the answer. "There's no way I'm jumping down there. We'll just have to find some other way."

Grumbling and muttering dwarven oaths, Calyx started to storm back out from under the giant web when a sudden idea struck him. Inquisitively, the smith turned his attention back to the silver strands hanging above him, a questioning finger plucking at one of the lines like a musician might pluck at the strings of his instrument.

Curiously, the dwarf swung his gaze to Taci. "What's this stuff made of, anyway?" he asked, still plucking at the thick lines overhead. "It's not normal spider's silk. Feels as tough as *gnaiss*."

Taci tugged delicately at the silver hoop piercing her right earlobe. "The web of Mother Many-Legs is as sturdy as some metals when heated over an open flame," the young girl replied. "When done properly, it will retain its shape indefinitely."

"So you people have done this before?" Calyx noted with some enthusiasm. "What about a rope? Do you think we could splice a few strands together and make a rope long enough to reach the top?"

Taci nodded, her pitch-black hair spilling down around her bare shoulders. "It can be done," she said. "Heat the pieces you wish to connect, and the web will grip one another tightly."

A look of awe flashed briefly across Calyx's mien. "You can solder it?" he asked in his sudden excitement. "It'll weld together like a metal?"

"It may be a little stiff at the joints, but the rest of your rope will remain flexible," the young girl replied. She touched at her earring again. "The *Kwau* have learned to make many things with the webs of Mother Many-Legs."

The admiration remained in Calyx's eyes. "I can understand why," the smith answered, prodding the silver strands above him with newfound respect. "This stuff's better than silver. Aitchley, come here and give me a hand getting some of this stuff down."

As Aitchley moved to help Calyx, an unexpected scream split the silence above them, and two figures suddenly came crashing down into the web. Even before the silver netting had stopped swaying, Sprage had pulled himself into a seated position, all but oblivious to the sticky lines and webbing that had tried unsuccessfully to keep him glued down.

In more shock than terror, the healer jabbed an accusing finger at the Rhagana beside him. "You . . . You pushed me!" he shrieked.

There might have been a brief darkening of shame across Gjuki's face, or else it was just the shadows from Taci's torch as the Rhagana answered, "I apologize most profusely, Healer Sprage, but there appeared little hope of finding any alternative. We certainly couldn't leave you up there all alone to find out what other giant creatures might inhabit these caverns."

The indignant anger that flushed Sprage's cheeks momentarily abated as he mulled over the gardener's words, but the shock remained as he swung his disbelieving gaze down through the web at those gathered below him. "Did you see what he did?" he asked them, seeking sympathy. "He pushed me!"

Calyx poked impatiently at where the healer sat upon the webbing. "Well, goody-goody for him," he remarked. "Now get the forge off the web; I'm making some spider-rope."

Before the stunned doctor could say anything more, a low rumble reverberated through the rock walls around them. Bluish-white light slowly filled the chamber with an angelic aura as Camera 12 descended lightly to earth, its gimbaled rocket lowering its great metallic bulk with a majestic ease and grace that belied its mass. Arrogantly, Trianglehead perched upon the construct's back, avian contempt in his milky blue eyes as he enjoyed the smooth ride down.

As Camera 12's rocket cut off and its spidery legs unfolded like the landing gear of some lunar pod, Trianglehead ruffled his red-violet feathers and cocked his head smartly at the gathering of people around him. "Zstupid humansz," the bird declared, then settled himself back down for another nap.

Shadows danced and frolicked across the dark blue stones of the labyrinthian corridors as Aitchley followed the light of Taci's torch, uneven splashes of illumination whitewashing his path down the winding tunnels and catacombs beneath the Shadow Crags. Worriedly, the young man tried not to think about the tons of dark rock pressing down above his head— tried not to think that the ceiling above him could just as easily cave in as the floor below him already had—but the weariness running through his body made it all that more difficult to suppress his natural tendency toward pessimism. It had been a long day, the young farmer thought tiredly to himself. From the early morning hour when Harris had first roused him from

sleep, to the climb across the western face of the Shadow
Crags, to the whole *battu*-thing that led to their journey
through the ancient caverns. It didn't help any either that Calyx
had loaded the young man down with heavy coils of thick
spider's web, and the added weight only served to help sap
him of strength he no longer had.

We've been walking for hours, the young farmer mused in
his fatigue. If we don't stop soon, I'm just gonna fall face first
on the floor and fall asleep where I land!

His demeanor worsening as his weariness grew, Aitchley
glared into the darkness of the seemingly endless tunnel before
them. "Aren't we going to stop for the night?" he wondered
petulantly.

Taci's torch cut a yellow-orange swath through the blackness. "It would not be *dhe*," she said. "Beneficial." She
threw a quick glance over a naked shoulder. "We shall rest
when the morning hour draws near."

Shuffling his feet like a disgruntled child, Aitchley threw a
cantankerous stare down at the stone path. "Why?" he
whined. "What's the difference? Why don't we just stop
now?"

"I must agree with the QuestLeader," Eyfura SpearWielder
remarked. "Without the sky above our heads, I see no difference in when we stop, and I, too, begin to feel the ache deep
within my legs."

Despite their protests, Taci continued forward. "To stop
now would be *eu*," the young *Kwau* explained. "We would
only be forced to stop again once morning came."

"Why?" Aitchley demanded, his fatigue making him short-
tempered. "We've been walking at least half the night! What's
so important about morning?"

Taci ducked beneath a beetling protrusion of rock and down
another shaft of dark stone, her torch momentarily flickering
out of Aitchley's view. "We head for the Canyon Between,"
she answered matter-of-factly. "None may cross at daybreak."

"Well, why the Pits not?" the young man snapped.

Aitchley couldn't have been sure, but he thought he saw a
nervous shudder pass through the girl's blue-grey form. "The
Canyon is a fearful place," she answered. "Not meant for
Kwau. It is spanned by only one bridge, and it is the place
where this world ends and the next one begins." Another

shiver tickled its way up her spine. "It is *magh*."

Some of the girl's apprehension succeeded in rubbing off on Aitchley. "What do you mean, it's the place where this world ends and the next one begins?" he asked anxiously. "I mean . . . you're not just being overly dramatic, are you? I mean . . . you really *mean* that!"

"Of course," replied Taci. "I have no reason to make light of this." She tossed another glance at the young man behind her. "I thought you were aware of the dangers that awaited you."

"Seems this is one particular danger that was left off our list," Calyx quipped with dwarven cynicism, "but I have to agree with the kid. What's the big deal? So this place is *magh* . . . or whatever. At least it's got a bridge. Why can't we stop now and cross it in the morning?"

Taci continued winding her way through the sloping tunnels of the ancient gallery. "You still do not understand," she said. "The Canyon Between is *magh*. A place of great magic." She trembled again as if cold. "It is the place where the sun rises between worlds and where the dead go to die. It is the farthest east you may travel before entering the *Kad*—the place beyond the gates of death—where there is no sunlight and the *reu'dheu* dream the Sleep of the Dead."

A look of smug arrogance etched itself across Sprage's clean-shaven features. "That's impossible," he declared with sudden hauteur. "The sun doesn't rise up from a canyon . . . it only looks that way. Scholars and scients have long since determined that both our world and the world of the sun hang in space in a kind of organized pattern with each revolving around the other. Ancient beliefs and myths that the sun grew up out of the earth every morning or was swallowed up by the sea at night are just that: ancient myths! They're no sooner viable than the belief that the sun and moon are two warring sisters punished by Gaal at the beginning of time."

Taci was unimpressed by the healer's intellect. "I know nothing of what you say," she admitted tersely. "I know only what is *deru*. What is truth. The Canyon Between spans our world and the *Kad* and is joined only by the Bridge of Mists, and every morning the sun rises between worlds to make its journey across the sky and burns away the bridge, making it

impossible to cross the Canyon at daybreak. One must wait
for the mists to reform."

The conceit remained bright in Sprage's dark brown eyes.
"The sun does not rise up out of a canyon," he corrected her.
He released an exasperated sigh. "Next thing you'll tell us is
that you believe in ghosts!"

There was a vague expression of deep thought on Gjuki's
wooden features as the gardener turned to regard the indignant
healer. "Perhaps this is one instance where we should defer
to Mistress Taci's wisdom," the Rhagana mused out loud. "If
this canyon is as great a place of magic as she says, who knows
what we can expect from such an unstable and volatile
source?"

"*What*?" Sprage blurted out sharply. "You can't seriously
expect me to believe this! Scients and scholars . . ."

"I don't care what you expect us to believe," Calyx rudely
interrupted the physician, "but if somebody had told me a year
ago that I would have been *walking* to Lich Gate, I would've
told 'em to go and clean out that empty space between their
ears!" He fixed beady eyes on the querulous healer. "You
gotta remember we're going to a place that's only been written
about from visions, Sprage," he continued. "We don't know
half the things we might run into, and the things that we do
know about might turn out to be something altogether different
than what we're expecting. Keyless Locks. Philters of Re-
newal. Eternal Guardians. If Taci says there's some sort of
magic bridge that crosses a canyon between worlds, well,
then . . . I believe her!"

"But the sun doesn't rise up out of a canyon!" Sprage continued to argue. "It's been proven that . . ."

"It's been proven what?" retorted the dwarf. "That a bunch of
fat men in robes can sit around a table throwing out different the-
ories until they find one that suits all their needs? Look . . . I
don't like the sound of this any better than you do—my grand-
father used to tell me things about magic, and, believe me, I
want nothing to do with the stuff!—but I think we'd better
listen to Taci here rather than a group of pithless scients sitting
back on their fat asses up in Solsbury. Her people have been
here five hundred years, and if they say the sun rises up out
of some magic canyon, then so be it!" He trudged resolutely
behind the blue-grey girl, his hand gripping nervously to the

hilt of his warhammer. "When we started this quest, we were advised to go with an open mind—something completely unheard of to a dwarf—but I think I'm beginning to understand what Liahturetart meant."

As Sprage dropped back to sulk, Aitchley's mind was left to carry on the argument alone. Like the healer, the young man had always believed in the universe as explained in the few, paltry books he had managed to read and struggle through, but Taci's story—Aitchley had to agree—sounded more like something out of a mythology book. Fables about the Great Gods' Sorcerer or of Yram the Chaste's enduring virginity . . . that was where he would expect to hear such a story. But now—supposedly walking toward such a place—Aitchley began to wonder about how much of the world he really knew. If there was a canyon that separated the two worlds—and if there really was a magical bridge made of mist that burned away every morning only to reform—then that meant magic still played a pivotal part in the natural order of things. And that meant, despite everything Aitchley had learned, magic had not completely faded four hundred years ago with the last of the true Wizards.

"Perhaps it is better that you not know everything," Aitchley could remember Liahturetart consoling them.

Yeah, the young man answered glumly to himself, but now it looks like I don't know anything at all!

They camped for only a few hours that night, making a small campfire in the middle of a great cavern almost as big as the Tridome. As tired as he was, Aitchley found it difficult to fall asleep, his own various aches and pains keeping him awake, as well as the revelation that everything he knew may have been wrong. As if it wasn't bad enough that he hadn't understood what Tin William had meant about tampering with certain things, now his entire view of the universe had been tipped on end. In addition, Calyx was making an awful lot of noise forging his superstrong spider-rope, muttering and grumbling out loud about how it probably wouldn't work but hooting and hollering with rare dwarven delight when the glittering coils of silver cable were finally finished.

It was no wonder the young man had trouble falling asleep. As the others all drifted off to sleep around him, Aitchley rolled himself over onto his back and stared up at the shadowy ceiling of the great cave, a frustrated sigh escaping his lips. He hadn't even bothered to set up Tin William's Envirochamber, since the volcanic grottos beneath the Shadow Crags were warm but not uncomfortably so, and the realization that magic might still exist only made him all the more wary of Tin William's wondrous items. Even though the man-shaped construct had promised the young farmer that his futuristic provisions had little to do with magic, Aitchley was no longer sure if he believed him. After all . . . the world as he knew it was beginning to make less and less sense the closer he got to Lich Gate.

"Can't sleep?" a soft voice suddenly whispered in his ear.

Aitchley started at Berlyn's unexpected comment. "I . . . uh . . . I mean . . ." The usual warm flush colored his cheeks. "I'm . . . Yeah," he finally answered.

Platinum-blonde hair spilling down around bare shoulders, Berlyn propped herself up on one arm to look at the young man lying beside her. "Me neither," she said, smiling. She threw an awe-filled gaze out across the dark cavern. "This is all just so . . . oh, I don't know . . . amazing."

The enthusiasm in the young girl's voice momentarily shocked Aitchley into a disbelieving stupor. "Amazing?" he parroted her when he finally found his voice. "We're heading toward a place that defies all laws of science, and you think it's amazing?"

An eager light gleamed in the scullery maid's beautiful eyes. "It's magic, Aitchley," she said breathlessly. "I've always wanted to see magic. True magic."

"It's bloody suicide, is what it is," Aitchely muttered darkly. "Who's to say a bridge of mists can even support our weight? We'll probably walk across it and fall to our deaths!"

"It supported the pilgrimage," Berlyn pointed out.

"We don't know that," countered Aitchley. "Taci said they showed them the way. She never said that anyone actually made it." The young man flung a quick glance at the sleeping form of their nubile guide, hoping his gaze didn't earn him a jab in the ribs from Berlyn. "Besides," he went on pessimistically, "that was nearly five hundred years ago. Taci's only telling us what's been handed down from generation to generation." He pursed sour lips. "And what's scrawled all over the walls,'' he added patronizingly.

Berlyn eyed the young man beside her, her expression clouding. "You know, Aitchley," she observed, "you have no sense of adventure. No sense of . . . fun."

"Oh, thanks a lot."

The blonde winced as she tried to find the correct words. "You know what I mean," she chastised the young farmer. "We're doing things no one's ever done before! Going places no one's ever been! Doesn't that interest you in the least?"

"Being chased by ravenous brown trolls," Aitchley sarcastically added to her list. "Attacked by giant spiders. Abducted by power-hungry priests." He shook his head philosophically. "Doesn't sound like my idea of a good time."

Berlyn drew herself up into a seated position, peering down at the young farmer with sudden mischief in her grey-green eyes. "And you'd rather be back in Solsbury?" she interrogated him. "You'd rather be back working the fields for the Tampenteire estate?"

The thought of his hometown with its barren fields and rundown hovels did not sit well with the young man, and he tried hurriedly to push the bleak memories out of his mind. "Well . . . no," he answered truthfully, "but at least it's safe."

It was Berlyn's turn to pucker her lips. "Safe," she echoed derisively. "I'll show you safe." Purposefully, she pulled herself to her feet, snatching up Aitchley's hand and pulling him up after her. "Come with me," she instructed, the mischievous glint sparkling in her eyes.

Aitchley was forced to sprint over the sleeping forms of their companions as Berlyn led him across the length of the amphitheater. "Where are we going?" he wanted to know.

Skirt billowing, Berlyn skipped playfully over Poinqart's sleeping form and tugged the young farmer toward a narrow corridor in the rock. "Just come with me," she repeated.

Questioningly—and having little choice—Aitchley trailed the young girl into the dark tunnel, the feeble glow of their campfire swallowed up by the engulfing blackness of the catacombs. Clumsily, Aitchley stumbled down the pitch-black corridor after Berlyn by feel, only able to use one hand since the other was being tightly clasped by the blonde. The two had only gone a few feet into the passage, but the impenetrable pitch made Aitchley feel as if they had journeyed a million miles away from their friends, and an unsettling dread began to crust about the young man's brain, sending a flock of epileptic butterflies fluttering about his stomach. Nervously, the young man forced himself to a stop, pulling Berlyn to a halt ahead of him.

"Berlyn," he said uneasily, squinting his eyes through the claustrophobic confines of the stone corridor, "this is stupid. We're going to get lost."

Dimly outlined by a faraway thatch of glowing lichen, Berlyn turned back to face the young man, her impish smile half-lost in the blackness. "You've got to learn to take some chances, Aitchley," she advised him, stepping back closer to the young farmer. "You're too young to be acting so old."

As his eyes became more and more accustomed to the darkness, Aitchley looked down at the young scullery maid in befuddlement. "Running down a cave in the dark is taking a chance?" he asked her scrupulously. "It just sounds stupid to me."

Unexpectedly, Berlyn's lips were suddenly pressing up against his, forcing him back up against the stone wall in his surprise. A liquid rush of warmth filled the young man's body—instantly chasing away his anxieties and fatigue—and his arms wrapped instinctively around the young girl before him, drawing her in closer as he returned her kiss with a passion he did not know he had.

Tauntingly, Berlyn broke off their kiss, grey-green eyes searching his face. "Think you can find your sense of adventure now?" she teased, pulling out of his grasp and taking a step backwards.

Aitchley's eyes went wide through the green-blue gloom as Berlyn's dress seemed to melt away off her slender body, the dim glow of distant lichen highlighting pale flesh and small, round breasts. A nefarious giggle sounded deep in the blonde's throat as she stepped daintily out of her clothing and tossed her discarded shift at the young man, turning sprightly on her heel and racing off further down the tunnel. Immediately, Aitchley was after her, a sense of unrestrained joy and hungry lust burning away his misgivings, his own clothes coming miraculously free as he ran.

He caught her in a kind of gentle tackle, lowering them both to the rough ground, their naked bodies meshing like the pieces of a puzzle. In between deep gasps of breath and her own laughter, Berlyn shifted herself more comfortably beneath Aitchley's weight, planting a light kiss on the young man's lips.

"Still sound stupid to you?" she jeered.

Aitchley returned the kiss, his hand running up the length of her naked thigh. "Now this sounds more like my idea of a good time," he said back with a smile.

Then there was no more time for talk.

17

Ancient Glyphs and the Canyon Between

Nothing could wipe the lop-sided smile off Aitchley's face. Not the lack of sleep. Not the featureless gloom and musty confines of the subterranean caverns winding deep beneath the Shadow Crags. Not even the aches and pains from the previous day's journey coupled with the scratches and bruises from last night. Aitchley Corlaiys was in love, and not even the dark, claustrophobic tunnels around him could detract from the joy and happiness he now felt. This, he concluded with seventeen-year-old affirmation, this is True Love. I love Berlyn, and she loves me. Nothing else in the world matters.

Smiling so much it hurt, the young man walked hand in hand with Berlyn down the sloping stone corridors of dark blue rocks, a contented sparkle in his blue-green eyes. He was unable to get the overpowering sensations and emotions of last night out of his head—not that he really wanted to—and, sometimes, his eyes would just glaze over and his smile would take on a trace of lechery as certain thoughts came, unbidden, to mind. Not even in his wildest dreams had he imagined it would feel the way it did, yet his body still tingled at the thought of Berlyn pressing up against him, her hair a wild splay of silver-yellow gold in the murky dark. The tiny gasps and deep throated groans that had slipped from the young blonde's lips to echo like an audible aphrodisiac about them.

The sharp stab of her fingernails against his back as they thrashed and wrestled with one another across the rough, vesicular floor.

Leering, Aitchley threw Berlyn a knowing look, feeling a flood of warmth fill his cheeks when the scullery maid met his gaze with a look of similar lasciviousness. A reciprocating warmth answered from between the young man's legs, and he had to look away or else continue walking in some discomfort, forcing overwhelming desires back down and having to content himself with memories.

Walking behind the two young lovers, Calyx tried to keep his own smirk off his face, coughing into a balled fist to conceal his grin from an overly suspicious Sprage. You don't have to be Harris Blind-Eye to figure this one out, the dwarf thought amusedly to himself. There's nothing like pumping the old bellows through the stokehole to put a smile on your face, but I just hope the kid doesn't lose sight of where we're going. If there is magic up ahead of us, we're in for some serious trouble, and I don't need the kid playing middle-leg hopscotch when he should be paying attention. That's a good way to get dead . . . real fast.

A concerned expression succeeded in wiping the grin off the smith's face as he swung a quick glance at the half-troll waddling beside him, motioning the hybrid over with a curt wave of one hand.

A mix of human naivete and trollish curiosity glistened in the half-troll's yellow-black eyes as he approached the dwarf. "Mister Calyx-dwarf wishes to speak-see with Poinqart?" the hybrid queried.

"I have a secret mission for you, Poinqart," the smith replied, throwing a wary glance at the happy couple ahead of him. "You see Aitchley and Berlyn up there? I want you to keep a special eye on both of them. They're a little . . . uh . . . preoccupied right now, and I want to make sure nothing bad happens to them."

A crooked smile stretched the hybrid's ugly features. "Mister Aitch is in kissy-face-love," the half-troll declared.

Although this was obvious to him, Calyx was surprised by the half-troll's powers of observation. "Uh . . . well, yeah . . . you're right," he answered somewhat hesitantly. "Mister Aitch is in kissy-face-love, and we want to make sure he stays that way, don't we? It's your job to make sure nothing bad happens to him.'' He fixed the hybrid with a rigid stare. "Do you think you can do that?"

Poinqart drew himself up proudly. "Poinqart can do," he answered with hybrid certainty. "Mister Aitch and Missy Berlyn are Poinqart's friends. Poinqart will not let anything nasty-bad happen to them."

Calyx couldn't help the smile that returned to his face. "Good. Good," he said. "You do that."

Even as the half-troll moved away from the dwarf to take up his position as newly appointed guardian to the two teenagers, Calyx could feel the mocking stare from the long-haired healer beside him. "You?" Sprage asked in exaggerated shock. "Worried?"

Scowling, the dwarven smith shrugged indifferently. "Just taking precautions," he said in his defense. "I'd hate to think all that training was wasted just 'cause the kid was too busy making goo-goo eyes at his girl to be paying attention."

Sprage nodded with overenthusiastic agreement. "Oh, definitely. Definitely," he jeered. "You wouldn't want somebody to think you actually cared, now would you?"

Calyx's scowl pulled downward into a heavy frown, but he couldn't keep the slight red tinge of the embarrassment from darkening his already ruddy complexion. "You know, Sprage," he remarked with well-rehearsed cynicism, "I liked you better back in Ilietis."

"I wasn't with you in Ilietis," corrected the healer.

Calyx's frown inverted. "I know."

Dark blue stone wound interminably through the insalubrious depths of the Shadow Crags, corkscrewing and writhing like great serpents of hollow rock. Shadows leapt and shifted across the rough-hewn walls, and Taci's torch was the only pinpoint of light in the dreary, murky confines of the ancient caves. Even the phosphorescent patches of green-blue lichen growing upon the mafic rocks had begun to lose their glow, leaving only dark, clustering clumps of dead cells clinging tenaciously to the dark blue walls.

Completely lost—and wondering if even Taci knew where she was going—Aitchley followed blindly through the twisting, sloping passages beneath the basaltic mountain range. So long as he held Berlyn's hand tightly in his, there was nothing that could upset the young man—this was, after all, True Love, he reminded himself—yet, ever since their fall into the giant spider's web, Aitchley's sense of direction had been so bunged up that he could no longer tell north from south or east from west. Not that Aitchley had been very good with directions beforehand. There had been one day back in Solsbury that he and Joub had ventured into the central city to buy some supplies and had gotten irrefutably lost as the result of a short-cut Aitchley had tried to take—but now, deep underground without a sun or moon or even stars overhead to guide them— Aitchley's poor sense of direction was even more muddled than before. In Solsbury it had only taken forty minutes or so of aimless wandering before the young men had regained their bearings and made it home in time for supper. Now, however, Aitchley wouldn't even think of trying to take the lead. How Taci knew where she was going—or how she even knew they just weren't walking in circles—was completely beyond the young farmer. Maybe she was using the timeline of pictographs that accompanied them along the length of the dark blue walls, but, sometimes, even the crude glyphs carved into the stone looked as identical to one another as the very rocks they were carved in. And all the caves . . . ! Sometimes there were as many as three or more different openings, yet Taci never once hesitated as she continued guiding them further and further into the Shadow Crags.

Either she knows where she's going, Aitchley concluded somewhat pessimistically, or else she's damn good at faking it!

Allowing his mind to drift back to more pleasant thoughts—like being secure in the knowledge that Berlyn hadn't been faking it—Aitchley followed behind the young *Kwau* without a word of question or complaint. He didn't know why it was so easy to put his trust in the young girl— he had barely trusted Calyx the first time he had met him— but perhaps it was just his overall good mood. With Berlyn beside him, not even the gloom and stale air of the caverns seemed as oppressive as before.

They walked a few hours more, and Aitchley guessed it was about late afternoon from the hungry rumblings that came from his belly. A familiar ache began to throb at the back of the young man's legs, yet the lopsided smile remained on his face even though Taci showed no signs of stopping for lunch.

Unexpectedly, the blue-grey girl came to a natural archway and stopped so abruptly that Aitchley almost walked into her. Questioningly, the young man peered over the girl's bare shoulder and blinked in the flickering glare of her torch, blue-green eyes narrowing. He could barely see anything—the light of the torch refusing to let his eyes adjust to what lay beyond—but a faint glimmer of green-blue phosphorescence pulsed high above, hinting at a ceiling far higher than even that of Winema's massive chamber.

"What is it?" Berlyn wanted to know from over the young man's shoulder. "What's wrong?"

Pushing through a veil of cobwebs, Taci took a slow, awe-filled step into the dark chamber, blue eyes growing wide with astonishment. "It is the *perbru*," she said in a hushed voice. "The place of the first tribe."

Aitchley's own amazement grew as he followed the young *Kwau* into a cavern almost as big as the imposing Tampenteire estate back home. High walls rose straight up into the murky gloom around them, their surface scored and fractured into hundreds of vertical pillars by columnar jointing. Large, box-like stones of diabase stood at varying heights before the walls of columns, and the very floor beneath their feet was separated and divided into dark blue hexagonal patterns like the elaborate tiles Aitchley remembered seeing in the Tampenteire mansion. How plain rock had formed into such a uniform, tilelike pattern was beyond the young man—maybe it had something to do with the cooling of lava again—but it made the entire chamber appear almost manmade rather than the natural formation that it truly was.

There was a light tap on Aitchley's shoulder, and the young farmer looked in the direction indicated by Berlyn's pointing finger. Situated off to the left, infusing the enormous cave with an eerie aquamarine glow, sat a large pool of steaming water, its natural basin surrounded and enclosed by an architectural display of pale stalactites and stalagmites. A thick carpet of bioluminescent algae coated the subterranean lake's rounded bottom—its light distorted and rippled by the gentle motion of the water as it drained from its stony reservoir and cascaded down a series of travertine terraces before fading into the darkness.

Faint patches of green-blue lichen grew with more profusion about the giant cavern, creeping steadily up the basaltic columns that formed the great cave. Near the top of the cave—aided by the greenish-blue glow of the lichen—Aitchley could see where the naturally formed pillars abruptly stopped, replaced by dark blue stone that looked like some bizarre, giant mud sculpture. Natural walkways and alcoves also hung high above the hexagonal pattern of the chamber's floor, and Aitchley could see where higher levels cut through the main chamber, like the twisting staircases and higher floors that graced the Tampenteire foyer.

Neck craned back, Aitchley stepped further into the massive cavern, the other members of the quest moving in behind him with stunned admiration. Even Camera 12 seemed to show signs of robotic astonishment, pivoting and spinning on its spidery legs to try to get as many shots as possible in the dim, bioluminescent sheen of lichen and algae.

"This place." Gjalk's deep voice broke through his awe to echo around them. "I have never seen a place such as this before. What is it?"

In a kind of trance, Taci moved across the hexagonal stones toward a pair of basaltic thrones situated near the very center of the huge cavern. "It is the *perbru*," she said again, her voice still quailed by her surprise. "It is the place where my people first lived. The birthplace of the *Kwau*. Where there was both *gwenn* and *gene*, and we lived *oinowrios*. As one with the world."

Inspecting a flow banding that had congealed into a pointed outcropping of obsidian, Calyx pretended not to be as interested in their incredible surroundings as he actually was. "Sounds like a good place to stop for lunch," he remarked flippantly; he unslung the huge bag from his shoulder. "Who's hungry?"

After lunch, Aitchley leaned back in the glow of the subterranean lake and stared up at the distant ceiling of the enormous cave. Reflections of pale blue ripples shifted and wavered across the basaltic columns of the *Kwau*'s birthplace, and there were even tiny swarms of flying insects that appeared

to give off their own yellow-green glow. At least, Aitchley
hoped they were tiny swarms of flying insects. The sleeping
brood of albino bats Eyfura had spotted roosting among the
stalactites hinted that there must be adequate food present for
larger animals, and it also meant that there was an opening
somewhere nearby to allow the bats access to the outside sky.
What else the tiny sparkles of light could be, Aitchley did not
know, but, with the discussion of magic still prominent in his
brain, all he could do was hope that they were just bugs.

There was a sudden tug at the young man's hand as he lay
there, forcing him to lurch up into a seated position. Although
irritated that his rest had been disturbed, Aitchley was unable
to keep the smile off his lips when he stared into Berlyn's
eager face.

"Let's go exploring," the blonde suggested with childlike
excitement.

Aitchley felt his eyes go wide. "Exploring?" he repeated
with some surprise, mistakenly thinking she was referring to
the same kind of exploring they had done last night. "Now?"

The scullery maid continued to tug at the young man's hand.
"Yes, now," she replied. "Taci was going to show Gjuki,
Gjalk, and Eyfura around. Want to come?"

Aitchley tried not to let his disappointment show. "I don't
think so," he answered lazily. "I'm kind of tired."

A twinkle reminiscent of last night glimmered in the young
girl's gaze. "Come on, Aitchley," she playfully chided.
"Where's your sense of adventure?"

The lopsided smirk returned as the young man pulled himself somewhat reluctantly to his feet. "Oh, all right," he conceded.

He was rewarded by a blinding smile from the blonde as
she jumped eagerly to her feet and scampered to where the
three Rhagana stood clustering about Taci, dragging Aitchley
along by his hand. Sprage also stood nearby, head contorted
upward in the same pose he had held throughout much of their
journey through the Bentwoods, and Aitchley noticed Poinqart
come waddling after the two teenagers, a merry expression on
his hybrid features.

"Please stay close behind me," Taci was saying as they
approached. "I have never been here before and only have the

stories of my ancestors to rely on. I am not certain what we can expect.''

Some of the interest in Sprage's face faded as his color waned. ''We're not going to run into any more giant spiders, are we?'' he fretted.

''I do not think so,'' the young *Kwau* reassured him. ''There should be an opening somewhere nearby that leads to the outside, and Mother Many-Legs prefers the deeper caverns in which to make her *kei*. Her home.''

Aitchley felt some of his anxiety fade as he started after the shapely young girl. I thought would-be rapists and crazy priests had been bad, he mused somewhat sardonically to himself, but that had been before being chased by brown trolls and giant spiders. I'm getting tired of things trying to eat me!

They strolled leisurely about the enormous cavern for well over an hour, listening to Taci tell ancient stories of the people who once lived there. It was sometimes difficult to understand the young girl—retelling such old stories forced her to use more of her native tongue than usual, and Aitchley was beginning to confuse *kei* with *kel* and *dheu* with *dhe*—but he enjoyed himself nonetheless, the simple presence of Berlyn beside him and the feel of her hand in his overriding any confusion or befuddlement he may have felt. Poinqart walked clumsily beside them, his saucer-shaped eyes trained more on the young couple next to him than on the gargantuan cave around them, and Sprage did most of the talking, rattling off as many questions as—if not more than—he had back in the Bentwoods.

Pulling insistently at Aitchley's hand, Berlyn drew the young man away from where Taci was showing the others the small alcoves and scoriaceous niches that had once served as sleeping quarters for her ancient ancestors and directed the young farmer's attention to a blue-grey obelisk of basalt heavily decorated by ancient carvings. It was incredible to think that these pictographs had been chiseled out over five hundred years ago, the young farmer thought, but, without the constant barrage of weathering, the glyphs upon its surface appeared as vivid and as detailed as if they had been carved yesterday.

''Look,'' Berlyn animatedly instructed him. ''It's us.''

Eyebrows raised, Aitchley looked at where Berlyn pointed a dainty finger at a crude drawing of two figures—a man and a woman—standing side by side. "So what's it say?" he played along.

Berlyn drew in close to the obelisk, moving slowly around its width as if translating the ancient pictures. "It says, 'Aitchley loves Berlyn,' " she responded.

"That's it?" wondered Aitchley, pulling his own gaze closer to the dark stone. "I could have told you that."

The blonde continued to inspect the cairn. "Wait," she said, "it also says, 'Aitchley has the cutest smile I've ever seen.' "

Aitchley tried to hide the lopsided smirk that continued to pull across his lips. "Now I know you're lying," he scolded the young blonde. "I'll tell you what it really says."

Berlyn stepped back as the young man took her place at the base of the giant pillar, blue-green eyes examining each symbol with mock seriousness. He even went so far as to stroke thoughtfully at his chin, something Pomeroy used to do to try to make everything he said sound more meaningful. "What it really says is that you have the nicest ass in all Vedette," the young farmer teased his girlfriend.

Berlyn whacked him soundly across the shoulder. "Aitchley!" she scolded him.

The young man's grin widened lecherously as he pointed a confirming finger at one of the deeply grooved glyphs. "No, seriously," he joked. "See that symbol there? That means 'Vedette.' And see that one? That means 'jam-tart.' "

Berlyn smacked him again. "Oooh, you," she said in that way that only females could to make a simple pronoun sound like a reprimand.

Aitchley sniggered at his own prurient mischief. "And see that one?" he continued to jeer. "That one means 'plum duff' . . ."

His humor suddenly died as his eyes fell upon a glyph larger and more imposing than the rest. Even as crudely drawn as it was into the rock, there was no mistaking the graven image of the Dragon, its wings drawn back behind its massive reptilian body as it hovered above some undrawn horizon. Its massive rock mouth was depicted as wide open, and a jagged, forking stream of what Aitchley assumed was supposed to be flames was etched issuing forth from the creature's maw. It looked more like a zigzagging streak of lightning than a stream of fire, but its meaning was still clear.

Beside it—as austere as the Dragon glyph was elaborate—sat a pictograph of two triangles divided by a simple groove. Aitchley didn't know why, but the twin triangular shapes brought to mind an image of weighing scales, and he heard a sudden buzzing, inhuman memory reverberate back through his skull:

There are some things that were not meant to be tampered with, Aitchley Corlaiys. Be wary of Nature's scales.

The good humor and levity immediately drained out of the young man as the troubling memory returned to plague his thoughts. What had the strange metal man meant? he couldn't help wondering all over again. What clue was it supposed to be for that I'm too stupid to figure out? Did it have something to do with this rock? This cave? Did Tin William know that I'd come here and see this? No, that's impossible. Taci didn't even know we'd come here! How could Tin William have known?

Calyx's voice abruptly cut through the eerily lit cavern, resonating all about them and pulling the young man up from his distressing thoughts. "Come on, people!" the dwarf called to them. "Party's over! Time to get a move on!"

Dazedly—preoccupied by worries and anxieties thought long dead—Aitchley trailed wordlessly behind Berlyn to where the dwarf awaited them, ancient pictographs and glyphs burning into his mind.

Aitchley walked the rest of the day in troubled silence, hardly feeling Berlyn's hand in his. The blonde beside him was immediately aware of the young man's change in attitude but had no idea what may have caused it. She worried somewhat self-consciously that maybe it had been something she had said, but she couldn't recall anything she might have said that could have forced the young man to withdraw into such an unexpected bout of melancholy. Maybe it had been her comment about Aitchley loves Berlyn. Had that somehow upset the young man? Had he taken it the wrong way, or had it brought some kind of upsetting thought to mind that had forced the young farmer to draw in on himself? Berlyn wasn't certain, but it bothered her that maybe somehow she was the cause of Aitchley's abrupt depression.

Continuing on without discussion, the two teenagers followed the others through the narrow confines of the passageways east of the *Kwau perbru*. For a time they had trailed the gurgling stream of hot water down its multicolored tiers of travertine steps before turning away from the underground brook and following a sloping tunnel that climbed steadily upward. Even as they walked through the now familiar gloom of Taci's torch and the faint, greenish-blue flicker of the lichen, Berlyn could feel a cool rush of fresh air blowing through the narrow passageways, its gentle breeze lightly touching her bare flesh and moving softly through her hair. She could even smell a difference in the air—surprised at how used she had gotten to the stale, musty humidity within the underground chambers.

Lost in his worrisome thoughts, Aitchley walked beside the young girl, unaware of the gentle breeze or sweet smell of fresh air. He was far too concerned with whatever it was he was missing. Whatever it was he should have understood from Tin William's vague and enigmatic warning that had somehow slipped by him. This close to Lich Gate, the young man could no longer ignore the robot's cryptic message. Was it something to do with the Elixir itself? he worried. Or maybe the use of the Elixir? He had pondered such thoughts before, and they had not resulted in any easy answers then or now.

Maybe it's because there isn't an easy answer to this, the young farmer thought despairingly to himself. Maybe that's why Tin William's warning is so confusing. Maybe it's just not something you can come right out and say in so many words. But . . . it seemed so important to him at the time. The way he kept glancing around like he'd get in trouble. Or the way he had grabbed my wrist in such desperation. I just don't understand! *What was it he wanted me to know?*

The young man walked stiffly down the rocky corridor, legs moving in an almost robotic fashion. Scales. Balance, he continued to muse darkly to himself. What was it he had said about balance?

Although never very good at remembering things, Aitchley could hear the construct's words as if the metal creature were whispering them in his ear that very moment: "Life and death are part of the natural order, Aitchley Corlaiys. When a species interferes, disaster is the only result."

Aitchley frowned. No, that's not it, he chastised himself.

The doorways to his subconscious remained opened, and Tin William's voice sounded again. "There is a precarious balance at work in all worlds, Aitchley Corlaiys," the buzzing, droning voice said from the back of his mind. "A regenerative cycle. Birth and death. Growth and decay. Destruction and creation. But these are forces only Nature can control in its myriad ways. No single species must ever cause this balance to lose its integrity."

Aitchley's frown deepened. So what did any of that mean? he asked himself angrily. When a species interferes? Interferes with what? Life? Death? When a balance loses its integrity? What the Pits was he talking about? And why the Pits does that picture of the Dragon keep bugging me? What's that got to do with anything? I should have asked Taci what it meant!

Unexpectedly, the young man felt a chill wind rustle the hair beneath his hat, and he looked up to see that they had stepped out of the musty caverns beneath the Shadow Crags and out onto a mountain ledge overlooking an enormous chasm. The dark night sky hung black and swollen above his head—littered with a billion twinkling stars—and an ethereal mist churned and coiled around him like so many vaporous serpents, its moist touch cold and unearthly against his skin.

Dumbed, the young farmer stared out across the narrow ledge on which they stood, blue-green eyes going wide at the vast expanse of nothingness that met his gaze. Below him— hundreds of leagues straight down—the rock wall dropped sharply out of sight, blanketed by a frothing, churning ocean of living mist. He wasn't sure, but he thought he caught the faint glitter of stars below him as well as above.

Taci stepped to the edge of the cliff and swept a naked arm out before them. "*Ser, dwo kanna*," she announced, her voice echoing through the mist-filled chasm before them. "The Canyon Between!"

18

Bridge of Mists

Aitchley Corlaiys stood at the edge of the world and stared down into infinity. Thick, almost liquid wisps and streamers of mist coiled and churned around him, moving lazily through the air like large, bloated maggots of fog. The dark stone of the narrow ledge he stood upon felt real and solid beneath his boots, yet the impossible drop of the chasm before him sent wave after wave of vertigo and disbelief roiling through his system. Somber blue basalt faded into the ocean of shifting, burbling haze that filled the massive canyon, and—try as he might—Aitchley could see no rocky bottom. All he could see was the continuation of the night sky, tiny silver-white stars winking and flirting at him from above as well as below.

To his left—slightly north of where the young man stood—a ghostly white shape rose up out of the swirling mists, towering spires stretching skyward like some ancient castle keep. Tendrils and semitransparent scarves of endoplasmic fog continually melded with and separated from the spectral structure spanning the enormous canyon, and Aitchley didn't like the way that he could see a multitude of stars twinkling from behind the unreal construction of the Bridge of Mists.

It was unlike any bridge the young farmer had ever seen. Its misty, hazy form seemed to hover in an almost dreamlike state above the Canyon Between, and fog-formed trestles and beams of grey-white haze faded into brumous nothingness. Great, cloudy spires or towers of some sort rose high above the bridge itself—constantly wavering and shifting in the cold, polar breezes from across the chasm—and Aitchley had to blink a few times when he thought he saw people walking in a steady line across the misty length of the unreal structure.

Trying to force down the denial and disbelief that threatened to swamp the young man's rationale, Aitchley took a tentative step forward, blue-green eyes staring down into the unfathomable depths of the Canyon Between. There was a kind of thickness in the air, the young farmer noted. A heaviness similar to the overpowering humidity like that in the Bentwoods. But this went beyond mere water vapor in the air, the young man sensed. It went deeper than that. It was almost as if some preternatural instincts in the young man sensed the magic that made this place. The ethereality that made every movement or thought feel like it was trapped in some slow-motion mire of insubstantiality. The ghostly movement and unnatural thickness of the living, thriving mists around them. The impossibility of a canyon that dropped off into black, velvety space. And the madness and unreason that went screaming through the young man's mind as he tried to make sense out of things that would not—or could not—be made sensible.

This place truly was the end of the world, the young farmer concluded. At least . . . the end of the world as he knew it.

Calyx turned a wry look on a dumbfounded Sprage. "Still think this place doesn't exist?" he tormented.

Sprage licked dry lips. "I . . . uh . . . umm . . ." was all he could get out.

Settling herself comfortably on the ledge of blue rock, Taci sat with her back against the Shadow Crags, hardly showing any of the awe or disbelief the others displayed. "We will rest here for the night," she said. "It would be *sek*—too risky—to attempt a crossing now."

The color had even drained from Harris Blind-Eye's scarred and dirty face as he flexed his fingers, longing for the comforting feel of his knives. "Why?" he demanded, blue-black eyes glittering in a wild kind of fear. "What's gonna happen?"

Taci threw a cursory glance skyward, her pitch-black hair spilling down her bare back like ebon water. "I am unable to tell how deep the night is," she explained. "Legends say that the Bridge of Mists takes nearly a full day to cross. Were you to start across now, you might not reach the other side before the sun rises.''

"And when the sun rises, this bridge is destroyed?" Eyfura inquired, her tiny, pearl black eyes alight with inhuman curiosity.

"Until it reforms," replied Taci. "Still, that would do you little good while you are falling for all eternity.''

While the others' eyes all went wide, Calyx just snorted uncaringly at the girl's remark. "Or until we fall into the sun," he shot back. With a grunt, he plopped himself down beside the young *Kwau* and began his nightly routine of digging through his large sack. "You made your point, though," he continued. "If Taci says we cross in the morning, we cross in the morning.''

As Aitchley lowered himself to the ground—battling the vertiginous whirl in his head the whole time—he suddenly realized how painfully Berlyn's fingernails were digging into his hand. His own grip around her hand was tight and rigid as well, and he tried to flash her what he hoped was a sincere smile of reassurance as the two settled themselves on the rocky cliff and tried to get comfortable.

Even as the others made ready to camp at the rim of the canyon, Sprage remained standing by the entrance to the cave, dark brown eyes transfixed by the boiling, surging mists of the chasm. "Uh . . . Shouldn't we camp someplace else?" he worried, a tremor of fear catching his voice in his throat. "I mean . . . if this is the end of the world and all that, aren't we a little close? Won't we—you know—burn up if the sun rises here?''

Taci offered the physician a grey-lipped smile. "You still do not understand the *magh* that is at work here," she said dogmatically. A blue-grey hand swept out to encompass the unreality around them. "This mist . . . this place. It does not belong here. *We* do not belong here. This is a place for the dead, and what concern do the dead have of dying?''

Hardly convinced—but taking a small bit of satisfaction in his own examination of the unscarred rocks behind him—Sprage reluctantly joined the others on the cliff, choosing to remain close to the entrance back into the Shadow Crags. A similar shudder of apprehension wormed its way through Aitchley's innards as a million new worries went whipping through his head—What if the sun did burn them all up? What if the bridge wouldn't support their weight?—and he found it hard to relax no matter what. Not even the feel of Berlyn's hand in his nor thoughts of the previous night could help ease the anxieties and primeval fears in the face of such ancient magicks.

This is it, the young man could hear himself think. This *is* the end of the world. This is where magic still works. There are no rules here. No natural laws. No balance like in the Bentwoods. Whatever happens, happens . . . and there might be no way of ever explaining it.

The farmer frowned heavily. Bloody, typical Corlaiys luck.

As the familiarity of setting up camp drew the young man away from some of his fears, Aitchley was able to force down a few bites of supper and settle himself back against the scoriaceous wall of basalt. He tried not to stare too intently at the unreal canyon lurking in its hazy shroud of white mist before him—or at the way silvery starlight gleamed through the grey-white makeup of the bridge—and found his mind, instead, returning to the gnawing mental image of ancient glyphs.

Somewhat shyly, Aitchley forced himself to his feet—having to detach his hand from Berlyn's with a vague smile—and approached Taci. It may be too late to show her what I saw, the young man thought, but I can still ask her about it.

Taci looked up questioningly as the young farmer sat down beside her. "Is there something I can do for you, *bheidh* Aitchley?" she asked politely.

Aitchley flushed crimson. Near as he could tell, the word "*bheidh*" meant something like "consort to the queen." I guess we weren't as secretive as we thought! "I . . . uh . . . just wanted to ask you something," he responded coyly. He traced a finger in the ashlike dusting of the basaltic ledge. "When we were back in the *perbru*, Berlyn and I saw a symbol that looked like this." He completed his drawing. "Do you know what it means?"

Taci glanced down at the twin triangles Aitchley had sketched into the bluish dirt. "This?" the young *Kwau* asked back. "This is nothing more than a means of showing direction, *bheidh* Aitchley." She lightly tapped at the pyramidlike shapes and the line between them. "It represents the mountain range you call the Shadow Crags and my people call *kei*.

Home. Taken out of context, I am unsure if this were to mean 'east' or 'west'—for it must be matched with the previous or following glyph in order for me to make sense of it, but the line down the center indicates one such direction. A line across the top of both mountains would mean 'north' and, below, 'south' ''.

Aitchley felt an almost palpable sense of disappointment settle like broken glass in his stomach. "You mean it doesn't mean anything special?" he feebly asked. "I mean . . . it doesn't mean something like 'scales' or 'balance'?"

Taci's deep blue eyes looked up into the young man's own. "It is only a simple directional glyph, *bheidh* Aitchley," answered the young girl. "I am sorry if you thought it would mean more."

The bitter taste of disappointment strengthened like bile in the young man's throat and he started to push himself back to his feet. While, on the one hand, the discovery of the ancient symbol had rattled the young man's composure, he was also hoping it might shed some light on whatever it was Tin William had been trying to tell him. Finding out the scalelike symbol was used as a means of showing direction only heightened the young man's belief that he'd probably never figure out what it was the strange metal figure had been trying to warn him of until he bunged it all up anyway.

Even as he started to get up, an abrupt flicker of curiosity sparkled in the young man's eyes and he returned to his seated position in front of Taci. "What about the Dragon?" he asked unexpectedly. "I never knew the Dragon was seen this far east."

There was a momentary glint of confusion in the blue-grey girl's gaze as she blinked back at the farmer. "Why do you ask such an *aerere*? Such a question, *bheidh* Aitchley?" she asked back.

Aitchley shrugged noncommittally. " I saw a symbol of it as well," he explained. "Next to the other one." He sketched a crude drawing of the Dragon in the dirt similar to the way it had appeared on the ancient obelisk. There was a gleam of youthful curiosity in his eyes as he completed the lightninglike streak of fire coming from the monster's mouth and returned his gaze to Taci. "I always thought the Dragon had stayed specifically in Vedette. You know? In its own territory," he went on. "Gjuki told me it never came anywhere near the Bentwoods."

Taci stared down at the childlike scrawl, comprehension dawning on her blue-grey features. "In the time of my ancestors, the Mother Snake ruled your skies," she responded, matter-of-factly. "These symbols tell that the Mother Snake lived to the west. See how the drawings combine with one another to form meaning?"

The explanation of the twin triangles and the Dragon glyph did nothing to quell the abrupt bewilderment that had spawned at the back of the young man's mind. "Yeah," he replied, "but how did they know?"

Perplexity scrawled across Taci's attractive face. "I do not understand what you mean," she admitted.

Aitchley jabbed a finger at the Dragon glyph. "How did they know?" he repeated. "I mean . . . if the Dragon always stayed in Vedette—and your people always stayed here—how did they know there was a Dragon flying around to the west of here?"

"The Mother Snake came where she was needed," Taci answered. "The Great Trees where the plants walk as men never needed her influence."

"Her influence?" echoed Aitchley, befuddlement coloring his words. "What do you mean?"

What might have been exasperation marred the young *Kwau's* tone. "I am no *weid*, *bheidh* Aitchley," she said. "The words of your language escape me, and I am unable to make my meaning clear. The Mother Snake—along with all other creatures—has its place." She erased the two drawings with an absentminded sweep of her hand. "You would do better to talk to *weid* Kirima, our wise one, when you get back," she advised. "Although she does not speak your language, perhaps I can translate well enough for you to get the answer to your question."

Aitchley rose haltingly to his feet, a grateful—albeit lopsided—smile on his lips. "That's all right," he told the young girl. "It's not that important anyway."

Thoughtfully, the young farmer returned to where Berlyn was waiting for him nearby. He wasn't sure why the young *Kwau's* comment about the Dragon interested him so much—despite the fact that he had turned down her offer to perhaps learn more—but he had things on his mind other than if the Dragon had ever been seen this far east. If he understood Taci correctly, she was just talking about the same kind of thing Sprage and Gjuki had been talking about back in the Bentwoods.

Confounded, Aitchley lowered himself back down beside Berlyn and snuggled in close, sharing the warmth of his tattered and worn cloak that the blonde had retrieved from his backpack. Well, that did a whole Pits of a lot of good, the young man chastised himself. I find out the one thing that could have helped me figure out what Tin William was talking about turns out to be nothing more than a direction! Some scholar I am. So do I use the Elixir or not? What was it Tin William was trying to say? And since when did the Dragon have any kind of influence? I always thought it just ran around and killed people and burned things. Some influence.

Hating his own stupidity—his mind overrun by muddle of questions all without answers—the young man somehow managed to fall into the fitful, dreamless release of slumber.

Aitchley awoke the next morning to a raucous hissing and sizzling sound like that of gammon frying in a skillet. Half-awake, the young man cracked one eyelid and peered out through a sleep-encrusted gaze at the rosy orange glow of sunrise. Only this time, however, the sun was rising directly in front of him!

All sleep purged from his system, Aitchley bolted upright at the incredible sight that met his stare, scuttling back nervously toward the Shadow Crags as Sprage's worried words from the night before resounded in his head. The sky before him was a multicolored palette of bright reds, oranges, and yellows—all striped and marbled by swirling bands of agitated mists that hissed and fizzled as the sun's morning warmth touched its cold, ethereal strands. The stars overhead blinked out one by one as a familiar blue touched the heavens, yet Aitchley's gaze was riveted to the sharp drop before him and the increasing flare of reddish-orange light that slowly crested the rise of dark blue rock.

Blazing with a million shades of red, the sun rose up over the edge of the Canyon Between, searing away the unreal structure of the Bridge of Mists. Like some sorcerous dandelion, the misty bridge simply scattered into a hundred thousand fragments of twisting, coiling, protesting fog, starting at its base and slowly dissolving all the way up to its lofty, cloud-like spires. The crackling hiss of dissipating fog sounded harshly in Aitchley's ears, and he blinked in dumbed stupefaction as the pleasant, warming rays of the nearby sun touched his face, chasing away any lingering traces of last night's freezing winds.

As the enormous ball of flames climbed higher, Sprage clambered anxiously to his feet, dark brown eyes wide with fear and astonishment. "Inconceivable," the long-haired physician gasped.

Flaring, blinding radiance swelled within the magical canyon before them, scattering the last remnants of haze to the brightening sky. Of the bridge, there was no sign—only the arcing curve of the sun as it rose up gently in its place—and Aitchley continued to gape and stare at what he thought should have been an impossibility.

I always thought the sun was larger, the young man's shock-numbed brain somehow managed to register. I thought I once heard that a million Vedettes could be dropped into the sun and there'd still be room for more. But . . . But how can that be? How can something so large—something that looks big even from its place high in the sky—be rising up out of a canyon no more than ten or twenty leagues wide. Is the *magh* . . . Is the magic of this place really that great? And if the magic is so powerful here—at the very separation between real world and unreal—what's it going to be like once we actually reach Lich Gate itself?

Sudden fingers curled around the young man's hand, and he looked to see Berlyn sitting up beside him, grey-green eyes wide and unblinking. "How . . . How come it's not hotter?" the blonde asked in amazement. "How come it doesn't feel like it did back in the Molten Dunes? It feels more like a nice spring day."

Aitchley returned his glassy-eyed stare to the wall of color and effulgence filling the entire chasm. "Magic," he answered, awed.

Behind them—resting on his perch atop Camera 12—Tri-anglehead watched the sunrise with heavy disdain in his diamond-blue eyes. "You krossz that?" the young bird asked with some reservation.

Aitchley felt his head bob up and down mechanically. "We have to," he replied.

Trianglehead shifted nervously from one foot to the other. "Wasz wrong," the fledgling concluded dourly. "Humansz not zstupid. Humansz krazy."

Aitchley hardly heard the gyrofalc's words as he stared open-mouthed at the unreal dawn before him. Mist had already begun to re-form in the still, thick, unnatural air—writhing into existence as the sun rose higher out of the canyon and lifted steadily into the sky. Pale, wormy tendrils boiled up over the edge of the chasm like a saucepan overspilling, and Aitchley watched with heavy misgivings as the ghostly structure of the Bridge of Mists began to re-form exactly as it had been moments earlier, ethereal towers reaching up imploringly after the rising sun.

Taci pulled herself to her feet, smoothing out her snakeskin loincloth in an attempt to conceal her unease. "You had best hurry," the young *Kwau* said. "The bridge will only last until tomorrow morning."

A lance of panic inexplicably pierced Aitchley's breast. "You're not coming with us?" he understood, and he wasn't quite sure why he was so suddenly upset.

Taci tried to give the young farmer a friendly smile, yet she couldn't keep the apprehension out of her eyes. "It is *ta* for my people to cross before their time," she explained nervously, none of last night's calm left in her voice. "I was only supposed to guide you to the bridge—you must cross on your own."

Urgently shoving things into his bag, Calyx didn't even look up at the young girl when he asked, "Any ideas what we can expect?"

Taci shrugged. "It has been *gheslo* since the *Kwau* have dared to brave the empty plains of the *Kad*," she answered uneasily. "Many years." Her deep blue eyes flicked worriedly across the mist-filled canyon. "Beware the *reu'dheu*," she declared. "To awaken them from their sleep will surely mean the death of you all."

"The *reu'dheu*," Berlyn repeated with some hesitation. "You mentioned that before. What exactly is it?"

The fear in the blue-grey girl's frame grew more apparent as she stared out over the bottomless chasm. "The *reu'dheu*," she said again. "The Red Death. They will awake if they sense your presence."

Although Aitchley remained confused, he noticed the understanding nod that came fleetingly from Gjuki's direction. "The Daeminase," the Rhagana gardener explained when he spotted the young farmer's questioning stare. "Miss Taci must be referring to those that sleep the Sleep of the Dead. Those that are the Desolation of the Pits."

Taci's answering nod was one of firm conviction. "The *reu'dheu* will awake if they are disturbed," she went on, "and they will not return to their rest until you are dead. Many *Kwau* were dragged—still alive—into the *Peue* for disturbing the Red Death, and many others brought great disaster to their ancient *brus* by attempting to flee and leading the *reu'dheu* back to their *kei*."

"Another charming bedtime story," Calyx quipped, slinging his heavy sack over one brawny shoulder. "Now, are we going to cross the bridge or stand around here talking until it dissolves again?"

Taci stepped back as the impatient dwarf made his way up the ledge past her, purposefully heading up the sharp incline to where the hazy, shifting Bridge of Mists stretched out over fog-filled space. "I will await your return here to guide you back," the blue-grey girl told them. "May luck be with you."

Following Calyx diffidently up the hill, Aitchley heard the low raspings of his pessimism hiss within his cranium. Yeah, the young man's darker half jeered mentally, too bad it's all been bad.

Bloody, bunging typical!

Fog bubbled up around Aitchley's boots as he placed a tentative foot upon the nebulous Bridge of Mists, feeling his foot drop through the haze before coming to rest on something that wasn't quite solid but supported his weight nonetheless. Misty bands and hazy serpents spun and twisted through the air all about him, some melding seamlessly with the vaporous bridge while others tore themselves free and went spiraling off into the nothingness. Black, open space peeked through the cloud cover of gossamer mist beneath him, but Aitchley made sure not to glance out over the edge of the wide bridge. He had done so once already, and the resulting wave of nausea and dizziness that had assailed him had almost been sufficient to send him reeling over the misty railings.

He wasn't sure if the gauzy, unreal and mist-forged barriers along the sides of the bridge were even tangible, and he didn't want to be the one to find out.

Her hand locked tightly in his, Berlyn walked timorously beside the young man. Tiny beads of moisture clung to her bare legs like dewdrop anklets as she stepped delicately through the churning mists, and she didn't like the way gentle breaths of fog blossomed up into the air beneath their feet, rising up in great white clouds like disturbed blooms of dust. Any second she expected the ethereal ground to suddenly drop out from beneath her, sending her screaming and falling into the inky sky that hung hungrily below her. Sometimes it was difficult just to keep her bearings straight, what with a sky below her as well as above. It was no wonder there were no birds visible in either of the skies.

Aitchley risked a quick glance forward, trying to ignore his own peripheral vision. "How much further?" he asked anxiously.

Almost engulfed by the mist kicked up by his own feet, Calyx threw a sardonic look over one shoulder at the young man. "Why? What's the matter?" the dwarf wanted to know. "You feel like stopping for lunch?"

"No, I . . ." Aitchley stumbled when whatever it was supporting his weight dipped in an unexpected—and fog-hidden—slope. "No," he tried again, wishing the frightened quaver out of his voice, "I was . . . I was just wondering."

A familiar frown beneath his beard, Calyx sent another backward glance at where the sun had risen high over the jagged Shadow Crags. "'Bout halfway," the smith estimated. "I'm not sure." He gave the others an indifferent shrug. "It's gonna get dark a lot sooner than it should when the sun drops down behind the Shadow Crags."

"So how we gonna find our way across then?" queried Harris, a malicious smirk on his lips in an attempt to conceal his fear.

Calyx's answer was another shrug beneath his sack. "We

have torches," he remarked casually. "I've even got a lantern in here someplace."

Gjalk DarkTraveller leaned out over the bridge to stare down into the field of stars glittering below them. "But could that not be detrimental to our passage?" the ponytailed Rhagana wondered. "Might not the heat from a torch disperse the very mist that now holds us aloft? While I know this is not a natural mist, are we willing to take such chances?"

No rules. No laws, Aitchley could hear himself think once again. Whatever happens, happens.

A disgruntled expression contorted Calyx's face as he pushed his way through the thick, endoplasmic haze. "It was pretty warm this morning and the mist didn't seem to mind," he commented.

"Yet this would be a naked flame much nearer than the risen sun," Gjalk pointed out. "And we have seen the bridge dissipate in the face of intense heat."

"And forget about making our way across in the dark," Sprage said before Calyx could answer. "This is bad enough as it is!"

The dwarf's ruddy features darkened. "All right. So now what do we do?" he demanded. "Go back and call the whole thing off?"

Harris grunted. "Hey, you don't hear me complaining," he mocked.

A gentle voice—not much more than a whisper—sounded beside Aitchley. "Aitchley has a way."

Turning so quickly a bout of vertigo almost knocked him over, Aitchley stared open-mouthed at the petite blonde walking alongside him. "Me?" he blurted. "I do?"

"Tin William's lightstick," the scullery maid interrupted, flashing him a nervous smile. "It doesn't radiate heat, remember?"

Comprehension lit up the farmer's face as he remembered the odd, handlelike instrument that—when shaken—emitted a bright white light that had been given to him by the otherworldly robot, and he hurriedly dug it free from the maroon depts of his backpack and handed it to Calyx.

The dwarf took the plastic cylinder with a skeptical sneer. "Doesn't look like it'll give off much light," he snorted cynically.

"It's got a pretty good range," Berlyn responded, trying to be cheerful despite the drop to infinity beneath her dainty feet. "You just have to keep shaking it every so often to maintain it."

Bleakly, the smith tucked the pale white tube into his belt and continued on across the spectral bridge. The sky overhead began to tinge with deep purples and royal blues as the sun started its early descent over the ensiform peaks of the Shadow Crags—all nearly obscured by the wavering, thrashing strands of sentient mist—and the heavens above began to meld seamlessly with the blackness below. Eerie shadows splashed the unnatural bridge as Calyx tugged free Tin William's lightstick and shook it into phosphorescent activity, a brief glint of satisfaction sparking in his eyes at the halo of pale illumination that surrounded them.

They walked a few hours more, their way illuminated through the false evening by the magic lightstick. He wasn't sure if it was his imagination or not, but Aitchley felt as if there had been a subtle change in the air around them. He no longer felt the heavy thickness that had first touched his senses with such primeval anxiety outside the Shadow Crags, and the bridge beneath him seemed much more solid than it had earlier that morning. The winding, shifting banners of fog also appeared to have taken on a greater depth of tangibility—resembling pale white wisps of fabric now rather than tenuous haze—and, more than once, Aitchley thought he heard the hollow sounds of boots striking wooden beams as he continued across the cloudy expanse of the Bridge of Mists.

The young man felt Berlyn's hand tighten warily around his. "Aitchley," the young blonde suddenly whimpered. "Look."

Wordlessly, Aitchley peered up through the writhing, twisting coils of mist and fog at the eastern rim of the Canyon Between. It rose a million leagues above them—a sheer featureless wall of grey-white stone, and Aitchley wasn't sure whether it was made of rock or if an immense slab of grey ice towered before them. The bridge itself ended against the side of the wall, a craggy, toothlike cavern burrowing into the hoary glacier and disappearing into an unnatural darkness.

Sprage shivered as an arctic wind blew from the cavern's mouth like the breath of a million dead. "Is it my imagination, or is it getting brighter?'' he asked nervously.

Aitchley narrowed suspicious eyebrows at the increasing sheen of silver-white light reflecting off the pale, icy stone of the eastern rim. ''It does seem to be getting brighter,'' he agreed with some trepidation.

Questioningly, Calyx shook Tin William's lightstick, a look of vexed perplexity on his ruddy features. ''It's not me,'' he retorted, peering at the tiny nimbus of light between his fingers. ''This thing's as bright as it's gonna get.''

Eyfura's tiny eyes flicked over the edge of the nebulous bridge of fog. ''It would appear as if we have failed to consider one possible danger along this route,'' the female Rhagana remarked, staring down into the void.

Both Aitchley and Berlyn swung their gazes over the sides of the bridge; the canyon beneath them steadily burned with a growing white light.

Aitchley felt chill terror grab him around the throat. ''Moonrise!'' he screamed.

19

Columbarium

"**R**un!"

Aitchley needed no prompting from Calyx. The young man's legs were a blur of motion beneath him, kicking up large clouds of disturbed fog, as he raced frantically across the shifting, wraithlike Bridge of Mists, Berlyn's hand tightly clasped in his. Panic flowed through both their young bodies, and terrified thoughts filled Berlyn's head as she tried to keep up with the young man's longer stride, cursing as the hem of her dress interfered. The long tear up the right side of her shift offered her a little added freedom, but her skirt continued to get in the way as Aitchley pulled her along behind him, throwing anxious glances down through the churning clouds of the bridge at the silver-white orb of reflected sunlight steadily making its way up the Canyon Between.

"We're not gonna make it. We're not gonna make it!" Sprage chanted despairingly as he ran.

Although he had been leading the group, Calyx's shorter legs soon left him bringing up the rear. "Sure we will," he replied, his misplaced optimism surfacing.

"Perhaps the bridge will not fully disperse," Gjuki remarked, voice impassive and face expressionless despite the danger coming up at them from below. "Unlike the sun, the moon radiates no heat of its own."

"It's still gotta rise up out of the canyon," Harris snarled

back at the Rhagana. "I don't think the bridge is just going
to politely step aside!"

Pale, silver-grey light flooded the canyon with moonbeams
as the titanic satellite slowly lifted through the mist and fog.
"Less talk, more running," Calyx advised.

There was an unnatural creaking behind them as the moon
pushed up against the base of the Bridge of Mists, its pocked
and cratered lunar surface splintering the unreal fog like hazy
timber. An ominous shudder rocked the cloudlike floorboards
beneath his feet, and Aitchley stumbled in his mad sprint for
safety, nearly thrown from the misty bridge.

Berlyn wasn't as fortunate.

Unable to regain her balance while being pulled along behind the young man, the scullery maid felt her center of gravity
shift and sprawled forward, tumbling headlong into the swirling, boiling mist breaking up around her.

Agony shredding his shoulder, Aitchley felt his arm nearly
wrench free of its socket as Berlyn's sudden fall jerked him
backwards, pulling his feet out from under him. Frantically,
the young man clambered back to his knees, spinning around
to help Berlyn and freezing at the sight that met his gaze.

Behind them—not more than twenty feet away—the moon
crashed through the twisting, coiling haze of the Bridge of
Mists in its endeavor to rise skyward. Spinning, writhing fragments of fog tore and ruptured from the unreal structure—
squirming and spiraling in a kind of voiceless anguish—and
Aitchley could feel the cloudy surface beneath him swell and
bulge as the lunar surface continued to cleave upward in its
destruction of the bridge.

Strong, powerful arms suddenly hoisted both teenagers effortlessly off the hazy ground and carried them eastward. "No
time to stop-and-gawk, Mister Aitch," Poinqart teased the
young man. "Pretty-glowing-moon will crush-you-dead."

Hardly hearing the half-troll, Aitchley continued to gape as
the titanic moon rived through the ethereal composition of the
Bridge of Mists, struggling against the sentient fog that tried
to re-form itself even as it was torn asunder. Why Taci hadn't
bothered to warn them about the rising moon was beyond him,
the young farmer mused. Or maybe the young girl had thought
that they would be out of danger before the moon rose. Whatever the reason, at least the entire bridge didn't dissipate as it

had when the sun had risen. If they could make it across before the moon completely destroyed the spectral structure, they might be all right, but if they had gotten caught out on the bridge during sunrise . . . Well, there would have been hardly any point in running at all.

Sudden cold surrounded the young man as Poinqart carried them across the quaking bridge and into the cavernous maw of the canyon's eastern rim. Chill, grey ice engulfed them on all sides—dioptric in pale white by the glowing lightstick still gripped in Calyx's hand—and Aitchley shivered involuntarily as his breath escaped his lips in tiny caricatures of the mist outside. Beyond the cavern—obscured by fanglike icicles as thick as Aitchley's torso—the young man could still hear the crunching, rending dissolution of the Bridge of Mists.

Hugging herself in an attempt to stay warm, Berlyn surveyed the chill cavern. "It's so cold," she observed, lips turning a pallid blue. "What is this place?"

Distributing thick woolen blankets from the depths of his sack, Calyx gave their new surroundings a disinterested scan. "Ice cave. Glacier. Land of the Dead." He gave the scullery maid a shrug of impartiality. "What difference does it make?"

Buttonlike eyes focused further down the ice-formed corridor, Gjuki's deep voice resonated portentously around them. "I believe such a place is called a columbarium," the fungoid gardener declared. "It would suggest we are on the right path."

Pulling his worn cloak tight around his throat, Aitchley turned inquisitive eyes on the Rhagana. "A columwhat?" he wanted to know.

"A columbarium," repeated Gjuki, draping heavy blankets over his own shoulders. "A place where the ashes of the dead are stored."

An unsettling feeling of dread chilled the blood in the young man's veins as he turned eastward and stared down the grey ice tunnel of the columbarium. A single hallway—chiseled out of the recrystallized snow—sloped slightly upward and away, its cold grey walls and ceiling gleaming in the chemical glow of Tin William's lightstick. A few rimy puddles of water littered the polar-grey floor, and icicles formed clear blue stalactites and stalagmites in a mockery of limestone deposits along the edges of the cave. The cold wind groaned mournfully through the narrow shaft of glacial ice, whistling softly as it passed over a hundred thousand niches carved out of the walls of névé, rattling the black urns and vases that sat—alone and somber—in their frosty shelves.

Berlyn shuddered despite the heavy blanket draping her slender frame. "There are people in there?" she wondered squeamishly, eyes glued to the containers decorating the passageway.

"Cremation was a common practice a long time ago among kings and nobility until the Dragon made death by fire somewhat commonplace," Calyx remarked. "Now—what with all the plagues and such—it's kind of come back into style."

Aitchley took an apprehensive step toward the first urn standing erect in its niche of carved ice. "And these urns have people's ashes in them?" he asked distastefully, blue-green eyes trailing down the length of the hall. "There must be thousands of them."

Gjuki's own gaze traveled up the sloping path of grey-white cold. "Such is a columbarium, Master Aitchley," the Rhagana said with his usual equanimity. "It is a vault for the keeping of such remains."

"Well, it gives me the creeps," Berlyn admitted with another nervous shiver. "Can we get out of here now?"

Returning to his place at the front of their group, Calyx lit the way with Tin William's lightstick. "It's gonna get a whole lot worse before it gets any better," he prophesied, scowling.

Aitchley felt a sinking sensation in his stomach as his own pessimism echoed the dwarven smith's sullen words. Behind them—filling the tunnel with silver-white light—the moon rose up through the regenerating Bridge of Mists and ascended into the darkening sky.

There was no way to gauge the passage of time within the chill arctic halls of the unearthly columbarium. Even worse than the basaltic caverns winding through the dead volcanos of the Shadow Crags, the ice cave of the columbarium led straight into the heart of the glacial mountain, lined by innumerable, identical niches each housing a single urn. Some of the containers were large—ringed with fancy gold trim or inlaid with flecks of precious metals—but most were small, unobtrusive vessels . . . simple black amphorae with wax-sealed lids and rounded stands. It made Aitchley uneasy at the sheer, overwhelming number of urns dotting their path, and when the corridor began to branch out into immense rooms whose walls were row after row of funerary vases, the young man couldn't help but feel his spirits sink.

So many dead, he thought morosely to himself. Were these all the people who had ever been cremated or just those to die from the Black Worm? Or the Dragon? And what of the dwarves and Rhagana? Were their dead here as well, or was this strictly a place reserved for human dead? And how much more of this was there? Seeing so many niches and urn-filled alcoves gave the young man a morbid realization concerning his own mortality.

Ah . . . who am I trying to kid? he asked himself as the familiar self-doubt and despair rose to the forefront of his thoughts. We're all going to die and probably wind up here . . . in some tiny little vase stuck in some tiny little hole in the wall! And for what? Because I wanted to prove to Berlyn that maybe heroes can still exist? That maybe the Cavalier might do some good? What a cartload of mulch. The Cavalier can't do anything about famine or plagues. Daeminase Pits! He never even went so far as to go beyond Lich Gate and try to raise some two-hundred-year-old ancestor from the dead! And I'm expecting him to change the world? Hah! Not only am I probably going to wind up dead, I'm dragging Berlyn right along with me! At least I was able to show her how much I loved her before we all get killed by some runaway moon or get dragged—kicking and screaming—into the Pits by the Daeminase.

It wasn't the cold wind or ice beneath his feet that brought an anxious chill to the back of the young man's neck as he continued making his way through the bleak, featureless terrain of the glacial mountain.

Disconsolate thoughts passing endlessly through his mind, Aitchley followed silently behind Calyx, his hand still gripping Berlyn's. The hallways of the frozen columbarium melded into an indistinguishable blur—a repetitious expanse of somber blues and icy greys—and he could feel his fingers numb and swell before the bite of the arctic air. Even the insides of his nose seemed to frost up, giving the vicious chill a free path to his brain and creating a stabbing, lancelike headache at his forehead.

More rooms branched off from the main passage—other hallways glimpsed through the gloom and urn-lined shelving. Occasionally, glimmering, flickering sparkles of silver light— perhaps more swarms of those strange, glowing insects from the Shadow Crags—moved slowly as a single shape through the darkness, seen briefly, then gone. Aitchley didn't really care what the glittering silhouettes were—so long as they stayed further down the halls, they caused him no concern— but they added an even greater surreal effect to their surroundings, highlighting the distant corridors and hallways with fleeting shimmers of metallic splendor before disappearing into the darkness.

A great staircase carved out of the blue ice confronted them as they rounded a corner, each step slippery and treacherous with puddles of half-frozen water. An aching cold began to seep through the soles of Aitchley's boots as he plodded up the stairs after Calyx, his breathing coming in larger, more exhaustive puffs of haze. Berlyn shivered beside him, gooseflesh covering her bare legs, and she kept her heavy blanket drawn tightly around her, teeth chattering against the cold. There was even a look of intense discomfort on all three of the faces of the usually expressionless Rhagana, and Aitchley felt a pang of worry burn through him when he remembered the fungoid creatures had an aversion to extreme cold.

Struggling up the last step of carved ice, Calyx surveyed the cold, pale field of blue firn that lay splayed out before them. Large, icicle-draped monuments of recrystallized snow rose up like polar gravestones along their path—littering the wide hall with arctic cenotaphs—and shimmering, dreamlike shapes of swirling silver ingots moved and hovered lazily around them, floating slowly above the icy ground. Black urns continued to line the hoary walls.

Calyx sat down at the entrance to the garden of cenotaphs, rummaging through his sack for tinder and flint. "We'll take a short rest here," he said, "and then be on our way." He tossed a wary glance down the immense chamber of névé. "I don't know about you, but I have no desire to spend the night here."

Consenting nods and murmured agreements came from the

others as they gathered around a small fire and ate a brief meal. Aitchley didn't like the way their campfire caused small portions of the ceiling to dribble tiny cataracts of freezing liquid down around them—babbling like miniature rivers down the frigid steps before refreezing—but the invigorating warmth helped chase away not only the cold ravaging his system but some of his fears as well.

Feeling just a bit more at ease, the young farmer snuggled in close next to Berlyn and took advantage of their short rest, warming his rime-rimmed boots by the fire.

A silver shape of a hundred different lights glided smoothly past their campfire, glittering briefly in the glow of the naked flames before fading into the gloom of the cenotaph garden.

Resting her head against Aitchley's shoulder, Berlyn watched the glimmering silhouette hover by. "What are those things?" she wondered out loud, grey-green eyes watching the twinkling lights vanish into the darkness.

Aitchley could hardly rouse himself from the warm stupor he was slowly falling into. "Bugs, I think," he replied, eyes half closed. "I saw some back in the Shadow Crags."

Berlyn turned to watch another swarm of silver lights pass close to their campsite, seemingly drawn toward the glow of their fire. "Those aren't bugs," she answered. "Bugs can't tolerate cold like this."

"So these bugs can," Aitchley said with a shrug, accidentally jostling Berlyn's rest. "Look, this place is magic. Nothing has to work the way it usually does. If the sun can rise right in front of us and not make us all go blind, then a swarm of bugs can survive in the cold."

"But they're not bugs," Berlyn continued to argue. "Look at them. They almost look like they're trying to make a shape."

Drawn out of his rest by the certainty in the young girl's tone, Aitchley cracked one eye back open, staring with forced interest at the shimmers of metallic radiance moving through the hoary gravestone. While he still couldn't see any detail—couldn't make out any wings or legs of individual bugs—a sudden shock jolted him alert when he noticed they *were* trying to make a uniform shape. Each light—each silver mote—made up the whole, and the young man felt his jaw drop when he realized what that shape was.

"Aitchley," Berlyn whispered into the farmers's ear, "they're *people*!"

It was true. The hazy, unfocused shapes moving through the columbarium were the silvery afterimages of people. Aitchley could see them now. He could see where lines of silver light tried to form arms and legs—could just make out the fuzzy, glowing contours of doleful, unsmiling faces. Some were even detailed enough in their flickering resplendency to tell what kind of clothing they wore. And all of them floated eerily above the ice-covered ground of the enormous cavern—steadily moving forward without moving their translucent, spectral legs.

"Not people," Calyx grunted beside the two youngsters. "Ghosts."

Aitchley swung a startled look at the dwarf. "Ghosts?" he echoed in his disbelief. "There's no such thing as . . . "

Calyx gave the young farmer a cynical smile. "Watch what you say, kid," he interrupted with a grin. "I believe Sprage's put his foot in his mouth twice already on this trip."

Aitchley spun back around to gape at the luminous, diaphanous forms. "But . . . But . . ." he sputtered.

"We've been following them since the bridge," Calyx went on, beady eyes watching the slow meanderings of the silvery ghosts. "How else do you think I've known which way to go?"

"We've been following ghosts?" Harris Blind-Eye interjected, disapproval heavy in his voice.

Calyx shrugged. "What better way to get to Lich Gate?" he asked back. "I figured if anybody'd know the way, they would."

A faint shudder coursed its way down the southern-city outlaw's spine. "Yeah," he demanded, "but *ghosts*?"

Calyx offered another lackadaisical shrug. "Sure. Why not?" he responded. "They're not going to hurt us." He got up and waved a hand in front of a passing figure. "I don't even think they see us."

A skeptical look crossed Sprage's mien, but he held back his scornful doubt. "You mean—to a ghost—we don't exist?" he questioned with a hint of mockery underlying his voice.

Calyx started gathering back up his belongings. "No," he answered after a moment's pause, "we're probably just not important to them, is all. They belong here; we don't. What are we going to do? Kill them?''

With a few well-placed stomps, the dwarven smith extinguished their fire and slung his sack back over his shoulder, starting out across the desolate field of ice and frozen cairns. "Nap time's over, kiddies," he snorted to the others. "Time to move on."

Pushing himself to his feet—groaning as the cold crept back into his joints—Aitchley forced himself to stand, moving out after the dwarf through the hedgerow of cenotaphs. All around him—growing steadily brighter and more solid as they moved further east—the cadre of ghosts kept the young man company.

The chill wind stabbed into Aitchley's eyes like invisible daggers, leeching at his body's warmth and drawing all feeling from his exposed flesh. Berlyn stood close under his arm—trying to hide her face from the biting, searing wind of arctic cold—yet she still trembled fitfully as the frigid gale blew up around the tattered and worn hemline of her skirt, stinging her bare legs with its icy venom. Flakes of snow drifted tumultuously across the wind, whipping and spiraling over the wide plain of frozen cenotaphs, and large outcroppings of blue ice rocks—gnarled tumuli and dolmens—sat gathering heavy dustings of snow as the quest halted.

Frowning, Calyx stood on the banks of a frozen river, froth and spray held in pale crystalline jackets and frozen in time. A motionless waterfall of blue and grey ice tumbled down into the ice-choked river before them—fountaining down out of a high gap in the ceiling and spilling down an array of tiered rocks and icy crags. Constant pearls of melting snow dripped and gurgled down the motionless cascade—highlighted by an unnatural glow of white light streaming in through the hole in the ceiling. Across from them—on the eastern bank of the ice-congested river—the glacial mountain ended in a solid wall of bluish grey frost.

Calyx watched enviously as the procession of silver shapes and ghostly silhouettes floated effortlessly across the frozen river and melted into the eastern wall.

Dry sarcasm fairly radiated off Harris Blind-Eye's scarred and ugly features as he turned a mocking gaze on the dwarf.

"Now what?" the southern-city thief jeered.

Calyx's frown strengthened as he turned his attention to the cascade of frozen water on their right. Tiny rivulets of melting ice continued to burble down the transparent, sicklelike sheaves of suspended liquid. "Looks like there's only one way out of here," he concluded.

Aitchley tried to blink back his reservations as the dwarf stepped tentatively across the frozen river and approached the motionless waterfall. The light source—definitely not sunshine—beamed down through the broken ceiling like a warm spotlight highlighting some impressive sculpture, and Aitchley could feel the protests forming on his lips even as the dwarven smith neared the base of the hiemal-locked falls.

"You've got to be kidding," Sprage remarked before the young man had a chance to. "You can't seriously expect us to climb that thing."

Nonchalantly, Calyx began uncoiling the length of spider-silk rope he had crafted back in the Shadow Crags. "No, Sprage," the dwarf retorted without looking up from his work, "I'm jovially expecting you to climb this thing." He tied a loop in one end of the silken rope and returned his attention to the icy rocks and frozen water. "Now step back before you fall back."

Forced to retreat or else get hit by the whirling lariat in the dwarf's pudgy hands, Sprage took a few uneasy steps backwards, dark brown eyes filled with misgiving as the silver-grey lasso spun overhead. Skillfully, spidersilk snagged a jagged protrusion of icy snow high up along the tiered levels of the waterfall, and Calyx gave the cablelike rope a few cautionary tugs, making sure neither it nor the ice would break.

Beady eyes flicked to those standing around him. "Okay, who's first?" the dwarf queried.

Swirls of ice and snow seemed to blizzard through Aitchley's stomach when the dwarf rested dark eyes on him, but Calyx's gaze jumped from the young man and rested on the diminutive figure beside him, a rare smile stretching beneath his beard.

"All right," Calyx declared. "You."

White-hot terror pierced Aitchley's brain as Berlyn stepped purposefully away from him. "Anything to get out of this cold," the blonde replied.

Hardly being aware of it, Aitchley followed behind the petite scullery maid, staying protectively close to her. The waterfall rose high on their right—a motionless zigzag of ice and glacial rock—and Aitchley felt the cold trickle of melted snow soak through his already damp boots as he stepped across the frozen river, an unearthly chill scurrying up the length of his spine.

Calyx handed the length of secured spidersilk over to Berlyn. "Use the rope only for support," he instructed her. "You should just be able to climb from tier to tier."

Apprehension sent waves of warming adrenaline shooting through Aitchley's body as he watched the diminutive blonde make her way up the first of the englacial rocks. Cold water splashed up around her shoes—and the waterfall itself made some ominous creaking and cracking noises—yet Berlyn moved with determined swiftness to the next outcropping of ice and stone, her desire to be warm chasing away any other worries.

Aitchley hesitated at the bottom of the falls, staring up into the white light streaming in from above. The opening was at least twenty feet off the ground—maybe even six or seven feet above the highest-level steppe of the waterfall. Even if they could get up there, they'd never be able to actually climb out the top.

A rope suddenly dangled in front of Aitchley's face.

"Next?" Calyx said.

Frigid water and half-melted snow gurgled in a kind of sluggish rush over the young man's feet as he stood at the top of the icy waterfall, a painful numbness swelling his toes. Berlyn stood beside him—platinum blonde hair blazing silver in the bright light from above—and the others all made their slow and steady way up the frozen waterfall below them, each at varying levels. The cold wind continued to howl around them—clusters of snowflakes fluttering about their eyes like annoying clouds of hoary mosquitos—and Aitchley craned a disgruntled look skyward, frowning at the opening that, as he had guessed, was too high up to reach.

"So how are we supposed to get up there?" he grumbled out loud.

Berlyn shivered as the arctic breeze threw droplets of slush across her bare legs. "I can probably make it if you give me a boost," she observed.

"What?" Aitchley exclaimed, worry tainting his voice. "We can't send you up there all by yourself! We have no idea what's up there!"

"And we won't unless you give me a hand up," the blonde answered wryly. "Look, any place is better than here. Now kneel down so I can get on your shoulders."

Only complying because he couldn't think of a rebuttal quickly enough, Aitchley helped the young girl clamber astride his back, warm, shapely legs draping over his shoulders. He tried not to think about the firm flesh of her thighs pressing intimately against the back of his neck—now was hardly the time to be having such thoughts—yet it was hard to be concerned for the young girl's safety while lecherous fancies went whirling through his skull.

"Maybe we should let Poinqart boost *me* up there," Aitchley offered as a belated suggestion.

Tucking her skirt between her legs so it wouldn't get in the way, Berlyn attempted to stand on the young man's shoulders. "Don't be so ridiculous," she answered. "There's only enough room for two of us up here. Three of us might make the ice break."

Aitchley tried to keep his precarious balance in the rime and pools of slush as Berlyn's snow-damp shoes settled on his shoulders. "But . . ." he tried to protest.

"No buts, Aitchley," Berlyn interrupted. She rose unsteadily from her crouch atop the young farmer, tentative arms reaching upward. "Got it!"

A momentary flash of panic flooded the young blonde's mind as she latched onto the rocky aperture gaping above their heads, and she worried that the unnatural cold of the columbarium might have numbed her fingers to the point where she was uncertain of her grip. Struggling, the scullery maid pushed herself off Aitchley's shoulders—trying to use what little upper-body strength she had to pull herself up. Her legs dangled and thrashed in the cold open air as she managed to heave her upper half through the rounded orifice in the columbarium ceiling, and she was able to take some of the strain off her arms as she settled herself on her belly and wiggled through the ragged hole.

Aitchley watched with growing anxiety as Berlyn's feet disappeared through the opening. He waited for the girl to call down to him—to confirm her safety—yet her face never appeared at the stony maw. Bands of nervous sweat began to collect beneath the farmer's hat despite the frigid cold, and she stared up in silent trepidation at the columbarium ceiling and alarming quiet.

"Berlyn?" he called out, trying to sound casual but failing miserably. "Berlyn, are you all right?"

The lack of an answer caused a lump of fear to clog the young man's throat.

Poinqart was suddenly at the young farmer's side. "Never worry-fear, Mister Aitch," the half-troll declared with a cross-bred jumble of mixed emotions on his face. "Poinqart will send you quick-fast after Missy Berlyn."

Aitchley could hardly feel the half-troll's hands or his own feet as he clambered urgently across the hybrid's huge shoulders and all but launched himself at the opening. He caught the lip of the hole by pure chance, pulling himself up with red and numb fingers until he emerged in a warmth that purged the cold from his body. White light filled the immediate area with a corporeal vitality, and he found Berlyn sitting at the edge of the opening, grey-green eyes staring off into the distance at the radiance filling the purplish sky.

"Aitchley," the young girl whispered, hardly acknowledging the young man's presence, "Look at it. Isn't it beautiful?"

Aitchley threw a cursory glance at the high cliff walls that surrounded them. They had emerged in a narrow glacial trough of polished till and striated drift, sandwiched between unscalable cliffs and hanging valleys. Ghostly figures and silver shadows phased through the nearby rocks to rejoin them on the road, some—like Berlyn—stopping to stare at the nourishing gloriole of pure white light blazing on the other side of the glacial valley. Further up the steep slope—built right into the mountain pass of the grey ice valley—two huge gates hung open. Massive towering bars of yellowing bones and fibrous cartilage made up each gate—capped by an inhuman skull of equinelike shape and no eye sockets looming some fifteen feet above Aitchley's head. Each portcullis was held together by wispy, scraggly lashes of ropelike moss and stringy bands of red-black coagula. Tendrils of dried cartilage and gristle wavered in the polar breeze—intermeshed among the bone and ossicle—and yellow-brown flags of what Aitchley at first thought were leather flapped loosely in the wind.

That was before he recognized the loose folds of what had once been arms and legs.

Palefaced and nauseated, Aitchley turned back to where Berlyn still gazed at the hypnotic aura of white light painting the heavens. She hadn't even seen the ghastly constructs lurking menacingly at their backs, flayed skin flags billowing in the violet sky.

Calyx poked his head up out of the columbarium, beady eyes fixing on the horrifying structures of brittle bones and twinelike ligaments.

Although repulsed by the mere sight of it, Aitchley returned his wondrous gaze to the giant portals of empty flesh and viscera. "Lich Gate," the young man said in a low whisper.

"And it's open," Calyx commented casually, pulling himself free of the cave. A grim frown pulled beneath the dwarf's salt-and-pepper beard. "Looks like someone's been expecting us."

Dried skin fluttered like macabre banners in the breeze.

20

Beyond Lich Gate

T here was no sky above him. Stepping beneath banners of dissected skin, Aitchley Corlaiys walked tentatively through the massive skeletal portals of Lich Gate and into the Realm of the Dead. The air around him was thick and pluvial—smelling vaguely of coming rain mingled with the putrid stench of some faraway charnel house—and the freezing, arctic wind continued to pass over them, ruffling the dark brown hair beneath the young man's hat and bringing a portentous chill to his spine.

We did it, the young farmer thought, barely comprehending. We made it. We've actually passed beyond Lich Gate.

In a kind of horrified awe, Aitchley turned to inspect the World of the Outside, his curiosity battling with an antediluvian terror. Above him, an emptiness took the place of a true sky—a uniform bleakness smeared a dim, unpleasant violet, void of clouds but smudged like an artist's charcoal sketching. The ground was just as featureless, a cold, unearthly blue that was best described as an emotion rather than a hue. It stretched out for a hundred leagues in all directions—as flat and as arid as the Molten Dunes—melding into the distance with the blank, barren horizon in a kind of fuzzy, indeterminate haze. Here and there, boulders and stalagmites of dark indigo jutted upward from the empty earth, their pocked and ragged features resembling detailed carvings of human faces.

Aitchley shuddered without the help of the wind when he noticed all the rock faces were screaming silent, stony screams.

In stark contrast—to the young man's right—the air was filled with a warm, welcoming vibrancy that exorcised all fear and anxiety from his body. The eastern sky—or what passed for the sky—was completely filled by an enormous globe of pulsating white light, larger than the sun and ten times as bright.

A huge staircase, each step some fifty feet in width, rose up off the lifeless blue soil of the Outside, each step glittering with shifting, wavering flecks of inlaid gold. There were no visible supports for the stairs—they seemed to simply rise off the barren ground and curve in a gentle arc straight into the center of the blinding white aureole of light filling the pale, violet skies—and millions of shadowy, silver figures moved in long, unhurried lines up the massive staircase and into the albescent glow. It stung Aitchley's eyes to stare too long at the blistering white radiance that was the Uncreated, but the young man thought he saw what could have been a huge city beyond the eye-aching aura of effulgence, and he gaped in dumb stupefaction at the scores of opacious ghosts making their way up the gigantic staircase and fading into the white light of Oblivion.

" 'And I have seen the everlasting beauty of Oblivion—the Uncreated lands between lands, cities between cities, and worlds between worlds,' " Sprage quoted, also flabbergasted by the sights before them. " 'The kingdom whence no traveler save I have returned.' "

Calyx pulled his eyes away from the scintillating orb of sunlike intensity filling the vacant heavens. "Never would have taken you for a religious man, Sprage," the dwarf remarked.

Sprage managed to blink his gaze free of the Uncreated and flash the dwarven smith a sheepish grin. "I'm not," he answered. He threw an uneasy glance back at the Oblivion. "But I'm beginning to rethink my priorities."

Beside him, Aitchley's attention was disturbed by the sudden movement of Berlyn as she began to step forward across the uneven, barren stretch of dead ground that was the Realm of the Outside. Her grey-green eyes remained locked diligently on the white fire burning in the featureless firmament, and her legs moved stiffly—almost somnambulantly—as she headed toward the giant staircase.

Aitchley just barely caught her by the skirt, tugging her back before she could take another step. "Whoa! Hold on!" said the young man. "We're not going that way!"

Unaware of the young man's hold, Berlyn continued moving eastward, transfixed by the soothing white radiance pulsing before them. "Look at it, Aitchley," she breathed, taking another step forward despite the young man's fistful of skirt. "It's so beautiful."

Worn fabric started to tear in his hand as the young farmer tried to rein the girl in. "Yeah, it's nice, all right," he answered, consternated, "but we're not going over that way. We're going the other way."

Berlyn remained enraptured by the spired city silhouetted within the Uncreated. "But it's so beautiful," she said again. "Can't you hear them? Can't you hear the singing?"

Deep down from the center of his brain, Aitchley became aware of a lyrical melody that steadily rose in strength, filling his ears from the inside and bringing a soothing, quiescent tranquility to his thoughts. A choir of angelic sopranos—millions of voices in cantabile harmony—rang loud and clear, and Aitchley could feel their pull like something ancient and instinctive, an overwhelming draw more powerful than gravity itself. It was almost as if every pleasant emotion ever experienced by the young man existed just beyond that giant staircase . . . waiting for him so that they may be relived.

Aitchley took a single step toward the Uncreated, blue-green eyes locked on the blinding gloriole of living white light. He saw Berlyn within the city. Saw the night they shared in the Shadow Crags. Felt the sensations and emotions of that night tingling and throbbing all over again. Saw his father's face, and all the happy days of his youth. He saw Joub and all his friends who were either dead or gone. And saw the smiling face of a woman he almost didn't recognize . . . a woman he later realized was his mother.

Come, the voices sang inside his head. *Thou hast taken the road. Thou hast at last arrived. Join the Ones who possess the secret knowledge. Join the Ones who shine bright light in darkened places. Thy journey is complete. Join forever and forever you will be joined. One with All. All with One. At heart with All that is, was, or ever shall be.*

A primal compulsion to join overtook the young man, and he stepped forward purposefully. This was the missing piece of his life, he thought, spellbound, to himself. This was all the happiness denied him. All the love taken from him. This was where he belonged, and nothing would keep him from it.

This was his reward.

Something whacked him soundly on the side of the head, and the young man felt his tenuous grip on consciousness evaporate.

The singing had been replaced by a painful buzzing in his skull as Aitchley blinked himself back to consciousness, a curious hand probing tentatively at the bump that formed beneath his hat. Berlyn lay on the ground beside him—one arm draped over her face as if awakening from a drunken stupor—and, judging from the muffled groans made by the young blonde, Aitchley assumed she didn't feel much better than he did.

He glanced up through the distant glow of pure white light to see Calyx standing over him, heavy warhammer held ready in his hands. "Wha . . . What happened?" the young farmer managed to ask.

"You and your girlfriend had a religious experience back there," the dwarf grunted with dark humor. "Had to pop you one in order to bring you back to your senses." He smacked his hammer into the palm of his left hand as if to accent his words.

"You hit me?" Aitchley exclaimed, rubbing irately at the lump beneath his hat. "What the Pits did you do that for?"

Calyx offered the young man a fleeting—vaguely apologetic—smile. "Maybe 'cause Poinqart *and* Gjuki couldn't hold you back," he replied, "and when Harris started to blank out . . ."

"Harris?" Aitchley interrupted, still massaging the tender spot on his head.

The dwarf shrugged in response. "I don't know what it was you people saw in there, but only Sprage was smart enough not to look," he answered. "Our only alternative was to bop you on the head and hope that was enough."

As the dizziness started to leak free of his skull, Aitchley forced himself to stagger back to his feet. "So how long have we been out?" he wondered.

"Not long," replied Calyx. "Just a few seconds." He gave the young man another, more sincere smile. "I only hit you hard enough to get your attention."

Finding *that* hard to believe, Aitchley shook the lingering traces of his headache away and turned to inspect their surroundings. They had moved a little farther north of the staircase and sunlike orb of Oblivion, yet Aitchley could still feel the paradisical temptation to stare back into the Uncreated's white-hot depths. Now that he knew what feelings could be invoked by gazing into such otherworldly splendor, he wanted to experience them all over again, but he didn't even remember moving toward the light nor any of his friends trying to stop him. If the pull of Oblivion was that powerful, maybe it was better that he find something else to occupy his mind.

A chill breeze with icy teeth nipped at the young man from his left, and he turned to seek its origin. The flat, featureless terrain of the Outside stretched vacantly before him—empty and blue—yet a patch of blackness marred the wastes like a great lake of ebony. Questioningly, Aitchley adjusted the hat upon his head and took an uneasy step forward, blue-green eyes fixed on the sea of darkness.

Sharp rocks—dark blue stalagmites without a roof overhead to help form them—rose up like indigo fangs around the wide pool of blackness, their chiseled, human faces howling around the force of the arctic wind. Pale, tattered tendrils of lichen and moss dangled over the lip of the blackness, and Aitchley realized it wasn't a lake but a massive pit as wide as the Tampenteire estate. Thick, unnatural darkness filled it to the rim, and a sudden jolt of electrified terror arced through Aitchley's body as he recognized this place for what it was.

This is the Pits, the young man understood, fighting the near panic that rose up in his mind. This is the very Foundation of Chaos. The place where bad people go when they die. This is the entryway to the Catacombs of the Evil and the Red . . . the place where the Daeminase are, Dead but Dreaming.

The horror became almost tangible as Aitchley drew his gaze along the lip of the enormous Pit, fighting to keep his legs steady beneath him. Large poles of bone stood like yellowing sentries along the Pit's edge, towering an unnatural seven or eight feet in height, and each stake was crested by a decapitated head, mouth open in a silent, blood-dried shriek of eternal agony. Ragged strips of torn flesh flapped from the severed necks in the cold wind that blew up from the impenetrable Pits—waving and beckoning like the tentacles of moss and lichen hanging into the Pit itself—and Aitchley felt a wave of nausea clutch him around the throat when he recognized one of the preserved heads screaming voicelessly upon its sharpened pike.

Undying terror and ceaseless torment remained highlighted in the pale, gruesome death mask of Archimandrite Sultothal.

Sudden hands grabbed apprehensively around his arm, and Aitchley looked down to see Berlyn standing beside him. The blonde's eyes were locked fearfully on the massive Pit that left a deep black wound in the barren, featureless soil, and Aitchley could feel her trembling through just the simple contact of her fingers around his arm. The cold wind once again cut into Aitchley's very soul—trying to sap him of all strength and resolve—and the young man felt his legs go weak beneath him as he spied the destination of their quest beyond Lich Gate.

For there, growing up out of its impenetrable depths—situated right in the very center of the Daeminase Pits—stood the Cathedral of Thorns.

Aitchley blinked hard at the building towering before him. Twisting, serpentine spires of great thorny brambles stretched agonizingly into the empty lavender sky, their color the dark red hue of dried blood. An enormous bell tower speared the featureless heavens, writhing, coiling brambles as thick as Aitchley's waist intertwining with one another to form the structure. Even the elaborate tympanum that marked the cathedral's entrance was made up of a latticework of enmeshed brier, its huge double doors a network of bloody red thorns and crimson thistle.

Aitchley took a tentative step closer to the Pit, staring down at the thick pillar of winding, wreathing brambles that rose up out of the darkness to form the cathedral. Like the Canyon Between, Aitchley could see no bottom, yet—unlike the mists that had concealed the empty space of the canyon—the Pit disappeared into its own inky blackness. It was almost as if the enormous cathedral were an impenetrable fortress and the

Pit was nothing more than a velvet-filled moat of viscous dark.

Eyes the color of an ocean's waves glinted their puzzlement. How the Pits are we supposed to get over there? the young man wondered.

Boots scraped the lifeless soil behind them, and Aitchley turned to see Harris Blind-Eye step through the circle of decapitated heads and join the young farmer at the edge of the Pit. Calyx and the others followed close behind.

A grim frown came to the southern-city outlaw's lips as he peered out over the yawning black chasm. " 'Keyless Lock,' my backside," he snorted in disgust. "You don't need to lock a door that nobody can reach!"

Calyx gave the lockpick a dwarven sneer as he drew nearer. "Why do you think it's keyless, Blind-Butt?" he retorted.

Confusion still filled Aitchley's stare. "So how do we get over there?" he said, voicing his concern. "It's way too far to jump."

Calyx surveyed the wide stretch of liquid blackness that separated them from the Cathedral of Thorns with a critical eye. "My spidersilk's long enough," he mused out loud. "If we can get a line across, you and Harris can . . ."

"Him and Harris can what?" Harris Blind-Eye snidely interrupted. "Look, scout, if you're thinking of sending me over there, you can just think again. I didn't come here so I could fall into the Pits and be dragged off by the Daeminase. I'm here only because Fain put this bunging bracelet around my wrist, and, since you don't need me to pick any locks or deactivate any traps, I'm staying right where I am . . . safe and sound!"

A look of angry contempt contorted Calyx's ruddy features as he turned to confront the ponytailed rogue. "You think so, do you?" he snapped back, unimpressed by the brigand's well-practiced sneers and malevolent glances. "Well, let me tell *you* something, Harris Blind-Ass. Just 'cause that door's beyond our reach doesn't mean it's not locked, and just 'cause the *Kwau* probably deactivated all of the traps leading up to Lich Gate doesn't mean there aren't any traps inside the cathedral. Fain put that bracelet around your wrist for a reason, and this is exactly why he did it! Now are you gonna help us come up with a plan to get across, or am I going to have to remind you about a certain little necklace that sets that bracelet off?''

Aitchley actually saw genuine fear glimmer in the blue-black eyes of Harris Blind-Eÿe as the southern-city bandit threw a nervous glance back at the thorny architecture of the cathedral. The rogue said nothing more as he turned away—and Calyx rewarded himself with a smug smile of triumph—but Aitchley only felt a greater barb of anxiety stab through his breast. If Harris Blind-Eye is frightened, the young farmer realized with some trepidation, there must really be something to be frightened of!

Eyfura's deep voice sounded as she stared out over the unnatural blackness of the Pits. ''Perhaps if we used the QuestLeader's strange metal mount to ferry us across?'' she offered as a suggestion. ''It seems to have limited flight capabilities.''

''An ingenious idea, SpearWielder,'' Gjuki answered the female Rhagana, ''yet the creature called Camera 12 tends to make a rather loud roaring sound when it flies. Let us not forget Miss Taci told us not to arouse the Beasts of Nowhere . . . those that are called the Daeminase.''

Calyx stroked a thoughtful hand down the length of his black and silver beard. ''Still,'' he argued, ''the plan does have merit.'' He turned inquisitive eyes on Aitchley. ''Would your machine be up to it?''

The young man tossed a helpless glance over at where the arachnid construct sat crouching on it spindly legs, Triangle-head perching on its mesh saddle. ''I'm not sure,'' the young farmer responded honestly. ''Camera 12 does whatever it wants. I really don't have that much control over it.''

''Could you ask?'' Calyx wanted to know.

Aitchley shrugged. ''I don't know if it would even understand me,'' he replied. ''It's not supposed to interfere.''

Berlyn's grip suddenly tightened around the young man's arm, and he turned to see the slender blonde beside him go pale. ''Aitchley,'' she said in a tiny, little-girl squeak, ''look.''

Questioningly, Aitchley followed Berlyn's pointing finger out across the blackness of the Pits to where the Cathedral sat in its moat of lightlessness. Perplexed, the young man blinked a few times at the gigantic structure looming above him, unable to spot what had so frightened the young scullery maid.

Then he saw it.

Staked to the giant thorns that made up the Cathedral itself, Aitchley suddenly noticed a number of humanoid shapes dangling limply from the meshwork of nettles, their dark red flesh making them all but invisible against the blood-red hue of the giant brambles. Long, cadaverous arms and legs were impaled bloodlessly upon the enormous red thorns, and narrow, enlongated skulls slightly equine in shape lolled loosely against bony chests in a sleeping mockery of death. Gaping, grinning maws of needlelike fangs nearly tore the creatures' jawlines in half—stretching liplessly across the faces of the red monstrosities—and Aitchley could see neither nostrils nor eyes upon their otherwise featureless faces. They were all skull and teeth, and great rivulets of mucid saliva drooled steadily from between jagged, silver fangs to drip—endlessly and eternally—into the blackness of the Pits.

Seven disjointed fingers crested each gaunt hand—each finger long enough to completely encircle Aitchley's head—and spindly, lean legs as long as the creatures' gangly skeletal torsos made Aitchley guess that these creatures, when on solid ground, might stand seven or eight feet in height.

Trying to blink back his shock, Aitchley let his eyes trail down the thick width of thorny brambles that rose up out of the blackness of the Pits to form the base of the Cathedral. Everywhere he looked, every place he stopped to rest his gaze, he found lean, inhuman creatures of blood-red flesh and eyeless faces, all hanging—Dead but Dreaming—staked to the walls of the Cathedral of Thorns.

Harris stepped to the Pit and looked out across the vast sea of impenetrable blackness at the Cathedral growing up out of its center; he turned a snide look on the young man. "After you," he said mockingly.

Fearfully, Aitchley struggled his way across between the two lines of spidersilk rope, battling to keep his feet on the lower strand and not lose his center of gravity. They had decided using Camera 12 was far too dangerous with the Daeminase sleeping so close, and they had returned to their original plan: lashing two lines of spidersilk out across the unfathomable depths of the Pits, one stretched above the other. It was easier—according to Calyx—than trying to go hand over hand, and much more realistic than assuming anyone could tightrope their way across. Still . . . Aitchley was finding it increasingly difficult to keep himself steady on the bottom strand, guiding himself across by holding onto the upper rope and shuffling his feet after him.

Harris shot the young man a nefarious glare. "Quit shakin' the line, puck!" he barked in a harsh whisper.

Aitchley tried to regain his center of gravity, wishing the lower line would stop swaying up from beneath his feet and trying to throw him backwards. "I . . . I'm trying!" he shot back in a hushed voice.

Shaking—trying to compensate for each unsteady swing of the twin ropes—Aitchley made his way across the gaping black maw that was the Daeminase Pits. He had only looked down once—the same vertigo and nausea that had assailed him on the Bridge of Mists returning to almost knock him off his precarious rope—and he had only done so out of morbid curiosity.

He saw no torments of the damned below him. Heard nothing save the cold, mournful groaning of the wind. The Pits concealed their mysteries in a shroud of unnatural blackness.

Face slick with nervous perspiration, Harris Blind-Eye skipped off the spidersilk ropes and landed on solid ground beneath the shadowed recess of the briered tympanum. Aitchley followed, his boots making hollow-sounding thunks against the thick red brambles as he landed.

Harris spun on the young man. "Shhh!" he rasped. "Quiet!"

Grimacing, Aitchley looked up at the twisting, coiling branches that made up the Cathedral of Thorns; a gangly, inhuman Daeminase hung bloodlessly crucified not far above his head.

Licking dry lips, Harris returned his attention to the double doors of scarlet thorns before him. Like the Cathedral itself, the doors were made out of some fibrous, plantlike material, yet the bronze locks sealing the portals shut were very much solid metal.

Kneeling down to get a closer inspection of the lock, the southern-city bandit removed from his belt some of the twirls and betties used in his lockpicking trade. "The dwarf called it," he mumbled softly to himself. "The door's locked." Blue-black eyes glittered in eager anticipation. "Give me a minute, scout, and I'll get it open."

Nervously, Aitchley turned away from where the ponytailed brigand set about picking the lock and glanced back across the black ocean that was the Pits, squinting to make out his friends on the far shore. He could see Berlyn standing anxiously at the cracked and jagged lip of the chasm, Poinqart stanced protectively behind her. Calyx and the three Rhagana stood beside them, and Sprage kept himself safely behind Camera 12 and Trianglehead. The lengths of silver rope connecting the farmer back to the cold blue surface of the Outside rocked and swayed in each freezing gust of wind that blew up out of the Pits—looking frail and untrustworthy in their spiderweb construction—and Aitchley felt a disturbing lump of fear form in the place of his heart as he stared out over the pitch blackness of the Daeminase's home.

Only Harris and I could get across, the young man mused darkly, wishing he wasn't alone with the southern-city lockpick. Sprage could have made it, but he's afraid of heights—or so he says—and both Poinqart and Calyx are too heavy for the rope. Gjuki wanted to come, but the cold back in the columbarium really affected all three Rhagana pretty badly. It'll be a while before any of them are back to normal. So . . . here I am . . . standing with a man who's tried to kill me and about to enter into a place that no living person has ever voluntarily entered before.

The young farmer allowed himself a cynical snort to alleviate some of his fears. Hmph! he grunted to himself. Watch the Elixir not even be in there! Bloody, typical Corlaiys luck!

There was a subtle click that sounded like thunder in the young man's ear, and he turned to see Harris Blind-Eye rise to his feet, one of the red doors slowly swinging open. A self-assured smirk was drawn on the outlaw's face as he replaced the tools of his lockpicking trade at his belt, and he made a sweeping gesture toward the open door, bowing sharply at the waist like some personal valet or retainer.

"Haven't met the lock that can keep Harris Blind-Eye out yet," the rogue bragged in a low whisper. He swung serious eyes on the farmer. "You ready, puck?"

Aitchley slipped the Cavalier's shield off his back and onto his left forearm. "I guess," he answered apprehensively.

Right hand clutching his sword hilt, the young man pushed through the double doors and entered into the Cathedral of Thorns.

21

Cathedral of Thorns

*H*uge chandeliers of vertebrae and finger joints hung suspended from the vaulted ceiling by chains of red-brown ligaments, tiered with candles that burned but did not melt. Great rows of ligneous pews filled the large cathedral—rough-hewn and hard-grained like poorly constructed coffins—and high, arched windows allowed in the distant glow of the Uncreated, stained not by paint or metallic oxides but with the dried, red-black rouge of human blood.

Aitchley Corlaiys stepped across the crimson floorboards of the Cathedral of Thorns, nervous perspiration trickling down the back of his neck despite the chill in the air. Odd, twisted candelabras of costal cartilage and sternums lit his way, their candles filling the enormous room with the pale flickering tongues of yellow-white illumination, and ribbons of decaying, yellowed silk looped their way down the central aisle like the bunting from some long-forgotten wedding, interlaced with the shriveled and blackened remains of dead flowers.

Swallowing hard, Aitchley forced himself to take another step down the main aisle, one hand resting apprehensively on his sword hilt. There was something about the Cathedral—a feeling that hung in the stale, arctic air—that set the young man's nerves on edge. It was almost as if he somehow sensed the archaic emptiness that had once filled the great Cathedral, broken now by his presence, and the resulting indignity that radiated from the bramble-built walls themselves.

Until that moment, the Cathedral of Thorns had been untouched and unsullied by the pervasion of the living; Aitchley Corlaiys had changed all that.

The young farmer abruptly heard Harris catch his breath beside him. "Dip me in dung and roll me in piss," the outlaw swore in sudden astonishment. "I must be dreamin' 'cause a nightmare don't feel this good!"

Curiously, Aitchley turned his attention to the front of the cathedral, looking past the grisly decorations of gnarled bone and yellowing silk. He felt an unexpected rush of amazement blur his own eyes—causing him to blink once or twice to confirm what he truly saw—and, like Harris, he stepped forward almost automatically, drawn like a moth to a taper at the unbelievable sight before him.

Awash in a prismatic glow of gossamer rainbows, Aitchley stared at the front of the Cathedral, gaping at the greatest assortment of treasures ever compiled in one place. All about the chancel, enormous chests—larger and fuller than even those in Archimandrite Sultothal's chambers—sat clustered about the base of the thorn-forged altar like prostrate worshippers, their contents overflowing into one another in a continuous sea of emeralds, rubies, diamonds, and gold. Exquisite statuary embedded with precious gems ringed the area behind the altar—stone and marble busts of the Muse; clay sculptures of Hladgudd the Bloated; silver and gold figurines of the Twin Sisters; even a rare porcelain statuette of Yram the Chaste, beautiful yet virginal in her nudity, dark brown hair spilling down around her naked form like an ankle-length train.

Rare paintings and laboriously detailed engravings hung from the blood-red thorns of the Cathedral's walls, mixed in among brightly colored banners and silken tapestries from lands and times Aitchley had never heard of. The hilts and hafts of magnificently forged weapons protruded from the motionless waves of gemstones, half-embedded in hills of pearls and topaz, and a heavy woolen cloak with gold and silver trim hung suspended among the paintings, a large brocaded clasp embroidered with diamonds and garnets hanging about its throat.

Positioned all about the chancel—interspersed among the

full-sized sculptures and coffers of eye-aching wealth—glossy black pedestals of gold-flecked onyx squatted on all sides of the altar of thorns. Each pedestal displayed a treasury of rings, amulets, wands, and potions all glittering and gleaming with the unnatural, hypnotic aura of true sorcery; Aitchley even noticed a pair of magic gauntlets draped across a distant dais, their lames flickering with a silver-white glow all their own.

Yet—despite the splendor and grandeur surrounding him—Aitchley found his eyes riveted to the unobtrusive decanter resting on the altar itself, a celestial nimbus of light oscillating from around it. For there—situated atop the altar of thorns itself—sat the Elixir of Life, its container of jaded sapphire glistening in the sorcerous luster of its own contents.

Open-mouthed, Aitchley tried to blink some of the shock and wonder from his eyes, yet at the same time he was unable to shake a dire forboding that dampened some of his awe. There was something wrong, the young man concluded. Something he just couldn't put his finger on. Something more than just defiling a place that had never been contaminated by the presence of humans. Almost as if he had forgotten something . . .

A hungry flash went off in Harris's malignant blue-black gaze. "Whoo, hoo, hoo!" he snickered fiendishly to himself. "Look at it all! And it's all mine!" He sprinted down the center aisle, throwing a wicked glance back at Aitchley. "You know, scout," he jeered, "maybe coming with you wasn't such a bad idea after all!"

The unsettling feeling churning at the base of Aitchley's brain only increased as the southern-city lockpick neared the beguiling array of awe-inspiring treasures, wading hip-deep through the tide of crystals, amethysts, and bloodstones. "Maybe we should wait a second, Harris," the young farmer suggested, the uncertainty festering in his thoughts. "I don't . . ."

Greed and avarice inflamed the outlaw's mien. "Wait for what, puck?" he wanted to know. "You go grab your stupid Elixir . . . I'm gonna pick me up a few odds and ends to take home with me." He grinned with yellowing teeth. " 'A full share of anything of value we find on this quest,' remember?"

Even before Aitchley could respond, there was a sudden thunderclap of energy that plucked Harris Blind-Eye off his

feet and flung him forward, slamming him into the blood-red
brier of the cathedral's wall. An invisible wave of force also
smashed into Aitchley, lifting him into the air and hurling him
back down the length of the aisle. He managed a startled yelp
before slamming hard into a back row of pews, the cushioning
of Tin William's backpack probably saving him from serious
injury. Stars flared and went supernova behind his eyelids—
filling his head with a droning buzz of abrupt pain—and the
young man had to shake his head free of the sudden dizziness
that threatened to send him spiraling into the painless haven
of unconsciousness.

Dazedly—using the shattered pews to help him stand—the
young farmer clambered back to his feet. He could see where
Harris hung—limp and unmoving—against the far wall of the
cathedral's chancel, a sharp thorn as thick as a fist punching
through the back of the lockpick's left shoulder and holding
him upright like he was a broken marionette. Bright red rivulets of blood ran down the bandit's sagging body, and Aitchley was unable to tell if the southern-city brigand was only
unconscious or if another, deadlier thorn had impaled him elsewhere.

A sudden flash of light pulled the young man's attention
away from the motionless outlaw and back to the center aisle
of the Cathedral. Without any source of origin visible to the
young man, a cocoon of white fire manifested itself midway
down the silk-lined aisle, throbbing and shifting like the endoplasmic mists of the Canyon Between. White tendrils of
living, squirming iridescence pulsed and bulged, solidifying as
they intensified. Hazy, misty shapes congealed about the main
body—flaming with a dazzling effulgence through the cloud-
like aureole of light—and Aitchley blinked through the hurtful
fog of white-hot illumination as the wavering, surreal glow
coalesced into an icy thickness of solid light.

The fulguration dimmed only slightly as the protoplasmic
light coagulated into the misty, ghostly silhouette of what
could have been a man in blinding white armor. Arms that
weren't arms but, rather, the blades of swords and spikes of
halberds formed spectral rings around the humanlike shape,
and there were no eyes visible within the flaring white eye slit
of the thing's armet, only luminous daggers and dirks of solidified incandescence.

The Guardian! Aitchley unexpectedly remembered despite the disorienting buzz echoing through his skull. I *knew* I had forgotten something!

Berlyn jumped when an unexpected boom suddenly thundered from the interior of the Cathedral of Thorns, causing her heart to leap into her throat. A surge of adrenaline ran, scalding hot, through her slender body, and she stared out across the ocean of viscous darkness at the red thorn structure rising up out of the center of the Daeminase Pits, grey-green eyes straining to pick out any signs of movement from within.

Sudden hands were on the young girl's shoulders, forcing her down to the ground and obstructing her view behind a jumble of dark blue rocks. Irately, the blonde turned to give Calyx an acrimonious glare, but the dwarf hardly noticed her annoyance. His beady eyes remained locked not on the doorway of the great Cathedral but on the bramble- and brier-formed walls themselves, a white-knuckled grip tightening around the haft of his warhammer.

"Keep your head down," he hissed a warning to the girl. "I think I saw one of 'em move."

Electric fear smothered the ire in Berlyn's gaze, and she hunched down further behind the indigo boulders, a new apprehension gnawing at her insides. Timorously—trying to see without being seen—she peeked out from around her rocky cover. She could barely make out the gaunt, skeletal red forms hanging bloodlessly from the cathedral's thorns, yet a lance of icy terror thrust through her breast when she noticed some of the creatures were moving . . . vague, sluggish movements like a cat slowly coming awake. Long, insectlike fingers curled and uncurled in sleepy reflex, and lipless mouths quivered and slavered, drooling long strands of mucid saliva deep into the bowels of the impenetrable Pits.

Berlyn closed her eyes against the scarlet horrors shifting and stretching in their deathlike slumber. No, no, no, no, no, no, no, she mentally pleaded with herself. Don't let them wake up! Not with Aitchley over there! *Please!*

A sudden commotion of hushed voices occured behind the blonde, and she cracked open one eye to see Poinqart struggling with Gjuki and Calyx, a look of trollish anger and human anxiety on the hybrid's olive-green features. "Poinqart must go!'' the half-troll was muttering in a low grumble. ''Help-assist Mister Aitch, I must!''

Calyx tried, unsuccessfully, to keep the hybrid's flailing arms down by his sides. ''You can't go across now!'' he snapped in a gruff whisper. ''Even if the ropes could support you, the Daeminase might see you!''

''Poinqart cares not about ugly-fierce-*Eperythr*,'' the half-troll retorted, firm conviction in his gravelly voice. ''Mister Aitch could be in danger-trouble. Did you not make Poinqart his protector-friend?''

Calyx felt a momentary flush of embarrassment darken his ruddy complexion. ''Well, yeah . . . I did,'' he admitted. ''But . . .''

''The best way to aid Master Aitchley at the moment, Master Poinqart, is to stay low and bring no undue attention to ourselves,'' Gjuki calmly explained. ''It would not be anyone's best interest if our action brought the Daeminase down from their roosts.''

''But, Mister Aitch . . .'' the half-troll started to argue.

''We must have faith that Master Aitchley can succeed in this venture,'' Gjuki interrupted the hybrid. ''That is why he was chosen by the four lords of Solsbury.''

Poinqart's protests slowly faded, and he turned yellow-black eyes on the blood-red Cathedral sitting at the center of the Daeminase Pits. Berlyn, however, felt the fear and adrenaline continue boiling through her bloodstream, causing her hands to shake and her heart to beat faster. Even though the slow, groggy movements of the inhuman creatures had stopped—and the Daeminase appeared to have returned to their deathlike sleep—the young girl's worry and concern only heightened, leaving a cold, empty space at her breast.

Anxiously—grey-green eyes wide with fear—Berlyn turned a desperate gaze on the dwarf beside her. ''Isn't there something we can do?'' she implored.

A grave expression came to the dwarf's face. ''Know any minstral singalongs?'' he asked sardonically.

Trying to shake the persistent ringing from his ears, Aitchley steadied himself against the row of splintered pews and eyed the manlike shape of pulsating white light before him. His head still felt fuzzy—and the disconcerting buzz refused to vacate his skull—yet the young man stanced himself for battle, half-freeing his sword from its sheath.

The Eternal Guardian, he thought to himself despite the painful droning between his ears. Now what was it Liahturetart had said? Something about being everywhere and nowhere . . . ? Or was that the Daeminase? I don't remember.

Aitchley narrowed suspicious eyes at the pure white flame of man-shaped brilliance. Hundreds of luminous arms protruded from the creature's coruscating torso—radiating outward like the spokes on a wagon's wheel—and the white-light armor of its unreal form continued to shift and change, breastplate melding from bag form to peascod; armet reforming from sparrow's beak to pig-faced. Strange nozzles and funnels rose up out of the liquid light—weapons the like of which Aitchley had never seen before—and the young man wasn't even sure if the creature was looking in his direction or facing the altar where Harris lay . . . or both!

"Of no shape and of every shape it was, Eternal and Unfathomable, just as the Uncreated whence it sprang," Aitchley suddenly heard Liahturetart's ancient voice echo from the recesses of his aching head. "And it watched with a thousand eyes, and it listened with a hundred ears. And its arms and hands were the steel of knives, and all and none of the weapons Mankind had forged were a part of it."

A contemplative frown came to the young man's lips. Well, that tells me a lot, doesn't it? he jeeringly asked himself. How do you fight something that's made up of nothing? Or *can* you fight something that's made up of nothing? For that matter, can something created from the Uncreated hurt me?

His frown deepened. No rules. No laws, he thought darkly to himself. Whatever happens, happens.

Sabatons of solid light clomped ponderously across the wooden floorboards of the Cathedral of Thorns, heading purposefully to where Harris Blind-Eye dangled, unmoving. Swallowing whatever reservations he may have had, Aitchley launched himself forward, squinting through the haze of light to try to find a weak spot in the armor. He couldn't just let the Guardian kill Harris, yet—even as he ran—Aitchley wondered if his act of selfless bravery wasn't for the benefit of somebody already dead.

Unexpectedly, something hard slammed into the young

man's shield, picking him up and throwing him backwards. The deflective properties of his dwarven shield were all but useless against the strength of the Eternal Guardian, and Aitchley landed with a bewildered "oof," watching in stunned amazement as the creature turned to face him without turning, its front melding into its back and its back phasing through to the front.

Aitchley tried to chase the increasing buzz out of his head. Well, that answers that question, his pessimism wryly remarked. It *can* hurt me. Only question is, can I hurt it back? Fighting a creature made out of light sounds like trying to drink the whole Alocir Sea . . . Bloody well impossible!

Ignoring the pain reverberating through his skull and the dull ache of his left arm beneath his shield, Aitchley scrambled back to his feet, sword held ready. He tried once again to pinpoint a weak spot in the armor—some opening at the joints or between articulated lames—yet, instead of chainmail, the young man only saw flaming white light. He didn't think stabbing at the glow would do him much good—how can you hurt light?—and he threw an anxious glance at the open door behind him, weighing the possibilities of retreat.

No, he concluded bleakly. What good would that do? This is where the Elixir is, and it would be pretty stupid to run away now. But . . . what did they expect? I can't even bring forth a decent harvest! How am I supposed to kill something that's eternal? *Can* you kill something that's eternal? Damn it to Gaal! I wish I remembered what else Liahturetart had told us!

Sudden swords of meteoric intensity screamed over the young man's head, interrupting his thoughts and forcing him to drop to all fours. Frantically, the farmer scrabbled to one side, shield up as he tried to escape the barrage of dazzling white limbs. Something that felt like a solid-light version of Calyx's warhammer caught the young man on the silver crest of his shield, driving him up into the air and hurling him across the width of the Cathedral.

Aitchley slammed into the far wall, stars exploding behind his eyes. He heard his sword clatter somewhere noisily out of his hand—sensed more than saw the razor-sharp thorn protruding from the wall that missed his head by a few inches—and heard the unmistakable crunch and splinter of breaking ribs. Colors and lights leapfrogged behind his eyelids as the discomfort in his head increased, and he grabbed worriedly at his chest, wondering how badly he had injured himself.

He wasn't entirely relieved to see that he had crashed into one of the grotesque candelabras of bones and wax, the ribs he had heard breaking not his own.

Silver-white light blazed as the Eternal Guardian bulldozed its way through a row of pews after Aitchley, a whirlwind of luminescent morning stars and pikes forming out of its liquid form. Flames belched from one of its mysterious nozzles—and what might have been a blazing white bow momentarily materialized before fading back into its surrounding nimbus of light.

This is *not* going well! Aitchley grumbled to himself, lurching unsteadily to his feet. I'm gonna get killed if I don't think of something soon!

Blinding incandesence intensified as the Guardian neared, its hundreds of arms lost in the blurry haze of sweeping light. Desperately, Aitchley made a wild lunge for his dropped sword, snatching up the weapon and swinging blindly. Steel clanged as it struck the glowing armor, its blade slipping through the Guardian's right pauldron and into the light beneath.

The anguished howl of pain that resounded eerily from within the Eternal Guardian's helmet caught Aitchley completely by surprise. Glittering red rivulets of blood splashed down the front of the Guardian's breastplate—its arterially bright crimson staining the white-light armor scarlet—and Aitchley was still gaping in astonishment when a mace of solidified brightness connected with his shield and sent him somersaulting down the center aisle.

No rules. No laws, the young man reminded himself when he came to a bewildered halt near the chancel. Whatever happens, happens.

Encouraged by the blood-red trails burbling down the Guardian's vest of white-light steel, Aitchley jumped back to his feet and lunged again at the creature, his sword seeking out the vulnerable joints of its armor. Warily, the Guardian stepped back, unseen eyes analyzing the young man's attack. Optimistically, Aitchley pressed his advantage, thrusting determinedly for the Guardian's unprotected joints.

Twin blades of radiance suddenly clanged shut on Aitchley's sword, catching the weapon in a defensive cross and
trapping it between upturned quillons of solid light. The abrupt
snap of Aitchley's sword breaking in half shattered the young
man's sudden resolve, and he stared in horrified wonder at the
broken forte of his weapon, hardly acknowledging the bright
white ax blade that came screaming for his skull.

Blue-and-gold *gnaiss* reacted automatically, spinning the
young farmer around and blocking the deadly blow. The unexpected shock and inhuman strength behind the attack pro-
pelled the young man sideways, hammering him off his feet
and throwing him into the jumble of gems and jewelry surrounding the altar. The broken haft of his sword fell uselessly
to the ground—lost among the hillocks of diamonds and
pearls—and a jolting arc of pain lanced up the young man's
spine and centered in his brain as he crashed into a dune of
emeralds, the painful buzzing in his head threatening to swamp
him with the cold, enveloping blackness of unconsciousness.

Dazedly—as much surprised as he was hurt—Aitchley
forced himself to sit up, blinking eyes that were still glassy
with shock. The simple snap of his breaking sword replayed
itself over and over again in his ears—it didn't sound any
different from the cracking of a walnut—and the young man's
overwhelming shock numbed him to the approaching behemoth of living white light. He could hear the clink of flaring
sabatons as the Eternal Guardian waded through the ocean of
precious stones and artifacts about him, but the dizziness and
bafflement left the young man helpless. What was he to do
now anyway? He had lost his only weapon.

Aitchley looked up at the advancing Guardian. I'm dead, he
concluded pessimistically.

Unexpected hands—sticky with blood—clamped urgently
about the farmer's arm. "Give me my knife."

Stupidly, Aitchley directed his dumbed gaze toward Harris
Blind-Eye, a look of complete confusion marring the young
man's face. The brigand's shirt was a mass of red, and his
face was pale and drawn from loss of blood, but there was a
gleam of determined fury smoldering in the lockpick's eyes
that helped draw Aitchley up out of his own befuddled stupor.

Aitchley blinked hard. "Huh?"

Harris's grip tightened around the young man's arm. "My knife, puck," he hissed. "Give it to me."

Despite the menacing creature of solid light coming toward him, Aitchley felt a familiar mistrust rise in his breast as he stared into the bandit's eyes. "You . . . Your knife?" he repeated uneasily. "I . . . I don't have it."

Murder flamed in Harris's blue-black gaze. "Don't bung me cask, puck!" he snarled sharply. "I know you've got Renata! I recognized the wound back on the giant spider!" He threw a curt glance at the advancing Guardian. "Now give me my knife; I'll try and hold it off as long as I can!"

Hesitantly, Aitchley reached into the maroon-colored backpack and extracted the black steel of Harris's blade. Heavy misgivings continued to roil about the young man's stomach—this was one of the weapons Harris had tried to kill him with!—but then he redirected his gaze to the lumbering form of white-light metal coming toward them, hundreds of deadly-looking weapons coalescing and fading within its Uncreated aurora.

Aitchley slapped Renata's cold hilt into Harris's waiting hand. "Here," he said, quickly pulling himself to his feet. He paused as he turned toward the altar, an odd feeling of admiration flitting through his mind. "You might need this too," he added.

A small grin stretched Harris's pale features as he took the offered shield, sliding its enarmes over the blood-soaked sleeve of his left arm. "Go get your Elixir, scout," the southern-city outlaw said, turning to face the oncoming Guardian. "I'll be all right."

Fighting back any fears and reservations still plaguing his thoughts, Aitchley spun about and ran toward the altar of thorns, his boots slipping and sliding in the piles of gems as though they were dunes of sand. He tried not to think about how pale Harris was—or how ridiculously small Renata looked against the Guardian's glowing salvo of weapons—and focused his attention on the gnarled, twisting patch of blood-red brambles that made up the altar. If there was some way he could grab the Elixir quickly enough, maybe they could get out of there before they both got killed.

Skidding to a halt in a knoll of opals, Aitchley stopped before the altar of thorns. Before him—sparkling with eldritch

magicks that looked like bubbles of fermentation—the Elixir
of Life sat upon the altartop of brambles, its vessel of jaded
sapphire glistening blue and green among the blood-red thorns.
A faint tingle of energy seemed to radiate outward from the
bottle—penetrating Aitchley's flesh and gently soothing away
all the aches and bruises riddling his body—and a rhythmic
pulse of magical light, almost like a fluid heartbeat, throbbed
deep within the glass, filling the decanter with an unearthly
glow all its own.

Without caution or ceremony, Aitchley snatched the Elixir
of Life off the altar and shoved it hurriedly into his backpack.
He could hear the clash of weapons behind him—flinched
when he heard solid light strike hard against his shield—and
decided he could spend time marveling at the Elixir once they
were safely away from the Cathedral and the inhuman creature
guarding its many treasures.

There was a sudden sucking sound in the stale air above the
altar, and Aitchley turned to see yellow-green flickers of sorcery pop into existence, looking like sparks from a fire. Terrified—yet, at the same time, intrigued—the young man
watched as the crackle of magic broadened, filling the now
empty space above the altar with a dazzling array of color.
Unexpectedly, the noise and spangles faded as an elaborately
carved staff of blackened wood solidified out of nowhere, resting across the altar where the Elixir of Life had once stood.

Questioningly—his surprise still overriding his fear—
Aitchley stretched out a hand and took the staff. It stood nearly
as tall as the young man, its tendrils of carbonized wood coiling and branching around one another like some bizarre root
system. Gleaming silver capped the knob in an intricate display
of metalwork, and a similar ferrule covered the foot, crafted
to a dangerous, knifelike point. Detailed carvings and runes
decorated every inch of wood in between, and—as with the
Elixir—there seemed to be a warmth radiating from the staff
itself and flowing into Aitchley's fingers.

Another implosion of sorcery from above the altar pulled
Aitchley out of his contemplation of the staff. Yellow-green
fireflies of thaumaturgy culminated in an abrupt flare of sorcerous splendor, leaving in their wake a large, leatherbound
volume resting, open-faced, upon a small dais of crystal and
gold. Overwhelming surprise continued to cloud the young

man's mind as he stared at the sudden appearance of the book, his eyes scanning with puzzled awe the strange, alien words inscribed upon its open pages.

Every time I take something, something else shows up to replace it, he mused in his shock. So what do they all do? Are they all magic? If I took the book, what would happen? Would something else show up? And, if I took that, what then? Would this just keep going on forever?

A sudden voice of understanding resounded through Aitchley's head. No, not forever, he abruptly realized. Eternally.

Unbidden, the rest of Liahturetart's warning unexpectedly came to mind: "And it fulfilled its Task and Guarded that which was to be Guarded and hidden behind the Keyless Lock. And it Guarded Eternally, and what it Guarded was Eternal."

Aitchley returned bewildered eyes to the leatherbound grimoire open upon its dais. What it Guarded was Eternal? he repeated to himself, comprehension slowly burning through his perplexity. So no matter how many times I take something, there will always be something here? What if the same holds true for the Guardian . . . ?

Filled with sudden resolve, Aitchley turned to where Harris was barely holding his own against the white-armored sentry. "Kill it!" he screamed at the outlaw.

An expression of annoyed confusion marred Harris's face as he ducked a glowing broadsword. "Kill it?" he irately shot back. "How can I kill something that's eternal?"

Tucking the mysterious staff under one arm, Aitchley ran to help the southern-city lockpick. "So long as there's something to guard, the Guardian will always be here to guard it!" the young man hurriedly explained. "But it's eternal, not immortal!"

The look of befuddlement remained on the rogue's bearded features. "So what's the bloody difference?" he wanted to know.

Aitchley stumbled over a dune of rubies. "If the treasures can be removed and replaced, maybe it's the same for the Guardian!" he shouted urgently. "Just kill it!"

With a one-shouldered shrug, Harris flipped Renata over in his hand, gripping the blade between callused fingers as he readied to throw it. Unexpectedly, there was the thunderous chatter of machine-gun fire from one of the Guardian's white-light muzzles, catching the southern-city brigand across the shield. With a resounding crash, Harris Blind-Eye flew backward into a row of pews, Renata clattering free of his grasp, his tenuous hold on consciousness eluding him in the ruckus of splintering wood and solid-light ammunition.

Pure horror burned through Aitchley's nervous system. *"No!"* he shrieked in his sudden panic, skidding to a bewildered halt in a pool of topaz.

White light flared as the Eternal Guardian began to shift sideways, not so much turning toward the young man as molting. Horrified—staring blankly at the unmoving form of Harris Blind-Eye and the useless sliver of black steel lying beside him—Aitchley hardly felt his feet begin moving beneath him, propelling him down an incline of sparkling jewels straight for the monstrous figure of solidified light. His right hand instinctively snatched up a jewel-encrusted hilt sticking up out of the glittering debris of pearls and emeralds about him, and he swung his new sword once over his head, scarcely aware of how light—yet powerful—his new weapon felt in his grasp.

An unearthly scream resonated from deep within the Guardian's armet as Aitchley's new sword sliced down between breastplate and pauldron, passing through white-light armor as if it were water. Scarlet rivers splashed the Cathedral's floor—spattering crimson on crimson—and the blade leapt like something alive in Aitchley's hand, arcing back up and around, driving point-first through the Guardian's eye slit and into the white-hot light behind its visor.

Blood exploded in frothing scarlet tides down the face of the Guardian's bevor, numerous limbs thrashing and convulsing as Aitchley's sword pierced the blinding light of its unreal skull. Geysers of red painted the ligneous pews a ghastly vermilion—streaking both wood and farmer—and solid light began to dim, tentacles of twisting, protoplasmic luminescence squirming and writhing in voiceless anguish. Even the fountains of blood-red fluid began to fade, evaporating like moisture off the hot desert sands, and the Guardian's manlike shape grew hazy, fragmenting into a million embers of shimmering white light until only shifting, waltzing shadows remained.

Aitchley stood alone in the Cathedral of Thorns, jewel-encrusted sword held outward, fear and astonishment locking his muscles in place.

Weakly, Harris Blind-Eye pulled himself free of the wreckage, a dribble of red cascading down the right side of his head to offset the blood-smeared stains of his left shoulder. "We win, scout?" he asked blearily.

Still stunned, Aitchley slowly lowered his new sword, sliding its silver-grey blade comfortably into his sheath. "I . . . I think so," he answered unsteadily. He threw a nervous glance at the enormous Cathedral around them. "Come on, let's get out of here before that thing re-forms."

Helping Harris clamber to his feet, the young farmer assisted the wounded brigand toward the open doors of the Cathedral, a flurry of apprehension swarming through his brain. He could feel the reassuring warmth of the Elixir of Life from his backpack, and similar tingles of magical energy entered his palm through the thick staff of burned oak in his grasp, yet he couldn't shake the feeling that the Eternal Guardian would return before they were safely away. Then what good would any of these items be?

The young man frowned to himself as he helped Harris into the narthex of the Cathedral. Not that it would make any difference anyway, he thought pessimistically to himself. Here I am, stranded out here in the middle of the Daeminase Pits trying to help someone who's tried to kill me twice, and I don't even know if any of this is worth it! What's the point of getting a magic Elixir if I don't even know if I'm supposed to use it or not? I mean . . . what the Pits did Tin William want? Why help me if using this Elixir is going to throw something seriously out of balance? Or is that what he was trying to say at all?

Aitchley's frown deepened. Bloody, bunging typical.

Epilogue

The mountain path was overgrown by a tangle of knee-high grasses and flowering weeds, all turning brown beneath the strengthening glare of the summer sun. Brambles and thickets lined the dirt path—crowding a trail where thousands of feet had once tramped the soil flat—and large boulders stood poised like great sculptures among the chaotic profusion of green. Bees sipped hungrily at the nectar of wildflowers, and birds chirped and twittered among the safe haven of the brush, undisturbed for decades by the humans who lived below.

Weary footsteps trudged up the mountainside, shattering the stillness of a hundred years. Laboriously, Nicander Tampenteire made his way to the top of the hill, using what little strength remained in his exhausted body to pull himself upward. Streaks of dirt and half-healed sores covered his face and hands, and a heavy beard of dirty black hair completely hid what had once been youthful features. His clothes were mere tatters—filth-stained rags covered in refuse and ordure—and his shoes were coming apart at the seams, their soles worn thin and no longer protecting his feet from the sharp rocks and pebbles of the mountain trail.

Wheezing, Nicander followed the footpath up the crest of the hill, stepping free of the grasses and wildflowers and clambering over bare rock. Below him, Vedette stretched green in all directions, the lush thickness of Karthenn's Weald visible far below the mountainside. There was even a faint glitter—like a plateful of sparkling diamonds—from the faraway speck that was Malvia Lake. Yet Nicander all but ignored the view, his mind concerned only with his own survival . . . and that survival meant little if he could not make the climb.

On the verge of collapse, Nicander reached the summit of the mountain road, stopping before a great, empty cavern that tore a gaping black hole in the mountainside. Once, elaborate offerings had been scattered about this cave—hundreds of people a day visiting this most holy of places with gifts and sacrifices—clusters of beautiful virgins crying their eyes out over the hard, lifeless dirt. Food and flowers, gold and incense . . . offerings of eternal thanks had once filled the entrance of the cave, lining the enormous corridor of stone all the way down into its gloomy interior and surrounding the bronze and marble coffin that sat at the center of its naturally formed amphitheater. Nicander had never seen any of these things—they were events that had happened long before his time—but he had heard of them. Had heard of the many people who had visited this place on sacred pilgrimages and the objects of great wealth they had left behind.

Nicander scanned the empty hillside. No one came here much anymore, he observed.

Groaning, the young nobleman sank to the hard ground outside the enormous cave, leaning back against the jagged rocks. He could still not bring himself to believe that he had succeeded . . . that he was still alive. Four days ago he had caught and killed a rabbit, yet his clumsy, unskilled cleaning of the animal had almost cost him his life. Unable to properly eviscerate the beast, Nicander had accidentally punctured an internal organ and tainted the meat, the resulting sickness nearly killing him. How he had survived the two days of retching and vomiting was beyond him, and if it weren't for the tiny stream he had used to help restore some of his liquids he most surely would have died. Even now, the weakness and fatigue ran rampant through his body, making his legs and arms quiver as if there were no bones within them. And all because of Corlaiys.

It was all Corlaiys's fault.

Nicander lay back against the rock, closing an eye in eager

expectation. He would come, the young nobleman knew. Corlaiys would come. Not even LoilLan could cheat the young noble of the revenge that was rightfully his. No matter what dangers or foes stood between him and the farmboy, Nicander knew he would regain the respect that he was due. Then the world would see that Nicander was still worthy to be a Tampenteire, and Aitchley Corlaiys would be revealed as the worthless little mudshoveler that he was!

Smiling—his ravaged and weary body fueled by the bitter taste of promised vengeance—Nicander Tampenteire fell asleep outside the entrance to the Dragon's Lair, his feverish dreams vindictive and triumphant.

Captivating Fantasy by

ROBIN McKINLEY

Newbery Award–Winning Author
"McKinley knows her geography of fantasy...
the atmosphere of magic." —Washington Post

__THE OUTLAWS OF SHERWOOD
0-441-64451-1/$4.99
> "In the tradition of T.H. White's reincarnation of King
> Arthur, a novel that brings Robin Hood delightfully to
> life!" —The Kirkus Reviews

__THE HERO AND THE CROWN
0-441-32809-1/$4.99
> "Transports the reader into the beguiling realm of
> pageantry and ritual where the supernatural is
> never far below the surface of the ordinary."
> —New York Times Book Review

__THE BLUE SWORD 0-441-06880-4/$5.50
The beginning of the story of the Kingdom of
Damar, which is continued in The Hero and the
Crown, when the girl-warrior Aerin first learned the
powers that would make her a legend for all time.